The

BOY

with the

STAR
TATTOO

ALSO BY TALIA CARNER

The
BOY
with the
STAR
TATTOO

A Novel

TALIA CARNER

wm

WILLIAM MORROW
An Imprint of HarperCollinsPublishers

HarperCollins books may be purchased for educational, business, or sales promotional use. For information, please email the Special Markets Department at SPsales@harpercollins.com.

FIRST EDITION

Designed by Diahann Sturge

Maps by Noah Springer. Copyright © 2023 Springer Cartographics.

Library of Congress Cataloging-in-Publication Data has been applied for.

ISBN 978-0-06-332577-7

23 24 25 26 27 LBC 5 4 3 2 1

To those who dreamed the possible—
and to those who dreamed the impossible, daring to make it possible

To Ron, whose love has cocooned me so I
could emerge to spread my wings

This novel is a work of fiction inspired by historical events in France. While I stayed close to the facts, I took the liberty of constructing fictional stories and novelizing scenes of some real-life personalities. Mostly, I created a cast of imaginary characters.

For more about the historical background of the novel, please refer to the author's note at the back of this book and to the author's website at www.TaliaCarner.com.

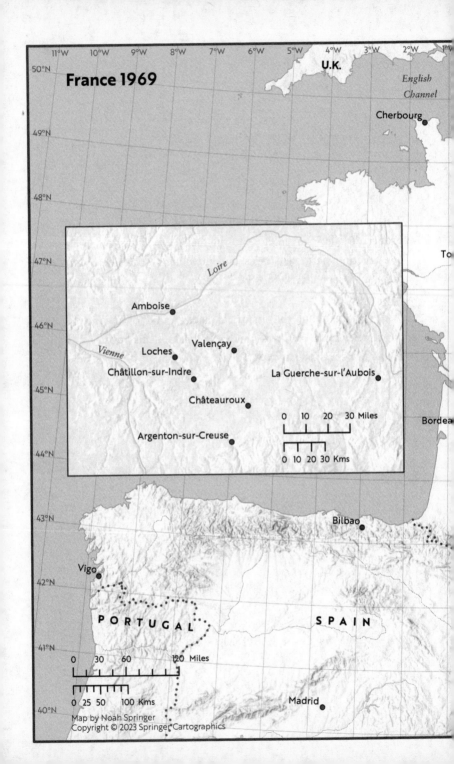

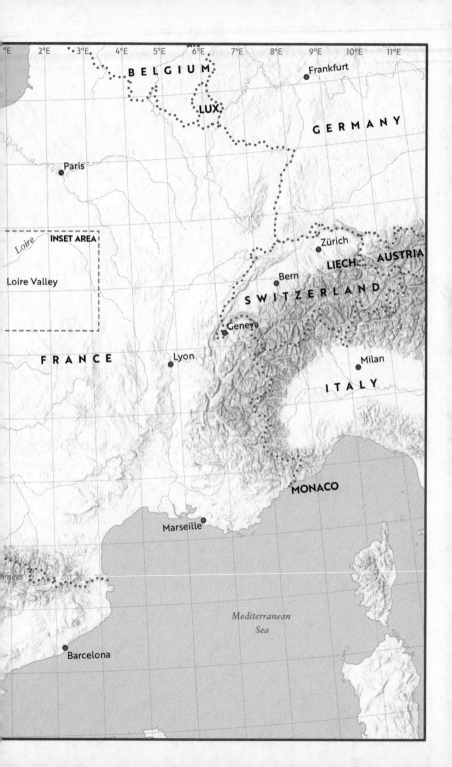

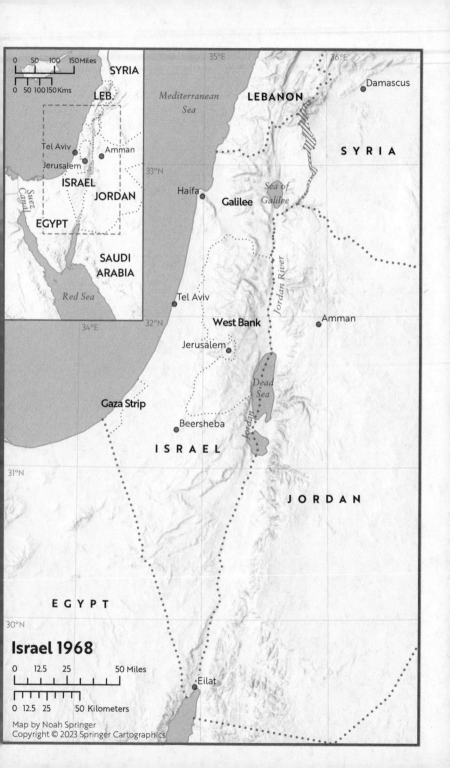

Israel 1968

Map by Noah Springer
Copyright © 2023 Springer Cartographics

A generation which ignores history has no past—and no future.
—ROBERT HEINLEIN, *TIME ENOUGH FOR LOVE*

Ability hits the mark where presumption
overshoots and diffidence falls short.
—GOLDA MEIR (ATTRIBUTED)

Prologue

Mediterranean Sea
October 1946

SHE CROUCHES ON the top deck, surrounded by hundreds of people squeezed together. All have fallen silent since the ship arrived at the easternmost reach of the Mediterranean Basin. In the moonless night, the sky and sea merge into one inky darkness. Judith's eyes strain to penetrate it and glimpse the shoreline. Oh, how her parents and sisters had prayed for this safe haven when trying to flee the Nazis' clutches. *I'm doing it for you,* she mouths, careful not to utter a sound. The ship's engines are quiet now. The hum that filled Judith's ears for nine days in this ancient vessel doesn't subside; it echoes in the pounding of blood in her temples. She has known fear. Terror has been her constant companion these past six years, since she was eleven. Now there's a new fear: of being intercepted by the British, who control Palestine and block the entry of Jewish refugees. Her yearnings to reach Eretz Israel might come to naught. What will happen to her then? The land is so close that Judith can almost taste the juice of its oranges.

A heavy chain is lowered with a muffled clatter, and Judith jolts with the ship as its anchor latches onto the bottom of the sea. Next to her, an eight-year-old girl whimpers. Judith hugs her against her side and places her finger on the girl's lips. They have practiced every night for this long hour of silence. The most difficult part is yet to come. The next steps will be filled with great risks—their only hope to reach freedom.

Anxiety hangs like a cloud over the passengers' collectively held breath. Judith passes her hand over the heads of the twelve children clustered around her like frightened birds. She mothered them in the Marseille displaced-persons camp and has bonded with them through her games and storytelling and playing her flute. They are all eight-to ten-year-olds except for one four-year-old boy, who is smart and obedient. The coming hour is the test that no one is allowed to fail. A child who panics and loses control puts hundreds of passengers in peril.

Salty mist rolls in. The ship bobs in the quiet night; the only sound is the lapping of waves against its sides. The calm is deceptive, auguring danger. The threat of discovery lurks in the soft breeze that caresses Judith's burning face and the sleek surface of the water—either might carry the faintest of voices to a British patrol boat.

In the tight space, Judith pulls the little boy onto her lap. He clings to her for comfort, opening in her an equal measure of love. Her lips brush his hair.

The muted strokes of paddles below the ship make her raise her head. Her group, composed of herself and the youngest children, will debark first. Someone touches her shoulder, and Judith rises, readjusts the straps that tie her bundle and the canvas bag holding all their shoes to her back. She lifts the boy and takes the hand of the nearest child; the rest of her charges form a tight chain behind her. The boy's father, one of the organizers, will be among the last to leave the boat, and Judith prays that he will make it to shore before they are spotted. In the darkness, a young man climbs up the ladder on the side of the ship and carries the boy down. At the railing, an Israeli woman silently directs Judith's other children to scramble down themselves. Judith follows.

Strong arms grab her back at the last rung and lower her gently onto a bench in a rowboat. More children and their leader quickly fill the boat. Two men her age take the oars, and Judith's heart swells with pride at the sight. These are Haganah members. Heroes. She trusts each one. Whatever else she does in her new home, she will strive to join their ranks.

First, though, she must guide her charges over the next crucial hurdles. If the British detect them on water or on land, soldiers will descend on them, force them back onto the ship, and send them back to the cursed Europe that loathes those it hasn't killed. Or the British will lock them up behind barbed wire in their newly built camps on the island of Cyprus.

After barely escaping the gas of the extermination chambers, they would be back in a concentration camp with no hope of escape.

Three empty rowboats skim by in the near darkness, bound for the ship to collect immigrants, as her small vessel makes its way toward the shore. Each swoosh of breaking water increases the thumping of Judith's heart. Will any of them reach safety before they are exposed?

Her journey began so long ago, on that summer day in Lyon when the police raided her Jewish school. Judith had been in the lavatory. She'd heard cries and peeked out to see her classmates being shoved into the yard. She ran up three flights of stairs to the roof. Below, parents rattled the locked school gates, screaming. As blood pumped through her veins, Judith vaulted onto the roof of the adjacent building. Her long, thin legs carried her from one roof to the next, past her neighborhood, until she no longer heard the screaming. She pried open an attic window and hid there for a day and a half, until hunger and worry for her parents and sisters sent her back over the rooftops.

The street was quiet when she reached her family's building. Light shone in the kitchen window. Her parents cried with relief and covered her with kisses. The Vichy government had a quota of Jews to deport, they'd told her, grief-stricken. Her twin sisters, two years younger, had been taken.

Next morning, their housekeeper bleached Judith's dark hair blond and took her to her own village. A business associate had made arrangements to hide her parents elsewhere, she was told.

After the war, Judith waited for them to come for her. They knew where she was. But they never showed up.

Suddenly, light floods the shore. A shudder runs through Judith at the sight of a searchlight bathing the white sand and gliding slowly across its expanse. Fear of discovery stifles her awe at this first glimpse of the land of her dreams. The light ascends a cliff, caresses its fissures, and casts ghostly shadows under boulders and clusters of shrubbery. The beam is still lingering on the cliff, searching, when Judith hears the lapping sounds of swimmers beside her boat. The four men and women each grab two of the smallest children and dash through the shallow waves to the shore. Judith tucks the hem of her skirt into her waistband, raises the bag of shoes, and lowers herself into the thigh-high water. It welcomes her with a surprising warmth. She quickly helps the rest of her children debark, then wades to the shore.

Their saviors are counting the seconds, she knows, so when a young man carrying the little boy guides them onto the sand and whispers to her in Yiddish, "I'll be in front, you'll bring up the back—run fast," she sprints with her well-trained children across the sand to the cliff, where he ushers them into a deep crevice.

She's dreamed of the moment when her feet touch the soil of the Holy Land, but now that it is happening, there's not a second to spare for a prayer of thanks. Her heart pounding, Judith squeezes the children against the sandstone rock. The wet, half-naked body of their rescuer is pressed against them as a new searchlight crawls along the beach they've just crossed. A thin rivulet of sand cascades onto Judith's shoulder. The seconds tick away in her head.

When the searchlight begins its arc upward, away from them, the young man touches Judith's hand. "Ready?" he whispers. His breath is warm, and a pleasant shiver travels through her as he hands her the boy. He scrambles up the steep crevice and stops on the first ledge to take the boy back from her, then grabs the arm of the next child that Judith pushes up. She climbs last. The cliff slopes away, and they crawl fast toward the flat surface.

They've just reached the top when their leader whispers, "Down!" and they all flatten themselves on the pebbly ground between clusters of knee-high prickly shrubs. Just then, a new beam of light bursts to life and plunges across the top of the cliff. It grazes their backs. They all hold their breath, their arms tucked underneath themselves, the curvatures of their bodies blending with the uneven surface. No one moves. A stone pricks Judith's cheek, breaking her skin. Her heart hammers so hard, she's afraid it might explode. She prays that the children will tolerate the stones' rough edges. If her group is exposed, it will doom all those who follow.

The searchlight goes dark, and blackness drops on her like a lead cape. She touches the nearest child, the agreed-upon signal, and they all get up. With no time to dust off the sand and pebbles, they break into a run across a plowed field. As her eyes readjust to the darkness, she sees the nearby silhouettes of more people rushing in the same direction.

A pinprick of a flashlight beam directs them to a waiting truck. Quickly, their rescuer helps them climb onto its bed. The wooden benches are not screwed to the truck bed. She places the boy on the floor, props him up between her legs, and puts her arms, like protective wings, around the kids beside her. *We're here,* she tells herself, hardly believing it. *Thank You, God.* She breathes in a lungful of the Holy Land air. The first of many millions to come, she knows.

More groups scramble up; children squeeze together to make room for arriving adults. Another truck rumbles away. The rescuers run back; hundreds of passengers are still waiting to be led to safety.

As the young man shuts the truck's low tailgate, Judith reaches over and touches his fingers. "My hero," she whispers. "Thank you."

"Welcome home," he replies, and she can hear the warm smile in his voice.

Part I

UNCERTAINTY:
*We sail within a vast sphere, ever adrift in
uncertainty, driven from end to end.*

—BLAISE PASCAL

Chapter One

SHARON

Tel Aviv, Israel
July 1968

SHARON ENTERS HER grandmother's apartment—her home— expecting to escape the scorching heat outside, but the air that greets her, aromatic with the smell of baking, is warm. The radio is playing "Jerusalem of Gold," the passionate song that became Israel's unofficial national anthem following the liberation of Jerusalem the year before. Sharon drops her carpet satchel and kicks off her sandals to soak in the chill of the marble floor. Her skin feels sticky from the bus ride back to Tel Aviv from the suburban home of her dead fiancé.

She's barely closed the door when Savta, her grandmother, steps out of the kitchen. "Someone from the navy was here to see you."

Sharon swivels on her heel. "Why didn't he go to the Golans'?" Since she hadn't yet become Alon Golan's wife, his parents are the next of kin. Thirty hours after the submarine *Dakar* sent its last signal, the commander in chief visited their house to deliver the troubling news. "The navy knows where they live," Sharon adds.

"He left a phone number." A bit of flour is smeared on Savta's forehead. Sharon reaches out and wipes it off.

"Did he say what this was about?" Sharon is exhausted from six months of mourning, of waiting for the sunken *Dakar* to be found and for a proper burial to take place. "It must be a mistake."

"Are you going to call?" Savta holds out the note.

"Maybe tomorrow," Sharon mumbles. Haunting images of Alon struggling for air, his fingers clawing at the iron walls of his tomb, rush through her mind. She's just spent another day in the only place she finds solace: his parents' home, where dozens of friends and relatives take turns dropping by daily, bearing platters of food. They brew coffee, serve cakes, empty ashtrays, refill bowls of nuts and pickles, and pass around pitchers of fresh-squeezed orange juice. The television is kept on day and night for any breaking news. The Golans' heavy silence in the midst of this activity suits Sharon's mood. The hollow gouged in her middle is unprepared to accept her friends' invitations for an outing of falafel and ice cream, a beach paddleball game, or a night's campfire, where she used to play her flute.

"The officer was clear that he needed to speak with you," Savta insists.

All Sharon wants to do now is drop on her bed and give herself over to a long cry. She kisses Savta's cheek in a pretense of a light mood. Despite the heat, Savta's skin is clammy and cold, smelling of vanilla. A flood of love washes over Sharon. These past two years, she's been wrapped up in her own life: her two-year intelligence service, the Six-Day War. Operationally, the war took not a mere six days but six months of her working around the clock, rarely having time to sleep, let alone come home. Now her mourning is a bottomless sorrow, a black hole from which no light—or emotion—escapes. She has given little thought to Savta's deepening loneliness following Grandpa Nathan's passing.

What would a naval officer want with her? Only once, within two weeks of the *Dakar*'s disappearance, did an officer come here rather than to the Golans' home. That social worker from headquarters, a woman, inquired whether Sharon was, by any chance, pregnant. No, Sharon wasn't, and she was glad not to be faced with the dilemma. She wouldn't have wanted to raise a child without a father. She was an orphan herself, and although her grandparents were devoted to her, they had already reared seven children and spent many days babysitting their sixteen grandchildren. Then, in 1948, in the middle of the War of Independence, between sirens, there was a knock on the door. Their twenty-three-year-old son, Amiram, and his young refugee wife, Judith, had been killed in battle defending their kibbutz. During a brief cease-fire, Sharon's devastated grandparents rushed to pick up the six-week-old orphan from Haifa, where the kibbutz's children had been evacuated.

"Have you eaten today?" Savta's fingers pinch the excess fabric of Sharon's calf-length dress. "You can't keep losing weight."

Sharon forces a smile. "It's the summer heat." She tasted only a few morsels from the plate someone at the Golans' pressed into her hands.

The phone in the kitchen rings. She lets Savta step in and pick it up. If it's any of Sharon's friends, Savta will take a message. Sharon will not call back.

"That officer." Savta's palm covers the mouthpiece.

Sharon groans. *Just take a message,* she mouths impatiently, but Savta holds out the phone.

A deep voice says, "Good evening, Sharon. This is Commander Daniel Yarden."

"I got your message. I'm sure you want to speak with the Golans."

"I'd like to speak with you. You and I met at their home."

Since late January, every week, officers of the various branches of the Israel Defense Forces, the IDF, have been dropping in at the Golans' house. Some sit silently, soaking in Alon's parents' grief; some engage in conversation with other visitors, all of whom have military experience in their past.

Sharon has been oblivious to the visitors. "What's this about?"

"It needs to be discussed in person."

"I told your social worker six months ago that I wasn't pregnant."

He chuckles. "How about I come by in an hour?"

"Can't it wait till tomorrow? Or next week?"

"If it's okay with you, I'll be over at twenty-one hundred."

She's puzzled by his persistence. She wants nothing to do with the navy. With a sigh, she stretches out the words, "All right."

"Is that about your intelligence unit?" Savta asks after Sharon hangs up.

"If they needed me, they'd send a telegram, not a naval commander." Sharon kisses Savta's cheek. "I'm going to take a shower."

Two carp are swimming in the tub in the bathroom. Today must be Wednesday, which is when Savta begins shopping for Friday-night dinner. Friday morning, she'll kill, gut, and stuff the carp for her gefilte fish.

"Hello to you too," Sharon says to the pair as she wiggles out of her dress. Rather than spending another day at the Golans', she should stay home on Friday and help Savta cook the meal for whichever family members show up—usually about twenty. Since Grandpa's long illness, Savta can't afford the daily Arab maid.

When Sharon steps into the adjacent shower stall, she realizes that for a whole three minutes, she hasn't thought of Alon's torturous death.

THE UNIFORMED VISITOR is tall, almost gangly, and wears rimless glasses. He politely refuses Savta's offer of coffee and a slice of poppy-seed cake.

The living room has a frosted-glass door and he asks Sharon's permission to close it. He pulls over a chair to face her while she settles on the sofa. Her long hair is still wet from the shower, and the dampness spreads across the back of her cotton frock.

He leans forward. His face is long, like the rest of him, and pleasing, except for the bulbous tip of his nose. His green eyes are enlarged by his glasses. A shadow in his cleft chin hints of a hidden stubble. He appears to be around twenty-seven. "Sorry to press you for this meeting, but I am about to go overseas."

"Spill it," she says. "I can't imagine what this is about."

"What are your plans for the coming months?"

"Are you serious? I'm waiting for you guys to find the *Dakar*—if you're even bothering to look for it any longer."

"I'm so sorry for what you're going through. The *Eilat* and then the *Dakar* hit us all very hard."

The destroyer *Eilat* was sunk last October by Egyptian missiles; forty-seven men were killed and a hundred wounded. Alon had trained with some of the *Eilat*'s seamen, and she accompanied him on shivah visits to the bereaved families. At least they had the consolation of burials. At least many of the boys who were injured survived. How could she have imagined that four months later she would be similarly devastated? The two stupendous losses extinguished the exhilaration over the unprecedented victory of the Six-Day War.

"Is that what you came to talk about?" Sharon asks.

"Indirectly, yes." His eyes meet hers. "We are rethinking naval warfare, overhauling the navy."

Why is he looking at her as if she has anything to do with naval warfare? Since he is, Sharon can give him a piece of her mind.

"I never understood the strategy of defending our long shoreline primarily from the air, treating the navy as a bastard child." Her tone heats up. "Which is also evident in the way you stopped searching for the *Dakar*."

"For the record, the navy and air force have not given up, but this is outside my work. I am in the process of recruiting people for another project."

She shoots out of her seat and paces the room. "Not me, that's for sure. First, I finished my IDF duty. Second, the only women in the navy are secretaries, and I can't type. Third, if you don't mind my being blunt, I hate your navy."

"Just listen, please." He gestures for her to sit down and waits until she lets out an impatient groan and settles against the sofa's cushions. "We've checked you out. You graduated from Alliance Française." Sharon nods, perplexed at the mention of her French-language high school. He continues. "We know that in Intelligence, you worked in Arabic, which we don't need at the moment. Besides English, don't you also know some German?"

She crosses her arms. Why is any of that this commander's business? Her eyes are drawn to the framed photo on the wall behind him: her parents on their wedding day. They stand in front of Grandpa Nathan's synagogue, the svelte bride holding a bouquet of white anemones against her straight, buttoned, and belted dress. The fabric is cream-colored, not as blinding in the sunny black-and-white photo as Amiram's white shirt. Savta told Sharon that Judith had no relatives and was attended by only one girlfriend. Relieved for two days of their duties at the kibbutz, the couple and the friend had taken the hours-long bus ride to Tel Aviv for the wedding.

Who was this woman, her dead mother, the Holocaust refugee? She must have had a knack for languages too, because when Amiram brought her to meet his parents a mere seven months after Judith Katz arrived in Israel, Savta was astonished at how fast the newcomer had learned Hebrew. Her mother must have also been musical; Sharon's musical talent certainly didn't come from her father's tone-deaf family.

How had her mother's touch felt on her six-week-old skin, the last time she'd held Sharon?

Sharon is stroking her own exposed arm as the commander's words pull her back. "The results of your psychometric exams before you joined Intelligence were later confirmed by your performance there," he says. "You are extremely resourceful, you work well independently, and you are detail-oriented without being bogged down by minutiae. You're able to juggle several pieces of information while assessing a situation. What others might call intuition seems to have led you to uncover crucial intel during the Six-Day War, right?"

Blood rushes to her face. Isn't she a civilian now with the right to privacy? "Presumably, my unit's projects were highly confidential. How did the navy get access to them?"

"We didn't. Only to the personnel file. And we spoke to your commander."

"Why? Are you recruiting a Mata Hari?"

His laughter is rolling, pleasant. "It's only the Cherbourg project."

"What's that?"

"The Saar boats being built in France."

Of course. When the twelve boats were ordered a few years ago, there were some write-ups in the newspapers. Sharon only noticed that the first five had arrived because Alon pointed them out to her when they drove past the Kishon port on the way to Carmel Mountain.

A familiar surge of grief swells in her at the memory of that picnic in the forest. They'd made love on a bed of dry pine needles and fallen asleep to the music of the breeze rustling in the treetops. The pines' resinous aroma now rises in Sharon's nostrils. Doesn't this commander grasp that she is too distraught—and angry—to care about the revamping of his fleet?

She collects herself. "Cherbourg, as in *The Umbrellas of Cherbourg*?" she asks. The musical film starring Catherine Deneuve was a bore, yet it and its theme song had become international sensations.

"That's the one. It's a port city in Normandy. The *Titanic* sailed from there."

"Normandy has lots of cows," she says, recalling her introductory French textbook.

He laughs. "Sheep too."

She scratches her cheek. "Let me get this straight, Commander Yarden—"

"Call me Danny."

She won't fall for this tactic of familiarity. "Are you offering me a job in France in the middle of nowhere?"

"I didn't get to that yet, but yes, except that it's a lovely place—and only a five-hour train ride from Paris." He grins as if aware of the absurdity of touting such a long distance as a plus. "Most important, the navy needs you for a very interesting position."

His audacity infuriates her. "Are you kidding me?"

His left eyebrow arches. "Why else would I be here talking to you?"

"I'm not remotely interested in working for the navy that killed my fiancé. We were going to get married this October."

"Hear me out."

"What kind of job could your navy possibly offer that would make me want to be part of it?"

His tone turns persuasive: "We want you to take over some complicated, highly classified tasks that are too confidential for me to outline right now. Also to act as a liaison with our foreign contacts." He examines her face. "We are about twenty Israelis living there, some with families. A warm little community. You might find the change of scenery refreshing."

Sharon stands up. "Thanks for thinking of me. I'm flattered and horrified to have been the subject of such an extensive investigation. I can't imagine leaving Israel while I'm waiting for a funeral—nor having anything to do with your navy."

Equally, she's scared of traveling abroad, of the unknown. Grief has become a familiar landscape.

AFTER YARDEN DEPARTS, Savta tiptoes in. She wipes her hands on her apron. "What did he want?"

"Apparently, the naval brass met me at the Golans', did some digging about me, and came up with a ridiculous idea to get me out of here—for reasons I'm yet to figure out."

"Out of here to where?"

"France, but not Paris. Some job in a remote port." Sharon pauses. "I'm surprised that they have a rehabilitation program for fiancées, not just widows."

Savta sits next to Sharon on the sofa and takes her hand. Her brown irises are almost hidden under her drooping upper lids. Sharon reminds herself to pluck Savta's two stubborn chin hairs. "Listen to yourself," Savta says. "When did you become so cynical? This is a chance to change atmosphere, to see the world."

"It's not seeing the world. There are just cows and boats there, not the Paris Opera."

"Nothing is happening for you here. You've missed the university's registration deadline. While you're waiting for the *Dakar* to be found, you need to do something. Anything. Just don't spend more *months* sitting on the Golans' couch. It's killing me to see you so defeated by grief." Savta tucks a stray strand of hair behind Sharon's ear. Her glance shifts to the photo on the wall. "Even though you were a newborn then, you carried their loss in your heart. When you were little, you used to speak to them, tell them about your kindergarten friends." Savta's eyes redden. "You played your flute for them and twirled around to show them every new dress I sewed for you. Now Alon's death has broken you. What is there to do but pick up the pieces and soldier on? I lost a son, the apple of my eye. God forgive me, but Amiram was my favorite of the seven I was blessed with. I had to learn to breathe again. You helped—you gave me a new purpose. You're only twenty years old; the world is open for you. Find a purpose. You have choices that women of my generation never even dreamed of. Open yourself up to opportunities. Say yes to life."

Sharon lies down, pulls up her knees, and rests her head on Savta's ample thighs. How can she leave her grandmother? Savta strokes Sharon's now-dry hair, and tears that have been dammed behind Sharon's lids soak Savta's skirt.

"To be a Jewish woman is not to accept defeat," Savta says.

Chapter Two

SHARON

Tel Aviv, Israel
July 1968

I N BED AT night, with only the streetlamp's light seeping into the room, Sharon stares at Alon's photo. A cat meows, and the cover of a trash can clatters onto the concrete. The neighbor above drops his work boots upon his return from his late shift at the electric company. Sharon's mind churns with possible explanations for the *Dakar*'s disappearance. These obsessive speculations have plagued her from the start, but she never dares raise them in the Golans' presence. Could Alon still be alive somewhere, captive? But even the rabbis—so pedantic when it comes to identifying the body of a missing husband before they release a woman from her marriage—now accept the men's deaths. They are contorting their halachic logic to free the *agunot*, the women "chained" to their marriages. If not declared widows, the wives of the lost officers and sailors would forever be forbidden to remarry. Should they bear children, their offspring would be labeled *mamzers*, bastards.

At seven in the morning, Sharon is in the kitchen brewing coffee. Her eyes burn from lack of sleep. She places on a tray buttered toast, half a grapefruit, and a cup of coffee with a sugar cube in its saucer. She's about to take the tray to Savta in bed when the phone rings. Sharon vaults toward it; at this unusually early hour, it might bring the news she's been waiting for—and dreading.

She's disappointed to hear Commander Daniel Yarden's voice.

"I'm not far from you, heading to the central bus station. Would you join me for breakfast?"

"I won't change my answer." Despite Savta's encouragement, Sharon is certain that saying yes to traveling abroad—or to the navy—is not an option.

"Just a friendly chat in a café," he says. "We can't discuss yesterday's topic in a public place."

She understands his new tactic. She's used it herself. She recalls the night during the Six-Day War when an eleven-year-old Arab girl was brought to the tent that served as Sharon's field office. The girl had been found wandering in an olive grove. The soldiers, who had almost shot her in the dark, didn't know what to do with her. The girl wore a long dress, and her single possession was a hand mirror with a painting of a veiled belly dancer glued to its back. Sharon turned off the interception equipment she was using to listen to Arabic chatter and assured the girl that she was safe. She made her a chocolate-spread sandwich and gave her a glass of milk. The girl clutched the mirror in her right hand and used her left to eat and drink, which was odd, as Arabs always ate with the right hand. Although the girl seemed wise, she said she didn't know her name. By two a.m., her lids were drooping with fatigue. Sharon unrolled a mattress, tucked her in, and sang her an Arabic lullaby. When the girl was asleep, Sharon gently took the mirror and pried open the back. She discovered a list of people, their code names, and a hand-drawn map of their locations. She was furious. Someone had sent a child across enemy lines in the middle of the night. She could have been killed.

But Sharon's intelligence unit had obtained crucial information.

"Hello?" the commander says on the other end of the line.

"Sorry. I—" Sharon is about to repeat her refusal when it occurs to her that she can ask him the questions that have been torturing her. "All right," she says.

In this busy neighborhood filled with wholesale shops and small factories, it's hard to find a quiet spot in the café. The commander has secured a table in a corner next to a large window overlooking a city-block-long park where an old man scatters seeds for the birds. Soon, mothers will show up with their toddlers; Savta used to bring Sharon here.

Every station on the radio plays "Jerusalem of Gold" through-out the day. Sharon can't address the commander by his first name even when he is wearing civilian clothes; his khaki pants and button-down shirt are so neatly pressed that among the other café patrons in shorts and T-shirts, he might as well have been wearing his uniform. His prescription glasses have been replaced by aviator sunglasses, and she can't see his eyes.

They order breakfast, and the waitress brings them coffee. Sha-ron realizes that this is the first time she's sat at a café since *it* hap-pened. Life streams on. She puts two spoonfuls of sugar in her coffee and stirs. "Since you know so much about me," she says to the commander, "how about if you tell me about yourself?"

"I'm a kibbutznik from Ayelet HaShachar. Unmarried. I attended the naval academy in Acre. Additional training in Toulon," he adds, mentioning the large French maritime center on the Mediterranean.

"Neither the kibbutz nor the naval academy teaches French. How do you manage in that *Umbrellas* city of yours?"

"Actually, I was born in France. I was brought here by the Youth Aliyah. My new family made sure that I kept up my French."

Sharon gasps. She sets down her cup carefully, trying not to show her excitement. Youth Aliyah was the immigration organiza-tion that, twenty-two years earlier, had brought her mother from France to Palestine—and that is practically all Sharon knows about the woman who arrived here at age seventeen, married at eighteen, gave birth at nineteen, and was killed six weeks later.

When Sharon was little, every year her grandparents drove her up north to the annual memorial service for the fallen heroes of the Battle for the Galilee. She recalls her growing panic at age six as she circulated among the adults, all of them wearing the unofficial Me-morial Day uniform of a white shirt over blue pants or a skirt, their faces solemn. "Did you know my mother?" she asked each of them. She received nothing but soft strokes on her head and sad looks. "I'm sure she loved you very much," some said. "She was a true hero" and "She watches over you from heaven," others said. "How do you know if you didn't know her?" Sharon responded, her throat constricting as she held back tears, intent on her mission to find at least one person who had known Judith Katz.

Finally, Grandpa Nathan gathered her into his arms and sat her on his knee. "The entire group was killed in the battle," he whispered. "These people are here to honor their sacrifice and their memory, even if they didn't know any of them personally. 'In their deaths they willed us life,'" he said, repeating the line carved on the earth-toned marble memorial they were facing and that she could read herself. "You have one thing that these people don't know about."

"What is it?"

"Your mommy's beautiful face." He kissed her cheek. "And her cutest dimple."

Sharon would never know her mother, but the second-best thing would be talking to people who'd lived through her mother's experience of Youth Aliyah. That never came to be. Growing up in a city, she never met any of the tens of thousands of rescued children—all older than she—because they had been, like the commander, absorbed in kibbutzim and agricultural youth villages.

Treading cautiously, she asks him, "What happened to your parents?"

"I don't know. It was during the Nazi occupation of France."

"Who took care of you?"

He shifts in his seat. For the first time, she sees him lose his composure. "Maybe the underground at first. Then I was adopted by a French couple."

"What underground?"

"A French network of anti-Nazi men and women hid Jewish children. When things heated up, they transferred the kids to a new hiding place." His tone turns more energetic. "It's all in the past. I focus on the future. We face an existential threat not only from our Arab neighbors but from Russia. After centuries of official anti-Semitism, they've found partners who share their sentiments outside the Soviet borders—and right on our own."

She knows all of that, but his words remind her how self-centered she's been these past few months, as if losing three people means she's sacrificed enough. Except that their deaths haven't brought security. The threat of a second Holocaust, another genocide committed by Israel's neighbors, forever lurks about.

The electric fan above Sharon's head lets out a small screech with every turn. For a while, neither she nor the commander speaks. Outside, light saturates everything it touches, although it fails to brighten her mood.

Their breakfast of chopped salad and fried eggs arrives. Sharon restarts the conversation by mentioning the names of Alon's officers who graduated from the naval academy. The commander knows them and recounts a three-month voyage to India on a commercial tanker he'd taken with one of them the summer after he graduated and before he enlisted.

"I want to ask you something I can't bring up in Alon's parents' presence," she finally says. "What if the *Dakar* didn't plunge to the bottom of the sea but was seized by Egyptian or Russian forces, and the crew is not dead but captured?"

"International diplomatic channels have plowed through such a possibility."

"Here is another scenario." She takes a deep breath. "Isn't it possible that the American navy sank the *Dakar* in retaliation for the USS *Liberty*?" The American destroyer was hit in the middle of last year's Six-Day War when Israel mistook it for an enemy ship. Explanations and apologies failed to placate the enraged Americans. "I mean, not officially, not by a US government order, but by some low-level officers to avenge their brothers?"

The commander pushes his plate to the side and places both his elbows on the table. "Sharon, rumors are bound to float around. There's absolutely no basis for such a theory."

"I learned in Intelligence that until there's a solid explanation, all possible theories are valid."

He smiles. "One more proof of how well you'll fit in on our project. By the way, did I tell you that a civilian's salary is on the French union scale, not the Israeli government's? That's quite a bundle."

Sharon doesn't show that her interest is piqued. Savta is struggling financially after Grandpa Nathan's long illness, which depleted their assets. Sharon hasn't yet contributed since her military basic pay covered only the cost of mascara. She'd planned to seek office employment between her expected release from the military in February and the start of the university semester in November. Even if she had done that, she couldn't have mentioned her intelligence service. With no formal work experience other than some drafting and billing at her uncle's factory during school breaks, she would have started at the lowest end of the pay scale. She is flattered that the commander views her potential through her qualifications, not her nonexistent work history.

"Sounds good, but it's not about money," she tells him.

He rises, pays the bill, and motions with his head toward the garden. "Shall we take a walk?"

The outside air wraps around her like a wet, hot towel. Dust rises from the path at her first step. It will be another blistering summer day. Sharon contemplates taking the bus to the city pool for a long swim and is jolted by the notion that she is considering doing anything other than joining the Golans on their couch.

"Look," she says to the commander while her mind digests her sudden craving to dive into cool water. "You're wasting your time on me."

"I don't think so. You care deeply about Israel's security." He pauses. "Do you know that the *Eilat* was hit by a Russian-made Egyptian missile? It was the first such missile ever shot at our ships, and it proved how dangerous its range and accuracy were."

Sharon's heart lurches. She's transcribed the minutes of enough intelligence meetings to understand that, given the missiles' improved distance and accuracy, it is only a matter of time before one of them hits the spot where she now stands, in the middle of Tel Aviv.

A bus puffs out black soot, and its acrid smell wafts toward the garden. The swallows chirping in the treetops are shocked into a momentary silence before they pick up their song again. These small, valiant birds, Sharon thinks, have adjusted to the urban pollution instead of seeking a greener neighborhood. When she's not floating in her bubble of grief, she notices the world. She cares—and worries.

If only it weren't the navy that was asking—and expecting her to travel into the unknown.

"I'd like to make it clear," the commander says, "the Saars project is highly classified. You may not share our conversation with anyone."

"How can it be classified if it was in the media when we ordered the boats, and five are already in Israel, docked in full sight?"

He raises his fingers to tick off the reasons. "One, they have special features that are, let's say, unique. Two, our team's presence in Cherbourg is not reported anywhere—not in France or Israel. Three, the Saars' final designated use is the issue. They are being built as oil-exploration boats. No weapons are being placed on them."

"In that case, the arms embargo shouldn't apply," she states. President de Gaulle's arms embargo, reinforced by the recently elected prime minister, Pompidou, was a blow to Israel. France had formerly been a friendly supplier of tanks and planes—it had even helped in the development of Israel's nascent nuclear power. But after tiny Israel was attacked by four mighty Arab nations and won the war in a mere six days, France chose to side with the Arab states. The fifty French Mirage airplanes that Israel had fully paid for were not delivered. With France refusing to sell Israel spare parts for its French-made tanks and planes, the nation's military vehicles and aircraft are fast going out of commission. The country is being choked, and the defeated Arab countries are gearing up for another round of war.

"The arms embargo is not *supposed* to apply to boats built as platforms for oil exploration," the commander tells her. "But these Saars are constructed of steel, not wood, and they are too fast, sophisticated, and expensive to serve a civilian purpose. That leaves a gray area for France's interpretation—and ours." He removes his sunglasses and looks at her. "If you were the French minister of defense, what would your take on it be?"

Why is the commander testing her when she has no intention of joining his team? "I would wonder why the Israeli *navy* is directing what is supposed to be a commercial enterprise," she replies. "In which case, the Saars operation must be conducted in secrecy even in France?"

A small smile quirks his lips. "Let's say, under the radar."

They pass by the sandbox, where a woman empties a bag of plastic toys for two little boys. Sharon watches her. What kind of a mother would Judith Katz have been? Her name was so common that Sharon's efforts to locate information about her in the Youth Aliyah's messy archives had been futile. Was Judith funny, introspective, impatient, reserved, shy, giving? All Savta could tell Sharon about her daughter-in-law, whom she'd met only twice, was that during the Holocaust, Judith's family lived in France. They had been deported and had presumably perished. Orphaned, bewildered, and homeless, Judith was seventeen when an Israeli team searching the countryside after the war for lost Jewish children found her. She helped care for a group of rescued youngsters and accompanied them on an immigrants' ship to what, two years later, would become Israel. Amiram, four years older than Judith, met her on her arrival.

"What do you remember from your Youth Aliyah voyage?" Sharon asks the commander.

He chuckles at the turn of the conversation. "I was fascinated with the ship and the sight of endless water. I hung around on the bridge and bombarded the captain with questions. He spoke no French, but he let me hold the helm. That's when I fell in love with the sea."

That's not the anecdote she's searching for. "Do you remember others on the journey?"

He looks at his watch. His tone is bored when he says, "It was so long ago."

She will dig for more if she gets the opportunity. The commander thinks he knows all about her. He can't imagine that she will make herself useful to him only so she can probe his Youth Aliyah memories. For the first time in Sharon's life, a window has opened for her to learn something about her mother's experience. All it will take is chutzpah—daring and audacity.

They stop in the corner leading to the street. A horse-drawn farmer's cart slows the heavy morning traffic. Irritated drivers blow their horns. The horse lowers its head as it tries to pull faster, harder. Sharon feels bad for the poor beast.

"By the way, did you know that the first Saar participated in the search for *Dakar*?" the commander asks her through the metallic cacophony of honking horns.

She didn't but won't admit it.

"Well, it was nice chatting more." He extends his hand. "Thank you. Shalom."

"Okay. I'll take the job," she blurts out.

A quick expression of surprise traverses his face, then disappears. "I'm glad to hear that. Sharon, you'll be channeling your pain into something constructive for Alon's memory."

No. She'll be deserting Alon, walking away from believing that at any moment, the submarine will be found. Despite the heat, a sudden chill zips through her. What has she done? Her emotions are too raw, already too taut, like a boil about to burst the skin. She can't afford to heap more stress and fear on herself.

Sharon walks back home, joy and regret clashing inside her. Come to think of it, nothing is holding her to her impetuous acceptance. When someone calls to make the travel arrangements, she should rescind it.

Chapter Three

CLAUDETTE

Loire Valley, France
Spring 1940

THE WINDS OF war in the east, where Germany had invaded Poland, were distant. They had nothing to do with France, Claudette thought. What felt real to her were the upcoming summer festivities. Young village women flocked to her grandmother's cottage, where Claudette refashioned and embellished old dresses. Come July, the village of La Guerche-sur-l'Aubois would celebrate both Bastille Day and the one hundred and fiftieth anniversary of the Fête de la Fédération.

Claudette sat on the upholstered chair in the front room stitching, her cursed left leg hidden under the sewing table. Three girls her age chatted excitedly about the young men with whom they hoped to dance. For one of those girls, Claudette would salvage an embroidered bodice from an old dress and attach it to a newer organza skirt. For another, she would stitch pearls around the neckline to emphasize the girl's alabaster skin. For the third, Claudette would alter the girl's mother's bridal dress by weaving colorful ribbons into the white lace.

Claudette kept her head down, bent over the silk roses she was cutting, and wallowed in her sorrow. No one, including herself, expected a cripple to participate in the merriment. She wouldn't even watch the dance from the sidelines with her grandmother Mémère and be subjected to looks of pity and the mockery of young men. Come the night of the festival, girls wearing her dresses, her creations, would twirl in the plaza and be courted and swooned over by handsome lovers.

All Claudette could do was stitch her sorrow into beautiful embellishments.

Just before nightfall, she grabbed her cane, hobbled out to the garden, collected ripened tomatoes, and unlocked the back gate for the peddler, a Jew, who made weekly rounds with his cart selling women's toiletries, detergents, sewing supplies, medicines, small tools, and kitchenware. When she was little, Claudette had feared this strange man with the funny accent who never took off his brimmed hat, whose face was covered with a beard, and whose eyes were hidden behind glasses. His people had killed Christ, so what was he capable of? Her suspicion had melted after he had cured Mémère's coughs with his elixirs.

Claudette was twelve when he began his weekly visits and discovered that, due to her disability, she had never been to school—it was too far to walk. He taught her to read. This medicine man had also given her holy water and instructed her to dab it on her knee twice daily, then lift her cursed leg ten times. Miraculously, the holy water worked and her leg strengthened. Unfortunately, once Claudette turned sixteen and her body filled in, the additional weight made her lose her balance. Her left leg, twisted at birth, had been further damaged from repeated muscle tears. In one of her falls, she had broken two of her front teeth. Since then, Claudette covered her mouth with her hand when she smiled.

The Jew led his cart into the barn, where his horse would keep Rosette the cow company. Claudette had concealed the man's overnight stays from her best friend, Solange, who claimed that all Jews were crooks. Since he slept in Mémère's bed, Claudette had a greater reason to keep mum about the Jew's visits. He was a widower with three kids, he had told them, and Claudette looked forward to the gifts he brought each week.

"I have something special for you," he told Claudette after he entered the house and politely accepted Mémère's offer of a meal as if it hadn't been their routine for years. He unwrapped a contraption of metal and leather buckles. "It's a brace. It will allow you to put weight on your leg."

The brace had two flat metal rods. A cobbler had fixed them to a shoe and added three buckled leather straps to circle Claudette's thigh and calf. After Mémère finished helping Claudette strap it on behind the dressing screen, the Jew presented the matching right shoe with a flourish of his palm.

Smiling, he watched Claudette take her first tentative steps. "You see? You'll stand straighter, and it will ease the pain in your back."

The contraption was heavy, and Claudette couldn't bend her knee, but she could put weight on her cursed left leg without it buckling under her. She loved how the new leather shoes shone. She sent the Jew a happy smile of thanks, but the word *merci* failed to convey the gratitude she felt for his care these past several years.

"Wear it in good health. May God be with you," he said.

His mention of God used to confuse her. The Jew didn't seem concerned about being punished for killing God's son. But Claudette had long since stopped trying to reconcile what the priest said about the evil Jews with this man's gentle ways.

"Does your son wear this brace too?" Mémère asked him while Claudette paced around the room, basking in the new freedom to move about.

He had told them that his son was afflicted with a similar disability, but Claudette had never met the man's three children. "Of course," he said. "At his job apprenticing with a printer, he must stand for hours setting up letters."

"Would you please bless Claudette?" Mémère said. "To help her walk." She had told Claudette that Jews, the Chosen People, were close to God.

Claudette stopped pacing. The Jew's hand hovered over her lowered head. "May God bless you and keep you. May God shine light on you and be gracious to you. May God turn toward you and grant you peace."

IN THE MORNING, as Claudette milked the cow and collected the eggs from the chicken coop, she thought about the Jew's son. Perhaps, sharing her infirmity, that boy would like her? If he was like his father, his gray, penetrating eyes would gaze at her with fondness, and his soft voice would be filled with kindness.

The warmth that ran through her at the image was like nothing she'd ever felt before.

Later, alone at home, Claudette fixed daisies to a blue chiffon dress and dared to try it on. The airy, sheer fabric felt soft against her skin, rich and sensual. She examined herself in the mirror that the Jew had installed for their customers. A longing swept over her. Her mind leaped into a fantasy starring his crippled son.

In her daydream, the two of them sat at the edge of a vineyard and just talked. If he was like his father, he would be wise and tell her anecdotes about the world outside this village.

She would be wearing this chiffon dress, and away from prying eyes, their bodies would sway in a slow dance. Or they might even kiss.

A CART HEAPED with woven baskets of all sizes stopped in front of the house, and Solange climbed down from it. "Wait! I'll get you," Claudette called out, happy to show her blind friend her newfound mobility. "Feel my new brace." She brought Solange's hand down to the metal rods, then guided her from the sidewalk into the yard and up the three steps to the porch.

"And I got so many new booklets," Solange exclaimed as they sat down. She withdrew from her skirt pockets novellas with tantalizing pictures on their covers.

Claudette had met the feisty Solange when she had first arrived in La Guerche to learn sewing from Mémère. Her father knew that no one would ever marry his lame child, and his seamstress mother could help Claudette find a way to earn her keep. Now, picking up the first booklet, Claudette was certain that the Jew's teaching her to read had been an act of benevolence directly from God. She could read to her blind friend the titles of the new booklets and describe the cover art of each. *The Stranger's Touch*, *A Rogue and a Pirate*, *Love's Tender Fury*, *Velvet and Fire*, *Unlikely Lovers*, *Blazing Hearts*, *A Night to Cherish*, and *Once More Forever*.

"Start with *Blazing Hearts*," Solange said. "Like when our princes will come and set our hearts on fire. Figuratively speaking," she added in a high-society prissy voice. Claudette burst out laughing at the words that Solange seemed to collect while her fingers were forever weaving.

When Claudette finished reading the story, the two of them dissected it and speculated about jealousy and love. Yet hovering in the background was Claudette's knowledge that neither of them would ever experience any of it. Only heartaches.

MÉMÈRE HAD LOST two sons in the Great War and was less insouciant than their young customers about the war raging outside of France's borders. There were mothers there too, mothers who were losing sons, she said, and they were all crying. When she and Claudette went to fetch beer at the tavern, Mémère questioned Monsieur Lefebvre about the battles. He had fought in the Great War, and since winter he had begun to wear the frayed military jacket that marked him as an expert on military strategy.

He hung a large map on the tavern's wall. "We need not worry about the Germans," he told Mémère. "No enemy will ever again invade France from the east." He tapped on the squarish shape that he said was France, and his gnarled finger traced a red line. "Here is the northeastern forest. Absolutely impenetrable. South of it, the rest of France's long eastern frontier is protected by the Maginot Line."

"What's that?" Claudette asked, alarmed. The distance shown on the map between that border and La Guerche was shorter than her forearm.

"An immense line of concrete fortifications, bunkers, and cannons stretching for thousands of miles to our southern shore. No enemy will ever again enter France from the east." Mémère's mouth pulled down in sadness. Claudette knew that memories of war were forever vivid in her head.

Indeed, horrible news arrived in May. The German tanks had plowed through the supposedly impenetrable northeast forest, and suddenly the war exploded inside France. Two million French soldiers were taken prisoner. Overnight, all the young men with whom the village girls had planned to dance enlisted. Probably the Jew too, because he stopped coming. Although he wasn't young, he wasn't too old to fight.

Mémère cried again for her two boys and for the French mothers who were wretched with worry and fear. The last of the Jew's elixir failed to lessen her anguish. Claudette stared at the grainy newspaper photo of captured French soldiers, and her lungs burned as if she had inhaled the smoke of gunfire.

La Guerche hummed with rumors of advancing German troops. Life was conducted in hushed tones among women and the few old men who remained in the village. In the tavern, Monsieur Lefebvre led the old men in devising military strategies to defeat the enemy. On his map, green pins marked the advancing Germans. A large blue pin marked La Guerche-sur-l'Aubois. He showed Claudette the Loire River, which, after heading north, made a sharp turn westward to reach the Atlantic Ocean. Their Aubois River was one of its many tributaries.

Like Claudette, Monsieur Lefebvre must have been dismayed by the proximity of the blue pin to the green ones because he organized the old men to patrol the streets at night. They donned their battered helmets and tattered military wool jackets and carried their tarnished rifles.

Claudette lay upstairs in the dark, her dog, Belle, curled against her, and listened for the guard. Only after she heard his tired footfalls on the cobblestones did she fall asleep, trying to believe that Monsieur Lefebvre's squad could keep the German tanks away.

The Germans went on to conquer Belgium, the Netherlands, and Luxembourg. The newspaper Claudette read in the tavern reported that the French government had abandoned Paris and relocated to Bordeaux. The pins on Monsieur Lefebvre's map shifted westward and southward. The Germans had conquered all of Normandy's shore with its strategic ports.

"The Brits are our only hope against the Nazis. The Brits and the Canadians." Monsieur Lefebvre dropped his head, probably planning a new military strategy.

Since spring, the word *Nazis* has been uttered with fear, the speaker's voice lowered a notch. It wasn't just the word *Germans* in newspaper headlines. Nazis were worse. They were so powerful that the only countries able to stand up to them were England and Canada. But Claudette knew that Canada was as far away as China, where the finest silk came from, and India, whose silk was sturdier and more colorful.

And counting on the Brits? Everyone ridiculed the ways of France's long-standing enemy. Claudette was vaguely aware of a centuries-old history of bloodshed between the two nations. Why would the Brits bother to save the French?

Chapter Four

SHARON

Paris, France
September 1968

How does one scout an airport? After the El Al Israel Airlines plane touches down at Paris Orly Airport, Sharon remains in her seat for a few minutes, baffled by her first assignment. Commander Daniel Yarden instructed her to lock her suitcase in the luggage storeroom, then spend an hour or two scouting the airport. It all sounds so foreign and chilling that Sharon's initial apprehension balloons in her chest. What has she done, accepting this job?

In the seat pocket, a flyer features a map of the airport and its gates. Sharon grabs it.

"Walk through the terminals, check each level, and get to know where the gates are and where each exit takes you," the commander told her. "Don't make any notes publicly. Memorize landmarks like stores and kiosks, broken floor tiles, and exposed ceiling pipes. Pay attention—some chains have more than one store in each airport. And in some European airports, gate numbers repeat in different terminals, so there can be a gate four in both terminal A and terminal C."

She cannot imagine what end this scouting serves. Surely the navy doesn't plan to take hostages or blow up an airport. Israelis design their operations abroad to avoid public drama; they don't grandstand like the Palestinians.

She exits the plane, the last vestige of the familiar. The whirlwind of emotions that roiled in her during this past month of preparations churns faster. She's on her own. The commander thought he had her profile charted, but he missed one crucial point: She's never been without a close ally—Alon, Savta, friends, or colleagues. By clinging to the Golans for six months of shared grief, she had staved off this crushing loneliness that now rises in her.

She has a job to do, she reminds herself. Determined, Sharon spends over an hour checking the corridors and gates, then she slips into a lavatory and writes notes on the airport map. She tucks it into her handbag with her voucher for a night in a Paris hotel and an envelope of francs. What if she missed some crucial information the commander wanted her to find?

Midafternoon, she checks into a small, charming hotel on the Left Bank with a wood-paneled lobby that smells of dusty fabrics and freshly brewed coffee. In her room, she throws herself on the bed; her outstretched arms almost touch the walls. She stares at the diamond relief around the small chandelier. She's in Paris! The commander gave her no further tasks, but her hotel voucher is for a single night. She has only the rest of today to explore the city.

Except that Alon is not here with her.

She brushes her hair, parts it in the middle, and ties a headband around her forehead. She changes out of her long, wide-sleeved caftan into a printed minidress and checks her image in the mirror. Her eyebrows are thick, and her irises are dark against the bright white surrounding them. Nothing reveals her apprehensions. *Paris, here I come!* she mouths with faux cheerfulness to fortify herself. She forces her lips into a smile. Yup. The dimple that Alon loved is still there.

Before exiting the hotel, she deposits her heavy skeleton key with the clerk at the reception desk. He hands her an envelope. "From the gentleman in room six oh four."

The commander is here? Sharon tears open the envelope and finds a note written in large, loopy letters.

Welcome to Paris. If you'd like to join me for a concert at Notre-Dame, please be at the entrance at 19:45. Otherwise, plan to talk at 23:00. Danny.

She misses music; she has been away from her flute for so long. Yesterday, before buckling her suitcase, she contemplated whether to pack it, but it was inconceivable that she would find it in herself to play music. Yet at this moment, so far from home, she knows she'll attend the concert.

On a map of central Paris, the clerk marks the location of the hotel and points to the icon showing the cathedral of Notre-Dame, several blocks away.

She has four hours before she meets the commander. Sharon walks around the district, taking photos with her camera. There is so much to see in the narrow cobblestoned alleys, where some old walls are kept from collapsing by cables and screws; in the magnificently ornate larger buildings in the wider streets; in the colorful boutiques and street markets. She stops at Place Saint-Michel, awed by its breathtaking marble fountain. But what's most striking to her are the hundreds of people her age who lounge about on the ground, seemingly carefree. Their attitude is such a contrast to that of Israelis, who are forever steeped in existential worries. Just this past May, the news on TV was filled with images of the French students' uprising and the violent clashes between them and the police. This plaza was the epicenter of the riotous protests that swelled when the labor unions all over the country joined the students with an all-out strike.

Sharon had felt so remote from the issues at the core of the events. Rebelling against the establishment? She and her generation in Israel had just won the greatest military victory in Western history— they *were* the establishment. Protesting against consumerism? Not a concern when 70 percent of every Israeli's income was taxed for the nation's defense. Enraged by capitalism? Israel was proud of the socialist policies that helped absorb millions of landless Jewish newcomers. Now Sharon watches the much calmer crowd; some sing along with a guitarist, others float in the serenity of hashish she can smell, still others engage in heated debates.

In Intelligence, she learned to be a "listener," to eavesdrop on conversations in Arabic. Now her training kicks in and she inches closer to a vociferous group and catches a discussion in French about

Wilhelm Reich's book *The Function of the Orgasm*. With the advent of the pill, one young woman says, it's time to acknowledge that understanding the intricacies of sex doesn't come naturally. "An orgasm is politics," the woman says. "It frees us from the male institutional domination." Sharon smiles to herself and moves away. She and Alon had never heard of an orgasm and didn't know where to look for it once it was mentioned. It had taken a book to show them the way. She's never thought of it as anything but a private matter.

Just then, a young woman with straight blond hair who's wearing a gauzy white dress floats over, tucks a daisy in Sharon's headband, and raises two fingers in a peace sign. Sharon thanks her, then locks eyes with a girl nearby, another member of the small universe of girls with daisies in their hair.

⌒

THE DOME OF the Notre-Dame cathedral rises above Sharon with its magnificent chiseled stone vaults and stained-glass windows. As people around her settle into their seats, she gazes at the architecture. She catches Danny glancing at her, smiling at her tilted head, and she smiles back to thank him for introducing her to the genius of the architect of eight hundred years ago who knew how to ignite awe in the hearts of believers.

Just then, the string section of the fifty-piece orchestra breaks into a swirling storm. The piano sends up waves of sound, ascending and descending scales, that are answered by the horns' valiant chords. Sharon closes her eyes as the swell of pure notes fills both the cathedral and her body.

Night has long fallen when she and the commander walk along the Seine, its ebony water sparkling with millions of pinprick lights. The arpeggio of the "Revolutionary" Étude by Chopin is still in Sharon's head, and looking at the water, she hears the graceful gurgling streams. She regrets having left her flute at home. Home and its sorrow are eons away. Savta was right when she urged her to travel.

Sharon and the commander descend a flight of steps to the quay and sit down on a bench.

"I wish you could spend longer in Paris this first time," he says, "but there will be other opportunities."

"Commander—" she begins.

"Danny. We'll be working closely together—and you're a civilian."

"Danny, you know that I will stay only until the *Dakar* is found." This also means that she must get to her agenda very soon. She must tread with caution, though, not press him.

"In the short term, we'll be facing a few crises," he replies.

"Since there's an arms embargo, why does the Saars project continue? Won't we lose the remaining seven boats the same way we lost the fifty Mirages? France didn't return the money either, which is outright thievery."

"You know the joke about the Jewish man who was sentenced to death, but pleaded with the king?" Danny replies.

"Which one is that?"

"'If you give me a year,' the Jew said, 'I'll teach your dog to sing.' The king was puzzled but agreed to postpone the execution. When the Jew returned home, his wife asked, 'How can you make such a deal? You can't teach a dog to sing!' The man replied, 'A lot can happen in one year. I may die, the king may die, or the dog may learn to sing.'"

Sharon laughs. "Meaning?"

"New winds may blow. De Gaulle didn't stay in power his full term. Now Pompidou is distracted by troubles in North Africa. Other problems might pop up. Or his fit of temper against us might subside. Who knows? In the meantime, the ban is not on building our boats, only on delivering them, and even that is unclear, according to some people in his administration. They see this breach of a contract that was signed in good faith by their government as bad for France's reliability as an exporter of armaments."

A barge passes by, its cargo covered with burlap, followed by a tourist boat bursting with lights and music. The people on the deck raise champagne glasses at them: *"Salut! Salut!"*

"Here's your first real assignment," Danny says when the jovial sounds roll away. "Tomorrow you'll catch the ten-ten train from Gare Saint-Lazare to Cherbourg. Arrive at the station forty-five minutes early and look for two Israelis, Oded and Gideon. They don't speak French, so when you find them, you'll buy the tickets. Once you're all on the train, there are a few rules for now and for all future trips: Don't all sit together, though you can sit with one of them, as if you're a couple. And don't read anything in Hebrew or speak it until you reach Cherbourg."

"How will I recognize these guys?"

"Are you asking how you'll be able to recognize two bewildered kibbutzniks?"

She laughs. They'll be wearing the standard-issue biblical sandals of double leather strips and the simple clothes that are sewn and distributed by one clothing cooperative, Atta. Kibbutz members are recognizable in Tel Aviv, let alone in Paris. Not Danny, though. This kibbutznik, again in civilian clothes, dresses impeccably.

"Where will you be?" she asks.

"I have an early meeting with Moka Limon."

Of course. Everyone knows the retired admiral, now in Paris as a civilian diplomat. Eighteen years earlier, he had been chief of the Israeli navy, then composed of no more than walnut-shell-like former immigrants' boats.

Sharon is about to ask why Limon is still in Paris when he can no longer procure arms, but then she figures it out: the legendary high-society literary salon his elegant wife has established in Paris. Both are close to the Rothschild family and their vast European connections. No one is better qualified or better positioned to command a spy ring than Limon.

How would Danny or the Cherbourg operation be involved in that?

"Is any of this illegal?" she asks.

"Picking up an electrician and a mechanic at a train station, buying tickets, and riding up to Cherbourg?"

She puffs hair away from her face. "You know what I mean. Anything in this Cherbourg project."

"The difference between legal and illegal sometimes can come down to a comma in a sentence." He smiles. "What do you call that comma?"

"What?"

"Chutzpah."

She likes the idea of chutzpah, although Alon said she had none of that audacious attitude. "What happens when my train arrives in Cherbourg?" Sharon asks. "Where do we go?"

"Cherbourg is the last stop. Someone will fetch you."

The last stop. One more step toward the unknown.

They walk in silence to the hotel, each deep in thought. Sharon has never sought adventure. She craved the opposite—no drama. She just wanted to belong. Her life path had been dictated by circumstances beyond her control, underpinned by her orphanhood. Her hunger for normalcy could never be fully satiated. Her six aunts and uncles included her in their families' activities. There she watched enviously as mothers taught their daughters how to jump rope and fathers showed their sons how to climb trees. All she had was the devotion of old grandparents, and she felt guilty for wanting more. When Sharon and Alon got together, when she was thirteen, his love anchored her into his family. She developed an easy banter with his mother, who often gave her small gifts, including the satchel now slung over Sharon's shoulder.

All this was over. For a split second, Sharon wishes that Danny would take her hand just so she could feel a human touch. She brushes away the absurd need. *It's time to grow up.* Sharon had never considered living away from Alon, and to be near him, she forfeited her dream of studying architecture. It would have required her to attend the Technion in Haifa while he studied botany in the Hebrew University in Jerusalem.

Now she's not only on her own in a foreign country, but tomorrow she will be responsible for two bewildered men.

SHE WAKES UP at six a.m. to inquire with the hotel clerk about the Métro subway. Though she is hours away from taking it, she descends the stairs at the nearest station. To her relief, she discovers a large wall map, and when she presses a button for her destination, Gare Saint-Lazare, the route lights up with miniature bulbs. Each of the two lines she should take is marked by a different color. Satisfied with her preparation, Sharon buys herself a French fashion magazine; she'll bury her nervousness in a light feast of makeup and clothes while improving her language skills.

What she didn't anticipate, she realizes a couple of hours later at the Gare Saint-Lazare, is how gigantic the station is, and how crowded. Where are her men?

Dragging her suitcase, she wanders for thirty minutes, checking the huge hall under the ornate canopy and then the many exits to the train platforms. Panic rises when she climbs the stairs to a second floor that seems to be a holding area for more waiting passengers. No sign of the two kibbutzniks. The huge clock tolls the half hour when she makes her way down again through people, porters, and luggage carts.

Someone taps her shoulder, and she turns. An old kerchiefed woman is holding a baby swaddled in a blanket, and Sharon is surprised when the woman asks for directions. Sharon is mumbling an apology that she's only a visitor when she feels the tug of a hand slithering into her satchel.

In a trained hard chop, she brings down the side of her palm on the arm. The woman yelps and retreats, leaving Sharon stunned with the rush of adrenaline.

She remains rooted in place, horrified. She'd come close to having her passport, money, and train tickets stolen by a pickpocket. Her initial surprise when the woman approached her should have alerted her not to fall for the woman-with-baby ruse.

She almost cries with relief when she spots the two men standing behind a column, befuddled as abandoned puppies. They're in their late twenties, their skin cured by sun exposure. Gideon, who has an unruly crest of hair, is a mechanic, and she notices the black oil embedded under his nails. Oded, shorter with broad shoulders and a shaved head, is an electrician.

"I'm Sharon," she says in English. "If you need to ask me anything, do so in English."

Oded whispers in Hebrew that they can't speak English.

"Well, no more talking, then," she replies in English. Anyone who studied under Israel's national school curriculum understands that much of the language. "That's an order," she adds in an officer's tone. Sharon hopes that the men will keep their mouths shut for the next five hours.

Walking to the train, she catches a glimpse of Alon. She stops and turns toward him. Of course the young man—of medium height and built, wearing a navy-blue uniform, a military duffel bag slung over his shoulder—can't be her dead fiancé.

Once they're all on the train, her charges—Gideon to her right, Oded a few rows down, facing her so she can keep an eye on him—fall asleep in minutes. Sharon sits by the window, and her breath catches at the lushness of the fields, woods, and hills. The emerald and jade patchworks of green look as if God had poured buckets of paint on the world. Farmhouses and silos are built from thousands of small fieldstones fitted together in a calculated but haphazard-looking way, what Sharon guesses is a centuries-old style that uses local materials.

She shifts her gaze back to scan the passengers on their way to and from the bar car. Could she have been followed?

Her eyelids droop, and she almost dozes off, then shakes herself awake. If only she knew what could go wrong, what she's gotten herself into—and what risks she might be taking.

Chapter Five

CLAUDETTE

Loire Valley, France
June 1940

CLAUDETTE LOWERED HER mending on the porch swing at the sight of a bedraggled family coming down the sloping street. Their horse, pulling a covered wagon, lurched down the hill, and all six members of the family used their combined weight to stop it from stumbling and falling. As their wagon rolled up in front of the house, Claudette noted their roughly sewn peasant clothes. An older man, shoulders stooped from exhaustion, asked her for water.

"Of course." She waved toward the well in the yard. She grabbed Belle's collar and commanded her to be quiet.

Everyone was on edge, even the dog. The French government had fled from Bordeaux to Vichy. Monsieur Lefebvre told the crowd at the tavern that at least, with the surrender agreement and the installation of the Nazi sympathizer Philippe Pétain as prime minister, the Germans would not invade the Loire Valley, where their village lay.

With this new development, Monsieur Lefebvre changed his military strategy. "The French Communists are our best recourse to chase out the Nazis. Every bridge blown up, every supply convoy ambushed—it's their doing or the Maquis'." The Maquis were guerrilla fighting groups that attacked the Nazis from the forest underbrush. Claudette would have left a basket of produce and eggs by the back gate for these brave men if she had known it would somehow reach them.

But if all France could do was rely on the despised British, the distant Canadians, and the local rebels, where was there hope?

Claudette went to the church daily to pray to God, Jesus, and Mary to save France.

The family pumping water in the yard hadn't finished filling their canister when Claudette saw a man walking beside a bicycle loaded with packages, from handlebars to the back wheel. Beside him, two boys dragged their feet in obvious fatigue. As they began their descent toward her, more people appeared at the curve in the road. Belle strained against Claudette's hold.

"Mémère!" Claudette called. "Mémère!"

"We are leaving," said the man in the yard. "Thanks for your generosity."

Mémère came out. She watched the family walk out, then, gazing up the street, went to the front gate and latched it. The neighbor next door did the same, sending over a look of warning. Released, Belle ran to the fence, barking.

"Quiet!" Claudette scolded her. Alarmed, she appraised a crowd now streaming down the road. They were dressed like her townsfolk, yet seemed deflated, and their carts were piled with furniture and farm machinery rather than produce. "Who are they?"

Mémère sent Claudette to fetch a tin mug from the kitchen while she filled a bucket of water, then she placed both outside the gate.

Up the road, a cart tipped over, spilling clothes, mattresses, housewares, and equipment. A cooking pot rolled into the ditch. The family bundled up only the blankets and trudged on, leaving the rest of their belongings behind.

By nightfall, over two hundred refugees had gathered in the market square. Claudette picked all the ripened tomatoes in their garden and brought up cabbage, onions, and potatoes from the cellar. Mémère sliced, boiled, and filled bowls with food, and the two of them walked to the plaza to feed the newcomers. Their neighbors also brought platters of food.

Claudette moved among the groups seated on the ground and

handed out pieces of bread to those too exhausted to stand at the makeshift food table.

"The Wehrmacht entered our village with their tanks. They confiscated everything—sheep, cows, chickens," a woman nursing a baby told Claudette.

"The Boche shoot anyone who defies their orders," added her husband, a man missing an arm. He lifted a piece of bread to his wife's mouth.

Wehrmacht. A new foreign word, as was *Boche,* the derogatory term for the German soldiers. The words made Claudette shudder.

"They moved into our home," said a woman seated on a blanket rocking a whimpering toddler. "My father couldn't walk much. He died on the road." She broke into sobs. "We had to escape."

This woman had left her father's body on the road? Stunned, Claudette sought Mémère's eyes for solace, but her grandmother, next to Solange and Solange's mother, Dorothée Poincaré, was busy doling out food.

Even though it was summer, the evening was cool. Some townspeople took in the refugee children for the night. As Mémère and Claudette walked back home, more figures appeared in the dark. When they reached the house, Mémère waited until they'd passed before she opened their gate, then she locked it behind them.

"Let's take in a family—" Claudette started.

Mémère cut her off. "They are desperate. I'm old and you are crippled. Let's be kind only to the extent that we can."

Belle barked all night at the commotion outside. At dawn, agitated and tired from lack of sleep, Claudette buckled on her leg brace and went out to milk Rosette. At her side, Belle jumped and yipped. "Stop it, Belle," Claudette snapped at her. "You're giving me a headache!"

She froze at the entrance to the cowshed. In the dim light, she saw a young man milking Rosette. Claudette yelped.

He jumped, grabbed his bucket, and, with milk splashing, ran, elbowing Claudette out of his way and knocking her to the ground.

Anger boiling in her, Claudette got up and hobbled to the cow. She hugged her neck as hot tears flowed from her eyes, feeling betrayed. Mémère was right to be guarded with the refugees.

FEAR OF THE Wehrmacht was overshadowed by the wave of refugees that turned into a flood. People were fleeing with no destination other than France's free zone. Some refugees rented rooms in people's homes. Many slept in the church at night on the condition that they would leave in the morning. Others built tents in the surrounding fields, now uncultivated, or camped and washed by the river. The quiet forest where Claudette had led Solange to pick mushrooms and fiddleheads in the spring now teemed with tents, people, and cooking fires. Drying laundry hung on tree branches.

Farm trucks chugged into the village; their drivers asked for petrol, but the station had run out of it. Luxury cars from Paris carried finely dressed people trying to find an open route to Tours or Orléans. Unsuited for all this traffic, the main streets became clogged. Mémère no longer kept the pail of water filled for the newcomers.

Their vegetable garden was picked through time and again. One by one, the chickens disappeared. Claudette kept vigil on those that were left so she could snatch their eggs before someone sneaked into the yard and stole them. Even though Monsieur Lefebvre's night patrol guarded Mémère's home, one morning the cowshed was empty. Rosette was gone.

Mémère broke down. "I raised her since she was a little calf," she said, sobbing. Claudette cried with her—for Rosette, who might be butchered for her meat, for their garden and chickens, for all of France's troubles.

On market day, few farmers' wives came—their husbands had gone to war—and there was little to sell. Claudette searched in vain for some produce so Mémère could start preparing for winter, but vendors from farther villages couldn't get through the checkpoints, and those in the free zone risked being robbed en route. How would Mémère pickle vegetables, cook her marmalade preserves, and layer containers of beef-and-goose pâté without ingredients?

Solange and her mother had one of the few stalls in the market. Everyone used woven baskets made of willow and seagrass to store or transport food, and now evacuees were buying large rattan ones to repack their belongings. Today, Claudette sat by her friend and listened to her amusing chatter while Solange's fingers danced on the straw and raffia she was weaving. In her blindness, Solange was attuned to people in ways that fascinated Claudette. She knew which customers were desperate and could use a discount and which ones were rich and could pay double.

That night, with no fresh produce, Claudette brought up from the cellar some of their cache of potatoes, cabbage, carrots, and string beans—the food they had stored for winter.

The next morning, she faced another disaster. The old baker, who kept his door locked and allowed only townspeople to enter—and charged them twice the price for half the number of baguettes—didn't open. A sign on the door explained that with no crops of wheat, the flour mill's supply had been depleted.

Except that smoke escaped the baker's chimney. Angry housewives banged on the door, accusing him of hoarding flour. He was still baking for his family, they yelled—and for those refugees who could pay an exorbitant price.

Claudette walked away, baffled by the prospect of the coming days without bread, the staple of life. She entered the pub, hoping to find an answer from Monsieur Lefebvre. At this early hour, he was already drunk. Worse, he had stopped planning new military strategies.

"The Nazis round up Jews, Gypsies," he said. He looked at Claudette pointedly. "And the crippled."

Her heart flipped. "What do they do with them?"

"You mean what do they do *to* them?" Monsieur Lefebvre raised his eyes heavenward. "You'd better hide."

Where could she hide if the Nazis swept into this village with their tanks? Could she climb up to the attic? What use did the Nazis have for *invalides*?

Not for the first time, Claudette compared her affliction with Solange's. The day they met, she had decided that blindness was worse—to be unable to thread a needle or bask in the beauty of perfect stitches; not to see the lush colors of silk or the intricacies of fine lace. Now, for the first time, she wished she had Solange's long legs to run fast.

"Don't listen to Monsieur Lefebvre," the tavern keeper told Claudette. "The French spirit and might will prevail." His voice turned to a whisper. "Mark my words. We'll organize a second army and defeat the enemy."

Two old men at the bar nodded and lifted their glasses, but their gesture was meek.

"The worst is yet to come," Monsieur Lefebvre said, his speech slurred. "The worst is yet to come."

Chapter Six

CLAUDETTE

Loire Valley, France
August 1940

THE DOWNTURN IN Mémère's health was sudden. Each coughing fit left her gasping for air. Her skin wasn't just pale; it was gray, as if she had ingested ashes. She no longer left her bed, and Claudette tucked a chamber pot under her a few times a day and fed and washed her. In church, she placed candles at Christ's feet. Aware of how preposterous it was to ask Him for this particular favor, Claudette nevertheless beseeched God in His mercy to send over the Jew and his elixir. Or, if the Jew had enlisted, could Mary at least protect him?

Before dusk, Claudette picked blades of sorrel weed in the garden for their soup. She straightened up and was arrested by the sight of the luminous orange-and-pink ribbons cast by the lowering sun. The beauty of the sunset never changed, regardless of the misery of the world below, and Claudette imagined assembling remainders of fabric in sunset hues to create a beautiful cape for a princess in one of the romance books.

Her reverie broke when a black car stopped by the back gate, the one through which the Jew used to enter to avoid detection. A mattress, a trunk, and suitcases were tied to the roof of the car. A man dressed in a cream-colored city suit stepped out, took off his hat in a respectful manner, and approached Claudette.

"Good evening, Mademoiselle. May I secure your kind permission to park here for the night? Perhaps use your well and outhouse?"

No one had ever spoken to her in the language of the romance books. Three months after the disheveled refugees had begun to stream in, a man more refined than anyone she'd ever met was standing in front of her asking for a favor.

He took out a thick roll of bills and peeled off two. Claudette stared at the beautiful woman in the front passenger seat wearing a fashionably tilted hat with a feather. Her arm rested on the open window, and the sleeve of her blouse was of expensive white silk. Curious to see the rest of the elegant woman's outfit, Claudette nodded her assent to the man but didn't reach for the money.

He took a step forward, holding out the bills. "Would you happen to have a room to let?" When she shook her head, he said, "We'll sleep in the car. Tomorrow I'll go search for petrol."

Claudette accepted the money and pointed to the cowshed. "It's empty."

After the man drove the car into the yard, a boy and a girl, about five and seven years old, bounded out. Just then, Mémère called for Claudette.

She rushed in to explain the visitors' presence. Mémère coughed and soiled herself.

By the time Claudette managed to come out again, it was almost dark. The family was seated on a blanket, sharing an open basket of food. The mattress and luggage were no longer on the car roof. Someone was moving about in the barn.

"Thank you for your generosity," the woman said. Her plaid skirt was spread wide around her, and Claudette could see that it had been cut on the bias. The woman had upturned lips that were finely carved, and her brown eyes were lovely. "May we ask you for another great favor?"

"What is it, madame?"

"Would you please let our children sleep inside? My boy is prone to colds."

There were two unused rooms upstairs. Claudette had been sleeping on the front-room couch since the start of the war, when the Jew's visits ended and Mémère needed her nearby. Claudette missed the Jew's quiet presence in the evening by the fireplace, where he read from his little book, his lips moving.

"Yes, madame," Claudette said.

An hour later, a heavyset woman led the children in. "Who are you?" Claudette asked.

"Their nanny." The children bounded up the stairs. With her heft, the woman could squeeze through the narrow stairwell only by turning sideways.

It was only for that night, Claudette told herself as she entered Mémère's room. She came out with the chamber pot and saw that the nanny had claimed her sofa.

"You're not supposed to be inside," Claudette said.

"I can't leave the children unattended, can I?"

They would all be gone tomorrow, Claudette told herself, and soon after, she crawled into Mémère's bed.

When she entered the kitchen in the morning, the nanny was working by the sink. Her large hips filled the small space, and Claudette couldn't get to the stove, which was taken anyway by a pot of porridge.

"Excuse me," Claudette said. "What are you doing?"

"Madame said to make the children's breakfast."

"Not here, though."

When the woman didn't move, Claudette called Belle and walked out to the yard. The elegant woman was washing her face in a bowl resting on the rim of the well.

"Good morning," she said to Claudette. "Thank you again. We were so exhausted from two days on the road. What a beast of a trip."

"Your nanny is in my kitchen."

"Do you mind? Please. My children haven't had a hot meal in two days. We're also out of provisions. Who could have imagined such a disaster? My husband has gone out to get some food and petrol. When he returns, we'll be on our way."

The man returned in the afternoon, his jacket folded on his arm, and from the way he swung the petrol can, Claudette could tell that it was empty. Back in her kitchen, they helped themselves to the oil and the sack of potatoes in the corner, then left money on the table. After supper, the couple sat in the front room and talked in hushed voices. The nanny had retired with the children upstairs, and Claudette was again relegated to Mémère's bed.

On the third day, Claudette protested to the man. "I never agreed to any of this. My grandmother is sick and I—"

He peeled more money off his wad of cash. "How much do you want?"

"It's not about money, it's—" Claudette could hear her own weak voice. Belle started barking.

"Do something about this damn dog. It frightens the children and gives my wife migraines."

"I'd like you all to leave. Please."

"Do you think we want to be stuck in this wretched house?" The corners of his mouth pulled down in distaste. When Belle continued barking, he kicked her.

"Don't touch her!" Claudette cried out. Belle retreated with a whine.

A week later, the family had taken over the house, discovered the storage cellar, and were eating Mémère's preserves. They hadn't bothered to tell Claudette their names. They didn't address her. They acted as if she were made of air.

"You are thieves," Claudette told them, and the man threw more bills at her. She shouted, "I don't need money—there's nothing I can buy with it!"

Only the children seemed to notice her yelling. Their mouths gaped in fright. The nanny told them, "Keep away from this witch, or she'll cast a spell on you, turn you into grasshoppers."

Their beautiful mother lowered her eyes whenever Claudette

passed by. She no longer apologized or asked permission to collect the one egg the last chicken had laid.

The mayor had gone to serve in the war. His wife, the town's midwife, had turned the town hall into a makeshift clinic with no doctor. "Armistice doesn't mean the end of war, only more ruthless occupation," she said to Claudette when she came seeking her advice. Her eyes were hollow from hunger. "I pray for it to end."

When Claudette went to the tavern to appeal to Monsieur Lefebvre, she found him drunk again. Fleeing soldiers who had dragged themselves into town filled the barroom, their stinking uniforms bloodstained and torn. A patron turned the radio dial as another manipulated the circular wire antenna. Crackling words came through with news: The Nazis no longer bothered taking French soldiers prisoner. They just beat them senseless and took their weapons.

Then a hush fell over the room as de Gaulle, in London, broadcast a call for French resistance: "Be brave. Together we'll defeat the enemy."

All Claudette saw was chaos and danger.

⁓

THE DAY'S HEAT was suffused with the dampness of a heavy rain. In her bed, Mémère shivered. Her skin had withered after her plumpness drained from underneath it. From the front room came the sounds of the two children running and squealing. "Who are the people in my house?" Mémère cried. "Are my sons back?"

"Squatters." Claudette placed at Mémère's feet a brick she had heated in the oven.

"Go fetch Dorothée Poincaré."

Rain pummeled the windows. The wind thrashed the trees outside. "Now? Whatever for?" Claudette plumped Mémère's pillow, which needed no plumping. Solange and her mother were supposed to be back from their week of traveling. The refugees bought woven boxes and suitcases, sturdier than their cardboard valises.

"Don't tire me with your questions." Another coughing fit seized Mémère. The phlegm she spat into a saucer was bloody. Her head dropped back on the pillow. "Ask for the priest too."

Not the priest! Not him—and not yet! A sob broke out of Claudette. The priest never told the children who threw stones at her and Solange that it was wrong. He never spoke of the cruelty of man toward man the way the Jew did, only about man's sins toward God. Claudette and Solange were *invalides,* the priest said, because they were being punished for some grave sins. The Jew, who almost never contradicted the priest's sermons, told Claudette that her and Solange's disabilities meant that God loved them more, not less.

Claudette crossed the front room, trying not to trip on the interlopers' mattress and valises. In the vestibule, she picked up her cane, put on her rain cape, and grabbed an umbrella.

Her shoes filled with water as she sloshed in the streams rushing down the cobblestones. She left a message for the priest with his housekeeper, then dragged herself to Solange's house on the other side of the village. Tilting her umbrella against the rain did little to avoid its assault.

Solange gave her a tight hug in spite of her soggy clothes. Dorothée hitched her horse to the cart, and twenty minutes later they all stood by Mémère's bed. Her teeth chattering, Claudette took off her wet coat and toweled dry her face and hair.

Mémère was short of breath when she spoke. "You know someone at Château de Valençay, right?" she asked Dorothée.

"The cook's first assistant, Lisette, is my cousin."

"Please show her Claudette's work. Maybe their seamstress can use help?"

Claudette's jaw dropped. A château? She selected a silk rose nestled between a pair of leaves and offered it to Dorothée. Since May, no girl had ordered alterations of a dress.

"Claudette, give her also my gabardine jacket." Mémère's voice was weak. "The repair is so perfect. No one can tell it's there."

"But you need it for church!" Claudette protested.

"The only way I'll get to church again is in a coffin."

Claudette handed the jacket to Dorothée. A stone crushed her heart.

Before Dorothée left with samples of Claudette's work, she addressed the man seated in the upholstered chair in the front room, smoking a pipe. His wife was reading a book. The nanny was keeping the children occupied upstairs.

"What if I get you a jerrican of petrol?" Dorothée asked the man.

He looked up, and his eyes narrowed. Blue smoke suspended over his head. "A full can?"

"I'll sell it to you, but only when you are all packed in your car to leave."

He glanced at the rain outside.

Dorothée started for the door. "I guess I'll sell it to someone else."

"No! Wait!"

Twenty-five minutes later, Claudette closed the door and leaned against it. The empty front room was suddenly quiet. The air smelled of pipe smoke. And now there was also the sour scent of the Angel of Death, waiting for Mémère to take her last breath.

Claudette hugged the dog and cried. If only the Jew would show up and make Mémère better. She wished for his quiet, reassuring presence, but she had no idea where his family lived. She didn't even know his name.

Chapter Seven

SHARON

Cherbourg, France
September 1968

A FULL-FIGURED YOUNG WOMAN, her hair gathered at her nape, waves to Sharon and the two kibbutzniks at the Cherbourg station. She rocks an infant in her arms and says in Hebrew, "I'm Rina, the Israeli mission's unofficial welcome committee." She lets out a small laugh. "And this is Daphna. My husband is at sea today, testing Saar Six."

The only other passengers disembarking at this last stop are the uniformed men with blue duffel bags. Noticing Sharon's glance, Rina says, "The naval port is one of the largest in the world. For security reasons, the French give us anchorage facility in their protected harbor. They also host our seamen in their barrack, *caserne*." She giggles. "They even supply our guys with heavy winter jackets so they won't freeze to death in winter."

Taking Rina's cue that it's now safe to speak Hebrew in public, Sharon asks, "Are you saying that the French host the Saars operation?"

A pleasant, toothy smile spreads over Rina's face. "Embargo or not, they love us here. Come to my Rosh Hashanah dinner Sunday and meet some of the French officers. They adore my matzo ball soup."

In Rina's car, Sharon settles in the passenger seat, the baby in her lap. She coos and jiggles her long, beaded necklace for Daphna, then tightens her arms around the fleshy, warm little body.

Rina maneuvers the stick shift. "She's ten months old. By the end of the year, God willing, she'll have a brother or a sister." Her hand flits over her bulging middle. She glances at the rearview mirror. "You guys have kids?"

"Three each," Gideon responds. "What's the rush to get us here? They literally pulled me away while I was milking a cow, told me to throw a toothbrush and some underwear into a bag, then drove me to the passport office. I'm not even navy—"

"They picked me up on the way," Oded says. "And I'm a tank commander. Can't even swim."

"Kidnapped and taken to France. How delicious." Rina chuckles. "Get your *kishkes* ready for days of sea testing when the weather isn't good, which is often. But we have fun too. With each launch of a boat, the French throw us a big party. They even grill whole lambs. Then, weeks later, once a boat's testing is finished and she's ready to leave for good, we organize a farewell banquet. Lots of champagne flowing." She glances at Sharon. "I guess you'll take the party planning off my hands."

Sharon wonders about the budget for this shipbuilding project. In her military unit, they saved paper clips and reused the disposable coffee filters. Here she learns of French-union salaries, travel budgets, and champagne parties. None of these war toys are free. Heavy taxes are borne by Israelis, even Savta, whose meager income from a rental property is slashed in half by taxes. Whatever money she manages to save is taxed again, taken outright from her bank account.

"I'm confused," Sharon says. "I was told that the Saars are built in a private shipyard, but you're talking about the French navy's patronage." Where is the utmost secrecy that Danny insisted on?

Rina tucks a tendril that has escaped her ponytail behind her ear. "Félix Amiot, the owner of Constructions Mécaniques de Normandie, what we call CMN, is an interesting former anti-Semite. In this small town, he's a friend of the navy brass, and he's also asked the local media not to mention us, so they don't."

"Can one be a *former* anti-Semite?" Sharon asks.

But Rina is navigating the car into a narrow street. Daphna is asleep, her fist clutching a clump of Sharon's hair. Sharon strokes with a tentative finger the baby's rounded cheek; it's like a ripened peach.

"Your invitation for Rosh Hashanah means a lot to me," she says to Rina. It feels good to know that the small community Danny talked about is so welcoming. "May I help with the cooking? I learned from my *savta*."

"Sure. My apartment is right above yours."

The narrow alleys are lined with three- and four-story homes, all with chiseled stone façades—so different from the rough, uneven fieldstones of farmhouses she saw on the way. Sharon cranes her neck to examine the picturesque masonry. Each window is topped by a lintel—a flat block that supports the load of the structure above. She smiles at the realization that traveling abroad will feed her interest in architecture.

Rina parks the car and selects a key to enter the building. The men bring the suitcases; Sharon carries her satchel and the baby.

Rina opens the door of a third-floor apartment to reveal a room with two plaid sofas and a pair of matching upholstered chairs over a maroon area rug. The polished teakwood dining table and eight chairs are in mint condition. Printed curtains flank the windows. There is even a television set on top of a bookcase.

"Sharon, take the small bedroom." Rina gestures to the left with her chin, then points to the short corridor on the right. "You guys share a bedroom. The men from the third bedroom are at sea today." She moves to the door. "See you for Rosh Hashanah dinner."

"You forgot Daphna." Sharon holds out the baby, still asleep.

"Oh, could you please watch her for a while? There's Gerber food in her diaper bag for when she wakes up." She smiles apologetically and pats her middle again. "With the new baby coming, I'm dying to take a nap."

The men, who have defined trades, seem unconcerned about their roles, but Sharon hasn't come all the way to France to be the mission's babysitter. She places Daphna on a blanket on the carpet. She's relieved when the baby wakes up and Oded changes her cloth diaper. He's an expert with safety pins. "In the kibbutz we take turns in the children's houses," he explains.

Sharon checks the refrigerator and, finding it almost empty, counts her francs. She wishes someone would outline her responsibilities. Surely she wasn't offered a generous salary for domestic services. Still, a bowl of fruit on the coffee table and fresh milk, eggs, cold cuts, and cheese in the refrigerator will make the place a home. She can almost taste the crust of a crunchy baguette.

"I'm going food shopping." She can't believe she's daring to venture out, but the men seem even less equipped for urban life. She swings the blue plastic shopping basket she found in the cabinet. "Want to share expenses?" They exchange a look. "Never mind. I'll buy for myself only." She turns to leave.

"No, no," says Gideon as he twists open a Gerber jar. "Sorry. We've never *bought* food."

"They've given us an advance." Oded pulls out a wad of francs and holds them at arm's length like he doesn't know what to do with them.

She withdraws three bills—as if she knows how much anything costs here.

"Buy us cigarettes too," Gideon says. "Gauloises, I hear, are the best."

In the street, Sharon checks the house number, then steps to the corner to memorize the names of the two crossing alleys. The pleasant smell of woodsmoke hangs in the air.

Twenty minutes later, she leaves the grocery store, but she must have turned left instead of right because within minutes, she is lost in a maze. The rural Normandy of her French textbook featured open meadows, not cobblestoned alleys. Why did she let herself take this job abroad?

After two circuits of the neighborhood, she musters the courage to ask a passerby for directions and finally locates her building.

When she enters the apartment, the baby is gone. Gideon takes the shopping bag and is at the kitchen counter dicing onions as Sharon opens cabinets in search of a vase for the red carnations that the grocer pressed on her as a welcome gesture. Gideon tosses the onions into a pan, breaks the eggs, and whips them up for an omelet. Oded chops vegetables into a bowl. His movements with the knife are quick and expert. Sharon is pleased with her roommates' domestic skills and with how easily the three of them fall into a comfortable companionship. It eases her loneliness.

Over dinner, she learns that Gideon and Oded live in neighboring kibbutzim in the Negev. They've occasionally made it to the desert city of Beersheba. They are even more befuddled than she is about traveling abroad. The meal over, the two men settle at the table for a card game.

Sharon showers and changes into her cotton nightgown, finds a Hebrew novel on the shelf, and takes it to her bed. She falls asleep to the sounds of card shuffling and subdued teasing.

She's awakened by voices. Her watch shows it's twenty minutes past midnight. Wearing only her nightgown, she steps to the bedroom door. Danny is in the living room with three men she doesn't know.

"Some very interesting developments." He grins at her, and she can't figure out why. "Which bedroom is available?"

"None." She points to the first door off the short corridor. "The one over there belongs to guys that are at sea."

"They aren't coming back." He directs the recruits to that room. "Please pack up their stuff," he tells them.

Another naval accident? Sharon's stomach contracts. She's about to get sick. She had noticed the absent roommates' clothes strewn about, an unfinished letter to someone's mother on the desk. She can't hold back the panic in her voice: "Danny, what happened to them?"

His tone is not ominous when he says, "I'll brief all of you together. Will you please get Oded and Gideon?"

She knocks on their half-closed door and steps in. "Guys," she calls into the darkness. Snoring stops. Sheets rustle. "Briefing time!" During her military service, she and her colleagues were awakened at all hours of the night for one emergency or another. Now three men have disappeared. She raises her voice. "Oded, Gideon! In the living room. On the double!" She flips on the lights to speed up their waking.

Danny puts the kettle on the stove and produces a bag of ground coffee from the top cabinet. His expression doesn't seem solemn. Behind her, Sharon hears the bathroom door open and close, then a toilet being flushed.

She's conscious that she's braless. Her breasts are small, but the nipples poke the thin fabric. She retrieves her cardigan and makes a mental note to shop for an inexpensive robe. She takes out the cheeses and the baguette, slices the apples, and carries it all into the living room.

The five men introduce themselves, stating their military ranks and former units. They are all officers on reserve duty, and they've left businesses and jobs for a month. One's wife is expecting their first child, and he'll miss the birth. "I'm here to do a job," he says.

"Sharon was in Intelligence," Danny volunteers.

"Only a corporal. I'm here as a civilian," she adds, her tone meek. These high-ranking men are anywhere from seven to fourteen years older than she is. What is she doing here?

Danny sits down and presses his palms together. "Here's the deal. Saar Six went out today on a test, as it has been doing daily for a few weeks. However, since the weather was good, the crew decided to just continue on to Israel."

There's a moment of silence; it's broken by one of the new arrivals, Moishe, here on his second one-month tour. "You must be kidding. No, I know you're not. But to pull off that trick, the boat had to have enough fuel, and after a day of testing, there wouldn't even be enough to reach Portugal. That means that they set out directly."

Sharon wouldn't have known the first question to ask. But she understands one thing: The challenge to Pompidou's embargo has been set in motion. The reaction will be fast and furious. Israel's gamble on its naval future is in the balance. The navy must get the rest of the boats or it won't be able to protect the country's western shore, not to mention Israel's southern access to the Red Sea, which is bordered by unfriendly Saudi Arabia, Yemen, Egypt, Sudan, and Eritrea.

For all Sharon knows, the French will clamp down on this Cherbourg project now, and her job will be over. She might be heading back to Tel Aviv before getting any answers from Danny.

Her glance takes in the faces of the men; their grave expressions reveal that they, too, are contemplating the political and military ramifications. Despite her initial reluctance to come here, she's not ready to go home.

Chapter Eight

CLAUDETTE

Château de Valençay, France
Summer 1941

THE DAY WAS bright, and the expansive windows of the sewing atelier were open to the breeze of back gardens, carrying in a fruity aroma. Claudette took her work to the window and sat on a plush settee to add a red lacy cuff to one of the duchess's black jackets. How easy it was to forget that battles were raging in the rest of France. The centuries-old walls stood as a fortress against the echoes of war.

The château's two perpendicular wings edged the huge terrace, where blue-aqua-and-green-feathered peacocks strutted between marble statues. The terrace ended with a sweeping balustrade and wide stone stairs descending to the reflecting pool, and past it, colorful flower beds. Claudette wished she could describe it all to Solange, now living with her husband in the occupied zone. The young man, a nephew of the priest in La Guerche, had been bound for the seminary when he visited their village. Unlike his cruel uncle, he was charmed by the feisty Solange and abandoned his plans for the priesthood. After they married, he penned a flowery letter to Claudette describing his wife's inner beauty. With her at his side, he had written, he would dedicate his life to doing good outside the priesthood.

Solange had found love despite Claudette's certainty that neither of them ever would. Claudette's happiness for her friend was mixed with envy. She couldn't fathom anyone wanting her; she didn't even have a pretty face or Solange's captivating chatter. None of the estate's more than thirty grooms and gardeners had even glanced in her direction.

Marguerite, the maid who twice daily dusted the wainscoting, wiped the mirrors, and polished the doorknobs, joined Claudette at the window. They watched the duchess's nine-year-old son, Mathéo, and his young tutor—a slight man not much larger than his charge—bending over some plants and fingering the leaves. The two were about to enter the double rows of aged oak trees when a tall, well-dressed man emerged from the walled garden and strolled by the reflecting pool.

"The duchess's new lover." Marguerite whispered this so Madame Couture, the seamstress who was pumping her sewing machine, wouldn't hear. "That's why she keeps her daughter in that British boarding school—she doesn't need her underfoot."

"You're being unfair and disloyal. The Boche are blitzing London, so how is the girl supposed to travel back home?" Claudette replied, her tone heated.

Marguerite giggled. "It's so romantic watching them."

Claudette objected to gossip about the duchess, a woman she idolized, but she too had been speculating about this gentleman. At dusk the day before, from her chamber window, she had studied him in his fitted brown jacket and leather riding boots as he paced the field that had been mowed after the harvest. He crossed the field's entire length, looking down as if measuring it.

Marguerite handed Claudette a romance booklet from a new series. Instead of a delicate heroine wearing a flouncy, lacy dress, this cover featured a woman in a commanding stance wearing a khaki-colored uniform. Claudette leafed through the pages and stopped at the drawing of a woman crawling under barbed wire. The next picture showed a huge explosion in red and yellow with the woman in the distance, her blond hair wild, raising an arm in victory.

Claudette had never imagined a woman in such a role. "A guerrilla fighter?" she murmured in awe.

"The Communists recruit women. I told Silvain Auguste I wanted to volunteer, but he wouldn't hear of it," Marguerite whispered, referring to the duchess's chauffeur. Rumor had it that he held a leadership role in the Maquis, although he hadn't quit his job to join them in the forest.

Claudette fished in her pocket and handed Marguerite a centime for the booklet. The maid had become her friend because her sister was also an *invalide*, although Marguerite's sister couldn't even sit up and had to be carried around.

"What will you do for the underground, blow up bridges?" Claudette whispered, glancing at Madame Couture to make sure she was not objecting—or listening—to this idle chat.

"The Germans are gentlemen; they aren't suspicious of women when they cross the checkpoints. I can deliver messages and ammunition."

Claudette envied Marguerite her courage; she never dreamed of performing heroic acts. All she wanted was for the war to be over so she could use her love of lace, colors, and silk to embroider shawls and embellish dresses for the duchess.

Duchess Silvia de Castellane, whose voice was soft and who smelled of lavender, was a beautiful woman, tall and slender like the models in the fashion magazines to which Madame Couture had subscribed before the war.

The wide gallery outside the atelier led to the duchess's apartment, and now the duchess and two friends entered. Claudette lowered her head out of respect for the visitors. Madame Couture's sewing machine came to a halt.

The duchess touched Claudette's shoulder. "Mademoiselle Pelletier is my treasure," she told her companions. "With no Parisian fashion available, she's transforming my mourning wardrobe."

Claudette blushed. The woman she idolized appreciated Claudette styling her clothes: a hint of lace encircling a blouse collar, delicate twisted piping on a jacket's cuffs, and discreet embroidery on a dress's pockets.

One of the guests handed Claudette a silk nightgown. It had a row of twenty covered buttons that had to be removed before it was laundered and sewn back on afterward. Claudette set out to work on it, loving the cool feel of the finest silk. She had not known such fine fabrics existed until she'd arrived here.

The guest asked Marguerite to fetch them coffee, and the three women settled on the velvet sofa to chat. Their conversation was a world away from the giggly chatter of the village girls in Mémère's home. Their Parisian accent was both nuanced and enunciated. These powdered, bejeweled, coiffed women who trailed scents of fine perfumes grumbled over losing their villas in the French Riviera and their châteaux in the Alps, now fallen to the Nazis.

"There's no one left in Paris," one guest complained. "My tailor, my cobbler, and my jeweler—the Jews are all gone."

Claudette's hand, holding a pin, halted in midair.

"The Jewish musicians from the opera have disappeared too," said the other. "At least the Nazis haven't bombed the building."

"They adore classical music," the duchess said, "but Wagner? It's so melancholic—"

"Frankly, I didn't mind the worldly Jews. They could pass for French. But the refugees from Eastern European countries? What a stinking mess," one friend said. "There were so many of them, you could trip over them in the street."

"Remember my Jewish neighbors, the bankers? They sold their art collection in haste. I was lucky to buy masterpieces for a few francs before the family was deported."

"Those rich bankers are probably on vacation in London," replied her friend.

The first woman shook her head. "No vacation. A new family has moved in."

The hair on Claudette's arms stood up. What did they mean by *gone* and *deported*? She glanced at Madame Couture, who was pinning a hem by her sewing machine. The jolly plump woman's lips were pressed together tightly.

A cloud passed over the duchess's brow. Her tone was uncharacteristically emphatic when she said, "The French Jews are French." She checked a fingernail and stood up. "I must find my maid."

The three women departed, but a sense of disquiet lingered in the room. Claudette didn't know what questions to ask Madame Couture. What had befallen the Jews? None of the refugees she'd seen in La Guerche looked like the Jew or had his foreign accent. Claudette knew no Gypsies, whom Monsieur Lefebvre said the Nazis were also deporting, but would the Nazis now come for the *invalides*?

Claudette's unease grew as she trekked the long distance to the kitchen for the midday hot meal. Unlike the insouciant atmosphere upstairs, here, the air of France's humiliation was thick, overpowering the rich smell of the root soup. The servants living in the village faced food shortages at home, made worse by the continuing flood of refugees. Two maids cried often for their fiancés in Nazi prisons, surely being tortured.

But here, at the servants' table, Claudette could listen and try to make sense of the events.

"What can de Gaulle do from London? Even the Brits dislike him," a butler said.

"Only he can form a strong new army here," said Silvain Auguste. "Jean Moulin, his deputy, is organizing the fractured Résistance cells. When the Nazis cross the demarcation line, they'll meet their match."

Alarmed, Claudette asked, "The Nazis will come here after all?"

"The Loire Valley is the breadbasket of France. Greed will make them break their agreement with the Vichy government," a footman told her.

Claudette's head reeled. She didn't know which of the four factions to put her faith in. The Pétainists in the free zone were committed to collaborating with the conquerors, trying to make the best of a bad situation. The Communists were despised because their allegiance was to Russia, a country that seemed to Claudette as distant as the moon. Then there were the Maquis, whose loyalty to France was different than that of the nationalists supporting de Gaulle. If only she knew which faction the duchess supported, she'd follow her lead—but the duchess was from Spanish aristocracy, had married German nobility, and was living as a Frenchwoman.

Monsieur Vincent, the business manager, rose. "We're issuing you all identity papers." He touched his potbelly as if that gave him even more authority than his lineage did—like Madame Couture's family, his had been in the service of the duke's ancestors since Napoléon's days. "A photographer will be here soon to take everyone's photos. Tomorrow, Silvain Auguste will drive you in shifts to the village hall."

"What do we need IDs for?" Marguerite asked.

"To show the *préfet* that your name isn't Jewish," he replied, referring to the local governor. "I've given him my word that no Jews are employed here."

"What about Gypsies?" Claudette asked.

He sent her a perplexed look. "What about them?"

Claudette heard sniggering at the other end of the table. Her stomach tightened. *"Imbécile,"* someone said.

They didn't understand that, because she was an *invalide*, her fate was tied to that of the Jews and the Gypsies. Her face burning, she murmured, "Uh, our enemies are the Boche."

"The Boche are the enemies on the outside, but the Jews are the enemies within." Monsieur Vincent withdrew a newspaper and read out loud: "'Jews are the vermin that have crawled to eat the flesh of our French society. Their constitutional nature is anathema to the French culture of decency, as they have brought nothing but graft and thievery.'" He added, "Thankfully, the Vichy police are sending them back to wherever they came from."

"Where is that?" Claudette asked, thinking of the Jew's funny accent.

"Who cares? As long as we protect France."

Chapter Nine

CLAUDETTE

Château de Valençay, France
October 1941–February 1942

A PACK OF DOGS barking as if they were out on a hunt awakened Claudette. She rose and looked out the window. In the side field that the duchess's lover had measured lay what seemed to be a huge elongated bale of hay. Claudette pressed her forehead against the chilled glass until her eyes adjusted and she saw that it was an airplane.

Visitors who had arrived in the night in a plane, not a carriage or an automobile? She wished she could peek into the reception hall, but Monsieur Vincent promptly dismissed any staff member found wandering through the château in his or her off-hours. And Claudette couldn't move quietly.

Two men unloaded from the plane a coffin-like box. She could tell it was very heavy from the way they struggled to carry it. They disappeared from sight, and two more men came and hauled out another similar box from the plane.

All was quiet. The dogs stopped barking until two men emerged from the back of the château. Claudette recognized the one carrying a lantern as a stable groom. His companion climbed into the plane. The groom set down his lantern and gave the propeller one strong push, then another.

Four men had arrived with two large boxes. Only one man left.

The engine's blast broke the silence of the night. With cracking reverberations, the plane rolled down the field, wobbly as a drunken goose. It lifted just enough to clear the trees and disappeared into the night sky.

Two days later, on Sunday, Claudette arrived early to the chapel on the ground floor of the château so she could pray at Jesus's feet before the duchess came in for the Mass. When she did, the household staff who lived on the premises would retreat to the back pews. Tears brimming her eyes, Claudette prayed for her own safety, for the blessed duchess, and for Solange and her family, who, like everyone in the occupied zone, must be going hungry. Kneeling with the brace was difficult on the hard stone floor, but the discomfort was a necessary sacrifice for the petitions she was making to God.

After Mass, she stood outside in the crisp autumn air gazing at the gardens that had lost their lush summer colors. She blew on her fingers in her knit gloves. Four maids who were setting out on a long stroll waved at her, then looped their arms through one another's. She watched them with the familiar pang of envy, wishing she had two good legs and could just wander around and think of nothing but the smell of the rain. She needed the ease and levity of girlfriends she'd had with Solange and even the customers at Mémère's home. With no place to go and no one with whom to spend her time, Claudette would pass the rest of Sunday alone in her room. She'd saved yesterday's newspaper from the kitchen, so perhaps she would finally understand this incomprehensible war.

Édouard, one of the groundskeepers, approached her, his hat crushed between two callused hands. "Would you like to see the new orchids?" he asked, pointing to the nearest greenhouse. "It's warmer in there."

Crimson flooded Claudette's face. No man had ever asked to walk with her. Édouard was a decade older than her, and his forehead was tilted forward, as if it were pulled by a string. She smiled. She loved the greenhouse, with its exotic flowers and smell of damp soil. She eyed the short distance and mumbled, "Yes, thank you." Perhaps, for the first time in her life, a man would present her with a flower?

But when they began to walk, Édouard's feet covered the distance as if he were in a rush.

Out of breath, Claudette called out, "You're too fast."

He cast a furtive glance around. "Oh, well, suit yourself," he said, and resumed his quick stride.

Claudette halted, stupefied, humiliated. He wanted only to trap her alone in the greenhouse; he did not want to be seen with her. She swallowed hard against the lump in her throat.

Back in her room, she fell on her bed and sobbed until she had no more tears.

MORE PLANES HAD come and gone during the winter, and with each landing, Claudette's euphoria at being a spectator in the theater that was the duchess's world had lost some of its sheen. The duchess's 1942 New Year's celebration for her two dozen visitors marked for Claudette only that the war was barreling toward them. The nightly BBC broadcast on Monsieur Vincent's radio repeated the same message: The Nazis were on their way.

They were surely coming for her. *Free France*, she prayed more and more frantically. *And protect me.*

Other staff members must have seen the planes, but no one mentioned them at the lunch table, probably taking heart at what seemed like the arming of the Résistance. But they could do their patriotic part by speaking out against the foreigners who were exploiting France.

"It's only right that the hundreds of thousands of Jews who have flooded our country should repay us by working at those labor camps," Monsieur Vincent said at lunch one day.

Claudette hated having nothing to say in defense of the poor Jews. The only Jew she had ever met was hardworking and generous and didn't exploit anyone. Had she missed what everyone else saw in these people? "What does a Jew look like?" she asked Monsieur Vincent.

"Luckily, I've never met one," he replied.

She pushed herself away from the table, mumbling about needing to get her work done.

Outside the dining room, Lisette, the assistant cook, pulled her aside. "Be at the kitchen back door tonight at ten o'clock," she whispered.

Claudette stared at her. In the almost two years since Lisette had shown samples of her handiwork to Madame Couture, the two of them had rarely talked. Like Madame Couture, who had a family in the village, Lisette walked or biked back home at the end of every day. What could possibly be required of Claudette at that late hour and in this part of the château?

At ten o'clock, Claudette was in the cavernous kitchen. Hanging polished copper pots reflected light from a lamp fixed over the serving counter that illuminated a bowl of fruit, a plate of crudités, and a tray of cheese and bread protected from mice by a mesh *cloche*. A bottle of wine and three glass goblets were set as if awaiting people of importance. Claudette gazed around the room and, finding no clues, stepped outside to the kitchen yard. In the dark, she sat on the stone bench where footmen took their smoke breaks. The cold of the air and of the stone beneath her penetrated her bones. She tightened her shawl over her coat. Only the bizarre nature of the request kept her waiting there.

High clouds hid the stars. Cats yowled. An owl hooted. Nearby, a tree branch snapped, startling Claudette. She smelled the mustiness of uncollected fall leaves.

Then she heard the scrunching of gravel. "Who is there?" she asked, her voice weak.

Two figures emerged from the darkness.

Chapter Ten

SHARON

Cherbourg, France
September 1968

IT IS ONE o'clock in the morning, and in the living room of the apartment, Danny discusses the new development.

"Are you saying that Saar Six departed without the blessing of the French?" Sharon asks him. She's been concerned about the possible illegal aspects of this operation, and now, barely a few hours after her arrival, she is in the thick of such activity.

"The local French navy is not in charge of us. Our relationship is merely collegial. Their permission has become a custom because they offered to host each Saar in their secure harbor while it was being tested." Danny's green eyes behind the glasses enlarge. He smiles at Sharon, then addresses the men. "Our crew of twenty-one men suddenly left. You're here to replace them since Saar Seven is about to launch. You were all handpicked. Each of you must stretch your gray-matter cells to absorb all that the local engineers can teach you. You'll work in the shipyard and start testing Saar Seven as soon as it's in the water."

"There are only five new men here, not twenty-one," Sharon says.

"Five new *officers*," Danny corrects her. His left eyebrow raises the way it does when he's humoring her. "More deckhands are coming from Tel Aviv in three separate groups. You'll meet the first at Orly tomorrow."

Sharon swallows. She just spent five hours on the train from Paris. Her arrival from Tel Aviv yesterday feels like a week ago.

Danny waves to the new men. "You've had a long day. Go shower and sleep. A car will come for you at oh seven hundred." To Sharon he says, "Can we talk in your room?"

She follows him in and settles on the bed, cross-legged, feeling discombobulated. Once she gets to Orly airport, should she fly back home?

Danny closes the door and sits on the only chair. "Three boys. Eighteen years old. Wet behind the ears, and they don't speak French. They weren't told their final destination in case they got lost coming out of customs and decided to ask for directions." Danny locks eyes with Sharon. "Take the train with them from Orly to Paris. As you already know, that train goes to Gare du Nord, so from there, take a taxi to Gare Saint-Lazare—it's shorter than riding two Métro lines—buy three tickets and put them on the train to Cherbourg."

Eighteen years old to her twenty. The demarcation between childhood and adulthood is her two-year military service and the intense months surrounding the Six-Day War. "Just send them off? Not accompany them here?" she asks.

"No. After you put them on the train and give them the no-Hebrew drill, you take the train to Brussels, where you'll meet three more guys—"

She interrupts him. "Brussels in Belgium?"

"Do you know another Brussels?"

Sharon's head is reeling. "After Brussels, will I be flying to the North Pole?"

He laughs. "Only to London, where you'll collect four seamen and take them by train to Portsmouth. That's in England." He waves in a direction that Sharon imagines is north. "From Portsmouth, there's a ferry to Cherbourg."

All this foreign travel and being responsible for groups of men, some of whom are only boys who can easily get lost—it's too much. Babysitting Daphna and doing domestic chores for her roommates suddenly seems like a more attractive option.

Sharon takes a deep breath. "Having spent eighteen hours in Paris doesn't qualify me to traipse from one European capital to another."

"Courage and wits," Danny replies. "That's how you and our army of eighteen- to twenty-year-olds won the most remarkable military victory last year. I'm sure that you'll do well."

Who assigned her to stand in for her entire generation's fortitude? If quitting now were possible, she would do it. "All this traveling in one day?"

He smiles. "Tomorrow night, you'll check into a hotel in the Brussels airport and meet the group in the morning. Day after tomorrow, you'll stay at a hotel in Heathrow. That's one of London's few airports. Are you with me?"

"Not at all. Let me write it down."

"It's all in here. Three groups, three airports—Orly, Brussels, Heathrow. We're spreading out the entries to avoid detection." He hands her a small notebook. "Most important, I want you to survey each airport and train station. Find your gate way ahead of meeting your charges. Since incoming flights from abroad go through passport control, wait outside that exit with the crowd. Don't push forward and get noticed."

She says nothing, certain that she'll mess up.

He goes on. "When you scout an airport terminal, locate its side and main exits and the nearest train station. Check the direction of the trains on each platform, because there may be different entrances." He scratches his chin, darkened by hair grown since his morning shave. "It's hard for people not to notice a tall, very pretty girl with exotic looks. Avoid engaging in small talk with, uh, strangers."

She doesn't think of herself as exotic. Although her hair, eyes, and eyebrows are dark brown, her skin is light. She wishes she had inherited her father's blue eyes. "I don't flirt, if that's what you mean."

"Good. And we don't want you fumbling about once you pick up the boys. Be confident where you're going, but look casual. No running, no drawing attention."

We. At her intelligence unit, officers from the navy, army, and air force met for joint briefings. The scenario Danny is laying feels like a Mossad project. The one thing she knows about such work is that there is no room for a single mistake. "This assignment is way over my head. I have no experience in any of it."

Danny lets a moment pass. "I trust you. Now trust yourself."

Sharon digs her fingers in her hair, looking down. She came here to probe Danny's Youth Aliyah experience, not for this. "I've asked you before, and I must check again. Am I expected to do anything illegal?"

"Not at all, but it doesn't mean that we want to broadcast our activities to the world."

What if one of her charges draws the attention of border police or airport security? Here, the embargo seems to be ignored by all. Will it become headlines because of her single misstep?

"Remember the comma?" Danny asks.

"Chutzpah?" She gives him a small smile.

Chutzpah should be her new mantra. If Danny doesn't doubt her ability to tackle this complex assignment in a foreign land, she should muster the boldness and daring to prove him right. Alon would have been incredulous at what she's being asked to execute. When she finished her one month of basic training in IDF, she was invited to sign up for the officer course. She declined. No way was she staying in that base for four additional months of rigorous field exercises. Alon hadn't encouraged her to see it as an opportunity to acquire leadership skills. Would she have become an officer if he had pushed her the way Danny is doing now? She can't blame Alon; he'd been young too and had taken her refusal at face value.

"Another thing," Danny says, and she looks up. "Don't let the boys make any stops in Paris on the way."

"What sort of stops?" she asks, alarmed.

"They'll have lists of shopping from their girlfriends, mothers, and sisters. They'll slip into stores. Make sure they're never out of your sight."

His words only add a new level of concern.

Danny glances at her suitcase, still unpacked on the floor. "Bring only your backpack. You'll be carrying a lot of cash." From his briefcase, he withdraws a money belt and an envelope filled with cash; he asks her to count the French francs, Belgian francs, and English pounds, then sign a receipt. He hands her multi-slipped airline tickets with blank spaces where the passengers' names go and watches as she folds the bills into small wads and tucks everything, including her passport, into the money belt.

She recalls the old woman who almost picked her pocket.

"Wear it *under* your dress," he says, "and use the stall in the ladies' room to take out what you need. Also, if you must take notes, do it there." Danny looks at his watch, large-faced with a metal-link band. "Get a little shut-eye now. Be at the train station in time to catch the six o'clock. When I leave, I'll tell the taxi dispatcher in the plaza to send you a cab. Next time you'll make all your own travel arrangements."

She hasn't even seen a plaza. "I have no idea where I am right now."

"You'll find a map in the living-room cabinet."

A thought occurs to Sharon. "Rina. Did her husband leave today too?"

"He's the captain."

"Did she know he wasn't coming back?"

"Oh, he'll be back in a couple of weeks, after he brings Saar Six home."

"So why do you need to train a second team if the first one will return before Saar Seven is launched?"

Danny smiles. "This question proves that you are the right person for the job." He rises. "Rina traveled more than an hour to buy you the airline tickets because we don't use the travel agent in Cherbourg. Naturally, he's in bed with the French brass."

Sharon is not surprised that Israel's friendship with the French navy has its limits. The distrust lends the operation another layer of caution that worries her. There's so much she doesn't know. Given how Danny evaded her last question, she's glad that she didn't make a fuss when the pregnant Rina left baby Daphna with her.

He hands her a note with a phone number. "Call our office collect. But not for routine reports. Only if there's a real problem."

She can't imagine a small problem, only a major fuckup. "You'll be hanging out here?"

"There's going to be hell to pay tomorrow when the French discover that Saar Six left without a champagne party. Someone has to take the heat."

"Here's a scenario to consider," she says. "What if this Saar Six's unauthorized departure heightens security in regard to all things Israeli? Passports are the first things to draw attention. What if our boys fall right into that net?"

"Call the acquisition office in Paris. They handle everything in the diplomatic channels. Do not mention our team here to the authorities."

So Moka Limon is behind this Cherbourg project? Saar Six's departure is challenging whether the embargo applies to platform boats designated for oil exploration, but it's also straining the diplomatic relationship between the two countries.

Suddenly, there is context to her job. Another purpose besides her own agenda, which is impossible for her to get into with Danny now. As difficult as her coming assignment sounds, Sharon no longer wishes to go home.

But what if she gets interrogated and has to lie to the authorities about being based here?

Chapter Eleven

CLAUDETTE

Château de Valençay, France
February 1942

"CLAUDETTE?" A MAN whispered, his voice trembling.

"Who is this?"

"Claudette, it's me." He approached her, then reached up to remove his hat.

Recognition hit her like a thunderclap. "The Jew?" Her arms reached out to hug him, then dropped. She had never before touched him.

He let out a soft chuckle. "You forgot my name?"

In all the years of this man's visits, Mémère referred to him only as "the Jew."

Before Claudette could reply that she had never known his name, he said, "It's Isaac Baume. And this is my son Raphaël."

His son. The crippled one? The one she had fantasized about? Claudette couldn't tell, since the tall young man wasn't moving. She finally found her voice. "Are you hungry?"

"Yes," Isaac Baume whispered, "but more important, we need a place to stay."

Stay? She couldn't speak. The man who had changed so much in her life for the better now stood in front of her in dire need himself. Her thoughts swirled. She owed him her gratitude, but how could she betray the duchess's trust and bring in strangers—and Jews at that? By arranging this rendezvous, Lisette had given her tacit approval. Surely, though, the assistant cook had no authority outside this kitchen. Or did the duchess, who allowed planes to land here, know about this? The answer was in Monsieur Vincent's statement: no Jews in Valençay.

"How did you find me?" Claudette asked.

"Your friend, the blind girl. Her husband helped us."

Claudette's heart warmed as she realized that Solange's husband was a good man. She glanced at the Jew's son, still standing two steps behind his father, shrouded in the obscurity of the night. All she could see was that he was almost a head taller than his father and that his arms were wrapped around himself from the cold.

The Jew—*Monsieur Baume*, Claudette corrected herself— shifted his weight from one foot to the other, visibly tired. He must be freezing. If Lisette had known about him and his son during the midday meal, the two of them must have been waiting in the forest all these many hours.

"Can you hide us? At least for a few days?" Isaac Baume's eyes scanned the massive wall that stretched away in what Claudette knew seemed like infinite possibilities.

She couldn't bear the pleading in his voice. He had been her grandmother's friend and healer. He had become family to Claudette. It was winter, and he had no place to go. She shivered. The château was huge and held centuries' worth of secrets in its thick stone walls, deep wine cellars, hidden chambers, and abandoned turrets. Her section in the massive tower had once housed wet nurses and governesses. The unoccupied chambers now stored rolled rugs, discarded toys, and trunks of old clothes. When these accommodations were built into the second floor of the round tower, an awkward corner had been forgotten. In her first month, Claudette had explored this storage space with a candle and at one end discovered a narrow, steep staircase.

"Let's go inside," she said.

In the kitchen, Isaac Baume took off his torn gloves and rubbed his hands together before he tore off two pieces of bread and passed one to his son. He mumbled a prayer, as was his habit before eating, then took a bite. She registered that his beard was gone, and there was a grayish tint in his sunken cheeks. Claudette busied herself

pouring wine into the goblets. She felt Raphaël's lanky figure somewhere behind her at a respectful distance.

"We can't delay here," she whispered, and started toward the
back corridor, then stopped. She couldn't leave the lit kitchen without getting a glimpse of the face of the only young man who'd ever
fired her imagination.

The light showed the same drawn cheeks as his father's, but
firmer, the jawline defined. A lot of uncombed wavy hair. Unshaven
face. Bright eyes that examined her with open curiosity.

Blushing, she patted down an errant strand of hair and signaled
the men to follow her.

They wove their way up the service stairs to a narrow corridor
hidden between double walls. Raphaël's uneven steps were discor-
dant with hers. He was trying as hard as she was to control the thuds
made by a leg that didn't fully obey. Their steps clattered in the
confined spaces, and the noise worsened when they cut through the
wide gallery to enter the tower. The duchess's chamber was down
the other end of the gallery. What was Claudette doing, taking this
risk?

"Let's crawl," she whispered to Raphaël, and they dragged themselves over the short distance to the tower, his father beside them,
carrying the food basket.

In Claudette's first months here, the duchess had asked a visiting
physician friend to check her. The man was surprised that her brace
had no knee hinges. He took meticulous measurements and, in spite
of the war, brought from Paris a brace complete with a new pair of
leather shoes. The padded, hinged knee brace had improved Claudette's walk and posture, reducing her backache. There had been no
limit to the duchess's kindness, yet Claudette had decided to betray
her patroness. *It's just for tonight,* she promised herself.

They entered the small vestibule in the tower. Claudette closed
the door behind them and breathed a bit easier. She pointed to another door. "The water closet has a sink," she whispered. The faucet

also had a handheld spray hose for personal hygiene; Claudette used it daily in the adjacent square floor basin, since Madame Couture insisted that there be no source of malodor in the atelier. Claudette flipped a switch to the water heater, a luxury she had never dreamed of at Mémère's house. "You may bathe when it warms up."

As soon as the water splashed in the lavatory, the pipes came to life with a blast of popping and crackling sounds, and Claudette realized that the noise reverberated downstairs. Anyone could hear it. She bit her nails, wishing that her guests would hurry up. This madness couldn't extend beyond tonight.

She retrieved blankets from Mémère's trunk, which also contained Mémère's coat, shawls, and sewing and knitting paraphernalia. Claudette had taken these when she left. Looters, she'd known, would empty the rest of the home long before her father came to claim his inheritance.

When she lit the candles she kept in case of power failure, she saw Raphaël's eyes—curious, kind, the color of fresh grass. She was glad that he couldn't see the heat flushing her face as she led him and his father to the nearby narrow door. At her signal, Isaac Baume forced it open. Carrying their candles and blankets, they pushed aside discarded nursery furniture and toys to reach the steep steps.

The room upstairs was as empty as Claudette remembered, though colder. Wooden cots were piled up, barely visible in the half-moon outside the four round, dusty windows.

"I don't know where else to take you," she said to Isaac Baume.

"This is good. God bless you for your compassion."

Raphaël untangled a few cots from the pile, and Isaac Baume unrolled the thin mattresses. Claudette assumed that no fleas infested them, given that there had been no human flesh to feed on.

Isaac Baume dropped onto the cot, and the two men began to eat. Claudette averted her eyes from their hunger and headed down to fetch a washbowl and a ceramic pitcher.

Navigating the staircase back up while carrying a water pitcher set inside a bowl was impossible for Claudette. Raphaël stepped down to take them from her. Their fingers brushed accidentally, and the touch electrified her with an unfamiliar sensation.

Upstairs, Isaac Baume was lying under a blanket. He tried to get up. "Thank you for all your trouble."

Again, her heart contracted at the humility of his tone. "Get some sleep," she replied, unable to add that it was only for one night. In her mind's eye she saw the duchess's face, and the guilt returned. "Where are your other children?" she asked.

"My daughter, they rounded her up because of me." Responding to Claudette's unasked question he explained, "I was born in Poland. Foreign Jews are being exiled."

"To where?"

"They say to labor camps."

"But your children were born in France, right?"

"It makes no difference even though I've lived here legally, and my children are French citizens." He added, "My youngest son is hiding at a monastery."

Claudette made the sign of the cross. "One day, I hope you'll all be together."

For the first time, Raphaël spoke. "My father told me a lot about you when I was growing up. I'm delighted to finally meet you."

Heat flooded her face. His voice was low and sonorous. It sent a shiver of pleasure through Claudette. The only man she'd ever fantasized about had dropped into her life in the middle of the night. No romance novel could have sprung a greater surprise.

She smiled, then covered her mouth to hide her broken front teeth.

Chapter Twelve

CLAUDETTE

Château de Valençay, France
February 1942

I N CLAUDETTE'S FIRST month at the château, the duchess had installed her in a room close to the atelier and ordered the cook to send Claudette a light breakfast and dinner every day to save her the trips to the distant kitchen. This morning, the breakfast tray that Marguerite delivered was laden—there was a pitcher of coffee instead of a single cup, three soft-boiled eggs, and bread and butter.

"Why this sudden appetite?" Marguerite asked, glancing at the three plates and three sets of utensils.

Claudette was shocked at Lisette's lack of discretion. She avoided Marguerite's eyes. Who else was in on the secret? How long before the duchess discovered her deception?

Marguerite turned to leave with a snap of her head that bounced the dark curls under her starched cap. Her demeanor stood in sharp contrast to their former easy bantering. She stopped at the door. "I wanted to do something for the Résistance," she hissed, "and of all people, you get to do it?"

The Résistance? Claudette almost blurted out a denial. Is that what Lisette thought too?

Marguerite looked at the closed doors of the unoccupied chambers, silent as sentries. Nothing revealed that Claudette had rummaged there at the crack of dawn for clean, warm men's clothes. Marguerite said brusquely, "I'll go tidy up the atelier."

All day, as Claudette embroidered the lapels of the duchess's jacket with silk, she was distracted. The tiny embroidery needle, as slender as the finest fishbone, pricked her finger time and again. And then she accidentally nicked the fabric with the tip of her scissors. Isaac Baume had given her these scissors, along with a matching thimble. The scissors' ring-finger rest, designed as a crane in flight, was like her soaring heart.

She repaired the tear and ordered herself to be more careful, although only an hour later, she singed a ribbon she was pressing.

"You act like a woman in love," Madame Couture said.

Was it love? Claudette told herself that it was no more than a village girl's infatuation. And yet, years before she met him, the thought of him had taken root in her. With his hobbled leg, he was a kindred spirit. He knew the frustration of an unruly limb. Now that she had seen Raphaël and heard his voice, she couldn't get him out of her mind. In the fabric she was holding, she saw the reflected glow of the candlelight in his green eyes. As the hours passed, the accidental graze of their fingers grew into a fantasy of his hand traveling up her sleeve to her cheek . . . The vision of his tall, thin figure hovering at the top of the steps that morning churned her insides with the sweetest sensations. His earnest thanks ignited her nerve endings—

Madame Couture's giggle landed Claudette back on earth with an almost audible thud. Embarrassed, Claudette bent over her embroidery. Yes, in the romance tales, love did happen just like that. A *coup de foudre,* they called it, a "strike of lightning," and it was so true. It was described as delicious torment, which was true too.

Claudette looked out at the cold, colorless fields and, beyond them, the Nahon River, its gray surface mirroring the overcast skies. In the quiet of the atelier, with only the sound of the burning wood crackling—the warmth kept Claudette's fingers supple—her worries mounted. What would Lisette do when she discovered that the people who had been sent over weren't brave Résistance members but hunted Jews? Would she confess to Monsieur Vincent, who would report the men to the *préfet*?

Marguerite's envy presented another danger. Would she explore the tower's uninhabited rooms for her Résistance heroes until she found the hidden passage? Would she, unaware of the disastrous consequences for Claudette, demand Silvain Auguste also give her an assignment, raising his suspicions?

As Claudette was leaving the kitchen after the midday meal, Lisette gave her a towel-wrapped bundle. "This must last until morning."

Claudette clutched the food to her chest and hurried up so she could steal time from her work. She was out of breath when she reached the hidden turret. The men, wrapped in blankets, were reading in the light that flooded the room in early afternoon. Raphaël closed his book and smiled at her. She blushed, put down the bundle, and offered to lead them down to the lavatory. In the foyer, she stood guard, beads of sweat dotting her forehead at the noises emanating from the pipes. She prayed that it wouldn't alert someone below.

She couldn't bring herself to tell them to leave tonight.

The men began to climb back to the turret. Raphaël turned toward her as if he wanted her to linger. How long could she keep this up? She was already exhausted by the physical demand. Yet rushing back to the atelier, she carried with her his last smile.

The sun had long since set on this short winter day when she returned to her chamber. She lit a kerosene lamp, then filled a hot-water bottle and brought it up to Isaac Baume.

"Could you tell us about your life and work here?" He was curled on his side under the blankets.

She put on her gloves and sat on the frame of a third cot. Her words formed a mist in the cold air as she told the men about the château, the late duke's wine cellars, and the duchess, who worked hard to keep the estate producing, ran a literary salon in the library, and hosted concerts in the music room.

After a while, Isaac Baume dozed off. His deep breaths were broken occasionally by a soft whistle. Answering Raphaël's questions, Claudette said she was refreshing the duchess's black mourning wardrobe and, because no new lingerie was being sent from Paris, she mended her employer's fine silk pieces.

Raphaël spoke about his work as a printer. He made Claudette laugh when he imitated his aging boss, who'd had to strain to see the pages. Isaac had helped him buy the business. As Raphaël spoke, his long fingers animated his sentences. He had liked setting the lead letters, he told her, one by one, upside down, the rows and spaces even, no mistakes. "As exact as your work," he added with a grin. His teeth were white and straight, like those of the men in the romance novellas.

He lifted the book he had been reading. "I printed this one. *Aesop's Fables.*"

She leafed through the pages. The letters and lines weren't as small as they were in the books the duchess read, which didn't even feature drawings. "'The Ant and the Grasshopper,' 'The Crow and the Fox,' 'The Tortoise and the Hare,' 'The Fox and the Goat,'" Claudette read aloud, glad that his father had taught her to read. "These are children's stories!"

"They seem so, right? Each is a lesson in life's philosophy. I read one fable at a time, and it helps take my mind off everything. I think about it for hours."

"Why are you on the run? We're in the free zone."

Raphaël looked at her. "The free zone is not free of old Marshal Pétain's hatred of us. He spews anti-Semitic propaganda. He's seizing Jewish property."

"But what can he or his government actually do to you? Aren't you better off in a labor camp, being fed and having a roof over your head, than you are living outside in the cold of winter?" She glanced at Isaac Baume. "What if your father gets sick?"

"The flyer, signed by Marshal Pétain himself, said that only foreign-born Jews were to be deported. Nevertheless, my sister was taken." Raphaël clasped his hands and looked at them for a long minute. "Afterward, I printed a fake document for myself and didn't wear the yellow star on my clothes so I could sneak to the train station, where the Jews of our town had been locked up, packed in like sardines. I went every day, hoping to find a way to rescue her. No chance. They wound barbed wire around the building, and the French police guarded them. Even from the outside, I could smell the stench. No food was ever delivered! My people literally starved inside. Then, one morning, all the children were brought out—even the babies and toddlers, who were snatched from their screaming parents' arms—and put on buses."

"Why?" Claudette whispered, horror filling her.

"Right. Why such inhuman cruelty? To what end?" He paused to let the image and the unanswerable questions sink in before he went on. "My sister was younger than me, but she was the smartest in the family. So kind, too, like a little mother since our mother died."

"What happened to her? Where is she?"

"Two days later, all the adults—my sister among them—were shoved like cattle onto a freight train. The cars had no seats or windows. They were bolted boxes! No light, no air, no food, no water, no sanitation. I'm having nightmares thinking what it was like in that tomb. How many hours and days could they survive in these beastly conditions?"

"Where were they going?"

"Maybe to labor camps in Germany? Am I to believe that after such brutal accommodations—if any of them survived—they were treated like royalty?"

Claudette curled into herself. "Why the children? What labor could they expect from infants?" Not unlike the useless *invalides*.

"Something is so terribly wrong, it's unfathomable. We Jews of France are no longer certain who is our worst enemy. That's why my father and I must stay on the outside: to figure it out."

In spite of the horrors Raphaël was describing, she adored listening to his voice. So masculine; no romance booklet could explain the effect it had on her. "The Boche are monsters," she said.

"Boche? No! I'm telling you that this is all our French government's doing. I saw not a single Nazi hat around, only blue French police caps."

Claudette bit her nails. Over the years, she'd heard people say they didn't trust Jews, starting with the priest at La Guerche, who'd called them Jesus killers. In the tavern, she had heard them spoken of with outright disgust, which was the reason she opened the back gate for Isaac Baume. Recently, she had heard the same vitriol from Monsieur Vincent and his quotes from newspapers. Yet how far could such hatred go? The Jews were the Chosen People, Mémère had said. When you met them in person, as Claudette had, you knew they were good people.

"Have they started removing the *invalides* too?" she whispered.

"Every time it seems impossible to imagine anything worse, it happens."

They fell silent. Isaac Baume's soft snores were the only sounds in the turret.

Claudette changed the subject, moving to safer ground. "In your shop, did you print romance stories?"

His laughter relieved the tension. "We had a whole storage room filled with them. When we left, I took with me only a couple of boring books." His eyebrows rose in a mischievous expression. "Had I known I'd meet you, I would have packed some."

She smiled, bringing her hand up to cover her broken front teeth.

"Don't," he said.

"Don't what?"

He touched her wrist and gently lowered her hand. "You have a lovely smile."

Heat rushed through her veins. His touch burned. No one had

ever said anything nice about her looks. Maybe Solange had, but a blind girl didn't count.

His hand still rested on hers. She turned her palm to touch his, and their gloved fingers laced. They said no more as they both rose and descended the steps to her chamber.

EVEN WHEN SHE had fantasized about starring in a romantic story, Claudette had never imagined the rapture that seized her the minute Raphaël's lips touched hers and the ecstasy that exploded when his hands ran up the sides of her body to the exposed skin of her neck.

She froze. Her body recoiled, and a tremor of her soul reminded her that this fleshly craving was strictly forbidden.

Raphaël stopped moving but still held her close. His warm breath was on her neck. "It's all right," he murmured. "I understand."

"I—I don't know what to do." She couldn't help pressing her heavy breasts under the wool cardigan to his chest. Her breathing grew rapid.

"Let's just hold on to this moment of refuge from the world, from the war."

The war. Death was at the door of so many, perhaps even hers when the Nazis came for the *invalides*. And right now, the taste of Raphaël's kiss was life. Claudette turned her face up for more. *It's a grave sin*, the priest's admonition echoed in her head, but it was so far away while the warm mouth traveling up along her throat made her melt.

They breathed hard as they helped each other out of their clothes, then unbuckled the leather straps of their braces.

Afterward, they lay still, basking in an aura that had never been described in her booklets: a glow, a bubble of happiness that she wished to hold on to forever, yet she knew its transitory quiver. She drank in the beauty of Raphaël's long, lean body, passing a finger over the sparse hair on his chest and the skin that was surprisingly velvety. Their useless legs—her left, his right—lay next to each other as if a third party were stuck between them, but they took nothing away from the moment.

"Are you uncomfortable? Does it hurt?" Raphaël's hand touched her lower abdomen. He picked up a washcloth and dipped it in the bowl of water on the dresser, and when she drew her knees together, he said, "Let me," and gently cleaned her as if she were a baby.

Then he touched a spot she hadn't known existed. Their lips met again, hungry for more. He propped himself up on his elbow. "Beautiful," he murmured as he passed his hand down from her cheek. He cupped her full breasts, circled her nipples, traveled over her soft, rounded stomach, then went farther down to her useless left leg. "Beautiful." He planted kisses on her emaciated thigh before returning to her private part.

It's wartime, she told herself, giving herself up to his ardor. Even God's rules had changed.

But what if they hadn't?

Chapter Thirteen

SHARON

Cherbourg, France
September 1968

THE FLIGHT FROM Tel Aviv to Brussels is delayed, and the agent at the airport counter has no information on when to expect it.

"Is it delayed or canceled?" Sharon asks.

"It's not in the air."

Three hours later, as she's pacing the length of the great hall, she remembers that she's not supposed to draw attention, so she sits down and pretends to read her French magazine. Her fear of a screwup has come true.

When the flight number finally appears on the arrivals board, it is clear that she won't be able to accompany the men on the next leg of their journey. The train ride from here to Paris's Gare du Nord takes over two hours. By the time they reach Gare Saint-Lazare, the last train to Cherbourg will be gone—and so will the last flight from Orly to London.

She can't leave her third group of men stranded in England. After some inquiries, Sharon reserves a flight for herself from Brussels to London, even though it will take her not to Heathrow but to another London airport; from there, late tonight, she will have to make her way to Heathrow so she can meet her guys tomorrow morning.

A new wave of anxiety washes over Sharon at the thought of finding herself somewhere in England in the middle of the night, searching for a hotel.

For now, though, she must solve the immediate problem: finding a way for the three seamen arriving here in Brussels to travel to Cherbourg on their own. With four train changes between two countries, they will surely get lost.

She is about to call Danny, but then she reconsiders. In her intelligent unit, a poster on the wall read LOSING YOUR HEAD IN A CRISIS IS A SURE WAY FOR *YOU* TO BECOME THE CRISIS. Her job is not to throw the problem back to her boss but to find a solution. He has shown her that if you delegate a task to an inexperienced person, that person can rise to meet the challenge.

She has only thirty minutes before her flight to London leaves when the three boys finally emerge from passport control. She rushes them to the baggage carousel. "Any of you speak French?" she asks them in Hebrew, keeping her voice low. When they shake their heads, she asks, "Do you know your final destination?"

They shake their heads again.

She points to a quiet area behind a thick pillar. "Let's huddle over there." The PA speaker announces that her flight to London is boarding. "You're staying in Brussels tonight, but your final destination is Cherbourg, in Normandy. That's in the farthest northwestern area of France. You'll change trains in Paris."

The men's eyes light up.

"To be clear, this is *not* a trip to Paris. Your schedule to get from one station to another is tight." She takes out three sheets of paper on which she's written clear instructions in Hebrew with the local names in French. "This will be a multipart trip. I'm assigning each of you one leg of it, and each man will be the quasi–noncommissioned officer, the NCO, in charge of his section. There will be consequences for fucking up." She locks eyes with each man before she distributes the money for their expenses. "Any questions?"

They look down and shrug.

"You are navy. This challenge is an opportunity for you to prove that you're extraordinary. We trust you." She hands the first boy the voucher for the hotel that she reserved at the hospitality counter. "So, where are you off to?" she asks to test him.

He points to the escalator, at the bottom of which is the subway they'll take to the center of Brussels.

"Your hotel is right at the exit. It's your job to make sure that all three of you stay in tonight. Eat at the hotel's restaurant. No touring the city," Sharon tells him. "That's an order." She instructs the second boy to call the office and report their delay. She hopes it's not the pregnant Rina who has been waiting at the Cherbourg station for hours.

Sharon hears the final call for her flight and starts to perspire. She quizzes the second boy about his responsibilities: buying the tickets for the early train to Paris, then getting the taxi from Gare du Nord to Gare Saint-Lazare. Once they're all there, the third boy is in charge of buying the tickets to Cherbourg, getting them on the train, and ensuring that everyone keeps his mouth shut for the whole five-hour train ride.

Once she's belted into her airplane seat, she exhales deeply. It's only then, as the plane is lifting off, that she wonders about the storm breaking in Cherbourg over Saar Six's stealthy departure.

———

Two days later, under sparkling blue skies, Sharon is standing on the bow of the ferry from Portsmouth, crossing the English Channel. As Cherbourg's shore comes into view, she takes in the harbors that fill the horizon from east to west, like the generous train of a bridal gown. What she had seen only in the flat town map stretches in front of her in all its glory. To the west is the French navy's port with its dizzying array of khaki-colored destroyers, aircraft carriers, and cruisers as well as dozens of coast patrol vessels and tugboats. At the east end are white passenger ships with hundreds of portholes dotting their sides sailing in and out of the harbor where the *Titanic* had stopped before its first—and last—journey.

And between these two, the mouth of the perpendicular harbor cleaves right through the heart of Cherbourg.

If only Alon could have seen this awesome sight.

The wind whips Sharon's hair, and she uses her headband to gather it into a ponytail. She's been questioning the decisions she made in Brussels. Could she have handled it better? She hopes that the young men have made it to their final destination.

The four boys she collected at Heathrow airport stand along the railing far apart from one another—according to protocol—all gazing out with the same awestruck expression. The other ferry passengers are Brits; they carry no luggage, only baskets, because they're crossing to shop for cheese and wine. Sharon can't fathom having such a peaceful coexistence with neighbors that shopping in their markets is a possibility.

It's hard for her to recall her trepidations merely days earlier about venturing out into the world. If she could, she would shout her glee to the wind.

DANNY MEETS HER at the ferry with a man he introduces as Kadmon, the mission's acquisition officer.

"Have all my other guys arrived?" she asks, breathless.

"They have. I expected nothing less from you," Danny replies.

In the presence of others, she is not about to expand on how this task almost spiraled out of control. Nor can she ask him about the drama involving Saar Six.

Kadmon sports a huge mustache. Although he is short, his posture is ramrod-straight. "Come talk in the office." His baritone voice is rich, like that of a radio broadcaster. He shakes her hand, then gestures to the parking lot outside the wire fence.

"Thanks again." Danny gives her a thumbs-up and leads away the new recruits.

Her mission is over. All her men arrived! She smiles to herself at Danny's praise.

The interior of Kadmon's Renault is clean, although it smells of cigarettes. He drives half a kilometer to an area surrounded by a high metal fence, passes a sentry booth, and stops next to a prefabricated building dwarfed by an immense hangar. Sharon is glad to discover that the mission has an office. From Rina's frenzied, unofficial role and her own hastily stitched-together assignment, Sharon assumed this project was run with haphazard informality, the Israeli way of executing things on the fly. She's impressed to find that this is an organized operation. They walk down the corridor, and Kadmon introduces her to two engineers whose office walls and draft tables are covered with blueprints of boats and mechanical parts.

In his office, Kadmon tilts back in his chair, rests his feet on the desk, and quizzes her about her trip. She briefs him about the setback in Brussels and her solution. Presumably, he's already heard about it from the boys, and she anticipates his criticism about the expense of putting them up in a hotel for the night. He only listens.

Thirty minutes later, he lets his chair right itself with a thud and laughs a throaty chuckle. "A little crisis gets your adrenaline flowing. A good way to stay focused."

She holds back a sigh of relief. The adrenaline that has pooled in all her joints is draining out.

"You charted your moves and took precautions," he goes on. "You solved a problem on your own. You did a splendid job. Welcome to the team."

Warmth rushes through her. "That's great."

He gestures with his chin toward a desk in the open area between offices, where a secretary would usually be seated. "Please write down every single detail. Draw maps with all the roads, stores, signage, whatever you can recall."

She rises. At the door, she hesitates. "One thing I'd like to add."

"What's that?"

"Whatever the goal of this operation is, its planning is full of holes. It seems to run outside the Mossad and its expertise. Something unpleasant is bound to happen."

"The Brussels flight scheduling?"

"That's just the start. You were careful about sending the men through different ports of entry, yet none of them had a backup story if they were questioned—and neither did I, since I wasn't supposed to mention Cherbourg."

"Thanks for your input."

She hates being brushed off. "In my intelligence unit, the mantra was 'Don't wait until you're in a crisis to come up with a crisis plan.'"

He looks at her pensively. "Very well. Please submit your recommendations."

Is he really asking her to outline a plan for bringing new recruits to Cherbourg? She'll do it, and she'll make sure it convinces him to take the issue seriously. At the desk, Sharon pushes the typewriter to the corner. After her IDF basic training, she resisted being sent to the typing course; she wanted to use her brain, not mindlessly type someone's memos.

She glances again at the machine, challenging her with its silent keys, the letters as disorganized as the ones on an eye chart. She's already conquered a greater trial. Tomorrow, she will type her report, even if it takes hours, and begin to design a program for future recruits' arrivals.

Right now, for the rest of the afternoon, she must draw the maps before she forgets the visual details. As she sharpens two pencils, Sharon grins to herself at the thought that in a few days, she traveled much farther than simply from Israel to Europe.

Self-congratulations aside, she shouldn't be distracted from the reason why she accepted this job. Getting Danny to speak about his past should be her priority.

Chapter Fourteen

CLAUDETTE

Château de Valençay, France
February 1942

WAR PUSHED ASIDE the guilt over sex without holy matrimony. War was also the reason she was in charge not only of the pressing needs of the two men but literally of their lives. It had been three days since they arrived, and she was torn between the exhilaration of her new love and fear of a discovery. The duchess would be disappointed and Claudette would be dismissed, but worse, the two men would be handed over to the Nazis at the checkpoint north of the Cher River. The BBC radio in Monsieur Vincent's office reported that the Résistance's ongoing attacks on German convoys, arms repositories, and bridges were being met by increasingly brutal Nazi reprisals against the local population.

The third night Raphaël spent in her bed, with only the moon slanting pearly light on his face, he revealed more about his flight with his father.

"My first mistake was following the ordinance to register with the local precinct as a Jew. I gave my father's Polish place of birth. It condemned us all, starting with my sister." Raphaël's voice broke. "Then I agreed to print Résistance leaflets for a customer. When he was arrested, I knew he wouldn't tolerate the torture and would give my name."

Raphaël and his father made their escape at dawn, leaving everything behind. Isaac Baume had long since stopped traveling and had sold his horse, cart, and merchandise. Fleeing, they took only a satchel each with whatever food they had on hand. They even discarded their blankets, since they were pretending to be regular Frenchmen riding to their factory shift.

Raphaël could ride a bicycle? Claudette had never considered it possible. "Didn't you have non-Jewish friends to hide you?" she asked.

"I couldn't ask anyone to risk the lives of their entire family."

She took it as a compliment that Isaac Baume had trusted her. She put her arms around Raphaël as he told her about being on the run for over a year, living off the kindness of strangers. "My late mother's jewelry paid for shelter at a farm, but then the underground bombed a bridge nearby, and the Nazis were searching for the culprits." A shudder ran through his body. "We fled and hid in a forest."

She couldn't imagine living out in the open, no shelter or food. The refugees who had flooded the roads in 1940 and raided Mémère's garden had lived in makeshift tents, but that was in summer weather. This was winter, and a particularly harsh one. There was hardly any coal to heat the château's vast chambers, which were almost impossible to keep warm even when fuel was available. The chopped wood that Marguerite brought up each day for Claudette's fireplace lasted only a few hours.

He continued. "In the fall, we lived in a monastery. We helped by fixing things and working in the gardens. Unfortunately, the nearby village was Protestant." Raphaël paused. "Protestants are helping Jews, but not when they can use them to get revenge against the Catholics, and the same is true for the Catholics. Both will snitch to the Nazis in the hope of harming their religious enemies."

"The Catholics would do no such thing."

"Not all of them, but yes, each faction will often betray the Jews that the other is hiding."

Two nights later, the chugging of a few airplanes wrested Claudette from sleep. She had figured out that they chose dark skies, nights of no more than a half-moon. However, tonight the full moon's light poured into her chamber. Raphaël was sitting up in bed.

She went to the window, and he joined her, his arm around her waist as they peered out. She wanted to give herself to this simple gesture of fondness and possession, but her attention was caught by giant mushrooms swaying down from the sky.

"Parachutes," he said.

Claudette had seen them in newsreels on the two occasions when the duchess sent the live-in staff to the village cinema. The grainy moving pictures were now real as, one by one, the slow-moving mushrooms reached the ground. Claudette's hands flew to her throat. "My God," she murmured, her heart beating hard. "The Nazis are landing here!"

"Not Nazis. Marshal Pétain makes the airports available to them. It's the Résistance in action, and its cell is active inside this château. Your duchess is cooperating with the organization, if not running it."

Claudette gasped. She had noticed large maps in the duchess's chamber but assumed they had to do with managing the estate.

She sank into a chair and began brushing her hair. The rhythm of the brush's strokes was the only steady thing in this large, ominous world that was pressing down on her.

Raphaël passed his hand through the hair cascading down her back. "Do you know if any paintings from the Louvre are hidden here?"

She shook her head.

"I printed a newsletter that had an article about the Nazis' impounding hundreds of paintings from the Louvre and shipping them to Berlin. One train car was opened at a stop along the way, the paintings removed, and the car sealed again. The Nazis only discovered it when the train arrived in Berlin."

She looked up at Raphaël's handsome face and waited for him to explain further.

"The article suggested that the paintings had been loaded onto a train heading to the Loire Valley and then hidden in a château."

"There are dozens of châteaux here," she said.

"Mostly farther west. This château is between the occupied and free zones. Its location makes it a likely stop. That's the same reason the paratroopers are landing here." Raphaël motioned toward the field outside. "The Nazis must suspect that there is a lot of activity in Valençay, and they would like to uncover it."

A shiver ran through Claudette. The war was catching up to her. The day before, at the midday meal, Silvain Auguste had translated an article from a smuggled British newspaper. It reported that the Nazis, disenchanted with France's puppet president Pétain, ignored him altogether and had begun to break the treaties they had made with him.

"The Nazis will arrive in the Loire Valley," Silvain Auguste had finished.

Raphaël knelt by Claudette's chair and buried his face in her midsection. His voice came out broken: "There's no telling who else saw the parachutes. My father and I must move on."

Claudette's breath caught in her throat. Terror and relief vied with each other. Her new love was smashed to pieces. "Where will you go?"

"I don't know. Our staying here is also too risky for you."

Her romance books said that hearts could break, but she'd never fully believed that. Now she felt hers cracking in pain—for herself and for the two men running for their lives. She grabbed his hands. "Can I come with you?" To be with him, she'd sleep in a cowshed, walk in the rain, live in the forest.

"Of course not." He hugged her, nuzzling her neck. "Please don't cry. I'll return for you after the war."

"You've taken a great risk," Isaac Baume said to her a few hours later when she delivered their morning coffee. "There aren't enough words to thank you. It's the respite we needed."

"I can't thank you enough for all you did for me when I was young and for Mémère." Sobbing, she withdrew her string purse from her skirt pocket. She had not spent the bills that her squatter had thrown at her, and she hadn't touched the salary she'd earned here. The money she handed Isaac Baume was half her savings. It might buy him and Raphaël shelter somewhere for the rest of the winter.

Isaac Baume protested, but his tone was unconvincing. She already regretted leaving the other half tucked under a loose wall panel.

The grief hollowed out her chest. Her tears flowed on and off all day. Madame Couture, who had speculated that Claudette was having an affair with one of the groundskeepers, asked whether the man had mistreated her. Claudette shook her head, to which the seamstress offered the only balm she knew: "It's better to have loved and lost than never to have loved at all."

Claudette's love for Raphaël was worth everything, even sinning. She wiped her cheeks and said nothing.

At one o'clock, Claudette entered the kitchen, headed to the stove, and whispered to Lisette, "They want to leave."

"Ten o'clock tonight, outside," Lisette whispered back.

Instead of eating, Claudette rushed to the church on the main floor and prayed for herself, for the Baumes, and for Free France. Communists, Maquis, Gaullists, or Pétainists—she was on the side of whoever would bring an end to the war.

WHILE HIS FATHER washed up in the water closet, Raphaël kissed her. He was wearing a uniform coat from the Great War that she'd dug out of an old trunk, and its coarse wool scratched her cheek. Even though Raphaël was much taller than she, he clung to her, and she felt the hunger and sorrow of their last lovemaking an hour earlier.

She was crying when she led the men back to the dark kitchen.

The underground operation was shrouded in mystery. Whoever took them away tonight might save them from death—or betray them once they realized that these two men were Jews.

A package wrapped in oilpaper and tied with string was resting on the side counter, and Claudette motioned for Isaac Baume to take it. Outside, freezing rain drizzled, and she tightened her cape around her. If only Raphaël and his father could find shelter in a dry, warm place.

Isaac Baume's hand, in a mitten she had knit for him from old wool, hovered over Claudette's head. "May God bless you and keep you. May God shine light on you and be gracious to you. May God turn toward you and grant you peace."

"Thank you for your blessing." Claudette's eyes teared up again.

He touched her wet cheek. "One day, God willing, we'll meet in peacetime."

Where?

Raphaël stood still under the door overhang, his sad green eyes boring into hers, and she could feel the heat of the message he was sending her. He loved her.

"I promise to come looking for you here after the war," he said.

She put her hand over her heart. "I promise that I will wait. Right here."

The sound of rolling carriage wheels coming from the direction of the vineyard grew louder. The carriage came to a stop, and a horse snorted and pounded its hooves on the gravel. The driver, a young man Claudette recognized as a gardener despite the oilcloth covering his head, asked, "Ready?"

Raphaël gave Claudette's hand a last squeeze before following his father into the cart. The rhythm of his uneven gait continued like music in her head after the cart had disappeared from sight.

She crossed herself and sent Jesus a silent prayer to protect these two Jews.

Chapter Fifteen

CLAUDETTE

Château de Valençay, France
September 1942

You HAVE NEVER seen any pregnant maids at the château," Madame Couture said.

Claudette wrapped protective arms around her protruding belly. Her morning sickness had given her away to Madame Couture early on. Lately, Claudette's back had begun aching more, a small punishment for her sin. First an affront to God, her sin was now an offense to humans, as Madame Couture's haranguing reminded her.

"A girl stays in the village until she can return to work," the seamstress said, "leaving the baby in the care of her mother or a neighbor."

Claudette looked down at the garment she was sewing. Madame Couture meant well; she was concerned about her. At La Guerche-sur-l'Aubois, whenever a girl married in a hurry and delivered a baby shortly thereafter, the stigma accompanied the child well into his or her school years. The disgrace of having conceived out of wedlock had become a part of Claudette, like her cursed leg. But unlike her disability, the baby growing inside her filled her with an inner glow. Her love for her unborn child was worth the shame. She had never expected to be a mother, and now the miraculous events—being loved by Raphaël and carrying his child—were two blessings tied together. She would raise their baby until the war was over, then Raphaël would return, and they would be a family.

Madame Couture opened the window, and Claudette breathed in the fresh scent of the lemon orchard. Her senses had become more acute, perhaps because she was smelling for two, bringing the outside world into her baby's safe, cushiony place. Yesterday, she walked outside to take in the fragrance of moist earth of the herb garden. It had been over two years since she worked the soil, and she missed growing her own vegetables. She would do it again once her baby was old enough to toddle next to her.

Apparently having had a new thought, Madame Couture turned to face the room. "Claudette, were you violated? Is that what happened?"

Claudette shook her head.

"Is he already married?"

"No," she murmured.

"Well, then, since it must be a staff member, why don't you let Monsieur Vincent take it up with him?"

Marguerite, Madame Couture, Monsieur Vincent, and even the duchess might believe her immoral, but they showed her kindness. That sympathy would evaporate if she revealed the truth. She couldn't risk getting fired and losing her protection at Valençay when the Nazis were at the door.

Sunday, Monsieur Vincent told Claudette to go to the village church instead of the duchess's Mass. "At least you can confess to Father Sauveterre," he told her.

The priest pressed, and when Claudette refused to name the father, he threatened her with eternal hell. "You're about to bring a bastard into the world. Your sin will forever brand both of you," he said. "Bastard," he repeated, spitting out the word.

Claudette cried, scared of burning in hell, yet she swallowed her secret. What choice did she have? *Bastard*. She wrapped her arms around her stomach to shield her baby from the unforgiving word. The only thing she knew for sure was that the child growing inside her was a sign that his father was still alive. Until they reunited, she had to keep herself safe for all of them.

Father Sauveterre changed his tone. "Child, isn't your disability enough of God's punishment for your stubbornness?"

Claudette sobbed harder. Of course she had been the cause of her own disability. She, no one else, had been stuck in her mother's birth canal, presenting her buttocks to the world and clinging inside with fetal fingers. Yet now, in her misery, she craved compassion and mercy, not this cruelty. She craved Jesus's comforting hand on her hair and Mary's motherly love.

Except that she couldn't repent. She would have loved Raphaël all over again. *Forgive me, Jesus, for not seeking Your forgiveness*, she prayed instead.

"THESE THINGS HAPPEN more often than people care to admit," Madame Couture told Claudette the day after Father Sauveterre's failed interrogation. "The man is forced to marry the girl and make the baby legitimate—"

Her lecture was interrupted when the duchess entered the atelier with a grand sweep of her silk robe's ostrich feathers. Accompanying her was a svelte woman with bobbed brown hair and deep-set eyes like the centers of poppy flowers. At first, the dresses draped over her arm concealed the small bulge of pregnancy.

"Please take out the seams to fit her condition, and would you please sew Madame Galvin a couple of comfortable frocks?" the duchess asked Madame Couture.

The guest threw a look at Claudette, probably comparing their pregnancies; Claudette was farther along. She suffered from back pain and was reclining in an upholstered chair, her feet propped up on a stool, her work in her lap. She tried to straighten up but her arms couldn't reach to lift her bad leg off the stool.

"Stay, stay," the duchess said, and turned to Madame Couture. "By the end of the month, I want her living in the village near the midwife."

After the duchess and her pregnant friend left, Madame Couture searched through the collection of fabrics in the armoire and muttered, "To think that my family's name is so debased that I must stoop so low as to sew for a Jewess!"

As if slapped, Claudette raised her head. "Madame Galvin is a Jewess? How do you know?"

"Her maiden name was Chiraze. The leather-goods family. Jewish. Why a Galvin would marry someone from that crooked tribe is beyond me."

"Where is her husband?"

"He stays in Paris to take care of his affairs, but Madame Galvin is living here in one of the posh guest rooms! She should hide in the cellar like the rats that the Jews are."

"Some Jews are good people. My *mémère* used to say that they were close to God."

Madame Couture snorted. "The duchess must think so too."

CLAUDETTE COULDN'T WAIT for Madame Galvin to return for a fitting. In spite of Madame Couture's distaste, she had sewn two frocks for her, and Claudette crocheted a pink collar for one and fashioned a silk poppy for the other. She'd stitched black-silk stamens to match Madame Galvin's eyes.

Madame Galvin collected the dresses, complimented both of them on their fine work, and hurried out. Claudette followed her.

"Madame Galvin," she whispered.

The woman looked back at her, her eyebrows raised in surprise.

Claudette gathered the courage to say the words for the first time. "My baby. It's—he's—Jewish too."

Madame Galvin smiled and turned to fully face her. "You aren't Jewish, are you?"

Claudette spoke fast. "His father is, and I want him to be Jewish too."

"In Judaism, the lineage goes through the mother."

Claudette narrowed her eyes at the blow. "I love your people. How can my baby belong to them?"

Madame Galvin shook her head. "First, *you'd* have to convert, and that's a long process of studying, requiring a rabbi." She softened her voice. "Anyway, this is the worst time for anyone in France to be Jewish. If your baby is a boy, you wouldn't want him to be circumcised."

"What's that?"

Madame Galvin blushed. "Jewish male babies go through a special cutting that marks our covenant with God."

"Oh." Claudette had noticed the difference between Raphaël's penis and her little brothers' from the time she still lived with her parents but had attributed it to physical variations, like noses. "Maybe something simpler, like baptism, but Jewish, so his soul can enter God's Kingdom?"

Madame Galvin shifted her weight from one foot to the other. "We have no such shortcuts. *Wanting* to be Jewish is not enough. Sorry. I must go. I wish you all the best." She started to leave.

"Wait!" There was so much Claudette wanted to learn from the first Jewish woman she'd ever met. "What's the most important thing for Jews?"

Madame Galvin stopped again. Her dark eyes looked at Claudette for a long moment. "To do good in the world. That's what God expects of us."

Claudette had witnessed that in Isaac Baume's unending kindness, a stark contrast to the village priest's cruelty. Even Mémère had looked favorably on Jews. Now Claudette had learned that they actually had a covenant with Him!

She lowered her head in reverence. Madame Galvin, like Raphaël, seemed oblivious to the fact that they were barred from paradise by original sin, since it hadn't been washed away by baptism. Instead, some inner strength sustained them; they didn't shy away from the religion that made the world hate them so.

Her thoughts swirled. She would inch closer to Raphaël's people through their baby. She would gift their baby's innocent soul to God by giving him both religions. The infant's illegitimate status would be diminished by the double consecrations.

Then an idea came to her. "I want to give my baby a good Jewish first name. It will be a blessing coming from you."

Madame Galvin let out a small laugh that was as delicate as she was. "I've picked Rebecca or Benjamin for my baby."

At that instant, Claudette's baby felt real. A name had been bestowed on him or her—a Jewish name, one that Claudette could whisper when the two of them were alone. "Those are beautiful names, Madame," she said, breathless with the magnitude of the moment. She took Madame Galvin's hand and kissed it with all the reverence she felt. "May God be with you."

Chapter Sixteen

SHARON

Cherbourg, France
September 1968

Two hours into Sharon's work on the maps, Danny appears. "I'm pleased, and Kadmon is pleased."

"I'm pleased too, in case anyone wonders."

He laughs and looks down at the map she drew of a section of Heathrow airport; it's filled with arrows and notes. "Wow, kiddo. You can draw well."

She chuckles. "One item that hasn't come up in your investigation of me: I did drafting during summer vacations at my uncle's factory." Had her father lived, he would have become an artist; everyone said so. Her own art was often displayed in the school's halls.

"A pleasant surprise." Danny pauses. "By the way, I've never asked you: How does an Ashkenazi girl who grew up in Tel Aviv and attended a French high school happen to become fluent in Arabic?"

She shrugs. "When I was little, we had a daily cleaning woman and a washerwoman who came every other day. They spoke Arabic, and when my grandfather realized that I was learning it, he bought a television set." They both know that there was no Israeli TV back then. The only available channels were broadcast from the neighboring Arab countries. "He spoke Arabic from having been raised in Jaffa, and the two of us watched together."

"Admirable flair for languages," he says. "And German?"

"I learned some from a neighbor, a Holocaust survivor, who lived alone. Every day my grandma sent me over to deliver a dish of food, and I stayed to hear the old woman's stories. She had no one else to talk to."

"Well, I'm glad that you're fluent in French."

Sharon hesitates. "Danny, what happened to the flak we were supposed to catch about Saar Six?"

He shakes his head as if mystified. "Our French colleagues here were upset, all right. It wasn't 'gentlemanly,' they said. To our astonishment, though, they weren't upset enough about it to report to Paris that the boat had left without their knowledge."

"Are they covering it up because it might seem like their own fault? Some internal problem?"

"I believe that it is our friend here who extracted a huge favor from them." Danny points out the window toward the giant hangar. To Sharon's perplexed look, he explains, "Félix Amiot. He averted a diplomatic confrontation."

"The *former* anti-Semite? Why would he do that?"

"It might have cost the town dearly had he been forced to halt production."

"Well, onward to Saar Seven!" She raises an imaginary champagne flute.

"Onward to seven through twelve," Danny replies.

It won't be so simple, she thinks. Seven's launch might challenge the embargo once more if the Israeli leadership pulls a similar gambit. Publicly embarrassing Pompidou yet again would carry severe ramifications.

Danny glances at Sharon's money belt, which is hanging off the back of her chair. She reaches for it and withdraws her expense list and the remaining cash. As he counts out the bills and coins, she asks, "While we're on the subject, may I get an advance on my salary?"

They go to his office, and he opens a vault built into the wall. She signs a form, feeling a bubble of pleasure. Her first earnings in

France. She'll buy a robe right away. She's not yet ready for a lipstick, but perhaps an eyeliner pencil?

"I suggest you deposit your passport in this safe," Danny says.

She glances at the three pistols and stacked boxes of ammunition in the safe. "Ready for any eventuality?"

"We're always concerned about a Palestinian attack. The crew members keep theirs in a safe on the boat they're working on." He smiles. "How is your gun handling these days?"

"Haven't touched it since basic training."

"There's a firing range where you could practice."

She shakes her head. "I didn't sign up for combat duty."

But as she walks back to her desk, her sense of safety is shaken. Should she retrain in handling a pistol? Be ready for a Palestinian attack here, in Cherbourg?

On her flight from Tel Aviv, she'd looked down from ten thousand meters at the blue sheet of the Mediterranean. Low-flying helicopters will surely locate the *Dakar* any day now, and her mission here will be over before any terrorist action. That also means that she's running out of time to grill Danny about his Youth Aliyah experience.

From the inside pocket of her backpack, she retrieves a black-and-white photo of her mother, the only picture of her she has other than her parents' wedding photo. The size of two postage stamps, it's a copy of a photo taken for her wedding certificate. Sharon has encased it in protective plastic. She examines the close-up and wonders yet again: Who was Judith Katz? The dark, almond-shaped eyes, the Cupid's bow lips, and the long neck—all so much like Sharon's—offer no clues. Was her mother witty and charming? Or shy and aloof? Was she a city girl or a farm girl? Did she have a sister to share secrets with, as Sharon would have loved to have? Judith Katz was surely musical, so what instrument did she play?

Would she have taught Sharon how to bake? Taken her on nature walks? Told her stories at bedtime? Sharon has heard from her aunts and uncles so many stories about her father—about Amiram's antics, his mischievous spirit, and his artistic talent. No one knew anything about her mother.

"Who are you, Judith?" Sharon whispers. "Who am I?"

AT SEVEN O'CLOCK, she's still drawing her maps when one of the engineers, Elazar, pops his head in. "I'm locking up. Come. I'll drive you home."

"I have no idea where my apartment is. I was there barely one night." Danny left a note with the address so she could call a taxi.

"You live right above me and my family. If you jump rope, we'll hear it."

She tucks her papers in an empty drawer, hoists her backpack, and follows Elazar to his Citroën. It's dusk, but there's just enough light for her to finally see something of Cherbourg.

Elazar takes the road that runs parallel to the canal slicing into the center of town. On Sharon's left are warehouses, boat-repair shops, and empty lots where fishermen's nets hang to dry. The opposite bank, though, is lined with four-story houses painted in muted beige hues. The small terraces with ornate iron railings have a distinctly European look. At street level, outdoor cafés with colorful awnings dot the sidewalk. *Bienvenue,* she thinks. *I'm in France.* It would be nice to sit with a book in a café on a lazy afternoon.

"This canal is an engineering feat conceived by Napoléon. Isn't it amazing? They had none of today's machinery." Elazar points to the cliff rising in front of them. "From that fortress, you can see the entire town and all the harbors. Imagine Napoléon standing there, looking down, and planning his naval strategy?

"The location of this canal, perpendicular to the two major harbors, is great for waiting out a storm. The English Channel is famous for its gale winds—they have claimed many ships over the centuries." He points east to somewhere past their office. "Napoléon also knew that, besides the naval war advantage, this spot opened up a commercial route to the Atlantic Ocean—to the New World—that didn't go through the Mediterranean." He sighs. "Before World War Two, thousands fled Europe through here."

She recalls Danny mentioning the *Titanic*. "No more ocean crossings?"

"People fly. Now there's a nuclear submarine plant instead." He throws a quick glance at her. "I hear that you speak French. What about German? Germany still sends their engineers over. Brrrr." He fakes a shiver. "That language."

His words jolt Sharon. How is it possible that that genocidal nation supports the defense of the country of the Jews? "I didn't know Germany was involved."

"Big-time. The Saar design was adapted from their Jaguar torpedo boat. They were about to start manufacturing when the Arab countries made their usual noise, and the Germans buckled."

"So here we are, in France."

"Helped by the former Nazi engineers. The hardest part is not to think of where each was twenty-five years ago. Like the owner of CMN, Félix Amiot."

"What's with him? Is he German?"

"As Froggy as can be, but he was a Nazi collaborator. He managed to avoid being executed afterward."

"How did he collaborate?" The *former* anti-Semite, she thinks.

"Isn't building over fifty planes and a ton of aeronautic engines for the Third Reich a collaboration?"

"Why would a Nazi sympathizer manufacture boats for Israel? He must suspect that eventually they'll be fitted with arms."

"Some say that life is not black or white."

"An anti-Semite is an anti-Semite."

"In fact, what saved him from the firing squad was that he took over his Jewish friends' business—Coco Chanel perfumes, no less—and even paid their debts, then after the war handed it back to them."

"While at the same time his planes dropped bombs on the populace in France?" Sharon adds in a sarcastic tone, "Can't wait to meet him."

She stretches and yawns. It's been a very long day. One of several very long days.

Elazar tells her that he's been stationed in Cherbourg since the start of the year. He left behind a son serving in the IDF. His wife and fifteen-year-old daughter are here with him; the girl is miserable over being uprooted, pulled away from her school and her friends.

"We have a great team here." He glances at Sharon. "The guys will fall all over you."

She scoffs. Moments later, she follows Elazar into the building. "You live on the second floor, I'm on the third, and Rina's on the fourth. Who lives on the first?" Sharon asks.

"It's been empty since the family got transferred after some juicy drama." Before she has the chance to ask for details, he stops at his door. "Come in and meet my family."

She's exhausted and hasn't had a chance to let Savta know that she's arrived safely. It was out of the question to send postcards bearing stamps from Belgium or England. She'll try sending a telegram tomorrow because an airmail letter will take two weeks to reach Tel Aviv.

"I'll come in just for a minute," she tells Elazar and is already being welcomed by a petite woman whose brown hair is gathered into pigtails that make her look as young as her teenage daughter, who sits in front of the TV. The girl's arms are crossed as if she's angry at the TV, and her expression is sullen.

"I'm Naomi," the woman says. "This is Pazit. Would you like to join us for dinner?"

The teenager doesn't react to the mention of her name, nor does she smile when the British sitcom booms with canned laughter. Sharon promises to come for dinner tomorrow and goes upstairs.

Oded and Gideon are playing cards with two of the three new

men. Israeli music is drifting from the cassette recorder under the TV. Sharon notices that the floors have been washed, and the dining table is cleared of dishes.

"Welcome back!" they greet her. "We were hoping you'd return to show us around."

How would she know this town in which she'd spent one night before being sent out? "Last I saw you, you were playing cards. Nothing more exciting has happened since?"

"A French colleague took us out to a disco. He drank so much that he couldn't remember how to bring us back."

In her room, her suitcase is still on the floor, still packed. So much has been crammed into her day, and now, when she expected a quiet evening, Israeli-style hilarity and camaraderie will draw her out.

They go to a bar around the corner, and her roommates recognize two Frenchmen they met at work and with whom they've developed a form of hand-signal communication. They all gather around small tables pushed together, and again, Sharon is the only woman. There is hardly a chance for a female friend close to her age.

"We heard we can order seafood," Oded says.

She laughs. "Let's live dangerously." She examines the mussels and oysters on the menu. In Israel, the Orthodox minority that controls the government through a political coalition enforces religious dietary laws. Only fish that have fins and scales are kosher. Israeli fishermen catch the same sea creatures that Italian and Greek fishermen do, but the Israelis must throw the nonkosher harvest back into the water before returning to shore.

Sharon turns to order mugs of beer from the waitress and spots Danny in a dark section of the room, seated kitty-corner to a young woman. Their heads are close together in intimate conversation. The woman's wavy blond hair and her jaunty tilted beret are clearly French, as is the elegance of the blue dress hugging her slim figure, her printed scarf, and the beige trench coat thrown over the back of her chair.

When the food is served, Oded's eyes widen. He stares at the plate. "The oysters are raw?"

"I call for a dare!" Gideon says.

"I'm in!" Laughing, Sharon lifts the first shell and sucks in the slimy creature. It is so slippery that it slides right down her throat, leaving a seaweed flavor. One of the Frenchmen raises his mug to salute her, the winner of the dare. Pleased, she samples the meaty mussels swimming in a warm garlicky wine broth, then dunks her bread in it. *"C'est délicieux,"* Sharon tells the Frenchmen.

From the corner of her eye, she sees Danny bring the woman's hand to his lips. She feels a tightening at the bottom of her stomach. How she longs for Alon and his spontaneous displays of affection.

She puts down her mug of beer and rises. "Guys, I'm beat. I need to sleep."

Gideon and Oded rise too. The latter holds a handful of coins out to Sharon; she scoops out their share to pay the bill.

The three of them run through the rain. Sharon's shoes slap the wet cobblestones, splashing water onto her calves. If Alon were there, they'd be holding hands and dashing through puddles, laughing in the rain. With him, she wouldn't have minded the water drenching her hair and making her dress cling to her body. Perhaps this is a scene in *The Umbrellas of Cherbourg?* The passion of Catherine Deneuve awakens in Sharon like a thirsty internal flower seeking to bloom.

Back in the apartment, she claims the shower. Then, with her freshly washed hair wrapped in a towel, she finally unpacks her suitcase and places Alon's framed photo on the nightstand. Twenty minutes later, under the wool cover, she stares at it, willing Alon's smile to turn into laughter that will infuse their night with love.

Rosh Hashanah, the Jewish new year, will arrive Sunday. She's looking forward to helping Rina cook, to the aroma of the matzo ball soup, and to the evening filled with whatever secular version of reciting or singing that Rina and the officers' team designs. Is she ready to mark the new year as a healing stage in her mourning process?

Chapter Seventeen

CLAUDETTE

Valençay Village, France
October 1942

THE SUDDEN ABDOMINAL contraction made Claudette gasp. This was too early! It had been only eight months since Raphaël's departure. Claudette had awakened this morning feeling odd; the room seemed out of focus, as if she had a cold. Even her teeth felt foreign in her mouth. But this?

"Léonie!" she called to the woman in whose house she was staying for her confinement. "My back is killing me."

As Léonie felt around Claudette's bulging stomach, a second contraction hardened it. "It's mild. They may stop. Pray that they will. I'll go get Madame Duchamp."

"Hurry up," Claudette called after Léonie in a small voice. She lay in her room, alone and frightened. Coming a month too early, her baby—Raphaël's baby—might not survive. She prayed to Mary, the Mother, who now stood by her bed, holding her hand. "Not yet, please. Let my baby grow a bit more inside."

It must have helped, because there were no more contractions until Léonie returned. Claudette heard her children whining when a third contraction seized her.

Léonie entered the room with a few folded towels. "Where is Madame Duchamp?" Claudette called. "Why isn't she here?"

"On her way. But your water hasn't broken yet. You have time." She left again, and Claudette heard her in the kitchen, pumping water into a pot.

She'd never felt so scared as she did when another sudden pain clutched her entire body, stronger than the previous ones. She gulped a lungful of air. Then a knife slashed her lower abdomen. Another knife stabbed her back. With a swoosh she could almost hear, a gush of warm water puddled in the bedding beneath her. She screamed as a huge contraction squeezed her abdomen. A guttural moan, like a roar, tore out of her.

Léonie reappeared. "Hold back. Just breathe out with each—" She stopped as Claudette had another contraction.

She panted so hard that her lungs emptied with a long growl.

"Jesus and Mary," Léonie said. "Please. Don't push." She peeked under the cover and pulled Claudette's legs up. "Just wait! Madame Duchamp is coming!" She propped a pillow under the left leg, which couldn't stay up.

Another huge contraction made all of Claudette's muscles spasm, and a wild groan emerged from her lungs, long and rumbling. Something slippery slid out.

"Oh no," Léonie said. "It's here!"

The air returned to Claudette's lungs. She was heaving, sobbing, and laughing. The perspiration that coated her face mixed with her tears. "What is it?"

Léonie lifted a tiny pinkish baby covered with waxlike white mucus; the umbilical cord dangled, not much narrower than the thin limbs. "You have a boy!"

FROM THE FRONT of the house flowed the sounds of Léonie's children. Claudette was in bed, the week-old baby snuggled in the crook of her arm, sleeping after being nursed by Léonie. Claudette was holding back tears. Her heavy breasts had failed to produce enough milk. Not only had her baby been born too small, vulnerable, but in his first few days, he hadn't stopped crying. The pitiful braying from weak lungs had torn at Claudette's heart. What was wrong with him? Could he die? She kept him latched to her nipple, and he sucked briefly, only to stop in frustration and resume his crying. Finally Léonie, whose two-year-old daughter still nursed, offered to try feeding him. It worked.

"You should continue to breastfeed," the midwife had told Claudette. "In a few days, you'll produce more milk. Let Léonie only supplement you."

Now Claudette examined her baby's fine features, each as perfect as a work of art. His miniature cleft chin was more pronounced than Raphaël's. Gently, she shifted Benjamin so he was lying belly-down on her chest and listened to his even puffs of air. He was content, trusting in her care. She breathed in his sweet milk-and-talc scent, and her heart broadened with so much love, she was unable to contain it.

Raphaël was present in their new baby, yet that made her feel his absence more acutely. "My baby. Raphaël's and my baby." She wept. By not producing enough milk, she was failing both her loved ones.

Outside, the late-fall wind assailed the trees, and rain pelted the window. Since coal was unavailable, and there was no man to chop wood, Claudette stayed in bed to keep warm. Where were Raphaël and his father? Were they at least in a dry barn? Or had they found a cave where they could light a fire? If only Raphaël were here to caress their baby's legs through the flannel swaddling and be grateful as she was that both legs were healthy. Madame Duchamp had assured her that in a year, Benjamin would walk normally. Claudette couldn't stop checking him to reassure herself that he had not inherited his parents' affliction, that his legs matched perfectly.

Madame Couture poked her head in the door. *"Coucou,"* she crooned. Smiling, she entered, carrying a covered dish. She gave each of Claudette's cheeks *la bise,* removed her drenched coat and scarf, and blew on her fingers to warm them. Then she leaned over the baby, who was sucking his fist. "Small, but handsome. Don't let him suck on his fingers," she warned. "It's bad for him."

Claudette lowered his hand and planted a kiss on the soft spot in his scalp under the fuzz of light hair. The pulse of his heart in the still-unfused dent made him so defenseless, so needing of her protection.

"What's his name?"

Claudette shifted him to reveal the side of his face. She wished he'd open his not-yet-focusing eyes. "Meet Benjamin-Pierre Baume," she answered with pride.

Madame Couture's smile vanished. "Baume as in Sainte-Baume?"

Claudette had never heard of him but liked the unintended association. "Yes. Like that."

"Since you're not married, your baby is a Pelletier."

Claudette said in a steady voice, "After the war his father will return, and we'll be a family."

"Until such time, he's a Pelletier." By Madame Couture's furrowed brow, Claudette could tell that the seamstress was mentally skimming through the list of the château's employees for someone named Baume. Who had been around last winter to father a child? A man who had disappeared, like so many, either fleeing to join the underground or, like Léonie's husband, sent to Germany for the obligatory labor service? "Well," Madame Couture finally said, "three more weeks until you return to work. There isn't much to do, but if you want to keep your post . . ." She let her words trail off.

"How can I leave my baby? Madame Duchamp says that I must breastfeed him several times a day or my milk would stop coming altogether."

"We've talked about it. All the château staff's children are being raised in the village."

"The mothers walk or bike back home every day," Claudette replied. "I can't do that."

"In that case, maybe the father of your baby can support you?"

At the sting, Claudette began to cry. Her emotions had been ricocheting since she'd given birth, hitting highs and lows so fast that she couldn't predict how she would feel from one moment to the next. One thing remained constant: she couldn't imagine an hour without Benjamin, let alone six days before getting her day and a half off.

"There, there, stop crying." Madame Couture stroked Claudette's arm, then touched the braid resting over her shoulder. "Father Sauveterre will baptize him this Sunday."

Claudette had already sprinkled some water on Benjamin to protect him, but a priest's blessing would be more effective, even if her last encounter with Father Sauveterre had left her feeling battered. This man who spoke about Christian compassion and mercy was as cruel as the priest back home. "I'll do whatever it takes to save Benjamin's soul," Claudette whispered. She would give him two religions to double protect him. "I love him so much!"

The baby gave a tiny smack of his lips.

Madame Couture pulled over a chair. "Some big news at the château. We've received a large shipment of sculptures."

"Sculptures? Why would the duchess buy them now?"

Madame Couture laughed. "Not *buy*. We are the proud protectors of the sculptures of the Louvre. You wouldn't believe the convoy of trucks that delivered them. They are giant, and we got so many that the gallery is full and more are set on the stairwell landings." She glanced about as if someone might hear their conversation. "Before you arrived, in 1939, the duchess hid hundreds of Louvre paintings in a sealed cave of the winery." She straightened. "But these sculptures are so visible!"

If Raphaël had been right about the paintings, Claudette wondered, had he also been right about the aggression against the Jews? And if the duchess was trying to safeguard a collection of sculptures, why put them in plain sight? The Nazis had surely heard about this transport from their spies in Paris or collaborators who spotted the convoy along the way.

That meant that Madame Galvin was no longer living in the

château. The duchess wouldn't risk attracting attention with such a public display.

Madame Couture continued to chat about the goings-on at the château's grounds. Children were now hired to fill odd jobs. Food shortages were felt more keenly because outsiders routinely broke through the fences and stole from the orchards and vegetable gardens. The henhouse and barns were now padlocked, and the few men still remaining at the château slept there, armed.

"What a nightmare." Madame Couture sighed. "The Nazis are coming, and there's no one to stop them."

"What about Jean Moulin getting the underground organized?" Claudette asked, recalling what Silvain Auguste had said of de Gaulle's emissary.

"That's our only hope." She lowered her voice. "I've been told in the utmost confidence that shipments of arms are being delivered by planes. There's going to be a big battle right here."

A battle right here. Claudette's hand tightened around the sleeping baby. "I saw the planes. They've been landing at night since last year."

"Since last year? And you never said a word!" Madame Couture tilted her head. "Is that how you got pregnant? By one of those visitors?"

Claudette hid a little smile that Madame Couture interpreted as a confession because she knelt next to Claudette's bed. "Let's pray for the brave men, for the duchess, and for France."

Jesus, please don't let the Nazis come here, Claudette prayed silently. *Mary, please watch over my Raphaël and Isaac Baume. Please make my milk plentiful.*

Chapter Eighteen

CLAUDETTE

Valençay Village, France
October 1942

MADAME DUCHAMP CAME to check on Claudette's recovery, and while she palpated her stomach, Claudette mustered the courage to ask the question that had been on her mind since her conversation with Madame Galvin. "What's that cutting for Jewish boys?"

The midwife stared at her. "What in the world does it have to do with you?"

Claudette burst out crying. "Benjamin's father is—"

Madame Duchamp rested her palm on Claudette's middle. "There were many Jews in my neighborhood in Lyon. I loved one of them once too." When Claudette didn't stop crying, she said, "Claudette, *chérie,* please understand that Jews don't enter the Kingdom of Heaven."

"Benjamin was baptized so that he will. Anyway, a baby's soul is innocent." She sniffled. "I must secure for him a Jewish covenant with God so that when his father returns, he'll know that I've respected who he is."

"I don't know what you imagine about your lover, but Jews stick together. With their own kind. My Jew's family wouldn't let him marry me."

Raphaël and I are the same kind. Claudette would forever remember how he had clung to her before departing. His lanky figure had wrapped around her short, plump one, drawing strength from their love. "We're both cripples."

"Even if I knew how to cut—and I have never even seen it done—the ritual requires a rabbi," the midwife said.

Tears continued to stream down Claudette's face. "I can't nurse my baby to keep him healthy in body, and I can't nurture his soul with the benefit of two religions. What a no-good mother I am."

"Motherhood takes sacrifice and patience. You're only at the beginning of a long road. By letting Léonie nurse him, you're thinking of what's best for your baby."

"He has to be Jewish too!" *Bastard*. Father Sauveterre had said that about her baby. That's what he was in the eyes of the church. A sin.

"This is an awful time for Jews. My niece in Lyon wrote that they were all taken away. What a catastrophe. It's a desecration of God's image to treat people like this." Madame Duchamp crossed herself. Then she blinked once, twice. "There's one thing I know how to do. I don't like it, though."

CLAUDETTE HELD HER baby down on a folded blanket and placed a few drops of red wine in his mouth. Madame Duchamp clamped down on his feet and dabbed mint essence on one to numb the skin.

Benjamin screamed at the first prick of the ink-dipped needle. Madame Duchamp made six tiny dots to mark the design. Blood spread quickly.

"He's bleeding!" Claudette cried.

Madame Duchamp dabbed cotton on the foot and continued to work. "I'm marking the six outlining dots."

Claudette bent to take a peek. "It's too big!" she said. "You said you tattooed beauty marks on women's faces!" Benjamin was supposed to have a tiny, jewel-like blue star, the kind of ornament Claudette might have embroidered discreetly on the duchess's handkerchief.

"The blood is only natural. It will heal fast."

"This star is too big!"

But more dots, intersecting with the first six, were already there.

Her heart breaking at Benjamin's cries, Claudette dipped her finger into the wine and placed it in the baby's mouth time and again. *It's for you, Raphaël, my love,* she said silently. Cutting the tip of their baby's penis would have been worse.

Benjamin continued to scream as Madame Duchamp worked quickly, connecting the dots with lines.

Claudette could take his pain no more. "Please stop," she cried. "I didn't think it would take this long." Nor be larger than her pinkie nail.

"Give him more wine." Madame Duchamp dipped the needle in the ink again. "Two more lines, then we'll be finished. One more. Voilà!"

Claudette pulled Benjamin to her breast. He latched on, stopped to bray, then latched on again. The bottom of the foot raised toward her was a swollen, bloody mess. Distorted by the curvature of the foot and the swelling, the Jewish Star of David was larger than a one-franc coin.

Bile rose in Claudette's throat, and her breakfast threatened to burst out of her. What had she done, marking her baby for danger? She gulped the rest of the red wine.

Perhaps this was God's way of bringing her baby into the covenant with his Jewish side?

Chapter Nineteen

SHARON

Cherbourg, France
October 1968

OUTSIDE THE LE Havre customs house, Sharon helps Danny haul boxes into a rented van. Yellow shipping forms in German are affixed to them next to green French customs forms she filled out. If anything about this Saars project seems bizarre, it's that a mere twenty-five years after Germany and France conspired to exterminate the Jews, the two nations are working together to ensure that the country of the Jews survives.

And survive they must. Intelligence Sharon glimpsed in the mail she opened for the team's head, Admiral Yaniv, reported that the Russians had increased land, sea, and air munitions to Syria, Jordan, Lebanon, and Egypt. Yaniv is a gruff man who often checks the envelope on Sharon's desk for the stamps she keeps for him from her Italian and German correspondence with suppliers of electronics and engine parts. He scoops them up while barely acknowledging her. With each report she reads, Sharon wishes even more to escape to a place that is free of the despair Israelis feel, of the fear of another Holocaust barreling down. Even if France relents and eases its sanctions, what are a dozen small new boats against all these huge armies with war machines?

Sharon climbs into the van and pulls the boxes from inside while Danny pushes them in. Even though these engine parts are relatively small compared to some refrigerator-size components Sharon has seen, they are heavy. Despite the autumn chill, perspiration soaks the band tied across her forehead.

She sits on the tailgate to catch her breath and looks up at the blue sky. All week she's been suppressing the sadness that threatens to drown her. Today, Tuesday, she and Alon were supposed to get married in his parents' backyard. Even to secular Israelis like them, Tuesday is known to be a blessed day because on the third day of Creation, God said "It is good" twice. Sharon had fantasized about the moment Alon would be waiting for her under the chuppah, his sheepish smile betraying his discomfort with formalities. Rather than wear his naval uniform, he planned to wear an open-collared white shirt. She, in her long white silk dress—a simple line, she had instructed Savta, no lace—would walk toward him barefoot, to feel the moist grass. An accordionist would have played the notes of "Erev Shel Shoshanim," the popular bridal song.

In her mind, she hears, *"An evening of roses / let's go down to the orchard."* A lump forms in Sharon's throat as the next line runs in her head.

"Are you all right?" Danny takes her wrist and presses a finger against her pulse. "You look pale."

He lets go of her, and she swallows hard and pushes herself back to her feet. She straightens her long cotton skirt, wishing Danny's hand stayed on her wrist. Her mind must be playing tricks on her— it's Alon's hand she misses. "I'm fine," she mumbles. "Just hot."

Danny bangs shut the van's double doors and turns the handle to secure them. "Let's grab a cup of coffee before heading back."

This is the first time she's been alone with him outside the office. Some evenings they socialize in the combined circles of Israelis and French—including his girlfriend, Dominique—fun-filled occasions that were not conducive to personal conversations. She's been waiting for a chance to tease out the details of Danny's past.

They settle at a corner table with a view of their loaded van. Sharon's gaze travels to the buildings in the street perpendicular to the port. In Cherbourg style, the houses are three or four stories high, creatively using the fieldstone she so likes or sporting leaves and pilasters carved into the limestone. She can never get enough of the charming old-fashioned construction. She loves the farmhouses they passed on the way here and imagines the interior coziness that turns each into a home: rough wooden ceiling beams, a large fireplace with an iron grille, and copper pots hanging over the kitchen counter.

"Does any of this seem familiar from your childhood? What kind of house did you live in?" she asks Danny.

He lets out a chuckle. "A filthy one, I heard."

"Where was that?"

"I have no idea. I was only four."

Only four? When he told her that the captain of his immigration ship had let him hold the helm, she assumed he had been older. Her entire reason for taking the job was to probe his memory. Her agenda is now blown to pieces.

"Did you know your last name? I assume it wasn't Yarden."

"Hey, what's with all the questions?"

She sits back, composing herself. "It's a good history lesson." She doesn't want to shift the conversation from him by mentioning that her mother was a French Jew and that she had no clue which village or city she'd come from. "In school we focused on the Holocaust in Eastern Europe. Three million Jews were exterminated in Poland alone. It happened all over Europe, but I don't recall a specific chapter about France."

"What was different here is that the Jews were rounded up by the Vichy police, not by the Nazis, and sent to a bunch of transit camps right here on French soil." Danny takes a sip of his coffee, then lets out a sigh. "Today, the French pride themselves on the fact that only a quarter of their Jews were sent to their death. They conveniently forget to mention that none would have been murdered if not for them. The French executed the entire operation—rounding up Jews, setting up four dozen transfer camps in France, and loading captured Jews onto trains to Auschwitz—without a single Nazi present."

She knew none of it. A shiver runs through Sharon. In Poland, Hungary, Austria, and other countries, although local populations served as Hitler's willing minions, the Nazis were always in charge, instigating. "Are you saying that anti-Semitism here was so deep that French people did that on their own?"

"The Nazis didn't even ask for the children. For extra points, the Vichy police deported thousands of them to be exterminated."

The hair at the back of Sharon's neck stands on end. This is what her mother must have escaped. Judith might have had siblings who perished. Danny could have been one of the children sent to be killed. She averts her gaze, looks at the shoppers walking in the street, then at the older couple seated at a nearby table. Her fingers are locked together tight, and her knuckles turn white.

"Are you unwell today?" Danny asks.

If he's referring to her menses, she wouldn't allow it to minimize what is really bothering her. "Such hatred. They unleashed such brutality on an entire group of people living in their midst."

"It's over. Don't take it so personally."

"How can you not take it personally, since they killed your parents?" And her own mother's entire family.

"Not only do I not forgive, I don't forget. But what good does dwelling on the past do me—or the Jews?"

Sharon hides her agitation by breaking off the crunchy corner of a croissant, and her fingers peel off the flaky center layer by layer. The older she gets, the more incomprehensible the Holocaust becomes— and the more important her unknown mother's life and experiences grow.

Danny gulps the last of his coffee. "In spite of it all, we established our own state so such atrocity will never happen again, and I'd rather dwell on the good things these former Nazi sympathizers are doing for us now."

"Are you referring to Félix Amiot?"

"Have you met him yet?"

"Just glimpsed him at CMN." She recalls an aging man of medium build, on the short side, with a full head of graying hair.

"He's an engineering genius with one hundred patents to his name. A visionary who built his first airplane at eighteen and from there went on to own half of France's aviation industry."

"And now he builds ships for Israel," Sharon says, not bothering to hide her distaste.

Saar Seven will be completed in seven or eight weeks. Danny will be its captain, and he will begin weeks of testing, going out to sea every day and returning every evening to the protective bosom of the French navy. In addition to that accommodation, Sharon collects from the friendly French officers valuable daily weather forecasts and tide maps.

The Saar's December launch will be celebrated when the moon and the sun align; the water level then will be ten to fourteen meters higher than it is at low tide. Several days later, the first night of Hanukkah will be marked with a second party. Sharon's anticipation of the double festivities is mixed with her concern over the imminent attack on Israel.

When they get back in the van, Danny starts the engine, pulls out, and makes a U-turn to head west.

"Doesn't Félix Amiot's wartime collaboration bother you?" Sharon asks.

"His story certainly tells you how complicated things were. Join us for dinner at his house Saturday after next."

Danny lights a cigarette. Sharon cranks down her window and rests her head on the frame to feel the ocean breeze.

"It's time you sign up for driving lessons. I need you to drive around," Danny says.

Learn to drive? What freedom it must be to be in control of where she goes. "Will the office pay for it?" she asks. In Israel, driving instructors are unionized, part of a corrupt system in which the testers from the motor vehicles bureau fail students at least twice so the students must pay for additional months of private lessons. Obtaining a license is a privilege of the rich.

"There are perks to working abroad, and the chance to get a license easily and cheaply is one of them," Danny says.

Obtaining a license is a fantastic perk, Sharon thinks, but can she commit to staying long enough? It's been nine months since the *Dakar*'s disappearance, and it will surely be found any day. In the meantime, her bank account in town is growing. She was able to splurge and join her downstairs neighbors Naomi and Pazit for a girls' weekend in Paris. Naomi was hoping that a trip to the City of Light would help shake the melancholy out of the forlorn teenager. After the three of them toured Montmartre and its Sacré-Coeur cathedral, took the elevator to the top of the Eiffel Tower, and clicked photos of the Arc de Triomphe, Sharon feasted her eyes on the splendor of Champs-Élysées fashion. For actual shopping, though, Naomi led them to the flea market. Even Pazit woke up at the abundance of inexpensive merchandise and copied Sharon's selection of corduroy pants, sweaters, and a short jacket for the changing weather.

At one point, Pazit went into a record store, and Sharon and Naomi sat in a café on Boulevard Saint-Germain watching the passersby. "What was the drama involving the family on the first floor of our building?" Sharon asked.

Naomi sipped her coffee. "The daughter of Yaniv's predecessor— she was about your age—came to visit her parents for a week. Danny made the mistake of taking her out a couple of times. Maybe there was more. The kid fell in love, stayed on, and badgered everyone to 'talk to him,' as if we could convince him to love her back."

"Must have been awkward all around."

"Her father was embarrassed by her behavior. Since his tour here was about to end anyway, he transferred earlier. Then Danny met Dominique, who's closer to his age and more levelheaded, and we all breathed a sigh of relief."

The story makes Danny seem more human, Sharon thinks now

as he punches the radio dial. Yves Montand's voice comes through, then the signal is lost.

"Let's talk about you," Danny says after a while. "Since you're doing drafting, any plans to study it?"

Between assignments, she helps Elazar, who instructs her on how to use drafting instruments. "I would have liked to study architecture, but I majored in social studies, so I didn't take the math classes I'd need to apply to the Technion."

"Not too late." Danny draws on his cigarette. "Winter here is long, cold, and dark. Plenty of time to hit the books."

"How exciting. I need tutoring, and I don't even have a math textbook."

"Mine is at my parents' home. I'll ask them to mail it." He smiles. "We're not short of engineers who can tutor you. I'll help when I can."

"Thanks." The time alone with Danny has lost its pressing purpose. Her hopes to penetrate the mystery of his past have capsized like a dinghy in a storm. But she likes their growing friendship. "To be accepted in the Technion, I'll need more than a passing grade in calculus," she says.

"You're smart. Give it a shot."

Instead of a reply, she tries turning on the radio again. This time Edith Piaf's sonorous voice is clear: "Non, je ne regrette rien."

With the wind teasing her hair, Sharon thinks that she doesn't regret coming to Cherbourg even if her original quest has come to naught. She's growing, coming into herself—she will even learn to drive. Becoming an architect was such an elusive aspiration, she never considered it possible. Even today she would rather have married Alon.

Life has its own story arc. A huge hand drops from the sky to yank you out of your orbit and throw you into another. And here she is, part of history in the making, although its events are yet to unfold.

Chapter Twenty

SHARON

Cherbourg, France
October 1968

S HABBAT MORNING BRINGS brightness and warmth, as if yester-day's rain and chill were a mistake and now summer has reclaimed its spot on the calendar. The office is closed, and Sharon's four new roommates are out in a rented car touring the region. Sharon rose early and baked an almond cake for Rina and a poppy-seed cake for Naomi. The radio is playing "Indian Summer," and the words about a lost love swell up in Sharon. Longing for Alon rushes in to fill the space of his absence. She checks her map. To while away the coming hours, she plans to ride her new motorized bike out of town.

She walks down to Naomi and Elazar's apartment to deliver the cake. "Hey, I'm going to a scallop festival," she tells Pazit when the teenager opens the door. "Would you like to come along?"

"No, thanks."

The British TV station blares in the background. "C'mon. It will be fun to see something new together, like we did in Paris."

"No. I have homework."

Sharon sympathizes with the misery of this lonely teenager, cut off from her boyfriend and school and drowning in a new language. "May I help you with your French homework?"

"What part of the word *no* don't you understand?"

Sharon climbs the stairs back to her apartment. She can't imagine how hard it must be for Pazit's parents. Are Naomi's sacrifices to support her husband worth the cost of her resigning from her job running a lab at a Haifa hospital, leaving a son in the IDF without his family, and making her daughter miserable?

Merely a few years ago, Sharon was a teenager, and she recalls the license some of her friends took with their parents. It dismayed her to hear them talk back. Rebellion and impertinence were never an option for her. As frustrating as her aging grandparents could be, so out of step with her fast-moving world—Grandpa Nathan forbade her to play Elvis Presley and Beatles music, claiming it corrupted the soul of Israel's youth—Sharon was forever cognizant of the efforts her grandparents made to raise her. Luckily, since age thirteen, she'd had Alon's parents as her second family. In their laughter-filled home, the latest Top 10 songs always blared in the background. Of course, Sharon was also on her best behavior. Perhaps there's some unexpressed pent-up angst and rage hidden in each teenager, like noxious fumes slithering under the surface in search of an opening.

Are insolence and impudence the luxury of only those who grow up with their own biological parents and feel safe lashing out?

When she enters her apartment she hears honking from the street that sends her to the window. Danny is standing by his car. The canvas of the roof is rolled away, and Dominique waves through the opening. Another feminine hand joins the wave, but that second woman remains hidden.

"Come join us for a picnic," Danny calls to Sharon.

"Bring your bathing suit," Dominique adds. "It's warm enough."

The beautiful Dominique is a reporter for the regional paper; she covers women's interests, from news on market days to the openings of beauty salons. Her column also offers recipes and beauty tips. Sharon is in awe of the Frenchwoman's chic.

She is touched by Danny's efforts to include her. This week he left an Eiffel Tower snow globe on her desk along with a list of places she should visit on her next trip to Paris.

She puts on a bikini, a cotton shift, and a cardigan and runs downstairs. In the bag she uses for food shopping, she has a rolled-up towel. She's thrown in the cake she baked for Rina, a water canister, and two apples, the only fruit left in the bowl; her new roommates devoured everything else.

The day is indeed unseasonably warm. Sharon wants to throw her arms up in the air and let the sun envelop her.

"Meet Rachelle, a colleague of Dominique at *La Presse de la Manche*," Danny says, then adds with emphasis, "She's researching her Jewish family history."

The small, full-figured woman greets Sharon with *la bise*—the French double air kisses—and tells Danny, "Don't start with that nightmare."

The subject piques Sharon's interest, but with the Beatles blaring on the radio and then the wind blowing through the car's open roof, no further conversation is possible.

Danny drives east to a beach cove nestled among massive boulders. There, he opens an umbrella for the fair-skinned Dominique to sit under. The olive-skinned Rachelle slathers her body with tanning oil and stretches out in the sun. Sharon spreads her towel between the two women, her head and shoulders in the shade, her body exposed to the sun. Danny shucks off his clothes down to his bathing trunks and sprints into the sea, his arms aloft as he plunges in.

Unlike Dominique, whose beat for the newspaper takes her out of the office, Rachelle stays inside; she does research and fact-checking. Both women are four years older than Sharon, and she is intimidated by their sophistication.

The two women chat about colleagues, bosses, and male reporters. In her staff role, Rachelle knows about all the plum assignments the men get. Lying between them, her eyes closed, soaking in sun, Sharon breathes in the coconut scent of Rachelle's suntan oil. The women's chatter drones on, broken by the screeching of seagulls against the steady rolling of the waves.

The ocean, stretching all the way to Australia, is Alon's burial place. Sharon sits bolt upright, drawing the women's curious looks. Their conversation stops.

"Did you get stung by a bee?" Dominique glances about.

Sharon stares ahead to where Danny is bobbing in the water. Judaism doesn't recognize burial at sea. Somewhere, three thousand miles away in the Mediterranean, Alon's body is floating inside the iron tomb of his sunken submarine. It's the same water she's now looking at, so deceptively calm, with the same silvery froth contouring small waves.

"Did you have a *cauchemar*?" Rachelle asks. "I got them after I searched records of refugees."

The comment pulls Sharon back. "What refugees?"

"Before and during the war, you know, thousands of Jews fled Europe right through Cherbourg." Rachelle waves toward the harbor west of them.

"Danny said that you're researching your family's history."

"My father's family could afford only one ticket to America, so his father sailed there with the idea that he would send for the rest of them. My grandmother stayed here to wait." Rachelle makes a sad face. "She's still waiting."

Sharon's skin feels hot. She dares not ask how this man's wife and children survived once the Nazis broke through the Maginot Line and took over Normandy.

Danny surfaces near the shore, his sleek, military body dripping water. "Come on! Join me," he calls.

The three women rise. Dominique runs ahead and throws herself into his arms. Laughing, holding on to each other, they stumble into the water. Moments later, their heads and shoulders are pressed together. Sharon wants to shrink back into the towel.

"Let's go." Rachelle reaches for her hand, and they run and fall into the water. The cold shock numbs Sharon for a few seconds, then, invigorated, she hurls her body forward. Her arms curve and hit the water as she slices through it, and she and Rachelle swim parallel to the shore. When a high wave threatens to break over them, they duck under it. Sharon's eyes sting, but she likes the power of her stroke, the rhythmic movements, the exertion of her muscles. Her mind is in a trance, emptied of all other thoughts, focused on pushing forward.

She could swim like this until she reaches Le Havre, she thinks, but then Rachelle signals to her, and the two of them turn ninety degrees to the shore.

When they reach the beach, the umbrella is a far dot against the wall of boulders, and the sky above it pulses bright blue. Their feet scrunch tiny pebbles packed tight by the lapping waves.

"By the way, you have a perfect body for your string bikini," Rachelle says, her eyes taking in the three front triangles Savta crocheted.

Sharon glances down at Rachelle's full breasts. "Thanks, but I'm too skinny."

"I'm too ethnic. My coloring stands out."

"You'll fit well in Israel." Sharon redirects the conversation. "I want to ask whether you know anything about the underground. The people who hid Jewish children during the war?"

"That's how my father's younger brother was saved. My grandmother and my father were caught and sent to a transitional labor camp here in France. They were supposed to go to Auschwitz next, but thankfully, a priest issued them faked baptism papers, and they were released. Still, it was years before they reunited with my uncle."

"Where was he?"

"He got lost. The underground shuffled him around for his safety. Out of fear of discovery, no one wrote anything down. In that system, only one person knew the identity of the next in the chain."

"Then what happened?"

"At thirteen, when he should have been bar mitzvahed, the family that sheltered him baptized him." She pauses. "Fortunately, he knew his former name and address. When the war ended, he was fifteen and ran away."

"Thank God."

"It wasn't so simple. It took another two years of heartache before the three of them were united." Rachelle looks at the sky as if to pluck some facts. "It drives him nuts that he can't be 'unbaptized.' To snub the church, he became a practicing Orthodox Jew."

"What would happen to a young child who didn't know his name?" Sharon asks, not expecting an answer. "Such a tenuous chain."

"Thousands of Jewish children must have gotten lost. It was wartime. Chaos galore: bombs leaving millions of French families homeless and fleeing; Nazis seizing all farm produce; defeated French soldiers wandering about wounded and dazed; the Vichy government yanking half a million Frenchmen from their families and sending them to labor in Germany; fierce fighting among the Communists, the collaborators, and the Maquis. In the midst of that, who knew or cared about Jewish children?"

The salt water dries on Sharon's skin, tightening it. Her face stings when she rubs it. How had her mother survived? "What about monasteries?"

"It wasn't hard to hide one child or two or three, but you couldn't hide hundreds of them. Some orphanages operated, but most shut down during the war."

Sharon wonders how Youth Aliyah found thousands of children all over Europe after the war. Did its agents knock on doors of monasteries and farmhouses and ask to take the Jewish orphans to another country whose language the children did not speak? Her mother was almost an adult and could decide for herself, but who gave away the four-year-old Danny?

Then it occurs to Sharon: If Danny was four at the time he arrived, the year must have been 1946. It was pre-Israel, the same year her mother arrived—and many thousands of refugees in dozens of clandestine voyages.

When Sharon and Rachelle reach the umbrella, Danny and

Dominique are not there, nor are their heads bobbing in the water. Sharon assumes that they are beyond the curve of boulders, making love, and Rachelle's silence about their absence tells her that she shares the same assumption.

Rachelle takes out a rattan picnic basket and begins to spread its contents on a red-checkered tablecloth. A fresh baguette, sliced tomatoes, salami, dried figs, and three kinds of cheese. A salad of beans and grains in a bowl lined with lettuce leaves. She places the cheese on a cutting board and decorates the arrangement with a cluster of green grapes. The plates are china, the utensils stainless steel, and the wineglasses are stemmed. Sharon admires anew the way the French do everything with style, even a beach picnic, down to the matching red-checkered napkins that Rachelle hands her to fold into triangles.

Sharon adds her cake, still in its baking pan, mulling over their conversation. Even if records of hidden children were kept, babies became attached to their caretakers, and teens must have matured in the four or five years of war and moved on.

"The orphanages," she says. "Were they like in Charles Dickens's *Oliver Twist*?"

"Better, allowing for severe wartime shortages. At first, a Jewish humanitarian organization was permitted to operate as long as the Vichy government controlled it. OSE—that's Œuvre de secours aux enfants—smuggled many children to Switzerland. Then its leaders were arrested. Some children escaped. Others were sent to concentration camps."

Escaped and all alone in a hostile world. Where did her mother hide for years? Or had she survived a camp? Sharon pours water into the glasses.

Rachelle sips some. "There were also many state orphanages—not Jewish—and more opened after liberation. The country was in shambles, and parents couldn't feed their children, so they let the state take care of them."

"The 'orphans' weren't actually orphans? They had living parents?"

"Seventy-five percent of institutionalized French children had at least one living parent. Non-Jews might have lost their farms, but Jewish survivors of concentration camps didn't even have a change of clothes or the tools of their previous occupations. They'd been away from their children for years, tortured, and they were often too broken to bond anew with them."

Seventy-five percent. Could one or both of Danny's parents be alive? Sharon looks at the coarse sand around her. The Allies had landed on these serene beaches several kilometers east of this spot. She always assumed that with that audacious campaign, so costly in human lives, the misery ended. In fact, another stage of misery and anguish had begun.

WHEN DANNY AND Dominique reappear, their arms are so tight around each other that they keep tripping. Danny drops onto the sand, plucks up the bottle of red wine and a corkscrew, and deftly opens it.

They chat while eating. Danny and Sharon can't mention even the most innocuous details of their work or joke about an anecdote. Disparate pieces of information and coincidental stories might be woven together to reveal a scheme not intended to become public. Dominique, though, is a charismatic talker.

"You have no idea what went on here just five months ago. The students' revolution in Paris spread nationwide to labor unions. The whole country came to a dead stop. Here in Normandy, all the shipyard workers went on strike. Grievances bubbled up. School boards agreed to overhaul our archaic education system, but around here, they did nothing about it all summer. I begged my editor to let me expose their apathy." She flings back her blond curls and ties them in a knot. "He stole my idea and assigned it to a male reporter. The piece was so lame! It didn't address the fact that classes have resumed with the same old dogmatic and idiotic methods." She turns to Sharon. "You know what first-graders write on? Slate."

"Why slate?"

"Exactly. They are not taught to hold a pencil, only chalk to scratch on a Stone Age slate."

Were records of hidden Jewish children also written in chalk on slate?

After lunch, Danny and Sharon play beach paddleball, a popular Israeli game. They position themselves on the water's edge, where ripples flirt with the sand, leaving it tightly packed. The familiar *thwack* of the hard, small ball brings Sharon memories of long beach days with Alon. The two of them could volley back and forth in a long play reminiscent of their lovemaking.

Sharon begs off, claiming fatigue, and calls Rachelle to take her paddle.

She lies down under the umbrella, and she must have dozed off, because when she opens her eyes, Rachelle is resting nearby. The slow rhythmical rising and falling of the breasts that spill out of her tiny bikini top indicate that she is sleeping. The sun has moved in the sky, and Dominique and Danny are lying across from them, their upper bodies in the shade cast by the boulders. Only their feet are in the sun, their soles facing Sharon.

Her eyes are not fully open when she notices a blue stain at the bottom of Danny's foot. A jellyfish sting?

Alarmed, she calls, "Danny! Your foot!"

He sits up slowly and unhurriedly clears the sand off the blue stain. "Oh, yes, my foot."

Sharon stares at a tattoo of a Star of David.

Part II

ALIYAH—GATHERING FROM DIASPORA:
*And He will set up an ensign for the nations,
and will assemble the dispersed of Israel,
and gather together the scattered of Judah
from the four corners of the earth.*

—Isaiah 11:12

Chapter Twenty-One

UZI YARDEN

Marseille, France
September 1946

UZI YARDEN SCANNED his foreign surroundings. The huge Marseille port with its fleets of ships was now behind him, and he was walking along a row of gigantic weatherworn warehouses. Trucks chugged in both directions.

He stopped to stare at the landscape in front of him, then glanced at his map to verify that this was supposed to be the Jewish quarter. What had happened here? Where were the streets that ascended from the port, fanned out, and climbed up the hill? Piles of rubble stretched up the slope. A lone, distant bulldozer pushing white bricks, wood beams, and mangled iron was the only sign of life. Dread spread through Uzi. No use trying to guess which street would lead to the address where he would receive his momentous assignment: rescue Jewish orphans.

In his twenty-two years, Uzi had rarely traveled even as far as Haifa, eighty kilometers from his kibbutz, and had never imagined crossing the Mediterranean and landing in France, of all places. Nothing was familiar. The Haganah section leader in his kibbutz who briefed him had warned Uzi to expect the unexpected. How did one conjure up unexpected situations? What other scenes as shocking as the demolished Jewish quarter of Marseille might he encounter?

Uzi wiggled his toes in the leather shoes. They weren't new, nor were they his. One of the toughest parts of his mission in France, it seemed, would be getting used to wearing shoes. Even when he'd trained to defend the kibbutz from infiltrators, he wore only sandals, the same pair he wore daily in the orange orchard. Only for milking duties did Uzi stuff his feet into whichever rubber boots had been left at the door, his bare feet sinking into cool, unidentified muck.

He stepped farther into the piles of bricks, shattered tiles, and smashed beams and tried to absorb the devastation of a vibrant community that was no more. His eyes searched the wreckage. There had been a world here under the layer of white plaster dust, streets teeming with craftsmen and vendors and lined with synagogues and schools and health clinics. A community with its own newspapers, music, and theater. What happened to the thousands of Jews who had lived here? Uzi guessed at the answer: deported to their death.

But where were their children?

Something bright in the rubble caught Uzi's eye. He bent and picked it up. Even before he wiped off the dust, he knew that this small silver object was a mezuzah, a case containing a holy scroll that was attached to the doorway of every Jewish home. He closed his palm over it, felt its sharp edges, a symbol of this lost neighborhood, then put it in his pocket.

Uzi's apprehension about this assignment rose. No one at the kibbutz members' meeting had questioned Uzi's suitability for it. There was no one else to send—and no time to waste. The liberation of the Auschwitz and Buchenwald death camps eighteen months earlier had revealed the horrors of the Holocaust. The guilt of having done nothing while this slaughter was going on in Europe gnawed on the collective consciousness of the tiny *yishuv*, six hundred thousand Jews living in Eretz Israel. The only thing they could do was rescue those who'd survived, especially the children—traumatized and orphaned—and bring them home.

Uzi rechecked his map. One thing he was good at was navigation. He had tracked the footsteps of the fedayeen, Arab guerrillas who infiltrated his kibbutz and murdered a family in their sleep. He had participated in a raid on a British prison in Jaffa to release jailed Haganah comrades. Uzi's glance confirmed the sun's zenith, farther north than Israel's, then he placed his finger on the spot where he was now wasting time dawdling. He scrutinized the map one square centimeter at a time, reading the impossible-to-pronounce French street names. And here it was, rue Saint-Savournin.

THE WOMAN AT the orphanage rose from behind the reception desk of what once had been a small hotel. A map of the British Mandate for Palestine hung above the cubbyholes that had once held keys, the map's boundaries still showing what was today Transjordan. Uzi swallowed the lump that formed in his throat every time he saw this evidence of the British repudiating their mandate, handed to them by the League of Nations, to create a homeland for the Jews. Instead, the British handed 76 percent of that land to the Hashemites to create Jordan—and blocked Jews from entering the remaining 24 percent.

The plump, middle-aged woman wore a brown skirt and a cardigan and had an orange scarf tied at her neck. She hurled herself against Uzi. "The boy from the Holy Land," she exclaimed in Yiddish. "What a blessed sight."

He was relieved that she didn't address him in French. He was fluent only in Hebrew. The English he'd studied in school for eight years was used only on the rare occasions he dealt with his country's British rulers, which he'd done most recently to obtain a passport. The French words he extracted from the dictionary during his Mediterranean crossing were unpronounceable. At least he had picked up Yiddish from his grandparents' bickering.

"What am I doing speaking Yiddish? Here we learn Hebrew in preparation for immigration to Eretz Israel," the woman said in Hebrew. "*Shmi* Miriam." She held Uzi at arm's length to examine his face, then reached up and passed her fingers through his unruly curls the way his mother still did.

"*Shmi* Uzi," he responded. "Got instructions for me?"

"What's your experience?"

"Milking cows."

She laughed. "Who is experienced in recovering orphans hidden in a foreign land? It was never done in human history."

He smiled to conceal his apprehension. Resourcefulness had been the key in his upbringing. *You think on your feet. You assess the situation, come up with a solution—then you act on it. You learn fast by executing the task.* There was no blueprint to follow in this far-fetched project, but there was one certainty: the underground Haganah couldn't become entangled in bureaucracy. The official Jewish organizations acquiesced to the British rulers and their monthslong waits for entry certificates that weren't forthcoming. Just when Jewish survivors were crawling from the ashes with no place to go, the British had placed a quota on their entry. What were the anguished, bewildered, and scarred survivors supposed to do?

The only way to bring them into the Promised Land was to smuggle them in, which was why the Haganah had become involved.

"How do I go about collecting children," Uzi asked Miriam, "short of playing my flute like the Pied Piper?"

"You don't *collect*. You search high and low—and find them."

Her response gave him no clue on how to proceed.

Just then, a class was let out somewhere, and the squeals of children reached the room. Miriam stepped to the window and beckoned him.

"Look at them. They are alive—and they are ours. We won't let the Catholic Church finish Hitler's job. The gonifs want to steal our children. They think they can baptize them, and that's the end of the story? That our people will give up on our future?"

The only Christian Uzi had ever known was his father's Christian Arab friend who lived in Nazareth. "Isn't baptism just sprinkling water on the head?" Uzi asked. "Nothing permanent like circumcision, right?"

"A few drops of water and some Latin words, and it's their excuse not to hand children back to their Jewish relatives."

Uzi scanned the boys and girls running about, ranging in age from eight to perhaps fourteen, and tried to comprehend their devastated lives. Most were scrawny, their cheeks hollow. Yet they chased balls and took turns at the swings and the seesaw like children everywhere. He caught sight of a small boy standing alone, his back to the wall, his head bowed, holding a spoon. A girl with twin braids stood several meters away, talking to her spoon as if it were a doll.

"What's with the spoons?" Uzi asked.

"They're concentration-camp children. If you had a spoon, you could scoop from the soup bowl. No spoon and you starved."

The words churned in Uzi's head. He couldn't imagine the pain of these children, dazed and lost, their parents gone without a trace, struggling for survival all alone with a spoon as their only lifeline. *That's why I'm here*, he thought. *To replace the spoons with toys and laughter.*

Uzi rubbed his face, felt the prickling of his unshaven cheeks. How did one approach a strange child whose language one didn't even speak and take him or her to the Holy Land? He glanced past the yard. A jumble of run-down buildings showed the pounding of sea winds in the crumbling plaster of their façades, as they did in Tel Aviv and Haifa on the eastern basin of the Mediterranean. There was no answer in the sliver of blue sky hanging over them.

"I saw the ruins," Uzi said. "Shocking."

"Our cursed city. In January 1943, twelve thousand French policemen, by order of the Vichy government, evacuated the Jews. I was in the mountains with a Christian friend when twenty-three people from my family were sent to their death: my grandfather, my parents, my three brothers and one sister, my aunts, uncles, cousins—"

"Awful." The word seemed hollow to Uzi.

She pointed to the yard. "When you sail back, you'll take the older children with you."

"I don't see young ones."

"Sadly, we can't care for them here, so we relinquish them to OSE. That's the formal Jewish-French organization that runs orphanages. They send the little ones for adoption with Jewish families in England or America." She sighed. "I wish they'd send them to Eretz Israel, but they don't believe that we have any future there."

"Do you operate alone? Where are the adult refugees?"

A spark gleamed in her eyes. "The Americans helped us open the first Zionist displaced-persons camp in Marseille, and now two thousand people are preparing to immigrate to the Holy Land—"

She was interrupted by an aide who whispered something in her ear. Miriam turned to greet a woman wearing heavy makeup, her bleached hair piled on top of her head like a large bird's nest. Even Uzi, who rarely noticed women's attire, could tell that her bright pink dress was too tight and too short. She nudged forward a boy of about nine years old. His eyes were wide with fright.

Miriam exchanged barely a couple of sentences with the woman before she reached into her pocket, withdrawing a few bills. The woman accepted them and departed. Miriam crouched in front of the boy and talked to him, then the aide rested a gentle hand on his shoulder and led him away.

"Did you just *buy* this kid?" Uzi asked Miriam.

"You may call it that. Orphan hunters know that they can bring Jewish kids to us or sell them to people in another country. Children are the new postwar commodity. Poland, Romania, France, Austria, Greece—all European countries have suffered great population losses. They need to replenish their numbers quickly, and the only way to do that is to grab children of whatever nationality."

"How absurd, after what the children have been through."

"For them, children are *tabulae rasae,* clean slates on which each nation can engrave its identity."

Within two hours of setting foot in France, Uzi thought, he had learned more about war than he had ever known.

In the dining room, Miriam stepped away to separate two kids whose argument seemed about to escalate. She returned to Uzi and sighed. "The French are our worst rivals. The nationalists have the audacity to claim our children. Do you get it? They now love the same kids who escaped their clutches when they deported their families to Auschwitz! They want to make them French!"

An older teenager wheeled a cauldron around and children clamored with their bowls held out.

"Please eat with us," Miriam said. "It's not much. We can't afford the black market that snatches most available food."

Uzi accepted a bowl of soup. A few strings of what could be chicken floated among pieces of vegetables.

Miriam took a deep breath. "Do you know that cooked frogs taste like chicken? And if we're not careful, we may buy skinned dogs sold as lamb."

"How do I begin my work?"

She glanced at the wall clock, then clapped her hands. "Give the children a talk in Hebrew. You have a couple of hours before your train."

"My train to where?"

"A town called Châteauroux. It's in the Loire Valley, which was part of the free zone until November 1942. Many Jews fled south through there. Unfortunately, it didn't save them. You'll rescue their hidden orphans."

How?

Chapter Twenty-Two

SHARON

Paris and Cherbourg, France
November 1968

SHARON WALKS THROUGH the gate of the Rodin Museum in Paris and is welcomed in the front garden by the giant sculpture of *The Thinker*. The day is cold, a bone-penetrating chill like Jerusalem in winter, and Sharon feels its sting. Without proper winter clothes, she can't stroll through the sculpture gardens. She steps into the grand mansion and is soon entranced by the sinewy, sensuous bronze bodies with intertwining limbs. But what arrests her attention is the tenderness of white marble hands gently cupping some divine grace.

She gazes at it, feeling the power of the subtle emotion. By the end of her visit to Paris with Naomi and Pazit, she had ticked off her list most of the city's main tourist attractions—Place de la Bastille, the Louvre, the Palais Garnier, Pont Alexandre III. The three of them ate Nutella crepes in Le Marais and watched street performers outside the Sorbonne. Now, she's exploring the city alone before meeting new recruits tomorrow, and it makes the city her own.

Back outside, she realizes that there is no way to avoid buying winter clothes, although she hates spending money on items for which she will have no use in Tel Aviv. She heads to the flea market, where she buys leather boots and wool socks, rabbit-fur-lined leather gloves, and her first ever heavy coat: a secondhand loden in a popular dark green, lined with plaid fabric. Influenced by Dominique's and Rachelle's style, she purchases two printed scarves.

Finally warm, she wanders through narrow alleys where she glimpses small hidden gardens. She clicks her camera at the ornamental cast-iron lampposts and drinking fountains. Danny advised her to visit the Musée des Arts et Métiers, and she spends the rest of the afternoon awed by and absorbed in the displays of machinery and measuring instruments. By the time she leaves, she's filled with admiration for the aptitude, inventiveness, and reach of the human mind. She belongs in this world of industrial design. She understands why Danny sent her here.

Back at the same small, cozy, Left Bank hotel where she stayed on the day of her arrival in Paris, Sharon writes to Savta on a Rodin Museum postcard and asks her to send her wool suit and have her birth certificate translated. She needs it in order to obtain a French driver's license.

What a dream that is! Can you imagine that I'll be learning to drive? Yes, I'm staying here for a while, but I miss you and your cooking. More in a letter. Love, Sharon

The thought of Savta's loneliness weighs on her. She recalls their quiet times in the late afternoon on the veranda, the chirps and trills of the swallows in the background. Savta wanted Sharon to spread her wings; none of her letters has expressed how much that separation must hurt her.

Please pack my flute too, Sharon adds vertically in the margin. This afternoon, humming while walking, she caught herself tapping her fingers on her thigh. She craves the feel of the flute's mouthpiece against her lips, the intake and outflow of breath that causes music to emerge from her center. Depriving herself of her art won't bring Alon back, even if mourning for him will forever play a note in her head.

Nor will spending an evening in Paris alone in a hotel room.

She takes the Métro to Abbesses, the station at the foot of Montmartre, then challenges herself to climb the steep wide steps up the hill. She stops at each landing to drink in the view of the city below. Tourists stream up and down the wide landings, pose and point their cameras. When Sharon reaches the magnificent white church of the Sacré-Coeur, it is already dark, and she gazes at the panorama of the city lights stretching away to the horizon with the brilliantly lit Eiffel Tower as a landmark.

A side street leads to a large plaza filled with artists displaying their works. Music pours out of the unglazed glass of the cafés' wall-size windows. The place teems with people, lights, colors, fancy clothes, and delicious smells of food and tobacco.

From one of the *chansonniers* pours the joyful notes of an accordion, and a group of Spanish students seated by the wall of windows belt out songs at the tops of their lungs. A young woman with a mane of wavy black hair passes around a pitcher of sangria. Catching Sharon's eye, she motions to her to come in, and the others call out to her in Spanish, then English, then French. Sharon smiles. For the length of time she will spend with these people, their worry-free existence will nurture her illusion that life is simple.

She steps in. They make room for her on the backless bench, and someone shoves into her hand a glass of sangria with floating pieces of orange and strawberries. The accordion player switches to a French folk song Sharon knows, and she joins in, first humming, then giving herself over to full-throated singing. In the school choir, she sometimes sang solo. Soon, with the sangria flowing in her veins, she sings along with a pair of Italians who take over with a string of popular love songs.

Australian medical students on their summer break order platters of olives, cheese, and *boudin noir*, pig-blood sausage. Before long, one more table is pushed to the edge of theirs and four Germans join the group. Sharon cringes at the thought that their drinking songs will resemble those of their Nazi parents.

"Where are you from?" someone asks her.

"Israel."

"The heroes of the world." Someone raises his glass. "To Israel!"

"To Israel!" the others echo.

"Sing us one of your songs," someone says, and the accordion player begins to play "Jerusalem of Gold." Sharon sings, and the girl on her right puts her arm around her and sways to the rhythm. Carried away by the camaraderie, Sharon stands up and performs all four stanzas. Just for a moment, she is with all the students of the world, in spirit and in song, sharing with them the beauty of her country.

When the last notes fade, one of the Germans pulls over a chair behind Sharon, straddles it, and leans toward her. "The Six-Day War was a stunning victory of your tiny country against the mighty military of seven Arab countries armed with Russian weapons, tanks, and airplanes," he explains to her in English as if she doesn't know. "It took only six days for Israel to destroy those armies!" He raises his beer stein in salute, then offers it to her. "We love your country."

Twenty-three years after the Holocaust, you love *us?* She's never faced a German with Aryan liquid blue eyes, square jaw, and blond locks saluting her with a stein of beer, grinning. He can't imagine how deeply she feels the collective victimhood of her people—and she's tired of it. With the sangria flowing through the whole of her, Sharon understands why Danny is sick of thinking about the Holocaust. She is tired of mourning her murdered parents—and now Alon. She is tired of dreading the next war in Israel, of living in fear that she and everyone she knows may not survive. That Tel Aviv will be flattened by a shower of Russian-made missiles hurled by Egypt, Jordan, Syria, or Lebanon; or that Saudi Arabia, Oman, Iran, Iraq, Yemen, the United Emirates, or Libya will blacken the Israeli skies with their thousands of airplane bombers. It's exhausting to always be on alert.

She accepts the German's beer, gulps, and returns the stein to him. He throws his head back and empties the rest.

Laughing, Sharon orders a pitcher of sangria to share with her new friends.

BEFORE THE SHABBAT, she returns to Cherbourg with the new recruits and deposits them in the *caserne*. Upon entering her apartment, she finds a note from one of the reserve officers informing her of a group disco outing tonight. Tomer is yet another transient buddy, Moroccan-born with raisin-dark smiling eyes and magnificent white teeth.

Behind the sleepy façade of Cherbourg, the evenings come alive in the discos where the sailors dance. The reserve officers often invite Sharon to the Bull Casino as their "good-luck muse." The many men surrounding her know about her lost fiancé, which stops them from making a pass at her. Their respect for their fallen brother overpowers the usual Israeli male bluntness.

The midnight air is cold and suffused with the smell of rain when Tomer walks Sharon home. She gets a whiff of his cinnamon aftershave. In the cobblestoned streets, their footsteps echo.

"It's my last night here," Tomer tells her.

She giggles. "A month of laughter, beer, and dancing."

His gloved hand finds hers. "Also some essential work, but the most important thing is that I met you." He kisses her, and she responds.

Hunger consumes her—for lips and tongues to intertwine, for her body to press against the whole of him.

She stops. Her insides are churning, and she breathes hard.

Tomer's hand is still tight around her waist. She steps back. Her mind flashes on a day in school when she was eleven. For the dress-up festival of Purim, Savta had sewn Sharon a Tyrolean girl costume, complete with a doll wearing an identical dirndl. Sharon won first prize, yet she was willing to forgo it when the school photographer positioned her next to a boy dressed in Bavarian lederhosen and an Alpine hat. The boy, a year older, was equally mortified at their pairing and pulled Sharon's braids.

For two more years, he kept pulling her braids, and then one day he asked her to the movies. That was Alon. They had been together for seven years.

"I'll wait for your call when you return to Israel," Tomer whispers and kisses her neck.

Chapter Twenty-Three

SHARON

Paris and Cherbourg, France
November 1968

"ALL YOUR ASSIGNMENTS until now were merely a preparation for the big one," Danny tells Sharon.

She gives him a perplexed look.

"I never shared it with you, but what convinced me that you were the right person for our team here was what your commander told us about the case of the guys from Chad."

She's shocked that her former intelligence unit's major general broke the rule of silence. "My commander talked too much," she replies.

On her way to Orly to pick up two new reservists, she wonders about her former boss. As a corporal, she had minimal contact with him, but now she understands that he wanted to secure for her this job on the Cherbourg project. How many people in the periphery of her life have shown her their caring without her realizing it? That orphanhood again, forever making her feel like an outsider.

At the airport, she selects a postcard of Paris at dusk shrouded in pink hues to send to her former commander. As an afterthought, she picks up a dozen more postcards for Uncle Pinchas, the Golans, a former music teacher, and friends.

The Chad assignment had been unusual. Sharon was puzzled when she'd been pulled out of her intelligence unit, where she'd been listening in on Arabic phone conversations in neighboring countries. She was sent on a one-day loan to the Ministry of Agriculture as a French interpreter for dignitaries from the African country of Chad. Israel was isolated from most African nations by the Arab boycott, but it offered agricultural know-how and training to any country willing to ignore that boycott. Dressed in civilian clothes, Sharon joined the two Chad visitors on a trip to the Negev to inspect new greenhouse technology. The handsome dignitaries were muscular with bluish dark skin; she imagined they looked like the attendants who had accompanied the queen of Sheba on her biblical visit to King Solomon. The men sat with Sharon in the van's center row, and she pretended not to understand when they conversed in Arabic. In one brief exchange, they referred to a plan to get hold of night-vision equipment. A much-improved version, Sharon knew, was being developed by the Israeli military. Before any of them exited the van at the experimental hydroponic farm, Sharon quickly scanned the laborers through the tinted-glass window. All seemed busy, laying down hoses and unrolling plastic sheets, except for one man in Bedouin garb who was peeking from behind a shed.

"Don't let the guests off the van," Sharon said in Hebrew to the director of the Ministry of Agriculture, himself a former IDF officer. "Let's talk outside."

Minutes later, the guests were told that, regrettably, due to toxic vapors in the greenhouse, their visit must be rescheduled. The Bedouin was apprehended. A week later, Sharon received a letter of commendation for helping to avert a serious security breach.

Sharon had uncovered the plot of the Chadians, but her role then was passive—listening, figuring things out. The new project Danny has assigned her hinges on her resourcefulness.

The two reservists she picks up at the Orly airport are cousins, tall, blond, blue-eyed Israelis born to German Holocaust survivors. They grew up in Israel, studied engineering in Germany, and speak English and French with accents that can pass for Scandinavian.

Sharon takes them shopping at Le Bon Marché, where, under a magnificent, seven-story-high stained-glass dome, a suave salesman fits them with Italian-cut suits, soft fabric shirts, and leather shoes. He adds ties, pocket handkerchiefs, and silk socks for when the men sit down and the cuffs of their pants rise. Acting like the girlfriend of one of the men, Sharon instructs them in her broken German—in case the salesman catches snippets of talk—to make sure they select different designers and styles; their outfits shouldn't look like unnatural getups.

She chokes at the exorbitant bill, but this is the cost of creating a façade. The men are supposed to be Norwegian businessmen from Starboat, a fake company, interested in purchasing the kinds of oil-exploration boats that CMN builds. They'll be meeting in Paris with executives of the French acquisition office for the approval of such a sale. Then the two "Norwegians" will head to Cherbourg for Amiot's guided tour of CMN. They'll have no contact with the Israeli team.

Never break a French law was a recent directive in a telegram from Secretary Meir—Golda, as the grandmotherly Israeli leader preferred to be addressed.

Never break a French law? Sharon faces this dilemma when she holds the men's fake Norwegian passports she collected from Moka Limon's office. Tourists must present their passports at the hotel check-in. What if her men used their legal Israeli ones, and tomorrow morning their courteous French host fetches them at the hotel? She imagines a reception clerk's polite smile as he tells the Frenchman, "Sure, sir, I'll ring the Israelis right now."

That you should not obey orders blindly was an important lesson from World War II. Should she obey the directive handed down to her from Limon, Yaniv, and Danny or follow Golda's policy? Which path is the wrong one? Which is the moral one?

One need not have an intelligence background to know that whatever the ultimate purpose of this ruse, the plan might collapse because of a reception clerk's slip. The political ramifications from Paris over the deception would be significant. Limon's diplomatic credibility would be questioned—and there could be no intervention from Amiot to avert a political crisis.

There is no choice. Sharon enters the men's mirrored dressing room, closes the door, and silently exchanges the Norwegian passports for their Israeli ones. She will keep them in her possession; they mustn't be found in the men's luggage, even by a curious chambermaid.

"Norwegians hold their liquor well, so only pretend to be drinking," Sharon whispers in German. "And if we bump into one another in Cherbourg, you've never met me."

What's the purpose of this elaborate ploy? Sharon knows not to ask, yet she feels like an important cog in a monumental scheme.

Chapter Twenty-Four

CLAUDETTE

Château de Valençay, France
November 1942

THE EMPLOYEES WHO lived in town, like Madame Couture and Marguerite, no longer showed up to work. Any minute, Nazi tanks might roll in or their bombs might drop from the air. The risk of being outside was too great.

Claudette perspired even in the damp chill of the grand rooms. Since returning to her job three weeks earlier, she had been working feverishly to help hide the duke's ancestral treasures. She cut up flannel liners from garments and sewed them into dozens of pouches for silver pieces. They would be buried in the park, where no air would tarnish them.

Fear coursed through her veins. The enemy was closing in. Among the skeleton staff, she would be singled out by the Nazis as the *invalide*. What would happen to her baby, away from her in the village?

She recalled the shock two and a half years earlier when the Maginot Line had collapsed. Now, blocked by the Allies' counterattacks in North Africa, Nazis were advancing into the free zone. Despite de Gaulle's daily broadcast from London encouraging the thousands of brave spirits to free France from its conquerors, and despite Silvain Auguste's grand talk about the underground preparing to meet the enemy, Claudette had heard of no French army, definitely not one strong enough to deter Nazi tanks.

"Hurry up, before the Boche take the job off your hands," Monsieur Vincent told Claudette and the few remaining maids. All she wanted was to hold Benjamin and press him to her breast—except that what little milk she had been able to produce had dried up. Only Léonie could feed him. Claudette's arms ached with his absence.

In spite of the cloud of doom, the duchess held her back erect and kept her voice gentle yet commanding as she supervised the staff's work. Paintings were taken down from the walls. Hundreds of fine cloisonné jars and porcelain trinkets were carefully wrapped and hidden in the basement behind a false wall. Crystal chandeliers were hung inside wooden crates along with antique furniture in the wine cellars. Claudette packed the ancient uniforms, swords, and medals—the paraphernalia of aristocracy—for the duchess's son and his future offspring because, the duchess said, gentility stood firm against shifting political winds.

Only the monumental sculptures from the Louvre remained visible. Claudette passed these marble Greek goddesses in the gallery when she went to her tower room to wash. When would the Nazis come to haul them away—and find her?

Monsieur Vincent ran the staff through air-raid drills. At night, they slept on mattresses in the wide passage parallel to the kitchen. Some nights, just before dawn, a group of men smelling of sweat and gunpowder entered the kitchen, fell hungrily on the cauldron of soup, and dropped to the floor to catch some sleep.

Then it happened. A devastated maid from the nearby Château de Chenonceau bicycled to the estate with the news that men in armored vehicles had taken over the château. The medieval building spanned the Cher River, which had been designated as the demarcation line between the free and occupied zones. The Nazis suspected that Chenonceau operated as a transfer bridge for fugitives and art. Hiccupping, the hysterical maid reported that when the estate manager denied the accusation, the Nazis shot him in front of the staff.

Next, the Nazis plundered Château des Bouffards. Midmorning, Claudette and the others gathered around the radio to hear the transmission by the BBC: "Dozens of German trucks were filled with every stick of furniture, every painting, every piece of china and silver;

even silk and brocade curtains were confiscated." Claudette wanted to put her hands over her ears, to block it all, but she couldn't stop listening. "First the Nazis emptied all the cellars of France's great wines and champagne. Now they're emptying France of all its art treasures and transporting them to Germany," the reporter continued.

The staff debated whether the brutal Boche would bomb Valençay into a pile of rubble or spare it because of the Louvre sculptures they wished to loot.

But no one doubted that they would come.

The duchess's maid had escaped, supposedly heading somewhere west with her mother, but the talk was that in fact she had run east with a German officer. Claudette was left to see to the duchess's needs. Her dream was realized, but it was no longer what she wanted. All she could think of was Benjamin.

"The Boche are not interested in infants. Your baby is in good hands with Léonie," Monsieur Vincent told Claudette when he came upon her crying.

What did this aging man know about the feel of Benjamin's tiny, warm body against her chest, his warm skin next to hers?

Léonie had rented out Claudette's former room to a Parisian couple, both university professors, and their twelve-year-old daughter, Emmaline. When Claudette visited for a day and a half each week, she slept in the front room. If the day wasn't too cold, she took Benjamin outside to be alone with him. She told him about her week, and his wise eyes—their greenish hue like Raphaël's—followed her lips when she spoke. When she departed, Emmaline cradled him in her arms and sang to him, which gave Claudette some comfort.

The morning Claudette heard of an air bombing of the village of Vendôme, she could take the separation from Benjamin no more. The attack had left many dead and injured, the surrounding houses and farms flattened, and the Vendôme château barely spared from ruin. Keeping her job was no longer an option. Claudette approached the duchess in her sitting room.

The green silk that covered every inch of the walls showed the unfaded areas where paintings had been removed. The wood floors were discolored in places where furniture had once stood.

Her voice trembling, Claudette said, "Madame la Duchesse, I'm so sorry to let you down, but I must go to my baby."

"Such a difficult time for all of us. I wish that I could protect Mathéo, send him away." The duchess sighed. "Monsieur Vincent will pay you the balance of your wages for the month. Ask him whom he can spare to drive you."

"Thank you, madame. I'll never forget your kindness."

"God be with you, dear Claudette. God be with all of us."

Claudette rushed to her room and gathered clothes, toiletries, and Mémère's sewing kit. She removed her money from behind the wood panel and tucked it into her brassiere and vest pockets. There was no question of lugging Mémère's heavy trunk; she could take only a large canvas bag. Dragging it on the floor, she made her way toward the business manager's office.

She emerged from the side corridor to mayhem. Marguerite, who hadn't come in for weeks, screamed in horror. The staff gathered around her.

"My sister." Marguerite hiccupped the words. "The Nazis!"

Claudette broke into the circle and put her arm around her friend. "What?"

"They're combing through the houses." The maid gathered herself. "They found Jewish refugees next door and dragged them out and beat them. They ordered us all to stand outside as they searched our homes too. When my sister couldn't move, they just shot her in bed!"

A black cloud filled Claudette's head. Her tongue thickened in her mouth. No one would drive her to the village now. The Nazis had finally come for people like her. To shoot them.

She had to live for Benjamin.

Chapter Twenty-Five

UZI YARDEN

Loire Valley, France
September 1946

DISHEVELED AND DISPIRITED people dragging cloth bundles and cardboard suitcases filled the stations. When a train arrived, they jostled for spots in the cars, ignoring the unshaven, wounded soldiers wearing tattered, bloodstained uniforms. Uzi changed trains three times and rode standing in a crowded bus on the last leg of his trip. The bombed railway to Châteauroux hadn't been repaired.

The town looked like a picture postcard. Green forest surrounded the château rising on the opposite bank of the fast-flowing river that could have irrigated the entire land of Israel. Using Miriam's directions, Uzi made his way down a cobblestoned street the width of a horse-drawn cart. A narrow channel carved in its center carried wastewater.

"Your first stop will be a Protestant house of worship. Its religious leader is called a pastor," Miriam had said. "Don't confuse him with a Catholic one, called a priest."

Uzi had no knowledge of the differences between the Christian denominations, only that they disapproved of one another. Then he saw their churches. A magnificent, sky-high cathedral dominated a wide street and drew the eye heavenward with its spires, steeples, and stained-glass windows. That street intersected with the main thoroughfare and narrowed to an alley only partially paved. There, still in sight of the cathedral, stood a humble, whitewashed, rectangular one-story building with a pitched roof. A marked difference, though both religions claimed to be monotheistic. How did that work with worshipping Jesus and a host of saints? Not that Uzi cared. He didn't believe in a divine entity, only in people and their innate strength. Not in all people, for sure, only the good ones, those who treated their fellow humans with decency, dignity, and kindness.

A sculpted open book mounted on the pediment above the door was the only decoration. Uzi pulled the string of a doorbell. Climbing vines in riotous autumn reds covered the wall of an adjacent garden.

"Welcome to the Land of a Thousand Châteaux," Pastor Gaspard said in English when he opened the door.

Uzi smiled and shook his hand. At least the pastor spoke English. Uzi would have to put forth some effort to utter the sentences in a language he was better at reading. Châteaux? This building certainly wasn't one. "Nice to meet you," he said, forming his words with care.

Pastor Gaspard raised his voice as if to make himself better understood. "An exaggeration, of course, but there are dozens of châteaux in the region. Some have been in ruins for ages; others were recently bombed. Many are still intact, but their heirs can no longer afford to maintain them."

He led Uzi into a room with an unlit fireplace that smelled of ashes and offered him tea and a sandwich. While Uzi ate—his first food since the soup the day before at Miriam's orphanage—Pastor Gaspard explained, speaking slowly, that he was a Calvinist devoted to rescuing Jewish children and uniting them with their culture and biblical mission of life in the land that God had given them. "We are an isolated enclave of Huguenots. Most of us are in the south. Our people have been prosecuted, like yours. Murdered for our faith. We know what it's like."

"Thank you. We can use all the help we can get," Uzi said.

"It's God's work. For us Protestants, the Bible is the highest authority—and you surely know what it says about your people. Chosen."

"What do you mean, *chosen*?"

"Chosen by God. You are His special people."

Uzi had never heard this. Or, rather, in his twelve years of Bible classes, which were part of the national curriculum—the Bible taught as a book of poetry and history, not as God's word—no one had ever taken this *chosen* nonsense seriously. If Uzi had reported this conversation in the kibbutz dining room, they all would have had a big laugh. Chosen for tsuris—troubles—would be the consensus. *Thank You, God, but could You please choose someone else?*

The pastor went on. "We reject the Roman Catholic doctrine of papal supremacy. We treat all religions as equal. Now there are custody battles in courts between the children's Jewish blood relatives and the adoptive Christian families who refuse to relinquish the children they've baptized. We make our stance clear: We honor the wishes of the dead parents."

"Thanks. Where do I start?"

"The children you are looking for live at farms and monasteries. They may be attending regular schools in the village, ignorant of their real identity. With the help of the underground, we tried to keep lists. Often we lost track, because there wasn't a single person or organization in charge." Pastor Gaspard stopped as if mulling over the dilemma anew. "Some children matured during the war years and moved to hunting cabins on deserted estates or found work on farms. They are out of our reach unless they seek our help. There are many caves in the region where people found refuge during the war, but there is no access to food, so I doubt that anyone lives there now. Anyway, I'm warning you that should you get lost in one, we have no search team."

The more Pastor Gaspard spoke, the more eerie and otherworldly this project became.

He told Uzi to bring the children in transit to him, and he and his wife would care for them in their home behind the church. Then he led Uzi to a house in an alley a block away and introduced him to Hilda Berkowitz. "She's the social worker keeping track of the Jewish children," he explained.

The conversation in English had given Uzi a headache. He was relieved that Hilda, a thin, bony woman almost as tall as he was, spoke Yiddish.

At her invitation, he sat down at her dining table. "It's been thirty hours since I arrived in Marseille, and I've accomplished nothing," Uzi told her after the pastor had left. "Where do I go first?"

"Jugendliche," she said. "Youth. Don't just burst through a door. Get the lay of the land. Get to understand each case and strategize your moves." She pointed a long finger at Uzi's chest. "But don't dawdle. We are grateful for the heroism of local people who sheltered and saved our children, often risking their own families' lives, but it's time. We fear for our children's Jewish souls."

She opened a ledger. Written in the columns were squiggles and symbols, not words. "It's coded," she explained. "For some children, we forged new identities but kept records of their parents' names. For their safety, the underground moved them from one hiding place to another. The problem is that only one person knew the next person in the chain."

"Might as well have used bread crumbs."

"You'll follow those bread crumbs." She took out a map. "I'm assigning you to the areas surrounding two villages."

Uzi thought of his experience tracking the Arab infiltrators; their footprints in the dusty path had been erased by the wind, the sand whipped up into feverish cones. In Eretz Israel, he knew the Arab villages and terrain in his area, knew the contours of the rocks and the shadows in dry wadis. When he was a child, neighbors had been united by the shared hardships and occasional joys of agricultural life. His father had taken him along on visits to Arab friends—until they turned into enemies. But how did one track here? From the window, Uzi glimpsed the adjacent house. A child could be hidden in there and Hilda would have no idea.

Deciphering her own notes, Hilda described to Uzi a few cases he should target, and he wrote down the details in his notebook. "What about the young ones?" he asked.

"It's our priority to keep siblings together; we don't want to separate them from their only living relatives. That said, we can't handle kids who are too young to care for themselves. Also, as you are well aware, getting out of France is the easy part. Entering Palestine is dangerous." Her eyes locked with Uzi's. He knew she was referring to the clandestine landings of immigrant boats. He'd helped evacuate the refugees from the beaches on dark nights, which was why the Youth Aliyah operation was populated with Haganah members. Hilda continued, "We focus on rescuing older children so we can salvage what's left of their stolen childhood—and before they are lost to our people." She paused. "Ready to go out and ask questions?"

"Except I don't speak French."

She lifted a stack of flash cards like the ones he had used in English class.

He mouthed words as he wrote down the translation of each: *Enfant juif. Je suis de Palestine. Puis-je payer vos dépenses?*

"'May I pay your expenses?'" he read.

"You'll be surprised how well money works."

Uzi shifted in his seat. "Is it ethical?" In the kibbutz, he had been spared the repugnant task of handling money. The secretariat purchased everything, even the underwear that the laundry shed distributed weekly according to size, since no clothes were personal property. Now he was about to buy children the way Miriam had done the day before.

"Are you asking me whether it's ethical to reimburse the children's protectors for the cost of their upkeep when this country was starving? Money demonstrates our deepest gratitude for what they have done." She pointed to the next card. "*Parents*. It's spelled like in English. Pronounced differently, and it means any relative. If you say you're the child's *parent*, it might mean that you are her relative."

"But that is a lie."

"Not in the grand scheme of things. We are all the family these children have left."

"What do I do if a child is happily living with a Christian family? If he or she is loved?"

"Try to persuade this family. The mood in France today weighs heavily toward national identity and reviving France through the next generation. One's family comes second, and many people can understand that—with some persuasion." She withdrew money from the sideboard drawer and counted bills. "If you don't take that child, another organization will. They might even kidnap her. What will they do? Place her in an orphanage. The question is only which organization and what it ultimately offers to a growing kid. So, yes, it's either us or them, and Eretz Israel is the best future."

"Kidnap?"

"A couple of weeks ago, a father, a camp survivor, whose twelve-year-old had refused to leave her new Christian family, kidnapped her to Palestine. He and his wife were crushed over the loss of their two other children. They weren't about to give up on this one. Can you blame them?"

"I hope I'm not expected to help in such an operation," Uzi stated. "In the first wave that arrived last year, each child *was* an orphan. The entire kibbutz movement is mobilized to absorb displaced kids who *need* a home."

"But all the children live in separate children's houses."

"By age group, but they spend time with their parents every evening. It's no different from city parents who work, except that on the kibbutz, my mother never has to cook. She has more time for her children. At night, parents rotate sleeping in the children's house."

"How did that work for you growing up?"

He chuckled. "I felt bad for city children who didn't have their own house with a classroom and recreation areas." He added, "My girlfriend and I still have dinner with our parents in the common dining room. And my classmates are forever my siblings."

Hilda handed him letters typed in French on official-looking stationery and signed each. "These authorize you to retrieve the children on our behalf."

IT TOOK ALMOST three hours for the bus to reach Châtillon-sur-Indre, which was to be his home for the week. The bridge had not been repaired after the Nazis bombed it, Hilda had told him. A temporary bridge served only pedestrians and bike riders.

Châtillon-sur-Indre was a small, sad village with only a few stores, now closed for the midday rest. A tall, narrow tower missing its top stood on a dell. Pigeons flew in and out of cracks in its windowless walls. As Uzi traversed an alley, he peeked through lace-curtained windows: A young couple was arguing in their kitchen. An older man was fixing a lamp in his front room. Three girls were sitting cross-legged on a bed, playing a board game. An ancient woman was lying on a couch near her stove. Where were the Jewish children?

Uzi knocked on the door of a cottage built of half-hewn timber and featuring a sign that read CHAMBRES. A kerchiefed proprietor in her mid-thirties showed him a room with a canopied bed and a bathtub. Uzi gestured to indicate that he would prefer a smaller room, and she led him to the attic, where tucked under the slanted eaves were a cot and a night table with a ceramic bowl. The lavatory was on the ground floor. Uzi nodded and handed her the francs she asked for.

"*Mon nom est* Uzi Yarden," he said.

"Madame Therrien." She made an eating gesture, then guided him downstairs to her tiny parlor, where she pointed to a card printed with squares. Understanding, Uzi presented the ration card that Miriam had given him, and Madame Therrien clipped a couple of coupons.

A small table in the corner of the room was covered with a lacy cloth, a black-framed photograph of a young man, a bouquet of flowers in a vase, and a lit candle. The wall above it bore a cross. A violin case rested against the table.

Madame Therrien served him soup rich with onions and cheese crusted on top. He soaked up the last drops of the soup with bread. An old woman shuffled in, crossed herself when she passed the small altar, and collected his bowl.

It was still afternoon, and he had work to do. Uzi got up. *"Merci,"* he said, and walked to the door.

He would not ask for Madame Therrien's help, not until he knew where her sympathies lay. He entered a store with a sign reading CHARCUTERIE that was filled with hanging salamis and smoked meat. He showed the proprietor the first address, which he'd copied onto a separate sheet.

Making a sad face, the man mimed airplanes dropping bombs and everything destroyed.

"And this?" Uzi showed him a second note.

The man pointed to an upward-sloping street. He mimed grazing sheep.

The chiseled steps Uzi took were bordered on both sides by stone fences. Small houses were built into the slope. Perhaps in medieval times they were subject to tax collection by the lord in his now-ruined tower.

Village life unfolded as Uzi walked on: A man hammered a long nail; a girl played with a toddler; a teenager led two goats. A chicken that had escaped a yard darted into Uzi's path, and he caught it and gave it to its owner, a woman who only glowered at him in return.

He was a stranger. They noticed his clothes, his hatless head, his unruly hair, and possibly his ramrod-straight posture. They had probably never encountered a proud, unapologetic Jew, although it's likely that they didn't know that he was one.

Uzi stopped by an old man sitting on a stool outside a low wooden shack. His face was turned toward the sun like a sunflower, soaking in its warmth. Uzi showed him the note. The man pointed to a green valley of alfalfa.

"Enfants?" Uzi ventured and raised two fingers. The twin boys, nine years old when Hilda had placed them on the list four years ago, must have been old enough to remember their parents' names despite their new fake identities. The man took Uzi's note and wrote down an address.

Twice more, Uzi's inquiries about the boys were met with recognition and directions. The boys were so near! Excitement made his feet light. He would rescue the twins whose parents had been deported to their death, whose only living relative at the time, an uncle, had been unable to care for them when he went into hiding. Bewildered and traumatized, cut off from family ties, the boys must be waiting to be brought back to their people.

Yet Uzi had to traverse woods of oak, maple, and birch, walk along a field of dried sunflowers, and cross a rickety rope bridge over a ravine. The scale of the area map Hilda had given him was woefully useless for the details of this countryside. Uzi stopped to draw a map of his wanderings so he could find his way back.

At last, he arrived at a building set on a dirt road with a sign above the door reading TAVERNE.

In the dim room under a cloud of cigarette smoke, a few patrons were scattered around small tables. He stepped to the counter, took out his pocket dictionary, and pointed to the word for "juice." The man behind the counter guffawed, revealing what remained of bad teeth. He pumped beer from a keg into a mug. Slamming it on the counter, he said, *"Jus français."* French juice. A patron nearby chuckled. Everyone was watching Uzi. This stranger who had walked into their midst was probably the only novelty of the day. Uzi lit a cigarette. Whatever conversations had been interrupted when he entered didn't resume. He smiled and raised his mug in salute. No one reciprocated. He disliked the smirk on the tavern keeper's face.

He tasted the frosty ale—darker than beer—then took a second gulp while scanning the room. There was no boy, let alone two, and in the thickening hostility he wasn't about to inquire about them. He ground out his cigarette in the ashtray with care and placed the unsmoked stub back in the packet. *"Bonsoir,"* he said, and turned to the door.

No one responded.

Chapter Twenty-Six

SHARON

Cherbourg, France
November 1968

SHARON LEARNS THAT at Félix Amiot's dinner, the half dozen officers of the Israeli permanent mission will be wearing their dark blue winter uniforms with multiple gold bands at the cuffs. She imagines herself in Rina's oversize black dress sitting in the formal dining room with the crisply dressed French and Israeli senior officers. The dress could be cinched with a belt, but that would only emphasize how unsophisticated and graceless Sharon is. Savta would be appalled.

There's no time to travel to Paris this week. Cherbourg's store windows, which displayed fashionable apparel in the Catherine Deneuve film, show matronly dresses that would look outdated even on Savta. As Sharon ends her rounds in the plaza, she spots Rachelle at a coffee shop wearing one of her stylish silk blouses.

Sharon plops down on a chair at her table. "I've been everywhere looking for a decent dress for dinner at Amiot's house," she says. "Where do you shop?"

"You're going to Fort du Cap Lévi?" Rachelle's voice is flat.

"You're not a member of Amiot's fan club?"

"I appreciate what he's done for this town. But can one ever erase his past?"

"Wow," Sharon says. "Everyone I've met so far admires him."

"Now you've met one who hates him. If time forgives Nazi collaborators, it is up to people like me to remember what they are capable of." Rachelle stands up and drops a coin for the waiter. In a softer tone she says, "Let's shop in my closet."

Sharon can't imagine how clothes belonging to the shorter, full-figured Rachelle would fit her, but she follows her home anyway.

She is warmed by the eclectic décor of Rachelle's living room. A purple shawl is thrown in calculated casualness on a red velvet couch, plants hang from the ceiling by macramé ropes, and glass balls are suspended on invisible wires in front of the windows to break up the sun's rays. A tall blue glass hookah rests on the floor between two leather beanbag chairs.

In her bedroom, Rachelle withdraws from her armoire a sky-blue chiffon dress.

Sharon's skepticism evaporates when she puts it on. The fabric, cut on the bias, hugs her slim body; the skirt flares out at her ankles. Rachelle throws a sheer shawl over the dress, the front of the airy fabric resting against Sharon's throat, the long ends trailing in the back.

"This is too beautiful." Sharon passes her hand over the soft fabric. Only the French can make the simplest cotton-and-silk blend look so expensive.

Rachelle hands her a pair of high-heeled sandals, and while Sharon tries swirling around the room in them, Rachelle examines her with pride.

"I have topaz earrings," Sharon says. It's a pair Alon bought her for her nineteenth birthday. She hasn't worn them since she and Alon attended his cousin's wedding last December. Eleven months later, that seems like a lifetime ago. Wearing the earrings, she'll feel Alon's comforting presence throughout the evening.

❧

LATE SATURDAY AFTERNOON, she steps out of Rachelle's building. Her hair, pressed on Rachelle's ironing board as if it were a skirt, fans behind her like a sheet of dark silk.

Danny lets out a low whistle. "You're looking sensational." He opens the car door for her with a flourish. Not for the first time, Sharon wonders where he acquired his European manners—surely not on the kibbutz, where equality of the sexes means the elimination of male chivalry.

Minutes later, they are on the scenic drive that winds along the Atlantic coast, rising over cliffs and dipping back again close to sea level.

"Tell me about Félix Amiot," Sharon says. "What happened between the time he built airplanes and the time he switched to ships?"

"Here is my take: Imagine World War Two. The man has huge aeronautical factories employing tens of thousands of people. He can continue to retain them under a contract from the Nazis, or he can shut down and watch his men get taken by force by the Vichy government, which had committed to supplying Germany with half a million French laborers."

Sharon mulls over the moral dilemma. A tough one.

Danny goes on. "That's why, decades later, his employees call him 'Papa Amiot.' He's extremely loyal to them, and they adore him in return."

"Presumably, decades later, those are not the same employees, but it is still the same man," she retorts, thinking of Rachelle's hatred of him. "With your logic, can we assume that Amiot's dedication to building our Saars is more out of his concern for the employees in Cherbourg than his interest in helping Israel?"

"He's the type of innovator who is fascinated by the engineering challenges that our Saars present. Besides, he does a lot more for us than his duty calls for."

"Let's see. Giving the Israeli mission two apartment buildings to house the staff? It's part of his cost of doing business." Sharon is emphatic. "What's more obvious is that twelve hundred Cherbourgeois are employed in CMN. You told me that he defused the Saar Six diplomatic crisis out of economic concern. That means that he would have done the same had Egypt been his customer."

"Egypt didn't contract with CMN. We did."

Sharon recalls their previous conversation and Danny's pragmatic view of facts on the ground—or in the sea, for that matter. Is it his training as an officer or his mindset that made him choose, as he put it, not to let the past cripple his perception of the present or alter his vision of the future?

She is guilty of not letting go of the past—and she does not want to. It defines who she is: a woman seeking to know her roots, to understand who she is as the mysterious Judith Katz's daughter.

At a sign reading FERMANVILLE, Danny veers onto a dirt path. Sharon takes an instant liking to the modest fort perched on a low cliff that drops into the English Channel. Farther up, in the undulating green pasture, sheep are grazing.

"Nice, eh?" Danny asks. "Couldn't be farther away from Israel."

She knows that he's not referring to the bright blue of the water or the pastoral scene on the knoll above but to the tranquility that lies before them. There is beauty in their homeland, but also daily chaos, existential anxiety, and emotional turmoil. Sharon looks at the sun still hanging in the sky, flushing the world with color. If only she could share this scenery with the Golans to ease their anguish.

The fort is only two stories high, its modest stone façade far less imposing than the buttressed fortresses she's seen along the shores of Normandy. Blooming pink rosebushes, likely delivered from a greenhouse for the occasion, flank the double wooden doors. They soften the high walls that extend on both sides, punctuated by twin towers, one at each end.

When the car stops in the circular gravel driveway, a valet opens Sharon's door and extends a white-gloved hand. She readjusts the blue wool cape Rachelle insisted she take against the chill and steps out, gathering the hem of her gown. The borrowed velvet string pouch dangles from her wrist.

On the other side of the car, Danny pinches the crease in his pants and puts on his white officer's peaked cap. Familiar as Sharon is with the uniform, she can't help but admire it. It has elegance and authority, especially on the tall Danny.

A butler shows them into a reception hall with bare terra-cotta floors and Moorish-style furniture. The ruggedly carved dark pieces are so different from the gilded fine antiques Sharon saw in Paris's Musée des Arts Décoratifs. She likes this sparse décor—a few well-placed couches upholstered in striped brocade, some brass side tables, wrought-iron torchères on the walls, and a single silver bas-relief chest beneath an ocher-colored antique tapestry that features a hunting scene. The masculine choices tell Sharon that this home has no lady of the house.

The style seems to match Félix Amiot, who disengages from a group of dignitaries and walks toward them, smiling. A red handkerchief tucked into his suit's breast pocket adds panache. As he shakes Danny's hand, the industrialist's other hand cuffs his shoulder. Then he turns smiling gray eyes toward Sharon.

"Meet Sharon Bloomenthal, our team's assistant for special projects," Danny says.

"Enchanté." To Sharon's surprise, Amiot brings her hand to his lips. She lets out a short, embarrassed laugh and wonders whether she's supposed to curtsy. Despite his formality, there is something warm about the man.

He signals to a passing waiter carrying a tray of fluted champagne glasses, takes three, and hands one to her and one to Danny. He lifts his own and says in English, "As we say here, *L'chaim.*"

She is even more curious about the paradox of this congenial man. Isn't Amiot risking the ire of his government by continuing to build boats for Israel? Or has he convinced the powers that be that after the recent nationwide civil unrest, it is in the government's best interests to see to the welfare of this town by keeping its people employed?

"L'chaim," she responds, then adds in French, "Coincidentally, we say the same word in Israel."

He bursts out laughing. "You speak French? How refreshing! So tell me, what project did you work on today?"

"Today?" She giggles at his specific interest. "Would you like to hear about the dozens of cups of coffee I've prepared or about the written mechanical instructions I translated from French to Hebrew for our crew?"

"Sure. And yesterday?"

She laughs again. "I helped the designers with some drafting."

"Ah, drafting!" Amiot seems to be in no rush to entertain his other guests. "When holding a pen to paper, that's when the best ideas flow. That's when I discover solutions that can't be imagined when lounging around a conference table."

Sharon smiles politely. Her host is too important and too rich to be interested in chatting with her. She's relieved when Yaniv and Kadmon approach to shake his hand. They loop Danny into their conversation, and she starts to glide away.

But Amiot half turns toward her. "Tell me later what you think of my *mouton salé*."

Mouton salé? It means "salted lamb." A dish or a wine? Or is it a new boat design? She wishes Rina and Naomi were here to explain, but they'll arrive later. After baby Daphna goes to sleep, Pazit will watch her, relieving both mothers. Sharon selects a miniature quiche from the tray of a passing waiter and steps through the back glass doors to the courtyard. In the small fort, stringy vines, now leafless and dry, cling to the walls in areas protected from the wind. She would have liked to climb up the boulders to the ramparts and imagine what a scout in the old days would have seen when all he had was a spyglass.

The architect, she thinks, could have added coned tops to the short corner towers, giving the battlements more power, but he resisted the grandiosity.

"Here you are!" A teenage girl emerges from behind Sharon. "I'm Christine, Félix Amiot's favorite granddaughter—actually, the only one." She chuckles and loops her arm through Sharon's as if they are longtime friends. "You're the only young woman here and, thankfully, not a naval officer. Are you a spy?"

"A detective, perhaps." Conversation is easy with the charming Christine, who's only four years younger than Sharon but far more refined. She tells Sharon that she attends a Swiss boarding school and is visiting for the weekend, having been flown here in her grandfather's private plane. As the girl chatters about the royalty and European elite at her school and the safari trip to Africa she'll be taking with her grandfather, Sharon feels the yawning gap expand between herself and this cosmopolitan, self-possessed teen. Her expression must show her bewilderment because Christine turns serious. "I'm sorry. I was just trying to cheer you up."

Taken aback, Sharon asks, "Do I look like I need cheering up?"

"Your fiancé. I heard. Sorry."

"Oh. I'm fine." Sharon is piqued at the label applied to her: *The poor woman is awaiting news of her fiancé, whose submarine was lost at sea.* In a light tone, she says, "What's *mouton salé?*"

"My grandfather's famous sheep up there." Christine points to the bluff, now shrouded in bluish mist. "The ocean salt clings to the grass, and the meat of the sheep that graze on it is both tender and salty."

"Like our kosher meat," Sharon says, "minus the tender part."

The meal turns out to be delicious. Sharon is seated next to Rina, who is poking at an asparagus spear when Sharon asks her, "What's the story with Amiot? A good guy or a bad guy?"

Rina strokes her protruding belly. "I live in a house he owns and I eat the great food he serves. I don't single him out as a Nazi collaborator. I hold *all* French people accountable for the fact that just twenty-five years ago, they rounded up Jewish *children*, whom even the Nazis were sparing, and sent them to their death. What kind of horrible people would do such a thing? We are living in a cesspool of anti-Semites, so let's just exploit whatever we can."

Sharon shivers at the reminder of the world of hatred her mother must have endured—and escaped. How? Did she have siblings who perished? Where did Judith Katz hide to survive the war that hadn't spared her parents? Sharon could have had grandparents, aunts, uncles, and cousins right here in France had they not all been murdered. Murdered by French people.

The next sip of champagne turns sour in her mouth.

Chapter Twenty-Seven

CLAUDETTE

Château de Valençay, France
November 1942

B ACK IN HER tower room, terrified for herself and for Benjamin, Claudette prayed with all her might until a rumble below sent her to the window. A convoy of canvas-topped trucks pulled through the porte cochère in the front wing and stopped in the inside courtyard. Men in green-gray uniforms poured out of the trucks, shouting orders in a harsh language.

The enemy was here, bringing their barking dogs. Claudette's mouth tasted sour. The men and dogs streamed into the building, and she could no longer hear them. They could be anywhere in the vast château. A paralyzing terror washed over Claudette along with a primal instinct to live for her baby and protect him. Never before had she felt the burden of being crippled so acutely.

How long before the Nazis entered her chamber? Would she be better off climbing to the turret? Not with the dogs sniffing. There was no place to hide. She washed her face and sat down to wait, hugging herself. *Benjamin, my baby. I will do whatever it takes to stay alive for you.*

At three o'clock, when the gold sunlight was fading, screams and keening outside made Claudette rush to the window.

At first, her brain didn't register what her eyes saw. Among the five people pushed toward a truck was the pregnant Madame Galvin, whom Claudette hadn't seen in months. Peeking from beneath the coat that didn't close across a belly at full term was the blue frock with the pink collar Claudette had crocheted. A soldier shoved her, and she fell to the ground. An older woman leaned over to help her.

An officer in shiny knee-high black boots pointed his handgun at her forehead. The woman's hands rose in supplication. The officer shot her.

Claudette shrieked, then clamped her hand over her mouth. Nausea rose in her at the sight of the three people—Jews, she realized—being shoved onto the truck. Madame Galvin rose from the gravel and, her arms supporting her stomach, stumbled to join them.

Claudette rushed to the bowl on her nightstand and vomited. Were these Madame Galvin's parents, the leather-goods magnates? Had the Chirazes been living here, possibly as long ago as when she had hidden Isaac and Raphaël Baume?

The Nazis shot anyone who hid Jews. Now that the duchess's crime had been exposed, she would be executed. A choked cry escaped Claudette's throat. She knelt by her bed. Her prayers came through her whimpering as her ears tuned in to hearing the shots of a death squad.

The kind, beautiful duchess—her protector—was about to be killed!

The sound of thudding boots in the long gallery made Claudette freeze. Still on her knees, she shrank into herself, anticipating the dogs. No barking, only the boots' clomping as they receded from her tower. She crawled stealthily to the storage space near the stairs Isaac and Raphaël had used and curled up in the dark behind discarded furniture.

MUCH LATER, SHIVERING in the cold, she heard the tower door open and the squeaking of leather boots. Someone stepped into the small vestibule. One by one, he opened the doors to the rooms. Soon he would find her. Claudette panted hard, certain that he would hear her.

The door was yanked open, and a ray of light slashed onto the floor and the pile of furniture. Claudette held her breath. Seconds passed. Her lungs were about to burst.

She heard him step away, leaving every door open. Any dog might wander in from the gallery, sniffing her fear. *Benjamin. My baby.* She had to stay alive for him. Her teeth chattering from the cold, Claudette remained in the hiding spot. Had she missed the shot of the duchess's execution? She prayed hard to be saved for Benjamin.

How many hours had passed? She relieved herself in a discarded bowl. More time passed. All was quiet in the tower and the vestibule. She crawled out, quietly closed the gallery door, and entered her chamber.

She pulled herself up and peered out the window. The full moon's position indicated that it was about midnight. There was no sign of the duchess's body lying in blood. The trucks were still parked like discarded shoes. Some soldiers stood nearby, smoking, dogs resting at their feet. A dog raised its head and looked straight at Claudette as if detecting her gaze. She lowered herself onto her bed and wrapped herself in Mémère's down comforter.

A tapping on her door made her drift upward from a fretful sleep. She had been swimming at the bottom of a river of dead bodies while struggling to reach Benjamin, who floated above her, babbling his throaty gurgles. She sat upright, her heart pounding.

Another quiet knock on the door was followed by a mild press on the handle, too soft for a Nazi. Claudette opened the door a crack. In the darkness, she saw Mathéo.

"My *maman* says for you to come," he whispered.

The duchess was alive! "Is she all right?" *Alive!*

"She says to bring your things and be as quiet as a mouse."

Somewhere, a clock struck three. In the night air, Claudette shook from chill and dread.

The duchess's chamber was unlit; the fireplace emitted a smell of dead ashes. Claudette made out the duchess's silhouette by the open window and was so relieved to see her unharmed that she fell on her knees, clutching the duchess's ankles. "Jesus heard my prayers."

The duchess helped her up. "They are not arresting me because the Duke of Sagan is a German title. It saves me from prison or worse." Her voice trembled. "The commander permits me to leave for Spain to stay with my de Castellane family. Spain is neutral, and my son will be safe there."

Claudette was devastated all over again. The duchess was alive but about to leave, to desert her. How could she manage here on her own? The Nazis would surely shoot her the way they had Marguerite's sister.

And Benjamin? The consequences of his tattoo hit her as if she'd collided with one of the Nazis' trucks. She had marked him as a Jew! What insane state of mind had caused her to make such a grave mistake? She had been crazed with longing for Raphaël, she knew, and too emotional to think straight. But the midwife hadn't understood that all Claudette had agreed to was a tiny jewel-like star.

"You must be strong now," the duchess said.

"I must reach my baby." Claudette's voice quaked. Where could she hide with him?

The duchess poured something from a decanter. In the moonlight, a crystal glass glistened as she handed it to Claudette.

The cognac burned Claudette's throat. It failed to stop her shaking. "My baby needs me." She would hug him and keep him safe—except she couldn't even feed him. She could barely walk properly, let alone run with him to safety. She couldn't protect her child.

"You are too talented to be left here," the duchess said. "Come with me."

"To Spain?"

"We don't have much time. Monsieur Vincent is preparing my car."

"But Benjamin." Claudette's eyes had adjusted, and in the darkness she registered a movement. She snapped her head to see Mathéo's tutor, Jules Hallberg.

"No one can reach the village. Jules is coming with us. You should too."

"I can't leave Benjamin." Claudette whimpered.

"You're an *invalide*. I don't want the Nazis to see you."

"He's only six weeks old."

"Monsieur Vincent will take care of the arrangements with the nursemaid. I trust him."

Claudette shook her head. "I can't. I just can't."

"By offering you a chance to escape with me, I'm assuming a grave risk." The duchess touched Claudette's shoulder, then gestured to Jules to head to the window. "We're in a rush. There's a rope to take you both down."

Escape through the window? The duchess was truly convinced that the Nazis shouldn't glimpse this crippled woman. What if they saw her baby's blue star? "My baby—"

"Save yourself now so you can raise him later." The duchess tugged Claudette to the window. "That's your only option."

Claudette watched the tutor climb onto the window's low sill. Madame Duchamp had said that motherhood took sacrifice, but Claudette had never imagined the kind of sacrifice she would be asked to make so soon.

"Stop whimpering or you'll weaken your grip. Now move!" the duchess ordered in a tone she'd never used with Claudette before. Her hand pressed on Claudette's back. "Go!"

In a daze, Claudette stepped forward and sat on the windowsill. In her head she heard Marguerite crying over her sister and saw the Nazi officer shoot the old woman.

"The war will be over, and you'll get back to him. Alive." The duchess held out the rope and forced it into Claudette's hand. "Go now!"

Claudette looped the rope around her leg brace and, using all the strength in her arms, let herself slide down.

Hands caught her as she reached the ground on the château's north side. A minute later, the duchess lowered down her bag.

No! She couldn't leave. Claudette turned to look up the solid wall. No; scaling the stones buttressed against invading enemies was a feat for a young knight in a romance novel.

Monsieur Vincent ushered her to the waiting Peugeot. Several jerricans of petrol were strapped on the car's roof along with suitcases. Whispering, he instructed Claudette to remove her brace, then helped her climb into the trunk of the car. She had barely arranged herself in the tight space when Jules Hallberg slid in. He rounded himself around her folded knees, his feet next to Claudette's head.

"Once you're on the open road, the two of you can move to the back seat. You've got your IDs." Then Monsieur Vincent added, "God be with you."

The smell of petrol and old shoes filled Claudette's nostrils. "Benjamin!" she cried out in a low voice. "Please keep him safe from the Nazis."

"Of course I will. I've known Léonie Doisneau since she was a child. I promise to pay for his keep."

Claudette's heart was breaking as he slammed down the trunk. The sound of heavy breathing from the young man curled against her legs was mixed with the slapping of leather straps and the rattle of buckles. They were locked inside.

Chapter Twenty-Eight

UZI YARDEN

Loire Valley, France
September 1946

GET THE LAY of the land. Hilda's words echoed in Uzi's head. Rather than returning the way he'd come, he walked away from the road. Behind the tavern building was a small ravine, its grassy banks rising toward scattered willow trees whose branches drooped into the water. One nearby shack was a toolshed, the next was for laundry. Past them was a large stone shed with a fenced enclosure, and Uzi smelled the distinct odor of cow manure and wet hay.

He purposely didn't look back to see if he was being watched as he ambled, trying to appear aimless. He had to avoid confrontation.

And there, in the cowshed, propped on a one-legged stool, a prepubescent boy was singing a tune while milking a cow. Uzi had noticed these kinds of stools; a French farmer belted it to his backside and moved with it from one cow to the next, freeing his hands. Eight cows in two rows waited for their turns. Uzi couldn't see if there was another person in the shed.

"*Bonsoir,*" he said, realizing too late that he should have said *Bonjour.* The boy's singing stopped, but he continued to milk. Uzi picked up an empty pail, grabbed a stool leaning nearby, and settled next to the cow across the aisle.

The boy raised his eyes in surprise. Uzi smiled and began to milk. The boy asked a question. Uzi shrugged and released one hand to indicate that he didn't understand. A second boy, identical to the first one, appeared. He was holding a long, thick wooden stick, its end whittled to a point, like a sword.

Uzi rose, letting his unbelted stool fall sideways, and raised both

hands in mock surrender. *"Je suis de Palestine."* I'm from Palestine—
the French phrase he had rehearsed. The boy relaxed his hold on the
sword-stick, and Uzi pointed to himself, said, *"Juif,"* then pointed to
the two boys. *"Juifs?"*

They exchanged a glance, then shook their heads.

"Tobias? Elias?" Uzi said the names he assumed they hadn't
heard in a long time.

They recoiled. Uncertainty furrowed their young brows. Their
cheeks were pink and soft, and their upper lips did not show a first
fuzz. Under their work shirts there was no muscle mass. This was
a good stage for them to arrive in Eretz Israel; there they'd develop
and become men.

Uzi searched his pocket for the flash cards and showed them the
one that translated to *Do you want to come to Eretz Israel with me?*
He added, "A kibbutz," and showed them a flash card that read
Une grande famille.

The eyes of one of the boys suddenly widened as he looked past
Uzi. Uzi turned and saw the tavern keeper and another man.

"What is going on here?" the second man asked Uzi in English.

"We've been looking for these boys," Uzi replied, relieved to
have an interpreter. "Their uncle left them in that village—" He
scrambled to find his slips of paper, wishing he could pronounce
the names of the places without them.

"Where is that uncle?"

Uzi took a guess. "Killed in the war. There are relatives in Palestine who want to raise the boys. *Parents,*" he added, using the
French pronunciation to strengthen his case. "If the boys want to
come, that is," he said, glancing at them.

From their positions by the cows, out of sight of each other, the
boys stared at him with identical childish, blank faces, as if they'd
been trained to show no emotion.

"I am their teacher," the man said. "Are you saying that I was
wasting myself on Jews?"

Uzi had never encountered anti-Semitism in its naked form. Arab hatred of Jews stemmed from mounting territorial disputes. What was the basis for it here? How had Jews wronged these people? Yet all over Europe, hateful words progressed to actions—to the murdering of Jews. Uzi had never felt the sting of such a hateful remark uttered with no shame.

Concealing his fury, he forced a smile. "You didn't waste your time, I'm sure. Are they good students?"

The teacher puffed a nonverbal reply and stepped away.

Uzi sensed movement behind him and turned his head in time to see half a dozen men from the tavern approaching. One burly man carried a pitchfork. They surrounded Uzi, and the stares they had speared him with at the bar exploded into shouts. Breath smelling of alcohol assaulted him. One man raised a fist four centimeters from Uzi's nose.

They would pounce on him the moment they spotted a twitch of fear on his face, Uzi knew. The first to throw a punch would unleash the crowd's aggression, and this Jew-hating mob might turn murderous. Recently, Arabs had lynched a Jewish merchant in the Haifa market.

Uzi hadn't come here to fight. It wouldn't deliver the children to him. But prepared he must be. He inched his foot toward the stick-sword that the boy had dropped. Uzi knew he was younger and quicker than all of these men, and he was an expert in *kapap*, the hand-to-hand combat developed by the Haganah in response to the British decree forbidding the Jews to carry arms.

Three men stepped forward.

In a flash, Uzi picked up the stick and planted himself in front of them, body taut, knees slightly bent. He held the stick with both hands, one on each end, and raised it in a defense-attack position. His eyes fired a warning.

Stunned at his quick maneuver, the men stopped moving. Uzi read a tiny loss of determination on their faces. The pitchfork was lowered. Uzi straightened and dropped one end of the stick but not his guard. He scanned the men's faces, locking eyes with each one in a message of his strength. He stopped at the tavern keeper and gestured with his chin to signal that the two of them should step aside.

The tavern keeper moved, and the men parted like the Red Sea.

Adrenaline still flowing in him, Uzi followed the man deep into the cowshed, where they stopped behind a pile of hay. Uzi selected the flash card that read *Puis-je payer vos dépenses?* He raised two fingers to indicate both boys. He didn't know whether they would go with him, but first he had to clear this hurdle. If the boys left, this man would lose two laborers.

"Cinquante mille," the man said. With his finger, he sketched the number in the air.

Fifty thousand francs? "No," Uzi said. That sum was several times more than what Miriam and Hilda had given him. *Two thousand?* he signaled with two fingers.

Eight, the man signaled back.

They settled on five thousand. Uzi opened his backpack and kept his hand deep inside while locating the bills.

They walked to the front of the cowshed, and the man shooed away the crowd. Only the boys remained. He spoke to them. They lowered their heads. Their chins trembled, and they put their arms around each other.

They glared at Uzi. *"Non,"* they said in unison.

Confused, Uzi wondered if he should just leave. He had ruined this life for them. Or had he? When the tavern keeper and his wife accepted the boys, they must have known they were Jewish. Going forward, though, the whole community would know it too.

He pulled out the dictionary and found the word for "morning." "I will return," he said, drawing an outward arch with his finger. Then he touched his own temple: *Think about it.*

IT WAS DUSK when he caught a ride with a farmer heading back to Châtillon-sur-Indre. In the horse-drawn cart's bed, two sheep were lying on straw. Uzi stretched out alongside them and closed his eyes, taking comfort in these familiar creatures that never hurt anyone. Guilt gnawed at him; he'd been warned not to burst through a door. For a while, the tavern and the farm had given the boys some permanency—but now a stranger had shown up and exposed their identities without the chance of bringing their parents back from the dead.

Uzi recalled the evening in the kibbutz's common dining room when the members had made the decision to send representatives to Europe to rescue children. One member, who had come from Poland as a child, was sent there; he spoke the language, though he knew nothing about the country. But whom to send to France? No one was fluent in the language or had any experience there, so the only useful skill the group could think of was ingenuity. And Uzi, already a young leader, was chosen. There simply was no one else.

No wonder that he'd failed in his first attempt. What hubris had made him think that removing two traumatized boys from their secure environment was best for them? But then again, they must have been circumcised, a practice Hilda told him was unheard of among the locals. In the long run, after a trying transition in Israel, embraced by their people, they would never have to dread exposure again.

Madame Therrien smiled widely when she opened the door, revealing a crooked front tooth. She gestured for Uzi to follow her.

Perplexed, he walked behind his landlady as she crossed her kitchen, where her mother was at the stove. She went out the back door and through her lush small garden shaded by an oak tree, the air suffused with the fragrance of thyme and marjoram. Her steps were quick, a reminder that, despite her mourning dress and tight hair bun, she was still young. She walked across the alley and entered another home.

The house was dark, the kitchen a deserted mess of piled-up dirty pots and dishes. A putrid-smelling garbage pail was overflowing. Madame Therrien led Uzi to the front parlor, where a man was sprawled on an upholstered chair, drinking directly from an uptilted bottle.

At his feet, a child of perhaps four years was playing with building blocks. His light hair was matted. When he lifted a dirty face to the visitors, it lit up with a broad smile. The man glanced at Uzi, then raised his bottle in salute.

Madame Therrien pointed to a photo on the mantel and nodded sadly heavenward. The photo showed a lovely bride wearing a hat over chin-length brown hair and holding a bouquet of flowers.

Uzi was certain that word about his inquiries had reached his landlady, but he doubted that she understood that his search was exclusively for Jewish children. This boy was too young anyway. Hilda had made it clear that the network didn't have the resources to care for small children, and in any case, you couldn't bring a young child along on a clandestine entry into Palestine—it would endanger everyone. Uzi lowered himself to the floor, picked up an arch-shaped building block, and placed it on the top of the small tower that the boy had constructed. A strong smell of urine hit him. While Madame Therrien carried more dirty dishes into the kitchen, Uzi played with the boy, gathering his thoughts. Judging by the filth and disarray, the widower could no more manage the boy than he could his home.

Uzi heard the back door close. Madame Therrien had left. The man on the chair closed his eyes and let out a loud belch.

The tower that the boy and Uzi were building collapsed, and the boy broke into laughter. He punched at the rest of the blocks with delight. His laugh was like bells, contagious, making Uzi laugh with him. The boy's eyes were wide, green, with long lashes. Despite the smeared snot and dry streaks of tears through dirt, he was beautiful.

There had to be a charity in town to assist this man and his child, or at least some neighbors who would help care for this boy. For now, all Uzi could do was wash him and change his clothes.

"*On y va?*" Uzi got up, extended his hand to the boy, and led him to the stairs. Discarded clothes, boxes, and tools cluttered the steps, and Uzi had to nudge them aside in order to climb up.

The tiny washroom consisted of a rusty sink and a hole in the rotten wood floor flanked by twin footrests. Judging by the stench, the bucket used to pour water from the sink into the hole hadn't been touched in a long while. Uzi removed a small dirty towel from a nail, rinsed it, and wrung it out. He dipped a hesitant finger in melted soap in a dish and washed the boy's face and hands. Since the boy seemed to enjoy his ministering, Uzi removed his shirt and rubbed the damp towel over his small body. The shape of his ribs was clear beneath his skin. The boy chattered, asking Uzi questions; Uzi, having no idea what he was saying, responded in Hebrew. The boy laughed as if Uzi had invented gibberish. What a sunny personality this kid had!

He helped the boy remove his soiled pants and immediately noticed the uncircumcised penis. Uzi was relieved—now there was no question of taking this young child with him. He lifted him to stand up in the sink, and the boy wrapped his arm over Uzi's shoulder for support and kept chattering in his sweet voice. The rusty sink made it hard to tell how much dirt came off him, but the skin that was revealed was pink. The water from the faucet turned cold, and the boy squirmed. Uzi placed him on the floor again and wiped his hair with the wet cloth. He took off his own shirt and dried him with it as best he could.

The boy put his small hand, so soft and trusting, in Uzi's and pulled him to a wall niche. It had a four-foot-long shelf with a mattress and a curtain made of a faded flowery skirt. The boy pointed to a trunk underneath the shelf, and when Uzi opened it, he found a few pieces of clean clothing. Again he wondered about the neighbors; he'd expected more from a village. Even a family feud couldn't justify such neglect. This boy was so lovable that Uzi already regretted that he had to leave him.

From downstairs came the clanking of pots and utensils. Uzi dressed the boy and put his own damp shirt back on. They descended the stairs.

Madame Therrien was at the sink, attacking the pile of dirty dishes. She had brought a bowl of vegetable soup and bread and placed them on the table. At the sight, the boy climbed on the chair and stuffed a piece of bread into his mouth.

Uzi handed him the spoon, and the boy began to slurp with it. He raised his green eyes to Uzi and pointed to the other empty chair.

This friendly child would be all right, Uzi told himself; he was gifted with strength of personality. Uzi made a sad face to convey that he couldn't stay and waved goodbye.

Holding the dripping spoon, the boy jumped up on his chair and clutched Uzi's neck. His little arms tightened. His neediness was heartbreaking. Still, there was nothing Uzi could do for him. He had to save children he could help.

He lowered the boy back into the chair, then took out a piece of hard candy and placed it on the table. Not knowing the word for "goodbye," Uzi said, *"Bonjour,"* and headed to the door.

"L'enfant?" Madame Therrien asked.

"No juif," Uzi replied.

"Oui, juif," she said.

Uzi couldn't explain about circumcision, certainly not with a hand gesture. Madame Therrien might have learned about his search for children, but Uzi doubted she knew the specifics. He pointed to himself, said, *"Juif,"* then to her and the boy. *"No juif. No juif."*

The woman said something to the boy, and he lifted his foot.

And there, centered in the arch, was an unmistakable blue Star of David.

Chapter Twenty-Nine

SHARON

Cherbourg, France
November 1968

TOMER, THE RESERVE officer with magnificent teeth, has sent Sharon two four-page letters describing his time-pressured life in Tel Aviv. He attends law school at night and labors in his father's garage during the day. He studies at stolen dawn hours and on weekends. *It's as if my brain is split—the academic part is given over to comprehending Ottoman, Talmudic, and British laws, and the mechanic part fixes cars and thrives on the smell of machine oil,* he wrote. *And then there's a separate chamber that fantasizes about what can pass between us when we finally meet again.*

She admires Tomer's facility with language, loves his imagery, and regrets not giving herself more to their passionate kiss. Yet in her responses she commits to nothing, especially since she's taken a liking to one of her "Norwegian" officers, who has returned for a second business trip.

"Jorgen," as she calls him playfully, traveled first to Munich. If his steps were traced back, he'd be remembered, since he met with a real estate agent about the possible purchase of an office building. Then he headed to Oslo, where he purposely registered with a travel agent to buy his plane ticket to Paris. Since he can't socialize with the Israelis in Cherbourg, Sharon meets him at his Parisian hotel.

She must take the plunge, she reminds herself when he helps her pull off her boots, then her sweater. His lanky body can't possibly feel like Alon's, and a polite man with European manners feels safe. The excitement of newness rises in her and propels her to reach for him.

Jorgen's body hair is so fair that she detects it only in the light from the bedside lamp, which she would have liked to keep on had it not inhibited his lovemaking. His prim, punctilious Germanic nature suits the role Yaniv assigned him, but Sharon craves the touch of a man who is expressive, warm, and open to laughter. After failing to loosen Jorgen up, she dozes off.

She leaves alone in the morning and takes her coffee in a corner café. The glass window fogs against the cold outside, and the air is saturated with the aroma of pastries baking, men's aftershave, and cigarette smoke. In her head, Sharon reviews the details of the night. She chose a man who would satisfy her body without involving her heart, but she hadn't expected the encounter to be so meaningless, like footprints on the sand washed away by a wave. *No regrets,* she tells herself. It had to be done, like swallowing bitter medicine.

On the train back to Cherbourg, she gazes at the rushing scenery, stone houses surrounded by the muted green of vegetation that is in hibernation until spring teases back its lushness. She recalls questioning Danny about his childhood home and discovering that he had left France at age four. As soon as she abandoned her agenda to probe his history, she discovered his tattoo. It has thrown her into a new orbit.

The image of his foot flits through her mind as it has since she first spotted it a few weeks ago. Someone must know something about this unusual Star of David tattooed on an infant's foot. It is a message, a traceable one, from his deceased parents. Or could it be an identifying mark from a parent who is still alive somewhere, aching for his or her lost infant? How Sharon would have pursued any thread, even as flimsy as this, leading to her mother's relatives. She cannot leave this sign alone.

LIKE A HUNTER in wait, she is on the alert for a chance to talk to Danny at a relaxed time away from the office. He's resisted her prying before, and she racks her brain for questions that would direct the conversation to his tattoo. These days, she rarely sees Danny. He's been spending hours in the hangar where Saar Seven is getting fitted with its communication and electronic systems.

Saturday afternoon, while bicycling across the town's plaza, she spots him through the glass window of a café. The top window in the church tower reflects the sun. On the ground, pigeons strut about, pecking at refuse left from the morning market.

Sharon dismounts her bike and steps inside. "Waiting for me?" She chuckles, guessing that Dominique will join him shortly, since the froth on his beer is still fresh. He gestures at the empty chair. "Coffee or wine?"

"Hot chocolate. Thanks." She keeps her coat on and releases her hair from the confines of her collar.

"Nice haircut." Danny's glance stays on her a second longer than usual, as if he's seeing her in a new way. "Very becoming."

"Thanks." She had her hair cut to just below her shoulders. Following Rachelle's guidance, she tossed her collection of headbands into the garbage and shed her hippie style in favor of a sophisticated look.

The waitress serves her hot chocolate, and Sharon lifts her mug. "To Saar Seven." Her smile masks her worry. Once the Saar is launched, in the dead of winter, Danny's twenty men will be taking it out for weeks of testing. The turbulent English Channel has, over centuries, swallowed thousands of vessels. She glances outside at the scattered November clouds. "The worst weather of the year."

"A smooth sea never trained a skillful sailor." Danny's gaze follows her to the sky. "Cooperating with the sea is about accepting its dominance and learning to navigate its moods."

In battling the sea, there is only one winner. Sharon doesn't say this; she scoops up the chocolate foam and brings the spoon to her mouth. When Alon volunteered for the submarine, she mistakenly believed that under the water, he would be safe from storms. So much for challenging this beast.

There's no natural segue to the topic on her mind, and she must broach it before Dominique arrives. "I've been thinking about your Jewish star," she ventures.

He straightens. "Sharon, enough!"

She swallows. "My mother also came with Youth Aliyah, but I can find no information about her."

"Sorry to hear that. There were thousands of us. Keeping records was secondary."

"So what's the message with your tattoo?"

He seems softened by her revelation. "Probably my parents couldn't have me circumcised."

"You weren't circumcised?"

"This will be my last word on this subject." Danny's tone is stern. She's brought him to the edge of his patience. "It was wartime. Either there was no mohel or my parents were in hiding or it wasn't a good idea to mark me in that classic Jewish way."

She's afraid to ask more, but he adds, "Just for the record, I corrected it later. At the children's home, you know."

"Ouch." In the kibbutzim, children are raised by age group, like siblings, boys and girls showering together until just before puberty. As a city girl, she was always appalled by the idea. "That took some guts," she says.

"It took less courage to do it than to endure the taunting." He sighs.

He is tired of her being a pest. She views him as a mentor and a friend. He views her merely as an efficient employee. When she falls in love again, it will be with someone like Danny but younger, so she won't feel as foolish as she does at this moment, knowing he must be regretting asking her to join him at his table.

She gazes at a couple with a little boy crossing the plaza. The parents swing him between them to his squeals of delight.

"Danny, you hired me because you liked my investigative skills."

"Who'd expect that you'd direct them against me?"

"It's not *against* you. I just can't leave the big question unasked."

"Which one is that?"

"The tattoo is not on your nose. It's convenient enough to hide. Who knew that you had it?"

"Meaning?"

"Why were you sent across the sea?"

"Sharon, that's two questions, and I've asked you to stop—"

She doesn't let him finish the sentence. "Your parents are dead, but many Holocaust survivors have found relatives. Maybe you have some too."

"Maybe." His tone is sharp, shutting down the possibility of the question's meaning. Relatives. Had she presented this probability at another time in his life, would he have wanted to explore it?

"Do you know where you were found?" she asks.

"I never asked."

He never asked? As a child, she pestered her grandparents, aunts, and uncles with questions about her parents. She still remembers her heartache during the memorial service when she walked among strangers and found that, unlike her late father, Amiram, an artist, a son, a brother, and a friend to many, her late mother, Judith, was only a name etched on the marble wall. Sharon traced the letters onto paper and handed it to those strangers.

"Do you at least know *when* you were born?" she asks Danny.

"Is that your fourth last question?" He shakes his head in desperation. "I have a made-up birthday. When I was issued a travel pass, my father selected that day as my birthday, October sixth, going back four years earlier, which is what he assessed my age to be."

"What do you mean, *my father?*"

"Uzi Yarden. He was the Youth Aliyah agent who found me." Danny's eyes narrow. His voice is angry. "Now are we done?"

She feels an engine revving in her. How traumatic it must have been for a little boy to be wrenched away from a family, from a woman he probably called Maman.

"One *really* last question? Why would your adoptive parents give a four-year-old boy to a stranger from a foreign land?"

Danny slams down his beer stein. "You know what the French say about onions?" He pushes himself from the table and heads toward the downstairs lavatory.

Onions. "Take care of your own onions" is what the French say when they mean "Mind your own business." Sharon stands up and fishes in her purse for coins to pay for her hot chocolate. If Danny didn't rely on her so much for work, he might have fired her. The mistake of pushing him too far was entirely her own. In evaluating a suspect's tolerance arc, an interrogator must assess the subject's emotional tipping point. She was wrong, and at this moment she'd better remove herself from Danny's sight.

She's still buttoning her coat when he returns. "It's your day off," she says. "Sorry to have badgered you."

"Wait." He sits, motions for her to sit back down, places his elbows on the table, and leans forward. She lowers herself just enough to perch on the edge of the seat, her satchel in her lap. "You're an orphan too," he says. "You know how we fantasize about what could have been or what even *was* to fill in the blanks in memories. I long ago decided not to let such unproductive thoughts interfere with moving forward in my life or allow them to affect the pursuit of my career." He pauses, and Sharon follows his glance outside, where Dominique is dismounting from her bike. He speaks fast as if to close the subject before his girlfriend enters. "I refuse to inhabit a body that is labeled *orphan* because I ended up with a great family. I'm the son of Israel, a member of kibbutz Ayelet HaShachar, and an Israeli naval officer with an extraordinary mission in life."

"Got it."

He gives her a stern look. "If you got it, then you'll stick to your assigned projects. Leave my life alone. Can we agree on that?"

She nods, and he gets up to greet Dominique.

Sharon feels her tongue pressing against the roof of her mouth, and her teeth clench. She rises for Dominique's *la bise* and says her goodbyes.

As she mounts her bike, Sharon ponders Danny's declaration. She admires his life philosophy and understands his rebuke. She has become a pest.

His increasing annoyance aside—and their agreement notwithstanding—the star tattoo remains a puzzle. What if he has living relatives? Somewhere, there's an answer.

Chapter Thirty

CLAUDETTE

Barcelona, Spain
Summer 1945

Liberation! It had been a year since the Allies landed on the beaches of Normandy. Claudette could barely breathe at the thought of finally being able to return to Valençay, to her baby. Four months short of his third birthday, Benjamin had to be talking by now. With his two perfect legs, he was running around, reaching with pudgy fingers to catch a butterfly. His eyes were surely green. Was his hair, so fine at birth, still light-colored like hers? Had it taken on a darker hue, the shade of Raphaël's? Did he have a favorite animal at Léonie's, perhaps a dog with whom he curled up? Léonie had to be telling him that the mother who loved him so much was coming back soon. Monsieur Vincent was paying the nursemaid for Benjamin's keep even if he couldn't transfer funds outside the country to Duchess Silvia de Castellane.

When Claudette first arrived in 1942, Spain was recovering from a civil war, and spirits were high. The duchess's relatives attended private concerts, flamenco performances, and bullfights. Set free from the solemnity of war raging in the rest of Europe, Claudette let her imagination soar as she created colorful and exotic embellishments for the women's wardrobes.

Overnight, though, political winds shifted, and the de Castellanes lost their wealth. Claudette had to move out of the compound and take in mending in order to survive. She lived alone for the first time in her life.

For months now, she had wanted nothing more than to set off on the road home. She listened daily on her landlady's radio to the transmissions from France—no longer from the UK—a great sign of France's liberation. Yet travel had been impossible while sporadic battles still raged in the South of France, and the German and American armies were exchanging prisoners after ending their war in North Africa. The Pyrenees crossings were dangerous; the main passes were clogged by refugees, and the local guides who ran the more treacherous routes through the mountains were themselves robbers. Nevertheless, Claudette had to rush back, not only to Benjamin but also to Raphaël, who would be looking for her in Valençay. All this time she had hoped that he and his father had stopped running and were safe in one of the labor camps. At least they would have had food and shelter.

Before strapping on her brace, she adjusted the two flat cloth pouches under each leather strap. They held all her money in paper and coins. No matter how harsh the circumstances, she had guarded this cache. On the duchess's advice, Claudette had exchanged the old francs for pesetas, reichsmarks, and American dollars. This money was her future; it would fund a new printing shop for Raphaël. For the expenses on her journey, she would carry only a few Allied-issued banknotes, because their value diminished as soon as they were printed.

The duchess fetched Claudette in her family's car, which was driven by Carlos, the chauffeur who doubled as a bodyguard when the de Castellane females left the compound. At the train station, he went out to purchase the ticket with Claudette's money. She watched with trepidation the hordes of people streaming in and out of the massive building that was about to swallow her into its cavity and spit her out on some train to a frightening journey, alone. Her stomach tightened at the thought of the bodies about to jolt her and knock her to the ground.

She wanted to pray to Mary and Christ and remind them of her years of devotion. But she had learned from Mathéo's tutor, who had escaped with her and turned out to be Jewish, that to adopt his faith, she must forsake Jesus and Mary. She must stick to the one and only God.

It had been a monumental decision. Declaring a wish to become Jewish was meaningless, Jules Hallberg said, confirming what Madame Galvin had hinted at. Claudette first had to give up Jesus and Mary.

How could she? They had been her saviors. They had comforted her throughout her growing-up years when she had been subject to the cruelty of her family and strangers alike. Jesus and Mary had stood up to both priests' hard judgments of her. She couldn't stop believing in their love; she could only force herself not to pray to them.

"Give this to Monsieur Vincent, please." The duchess's eyes reddened as she handed Claudette an envelope. "My late husband's German pension evaporated with the Third Reich's defeat. His title is worthless. I won't return to Valençay."

Not return? Disappointment flooded Claudette. She had counted on resuming her former employment and enjoying again the duchess's patronage. "Will you stay here?"

"Paris. Remember my old friend who married into the Galvin family? I'm waiting for word that I can sell cosmetics in their department store."

Claudette couldn't imagine the elegant duchess as a saleswoman serving her former high-society friends, who would sigh or snicker at her downfall.

"I was delusional to think that my good fortune could last forever. Whoever imagined that one day I'd be broke?" The duchess's voice caught in her throat.

Claudette held her hand. *Broke. Broke* wasn't the same as *poor*; it just meant rich people had less money than they were used to. "You still own Valençay," she offered.

"And how can I maintain it? With what money? My advisers tell me that I must gift it to the state in order to waive the taxes I owe."

"What about all the fine furniture and silver we hid? And the art? Can't you sell them?"

"I don't even know what the Nazis stole and what's left." The duchess blew her nose with a muslin handkerchief that Claudette had embroidered with her initials. "Anyway, who can afford to buy such relics? And the Louvre will soon claim back its own collections."

For a while, neither spoke.

Claudette broke the silence. "What happened to Madame Galvin? I saw her the afternoon she was taken. The officer shot an older woman who tried to help her."

"Her mother. It was a horrible day." The duchess dabbed at her eyes. "Luckily, her husband's family rescued her from the French labor camp and sent her to America before she was transported."

"Transported to where?"

"To a death camp in Germany or Poland." The duchess looked at Claudette. "Haven't you heard? The Nazis exterminated the Jews. Like cockroaches."

"Jesus and Mary." Claudette clamped her hand over her mouth in horror. "Killed them?"

"The news is coming out as concentration camps are being liberated. A huge number of Jews were murdered. Many of my Parisian friends were among them. Writers, musicians, painters, patrons of the arts—"

Tears filled Claudette's eyes. Raphaël had been correct to distrust those labor camps. How wrong she had been when she prayed that he and his father had found safety in such a place! Where did they hide, then? "That's awful," she whispered, now convinced that the Nazis had indeed murdered *invalides* too. But not Raphaël. He had understood the danger. He and his father must have hidden in some cave. Now she had even more of a reason to hurry back and set up house for them all.

The duchess's face was pale. "How naive we were when we saw the Jews being rounded up or just disappearing."

"But Madame Galvin had her baby in safety?"

The duchess dabbed at the corner of her eye. "A boy, may his soul rest in peace."

Shock radiated through Claudette's body. "She was planning to name him Benjamin." Her own boy would forever carry the Jewish name for them both.

A beggar banged on the car window, showing an oozing amputated arm. Claudette waved him off before the duchess could glimpse this hideous display. He thrust his swollen stump against the glass, then stepped away.

The duchess turned her gaze toward the armed soldiers guarding the entrance to the terminal and sighed.

WHATEVER CARLOS HAD done to obtain the tickets, he returned quickly. He handed Claudette the tickets and informed her that she would have to change trains in Toulouse and Limoges. It was unclear when or if there would be a train to Tours; the Maquis had bombed this main Loire Valley depot in November 1942 when the Nazis were about to cross the demarcation line. The Nazis had repaired only the tracks they needed to transport their troops southward, he explained.

"I wish you'd wait for the fall, when order will be restored to this mad world," the duchess said.

"More months away from my baby?" She let Carlos help her out of the car.

While he unstrapped her valise, Claudette stood by the open door and bent to kiss the duchess's gloved hand. "Thank you, madame, for your immense kindness and patronage." Mist clouded her vision as she inhaled for the last time the duchess's lavender scent and memorized the beautiful hazel eyes, the delicate nose, and the chiseled red lips of the noblewoman who had let her talent and creativity soar.

"God be with you and your child."

Claudette sniffled. "Please keep me in your prayers." Having the duchess pray to Jesus and Mary wouldn't be a betrayal of the Jewish God.

Carlos elbowed his way through the crowded terminal, guiding Claudette. Disheveled people were stretched out on benches, families were huddled on the floor among their belongings, and long lines led to the ticket windows. Beggars hounded people crossing the vast pavilion with its vaulted, decorated ceiling that had been built for glory, not for this horde of humanity with their rancid stink of sweat and piss. Carlos supported Claudette's arm with one hand and carried her valise in the other as they reached a gaping opening leading to train platforms.

"Be sure to tip the conductor so he'll help you with your luggage," Carlos said. "And get porters to carry it across platforms."

Claudette clutched her heavy satchel containing food for three days—tostadas wrapped in wax paper with cheese and salami and two apples—and hobbled along the length of the waiting train, bewilderment filling her. The valise that Carlos was hefting was heavy with folded fabrics; the duchess had suggested that Claudette invest in them because none were manufactured in France and she could sell them at profit. Without Carlos, Claudette wouldn't have known which platform was hers or what car to climb into. How would she manage two or three train changes?

This was for Benjamin, she told herself as Carlos pulled her up the steep metal steps into the car. He found her a window seat next to an old couple and hoisted her valise onto the shelf.

He touched the brim of his hat and departed. Her last protector was gone. Claudette clutched her wool shawl and two romance novels. She had no family, no friends. She was alone in the world. She had forsaken Christ and Mary. She couldn't imagine what she would find on her arrival at Valençay.

If only she knew where Solange lived with her husband. Had she passed the war safely? By now she must have a couple of children. How wonderful it would be to have their children grow up and play together.

THE PYRENEES WERE behind her. The Spanish border police hadn't asked for Claudette's ID; they had been happy to ease the pressure of too many European refugees in Spain. Claudette's body ached after a day and a night of bouncing in place. The roaring of the wheels underneath her rattled her bones and joints. The trips to the lavatory were treacherous; she had to balance over an opening above the speeding tracks, a hole eager to catch her foot. Afterward, she pushed her way down the cramped aisle, holding on to the backs of seats. There was no place to fall—the car was crammed with people and packages.

The only point of interest in the voyage was the passing landscape. On her flight south with the duchess, the driver had been trying to outrun the Nazis' southward advance, and Claudette had sat low in her seat. Now, heading back to her baby, she imagined Benjamin nestled on her lap as she narrated the sights: gorges dropping from the jutting cliffs, bridges and tunnels that must delight a little boy, and small fishing enclaves by riverbanks. How could she have explained the destruction the train was speeding by, the burned farmhouses, crumbled fortress walls, and bombed bridges?

As the train advanced north, the undulating green terrain became familiar. Claudette would have breathed easier except that she was about to reach Toulouse, where she would disembark, and get shoved into a sea of people in another huge terminal.

The conductor, whom she had tipped, came over. "I'll find a porter to help you locate your platform—if a train is scheduled. If not, well, you'll wait."

"How long?"

"Until the tracks are fixed or a route around it is available. It's a mess."

"Can you help me get my valise?"

"Which one is yours?"

She and the old couple rose while the train was still moving so Claudette could point it out. The conductor supported her arm while she looked up on the shelf at packages, boxes, and suitcases. None seemed to be hers.

"It must be stuck behind something." He rooted through the luggage and boxes, then searched to the right and left of her row.

Panic rose in her.

The train whistled. The syncopated chugging decelerated. The pounding of Claudette's heart accelerated. The train stopped.

"I'm sorry. I'll be back." The conductor rushed off to his duties.

She was left standing in the aisle, cold sweat erupting along her spine. A young man in a worn army jacket rose and checked the valises across the aisle and others lined up along the seats.

New passengers came aboard and tried to grab her empty seat. "Sorry to tell you this," the young man finally said, "but someone must have taken it."

Stolen. Her coat, her clothes, her collection of threads and patching yarns, Mémère's coat, her romance novels, the cloth she had planned to trade, and the two sweaters she had knit for Benjamin. All her worldly belongings were gone. How could she have been so stupid, so careless, as to let this happen? She recalled the refugees that had raided Mémère's yard—and the squatters. She should have known not to trust desperate people.

Whimpering, Claudette collected her satchel and wool shawl and let the man lower her onto the platform. A clock showed that it was ten thirty in the morning. The sky was clear blue, indifferent.

In the midst of people rushing in all directions, she leaned against the nearest column and the dam of tears burst. Her pent-up fear of this journey, this pilfering, the familiar tide of loss, indignities, and loneliness washed over her. Crying, she collapsed onto the ground, her cloth bag clutched against her chest.

No one stopped. No soft voice asked whether she needed help. In the aftermath of ruin, traumas, and chaos, what was a lone seamstress crying over the theft of her suitcase? She was mortified at herself, a human lump on the ground, like a beggar for whom she had never stopped to offer a charitable hand.

More trains passed in both directions. Her despair might make her miss her train home. Claudette scanned her surroundings and the platforms. The next train to Tours would be here, maybe now, maybe in five hours. She rooted through her satchel and took inventory of what she had left. The thief hadn't stolen her precious scissors and the thimble she had received from Isaac Baume. She had two handkerchiefs and a change of underthings, a hairbrush and strings to tie her braids. The last of her crochet needles was tucked into a roll of fine silk she had been crocheting into a lace collar she hoped to sell. Half a stale tostada was left.

The banknotes hidden in her brace still had some value, she hoped.

Most important, she had Benjamin waiting and Raphaël returning. She wiped her face and grabbed the column to pull herself up. No thief could steal the love in her heart.

Chapter Thirty-One

UZI YARDEN

Loire Valley, France
September 1946

THE FIRST NIGHT in Madame Therrien's attic room turned out to be comfortable. Uzi fell asleep under a soft down quilt while going over a list of French words. At three o'clock in the morning, he was awakened by the familiar call of the rooster. City people thought that a rooster welcomed dawn, but he crowed long before to wake up his flock so they could start foraging. The early bird got the worm.

And he must start working. The twins and, now, the boy with the star tattoo presented challenges that stumped him. He wished he could consult Hilda, although he already knew that for a little boy, clandestine entry into Eretz Israel was not an option.

Uzi opened his window onto a deep-blue sky strewn with unfamiliar constellations. After a pause for the rooster's aria, the night sounds picked up, a concert of grinding insects and restless birds. He inhaled the smell of cut hay and chimney smoke, comfort of the familiar in a world that was utterly foreign. He missed his girlfriend, Zehava, now alone in the room that the kibbutz had allocated to the two of them when they turned eighteen. There was never talk of marriage, a bourgeois custom. A rabbi-conducted ceremony was anathema to the secular kibbutz life. Religion was a relic of the Diaspora that the kibbutz movement had shed, along with the image of the cowering Jew. The ideology of building a new nation for the Jews, for healthy men and women working the land by the sweat of the brows, had replaced the blind following of archaic rituals.

Shortly after daybreak, Uzi was back at his table in the parlor, sipping a mug of tasty coffee with cream. Diagonally across the street, at the corner of the plaza, a grocer with an eye patch opened his store. He limped with what looked like a stick inside one pant leg. A boy of about fourteen carried out a box of leafy produce, went inside, and brought out a box of apples. Uzi observed him. He couldn't walk around assuming every dark, curly-haired boy he saw was Jewish.

But he could test a reaction.

He ambled over and stopped by a small pyramid of apples. The boy was trimming excess leaves off beets, and the tips of his fingers were bright red. *"Bonjour,"* Uzi said, and when the boy mumbled the same back, Uzi added in Yiddish in a low voice, *"Gut margn."*

The boy snapped his head toward him, then rushed inside.

Did he think that Uzi had spoken German? After France's tragic experience with the Nazis, Uzi must be careful. He would bide his time. Right now, he must check on the twins. The least he could do was take responsibility for the damage he had caused them.

On his way to the bus, he passed the salami shop, and the proprietor who had given him directions the day before waved him over. Inside, the man handed him a slice of salami with one hand and a note with the other.

"Une fille juive," he said. A Jewish girl.

Yes, word about Uzi's mission had burned through the village like fire in a field of dry thistles.

An hour later, Uzi reached the tavern. From a distance he could make out the small silhouettes of the twins seated on the doorstep, dressed in jackets. They had changed their minds and were waiting for him, he thought with glee.

His optimism evaporated when he neared and saw their sullen faces, their eyes swollen from crying. The tavern door was padlocked.

He crouched before the boys. "I'm sorry to bring you trouble," he said in Hebrew, hoping that his tone would carry his sincerity. *"On va en Israël,"* he tried, using his newly acquired French words. "Kibbutz?"

The boys shouted, *"Non! Kibbutz, non, Israël, non!"*

Uzi was at a loss for what to do next. Because of him, they were no longer welcomed in the only home they knew. He withdrew the slip of paper and pointed to the name Châteauroux. He could deposit them there with the Protestant minister. *"Israël, non,"* he said. At least not until Hilda or Pastor Gaspard convinced them that it was their best option.

They picked up a bundle each and began to walk. Their despondency gathered in their thin shoulders and their dragged feet. It pinched Uzi's heart. What had he done? How was it a rescue when there had been no threat of death?

As they cut through the field to the main road, Uzi spotted broken stakes of an old fence. He picked up one, grabbed both its ends, and held it straight in front of him as the boys had seen him do the day before. He pointed to more stakes on the ground, and after the boys had picked up one each, he demonstrated a *kapap* move.

Within seconds, they were into the game. He showed them how to protect their faces and another move to overcome an opponent's stick by twisting it and pushing him down with barely a touch.

"Kapap," he called out like a war cry.

"Kapap," they repeated. They faced each other and, shouting, showed off the new moves. They were back to being just children.

"I've messed up badly," he told Hilda when she opened the door.

"First let me speak with them." She rested soft eyes on the boys and addressed them in French. "Come in."

Twenty minutes later, she sent them out to the backyard to play. Uzi could see them through the window, practicing the *kapap* moves.

"Don't be so harsh on yourself." Hilda's thin face looked even pointier with her gray hair brushed into a neat bun. Her quick smile, though, was reassuring. "They had to be taken out of there. The future of the Jewish people hinges on reclaiming every last child."

"It's about these two boys," he replied, "not about world Jewry."

"What's the difference? Their parents were murdered because they were Jewish. Their wishes for how they wanted to raise their children were clear. The only question is what kind of Jewish environment is best for them." Her hand rested on an open page in her ledger. "Before deportation, the family was Orthodox, and the boys attended a yeshiva. Only when they went into hiding did they cut off their *peos*." She was referring to the long side curls. "We'll place them in an OSE Orthodox orphanage. Their schooling was interrupted, but they'll be back in a familiar cultural environment."

She brought Uzi a cup of coffee and a scone with berry marmalade. "Help me reconstruct their four transfers in case a relative comes searching."

When they were done, Uzi grabbed his backpack and got up. "Onward to the next kid."

He halted at the door. An open jeep came to a stop, and a soldier in an American army uniform jumped out. He lifted a box from the jeep's floor, smiled broadly, and headed toward him.

Puzzled, Uzi retreated back inside as Hilda stepped forward, a big smile on her face.

After Hilda and the American soldier had exchanged the double air kisses, she told Uzi in English, "Meet one of our angels, Robert Weintraub." Then she pointed to Uzi and told Weintraub, "And you meet one of our heroes, Uzi Yarden."

Her words gave Uzi no more clue about the identity of the soldier who excitedly pumped his hand. "From Ayelet HaShachar," Uzi said. "It's a kibbutz in the Galilee."

"From Philadelphia. It's a city in the USA."

They both laughed. They were about the same age. Robert's uniform was starched and pressed, and his shoes shone. Uzi was aware of his own limp cotton pants and frayed shirt, the hue indistinct after hundreds of washes in the kibbutz's laundry shed. His hair, streaked by the sun, hadn't been cut in weeks. He'd given up on the shoes, and his feet in the beaten leather sandals were unwashed.

"What's going on?" he asked Hilda in Yiddish.

"Jewish soldiers in the American army are helping us," she replied in English. "They are our liaisons with displaced-persons camps. They help with transportation and supply our network with food for our children."

"Speaking of food." Robert opened the box he'd brought and pulled out cans and packages. With a flair, he waved one dark brown packet labeled COFFEE, then withdrew a wrapped chocolate bar. *"Garçons,"* he called to Tobias and Elias, who were staring from the doorway. He broke off a piece for each, and when they put them in their mouths, their faces expanded with delight.

"This evening, Josh and I will bring provisions to Pastor Gaspard," Robert told Hilda. "Anything else?"

"Whatever medications you can spare."

Robert settled by the dining table on the chair that Uzi had left minutes earlier. The man didn't sit so much as recline, his legs spread a meter apart. Uzi tried to absorb this American insouciance, the body that was so comfortable in any space it inhabited. Kibbutz life was casual, but Uzi was witnessing Jewish spirit unrestricted by reproach or intimidation. Robert was a Jew who had claimed his legitimate place in the world.

While Hilda heated water for more coffee, Uzi bade them goodbye. The sense of relief he felt was boosted by the kinship he'd found with this American Jew. The tiny *yishuv* wasn't alone in its monumental task of saving Jewish orphans here, and his mission was not solely dependent on the ravaged, struggling Jewish-French community gathering up its shredded pieces. His Youth Aliyah network had the Robert Weintraubs of America as partners in salvaging what remained of Europe's Diaspora.

Uzi was waiting at the southeast end of the road, hoping to catch a ride with a farmer to Châtillon-sur-Indre, when Robert's open jeep pulled over.

"Hop right in," he told Uzi. "I have a couple of hours before chow."

Uzi was now familiar with the rutted road that the bus traveled for hours to get to Châtillon-sur-Indre. Robert flew over it, the jeep jerking from side to side over grooves, up and down into craters, each lurch and bounce threatening to throw out its driver and passenger.

Uzi remembered the note that the salami seller had given him. He signaled to Robert to stop. "Is this an address?"

Robert consulted his map—larger scale than Hilda's. "It's near your Châtillon-sur-Indre." He started the jeep again and veered onto a dirt path; twenty minutes later, he stopped.

On one side of the road was a murky lake with waterfowl and fishing dinghies; on the other side was an open meadow with white cows grazing.

Robert pointed to a distant farmhouse, then drove toward it slowly. "A military jeep still scares them. I give them time to see it's American."

The smell of damp earth and manure was pleasantly familiar to Uzi, as was the clucking of chickens. A woman emerged from the house before he reached the door; Robert stayed in the jeep.

"Bonjour," Uzi said. Then, failing to understand her response, he added, *"Enfant juif?"*

She led him right into the kitchen. A girl of about eleven was peeling potatoes.

Uzi crouched in front of her. She had large brown eyes. Her chestnut-colored hair was loosely gathered behind her neck, and unruly tendrils created a halo around her head. "Yiddish?" he asked.

The girl's eyes widened in fear. She glanced at the woman, then shook her head from side to side. Uzi got it. She knew what *Yiddish* meant. Her parents had come from Eastern Europe.

"Hab nisht mura. Don't be afraid," he continued. "I'm from the Holy Land."

The girl dropped the knife into the bowl. "Did my brother send you?" she asked excitedly.

Uzi had never seen such high hopes spark right in front of him. Unlike his experience with the twins, which still weighed on him, this girl presented a face for his mission. Her long eyelashes fringed eyes that looked at him with eagerness.

"Would you like to go there to find him?" he asked softly.

She rose and spoke to the woman. The woman smiled and hugged her.

"Take me to my brother," the girl said to Uzi.

"I don't know him, but in Eretz Israel, we'll do everything to find him. What's your name?"

"Charlotte."

"What would your brother call you?"

She hesitated. "Sarah."

The Frenchwoman seemed to have been waiting for the child to be reclaimed, yet two years after liberation, no one had shown up. She handed Uzi Sarah's ID, where her name was listed as Charlotte Blanchet. She wrapped a piece of cake in a cloth, kissed the child's head, and nudged her toward the door. She accepted Uzi's offer of two thousand francs for her expenses and kissed his hand in gratitude.

Uzi's heart was filled with pride as he led Sarah to Robert's jeep. One little girl would never again have to hide who she was.

Robert let Uzi off in the plaza of Châtillon-sur-Indre. Leaning on the door of the jeep, Uzi spoke to Sarah in Yiddish and Robert in broken French, explaining that Robert would drive her to Hilda and Pastor Gaspard.

"Other children are being cared for there until I come get you all. In about ten days, all of us together will depart for the Holy Land," Uzi told Sarah. He squeezed her hand. "We'll have a long journey ahead. I'm really glad that you'll be coming with me."

"Go find more children before anti-Zionist organizations do," Robert said to Uzi. "One day, when this is over, I'll visit you in Ayelet HaShachar."

"We'll be honored to welcome you."

"I heard the girls in Eretz Israel are beautiful."

"Maybe you'll find one to marry and settle there." Uzi picked up his backpack. "Thanks, and shalom."

"Here. For the kids you find." Robert handed him a packet of chocolate. He broke off a piece of another and handed it to Sarah in the back seat while he continued to speak to Uzi in English. "Let Hilda know if you need anything else. Our unit is under orders from high above to help."

"Thanks." At some point between his searches, he hoped to return to the little boy with the star tattoo, give him a piece of chocolate, and see the delight on that precious face.

Chapter Thirty-Two

SHARON

Cherbourg, France
December 1968

THE CHURCH BELLS are pealing. Families bundled in coats and scarves are making their way to Sunday services. At the entrance to Rachelle's building, several streets over from hers, Sharon pulls the bell string to her friend's apartment. She breathes in the buttery smell of the fresh croissants she just bought to go with the coffee they'll have before they head to the carnival.

Instead of coming down to unlock the building door, Rachelle opens her second-floor window. "I'm sick." She points at her throat. "Sorry to ruin your day. Take my car." She tosses Sharon the keys to the red Citroën parked across the street.

"Wait. I brought you a croissant."

"Can't eat." Her mane of dark curls is a mess, and her nose is red.

"Let me come up and make you tea."

Rachelle throws down the key for the main entrance. When Sharon enters the apartment, Rachelle trudges back to bed. Sharon finds aspirin and brings it to her friend with a glass of water, adjusts the radiator dial, brews tea, and places a plate with a croissant on Rachelle's night table. "Rest now. I will return later with a meal."

Sharon basks in the freedom of driving on the open road and takes the longer route west, hugging the shore. High waves roar and crash against a seawall in wild sprays that lash the car. In the fishing villages, lobster traps are stacked and tied down, wooden boats are moored and covered, and trawlers in the harbor struggle to break free of their anchors. Farther out, the sky and sea merge into a steel-colored blur that looks like the world before Creation. And this is not the worst of the weather. Twenty men, with Danny as their commander, will soon be testing Saar Seven in this ocean. Sharon turns the car to drive east, away from the shore hamlets, worry gnawing at her. Why has she agreed to bring herself so close to these life-and-death exigencies again?

In the Coutances village square, protected from the winds, the carnival is in full swing. People strut about in costumes, children ride the colorful carousel, and masked teens flirt. Under a makeshift canopy, a band fills the air with brassy music. Couples dance, wearing their coats. The cafés serve beer and wine, and, judging by their patrons' singing, they opened early.

Sharon sips her warm cider. The dancers form a snake line, and when they pass her, they sweep her along and weave through the square, grabbing more onlookers. Grateful for the distraction, she pounds her feet. The dancers continue through a second and third song. The merriment envelops her. For these transient moments, she is not merely a stranger.

She becomes aware of the young man behind her, his palms resting lightly on her waist as if he knows he needs to control his strength. When the music stops, the dancers turn to face the center, smile at one another, and clap.

"Are you alone here? Would you like to join my friends over there?" The young man waves in the direction of one of the cafés.

She notices his handsome face under the beret and registers that his accent is educated. Sexual warmth spreads through her, frightening her in its rawness. "Thank you. Maybe after I walk around for a while."

Humming the last tune the band played, she steps to the food market. It's one o'clock in the afternoon, and shoppers' baskets are full. Merchants begin to stack huge wheels of cheese in straw-lined wooden crates, untie necklaces of salami from makeshift rafters, and haul boxes of leftover produce into carts. She is tempted to return to the plaza and the young man. It might lead to the kind of wild sex she so misses—of limbs and hands and lips everywhere, of her passion unleashed with an attractive stranger.

To give herself time to decide, she asks a woman who is wrapping baked goods for crumbs and takes them over to the pigeons at the foot of a nearby monument. She watches them pecking. Life is so simple when the only concern is getting enough bread crumbs.

No need to complicate hers with an impulsive act she might regret. Or not. If the young man is in the café later, it will be her sign to go ahead.

The window frames of a café are painted burgundy. Below them, in planters, late-season purple cabbages are withering. Sharon enters and chooses a table overlooking the stalls. A musician approaches, pumping a French song on his accordion. Sharon examines it. She played the accordion for a year before settling on the flute. Hers had a piano-like keyboard on the right and eighty buttons on the left; this one has buttons on both sides. When she turns to fish for a coin in the satchel hanging on the back of her chair, she notices Félix Amiot watching her from a nearby table.

Since the dinner at his fort, she's seen him through her office window strolling in the shipyard with dignitaries in business suits or military uniforms. Catching her eye, he nods. She gives him a small smile.

He rises. "Mademoiselle Bloomenthal."

She's surprised that he remembers her face, let alone her name. "Monsieur Amiot," she responds. Does a woman get up for an older man? How old must he be for a young person to show respect without insulting him?

"Would you care to join me?" he asks. "We French appreciate good conversation around food."

She was planning to order potage Parmentier, the inexpensive potato-and-leek soup, for herself, and she brought Rachelle's tin container to get a heartier meal for her. "An honor. Thanks."

At his table, while she examines the extensive menu, Amiot asks, "Do you observe kosher?"

She shakes her head. "Our entire team here is secular. Orthodox do not serve in the army."

"I'm confused. All my Israeli friends here define themselves as Jewish, yet they do not adhere to any of the rituals."

"We care very much about our people's past, present, and future. We observe major holidays as our ethnic heritage rather than as religious practices. That's why we don't observe the stricter Orthodox Shabbat. Not even flipping a light switch because it's considered labor? That's an absurd, archaic leftover from when starting a fire required chopping wood. For us, the holidays are cultural." She adds, "I've never been to a synagogue."

"Nevertheless, all the galleys in your boats must keep kosher."

"Oh, that." She shrugs. "The minority Orthodox in our government keeps the entire country in its clutches through coalition agreements. Their religious dictates constrict the eighty-six percent of the population who are secular. The Orthodox are in charge of births, marriages, and deaths. They decide who is a Jew, which, by their definition, is only someone whose mother is Jewish. Even in Tel Aviv, a totally secular city, public transportation shuts down for Shabbat, and movie theaters are closed." She groans. "The entire IDF must keep kosher in case some soldiers are what we call Traditionals."

"What's that?"

"The Orthodox are fanatics who are exempt from serving in the IDF. By their choice, they do not integrate into our society, not school or work. The Traditionals adhere to a modern, modified version of observance—in private. They participate fully in Israeli society, including the army. They keep kosher at home and may pray a couple of times a day, but the men wear small knit yarmulkes, not the big black hard hats."

"Don't you pray?"

"I wouldn't know how." When there is a funeral for Alon, his mother will be forbidden by the Orthodox authorities to utter the religious text at his grave.

Amiot nods his head pensively. "Thanks for enlightening me."

Sharon giggles. "You must have noticed how our guys here binge on shrimp, mussels, and oysters. In Israel, a restaurant that serves that or pork is blacklisted by the rabbinical authority."

"Well, in that case," Amiot says, grinning, "may I suggest the fresh seafood today?"

Ten minutes later, a tower of layered beds of crushed ice with every sea creature ever caught by man materializes at the table. The mussels and oysters that she ate these past few months had no shells, antennas, claws, or hairy legs, unlike those in the collection she's staring at.

The waiter pours a tasting of white wine into Amiot's stemmed glass and, receiving his nod of approval, fills Sharon's glass halfway.

Amiot selects a shrimp. In one expert twist, he removes the legs, peels off the shell, and, holding it by the tail, presents it to Sharon. "Dip it in this sauce."

He continues to demonstrate how to crack or shuck each marine creature, explaining where it was fished and in what water depth. Sharon eats, amazed that this important man is expending so much energy to keep her engaged. Is it possible that, like her, in spite of being surrounded by people, he's lonely? Is his life tainted by the stigma—albeit well deserved—of having been a Nazi collaborator?

"Done any more drafting this week?" he asks.

His perfect memory no longer astonishes her. "An engineer friend taught me how to use instruments to create three-dimensional objects."

"Drawing each piece from all angles is critical before manufacturing it so no surprises pop up." Amiot tilts his head. "Any plans to use these skills in a future career?"

Maybe it's the wine in the middle of the day that releases her tongue. "I'm about to start studying advanced math for a higher-level test. Then I might apply to architecture school."

"Here in France?"

She can't even imagine how much a French university would cost. "The only place to study it in Israel is the Technion in Haifa."

"Oh, yes, your only port city. Unfortunately, my visit there was too short."

She takes another sip of the wine. How many former Nazi collaborators has her country welcomed? Since the early 1950s, when Holocaust survivors in Israel were offered remuneration from Germany for their suffering and losses, the question of a relationship with the former Nazi state was hotly debated in Israeli society—in living rooms and high-school classrooms, in the media and the Knesset. The arguments against accepting this blood money were offset by the urgent need for cash, crucial for the economy of the nascent country that had absorbed millions of newcomers.

"I'm sure that when all twelve Saars are finished," she says, avoiding the sensitive word *delivered*, "the military band will welcome you on your next visit."

He smiles. "How did you learn French so well? Your fellow Israelis are quite at a loss when it comes to our beautiful language."

"I went to a French high school in Tel Aviv," she replies, then adds the one thing she knows about Judith: "My mother had a great ear for languages."

"Had?"

"She died when I was six weeks old. In our War of Independence."

"I'm so sorry. How old was she?"

"Nineteen."

"Almost your age now," he states more than asks. Sharon is certain that he keeps a dossier on each member of the Israeli team.

"A Holocaust survivor," she says, then wonders whether he might take it as a reproach. Maybe, but why should she spare his feelings?

He shakes his head sadly. "The tragedy of your people goes on. And here we failed them so miserably. There's no atonement for what we did."

Is he implying that his own current extraordinary effort for Israel is his atonement? Sharon is angry at herself for having fallen for his charm, for having enjoyed this lunch and the wine that loosened her tongue. She opens her mouth to confront him about his Nazi-sympathizing past, to let him know that, unlike Danny, she understands Rachelle's disgust at what he did.

Her jaw clenches as she holds back the impulse to speak her mind. Israel needs the Saars—and this man's cooperation. As Rina said, exploiting these anti-Semites is the only moral way.

Only when Sharon drives away does she remember the handsome young stranger who might still be lingering in the plaza café.

Chapter Thirty-Three

CLAUDETTE

Loire Valley, France
Summer 1945

THE FARMER WHOM Claudette had paid to take her on the last leg of her journey entered the village of Valençay via the road farthest from the château. When she saw the destruction, her heart sank. She retained a flicker of hope until the cart stopped in front of what had once been Léonie's home.

She stared at the charred remains in despair. A smoky smell burned her lungs. Had Benjamin been in the house when it was set on fire? Léonie must have fled with all the children in time—but to where?

The house to the right had been burned down too, but the house on its left still stood. Its vegetable garden was covered with debris and weeds. Laundry on the clothesline flapped in the breeze.

"Madame, are you getting off?" the farmer asked.

"Please wait until I find out what happened here."

"I don't have all day."

"Please. I'll pay you." Her savings were dwindling fast. Merchants refused the Allied-issued paper francs, and some money had been taken out of circulation. Aluminum and zinc coins were worth more than ones of the same denominations made of iron. Her foreign currency was her best savings, but whom could she trust to tell her its worth? She would be robbed in any exchange; she had never learned to calculate beyond measuring a waistline or a hem. Nor had she anticipated the difficulty of arranging for transportation—or how much it would cost. Cars weren't an option due to a severe petrol shortage, and horses that hadn't died of starvation had been requisitioned by the Nazis.

The old woman who opened the door recognized Claudette and hugged her, sobbing. "They are all gone."

Claudette felt as if her heart would explode. "To where? Where's Léonie? And my baby? You remember him, right?" She pressed her palm against her chest. "What happened? Who burned the houses?"

Out on the road, the farmer clanked his bell.

"The Nazis found a Jewish family in the Doisneaus' house," the old woman cried. "They shot Léonie and took the couple away, but they burned the houses much later, when they retreated—"

Claudette cut her off. "Léonie is dead? For two and a half years now?" Who had been taking care of Benjamin? And the Parisian professors had turned out to be Jewish? Their daughter, Emmaline, had worn a cross on a thin gold chain. The professors must have glimpsed Benjamin's blue star, yet they had made no comment. "The children? Where are they?"

"Father Sauveterre took them."

Claudette sagged against the doorframe. At least they were alive; Benjamin hadn't been burned in a fire. By receiving the blessings of two religions, her baby might have doubled his chances of salvation!

"The girl too? Emmaline was about twelve." Wildly, Claudette hoped that the girl had protected him.

"She hid in our tree when the Boche arrested her parents."

But where had Benjamin been all that time? Where was he now?

Claudette kissed the neighbor's cheeks and rushed back to the cart. As the farmer helped her heave her body up, a sharp pain shot across her lower back. She groaned and bent over.

The farmer looked toward the setting sun. "I won't be out in the dark on a road overrun by robbers. Where shall I drop you off?"

The château's gates were surely locked at this hour. The neighbor had said that the priest had taken the children.

The area around the church was quiet, deserted, and mostly in ruins, like a ghost village. The damp charred-wood smell hung in the air. In one of the few houses still standing, a dim light glowed in a window. The barking of a dog broke the silence, triggering other dogs. Panting in panic, one hand pressed against her cramped back, Claudette lifted and dropped the iron knocker on the church's door.

An unfamiliar young man in a black cassock opened a wicket door set in one of the large wooden double doors. Claudette couldn't make herself coherent as she tried to explain through her crying that she was searching for her son. She knew she looked like a madwoman, bent over, her hair disheveled, and her clothes wrinkled from days of traveling.

"Come in, mademoiselle, and tell me everything," the young priest said.

"Where is Father Sauveterre?"

"Unfortunately, the Lord called him. I am Father Hugo. What's your name?"

"Claudette Pelletier." Breathing hard, she raised her eyes to him. His cheeks were round and his jaw still tight, but he was balding prematurely. "Do you have a record of the town children who were dispersed during the Nazi invasion?"

"We'll see what we can find."

She grabbed the doorframe, hoisted herself over the step, then followed him unsteadily through the church. She averted her eyes from the tortured Christ and His suffering mother. The holy space spun. She clutched the back of a bench as weakness overtook her. At her last stop, in her frenzied attempt to hire a cart, she had not wasted time hunting for food.

"Come this way." Father Hugo changed directions and entered a room with a long table in the center. Half a dozen people were eating. The homey smell of vegetable stew was in the air. "Have some nourishment first," he said.

"My baby—" she began, then swooned and dropped onto the edge of a bench. The knife-sharp pain in her back was like the agony of childbirth.

After a quick glance at her, the people at the table resumed eating. A kerchiefed woman smiled at Claudette and began to fill a bowl. Claudette dropped her head into her hands and reminded herself that she had to regain her strength for Benjamin.

The root vegetable soup with chunks of rabbit meat was the first warm meal she had had in three days. She soaked up the last of the broth with bread and sipped the red wine from the decanter passed around, hoping it would ease her back pain. When she pushed herself away from the table, she couldn't straighten. For the first time since receiving the Paris-made brace, she wished she had her old cane.

Father Hugo, supporting her by the arm, guided her to his office. "Here, sit comfortably and tell me what happened to your baby." He perched on top of his desk, facing her.

"He's gone." Claudette choked out the words. "Benjamin-Pierre Baume. He has a blue tattoo on the bottom of his right foot," she added.

"How were you two separated?"

She told him her saga.

Of course he had heard of the duchess. He raised his eyebrows. "She's not coming back? The livelihood of so many families depends on the château," he said. "I arrived here last fall, and I have been trying since then to take care of my flock. These people have gone through loss, fear, illnesses, starvation. Lifelong friendships and blood ties have been ruptured beyond repair by betrayals. Collaborators tried to get along with the Nazis, and collaborationists actually worked *for* the Nazis, spying and snitching on their own people. Who could anyone trust? Luckily, we have the Lord on whose everlasting care we can rely." Father Hugo walked to a filing cabinet and took out a folder. "Nine children were brought in on November twelfth, 1942." His finger ran down a list. "There's no Benjamin-Pierre Baume. There's a Benjamin-Pierre Pelletier. Like your name? Six weeks old."

"That's the one!"

"Born out of wedlock?"

Heat flooding her face, she nodded.

"Father Sauveterre's housekeeper cared for the children until June 1944."

Benjamin had been around one and a half then. Did that woman kiss his tears, hug him, tell him bedtime stories? "Then what?"

Father Hugo gave Claudette a strange look. "Don't you know what happened here?"

"The war intensified when the Allies invaded Normandy." Irrationally, from a distance, she had imagined that the battles raging all over the country were a matter for grown-ups only. "But where is Benjamin now?"

Father Hugo spoke slowly and loudly, as if she were hard of hearing. "German Waffen-SS troops plowed northwest, murdering our people. Have you heard of the massacres at Oradour-sur-Glane and Tulle? What about Maillé?"

"Of course." Claudette hung her head, recalling the horror of the reports she heard on her Barcelona landlady's radio. In retaliation for an attack on German soldiers and as a warning to the Maquis fighters against further acts of resistance, hundreds of innocent people had been gathered in village squares and executed in cold blood. "Those villages were far from here," she said meekly. "Where is my son now?"

"Far from here? The Nazis were advancing toward this region! People were fleeing, not knowing which direction was safest. I was still serving in Amboise, and the mayhem there was the same. In the midst of that, Father Sauveterre was on his deathbed. His housekeeper, with no one to help, had to protect not just one orphaned child but nine."

"Benjamin wasn't an orphan!" Claudette cried.

"Of course not. I can see that," Father Hugo said softly. He consulted the pages in the folder, then looked up at her. "You mentioned a tattoo?"

She lowered her gaze. "Yes," she mumbled.

"Of a Jewish star?" he asked, his voice low, compassionate.

"His father is Jewish." She sniffled. "I expect him to come back."

"No Jew has returned," Father Hugo whispered. "They were all, we presume, killed."

Not Raphaël. He knew how to protect himself. "So where is my Benjamin?"

Father Hugo leafed through the folder again. "Of the nine children, the two oldest were placed on farms. Four, including one of your friend Léonie Doisneau's children, were sent to a state orphanage. The three youngest were adopted."

"Adopted? By whom? Who gave permission when everyone knew I was alive?"

He pulled out a sheet of paper. "Here's a letter written by Monsieur Vincent Voclain—I assume you know him from Château de Valençay—ending his guardianship. That was required in order to release a child for adoption."

Monsieur Vincent? "He promised me—" Claudette broke into a deep sob.

Father Hugo let her cry for a while before he said, "Stay here tonight. Rest from your travels. For now, let's go to the sanctuary and pray for guidance."

In her grief, she was too broken to resist the comfort of Jesus and Mary. She asked for forgiveness for having forsaken them. "I hope that my suffering is not Your reprisal," she added. "Will You please, in all Your benevolence, help me find Benjamin?"

Chapter Thirty-Four

UZI YARDEN

Loire Valley, France
September 1946

IN FRONT OF a store, Uzi noticed a used bicycle with a price tag. Riding a bike would be more dependable and faster than taking a bus or hitchhiking.

He bought it and rode to the town hall, a low, one-story stone house with rosebushes along its front. A pleasant woman his age with a flowery bow holding back blond curls was just unlocking the door. She welcomed him and sat down at her typewriter, and he stepped over to the map on the wall.

Uzi was absorbed in copying a section of the map when he noticed that the typing had stopped. Glancing back, he saw the woman studying him. A sense of unease crept over him. Was she suspicious of him? Not long ago, strangers had terrorized this village. She must think that this stranger, copying the map, was up to no good.

But catching his eye, she smiled broadly, as if she knew him. She said something, and when he replied, *"Je ne parle pas français,"* she slid a finger beneath her dress's neckline and stroked herself under the fabric.

Heat flooded Uzi's face. Zehava had often teased him that his strong cheekbones and square jaw hinted at a Slavic ancestry that had been injected into the genes of Ashkenazi Jews. He exhaled and returned to his task but could sense the woman's eyes examining his back and shoulders. He forced himself to finish locating the farms and noted the number of kilometers between points.

"Merci." He started toward the door. *"Bonjour."*

She came around her desk to walk him out. She reeked of flowery perfume. *"A bientôt?"* She raised her face as if for that double air kiss. He shook her hand instead and rushed out.

TODAY HE WAS chasing a pair of siblings who had been moved: Martha, now twelve, and her brother, Manuel, now eight. Uzi hoped this search wouldn't turn out to be futile.

"I'm worried about them," Hilda had said when she gave him the details. "We can't assume that all our hidden children are in loving environments. Too many are being exploited as free labor. They receive no schooling or medical care if they are sick or injured."

At the start of the war, Hilda had deposited this pair of siblings with two widows, Madame Fournier and her sister, then sent them seven hundred francs a month for their care. However, when the Nazis invaded the free zone, the underground moved the children to a safer home. Since then—almost four years ago—no one had contacted Hilda for the monthly maintenance.

Madame Fournier's home was two hours away by bicycle. If this search failed, Uzi thought, at least it took him through breathtaking countryside. Narrow roads were bordered by overgrown hedges as high as city walls, alternating with muddy paths that cut through plowed fields and forests of birch, maple, and oak. Uzi stopped to pluck a cluster of barberries and savored their tartness. Why hadn't God led the Israelites another forty years and brought them to this fertile part of the world?

Uzi got back on a road that wound through vineyards stretching to the horizon and was awed when a fairy-tale castle popped into view, its pitched roofs made of solid gray slate. "Land of a Thousand Châteaux," Pastor Gaspard had said. Uzi pedaled along the wide moat hugging ancient, chiseled rocks and eyed the chained drawbridge over water on which water lilies floated. In previous centuries, the château had withstood armies' attacks from the ground. This century, it was only by chance that it had been spared attacks from the air.

What mysteries were hidden in the turrets and towers? Were there Jewish children forced to labor in fields and orchards, underfed? Were they housed in drafty barns?

He reached Martha and Manuel in the nick of time. Apparently, a year after the underground moved them, the children landed again with the aging Madame Fournier and her sick sister. Martha was now taking care of the women and her brother, cleaning and cooking. Madame Fournier had no recollection of how the children had first arrived, but she and her sister were about to move into her son's home, and he planned to deposit the children in a state orphanage.

The old women released the children to Uzi's care so quickly that he felt bad for the kids, yanked yet again from the life they knew. Madame Fournier summoned a neighbor with a truck, said a tearful goodbye, and coaxed the children gently onto the truck bed. Uzi climbed in too, hauled in his bike, and settled with his back against freshly hewn lumber. He held the weeping Manuel close. "You'll have a good life," he said in Yiddish to Martha, who sat at a distance. He couldn't express how exalted he felt about rescuing her and her brother from the horrors of a state orphanage. "You'll have a home and school and friends."

She nodded sadly, then dropped her head between her knees.

As the truck bounced on the rutted road, Uzi sang Manuel a Yiddish lullaby that his own grandmother used to sing to him. Perhaps something in the boy's memory would connect to it. From the slight tilt of Martha's hidden face, Uzi suspected that she recognized the song. After a while, she looked up. Uzi gestured to her, and she edged closer, her hunger for affection clearly outweighing her reserve. He covered the three of them with a rough wool blanket against the cold wind, and the two children fell asleep resting in the crooks of his arms.

The rolling hills Uzi gazed at were shrouded in the mist of the descending darkness. How had meeting Tobias and Elias, Sarah, and now Martha and Manuel changed him? he mused. He had begun his mission bewildered by logistics. Now his heartstrings were interlaced with the past and future of his charges. He was committed to healing these uprooted, lost little souls.

The thought brought him back to the little boy whose laughter rang in his ears even now over the chugging of the truck's wheels. How had he gotten his tattoo? Uzi had never heard of such a practice; to his knowledge, tattooing was strictly prohibited in Judaism. However, it was wartime, so perhaps the boy's parents had done the only thing available to them while in hiding. They'd wanted to be able to identify their boy upon their return. Unfortunately, two years after liberation, they weren't back. Whoever that drunkard the boy lived with was, he wasn't the biological father.

Uzi had told Hilda about the boy, and as expected, her response was emphatic: their organization had neither the facilities nor the staff for such a young child. She would inform OSE, she said. They would check the legal status of his adoption and explore the possibility of a still-living relative. "You're not the first agent to fall in love with a child," Hilda said. "You also must erect an emotional fence, like a doctor whose patient's case is outside his medical knowledge."

Except that Uzi couldn't forget the feel of that boy's little needy arms around his neck. How could he walk away and leave him in that neglected state? How could he subject the boy to the lengthy bureaucracy of OSE? It would be many months before his status was clarified, months during which the boy would be as lonely and unloved as he was now.

It was dark when the truck pulled up in front of Pastor Gaspard's church. Uzi joined the children for a late supper of soup and bread. As the minister's wife prepared to lead them to the dorm house, Uzi asked, "May I help tuck them into bed? It's their first night with strangers." When he was little, the rustling leaves of the eucalyptus tree, the screeching of cats in heat, and the shadows cast on the wall by the night guard's jittering flashlight made him quake in fear and wet his bed. What nightmares stalked these children who had already met the monsters that other children only imagined?

HE WOKE UP in the morning feeling energized. A storm had seized the world overnight, and it had left a peculiar silence of damp air so charged that it kept even the birds and insects quiet. Like after lovemaking, Uzi thought, wishing he could hold Zehava now and share his extraordinary stories with her.

In good spirits, he went to the home the boy shared with the drunkard. The kitchen was quiet, cold, and dark. He placed wood and newspapers in the stove and lit a fire. While the surface heated, he scrubbed a pot, poured in fresh milk from Madame Therrien's kitchen, and added semolina porridge he'd bought. Then he walked to the front room in search of the boy.

He found him curled up in the lap of the man, both asleep. Snoring loudly, his arms hanging at his sides, dressed in his shabby clothes, the man seemed inebriated. Uzi's heart contracted at the boy's pitiful need to draw security from an indifferent adult, passing the night with him without even a blanket covering them from the chill.

"*Boker tov.*" Uzi stroked the soft cheek. Good morning. "I have breakfast ready for you," he added in Hebrew.

The boy opened his eyes, and at the sight of Uzi, he smiled and stretched. "Maman?" he asked, his voice hopeful.

"It's me."

The man stirred; his snoring stopped. He didn't wake up as Uzi scooped up the boy in his arms and carried him outside to relieve himself. Then he led him back to the kitchen.

"Maman?" The boy scrambled up the stairs. His voice turned frantic. "Maman?" Upstairs, he broke down crying. "Maman!"

Uzi crouched and held him tight. "She's in heaven," he whispered, rocking him, helpless at the sight of such grief. "But she loves you and watches over you."

The strange language halted the boy's crying. He stared at Uzi with his beautiful, big eyes but didn't laugh as he had done a couple of days earlier.

"*Manger?*" Uzi asked in French. Eat? He carried him back downstairs and wiped the boy's face and hands with a damp towel. "*Dai'sa,*" he said. Porridge. He sprinkled brown sugar on it and brought a spoonful to the boy's mouth.

The boy smacked his lips at the unfamiliar taste, then opened his mouth for more. After two more spoonfuls, Uzi handed him the utensil to feed himself and guided the little hand to demonstrate how to scoop from the top.

"*Nom?*" Uzi asked. "*Je m'appelle Uzi.*"

"Daniel," the boy replied.

"Well, Daniel, I'm sure you know this song." Uzi broke into the Hebrew version of "Frère Jacques." Daniel giggled at the funny words and joined in French. Uzi loved his bell-like voice.

Breakfast over, he planted a goodbye kiss on top of the boy's matted hair. Tonight, he would give him a proper bath at Madame Therrien's. Afterward, Uzi would take his meager belongings and depart this village. There was nothing more he could do for him.

During his travels that day, Uzi decided, he would look for a toy seller. He pictured the delight on Daniel's face when he gave him a train. Uzi would teach him the Hebrew word for it, *rake'vet,* and sing him the train song. The onomatopoeic chugging of wheels and piercing whistle would be understood in any language.

Before mounting his bike, Uzi stopped outside the grocery store and picked up a rock-hard late-season pear. The paucity of good fresh produce in such a fertile land irked him.

"*Gut margn,*" he said quietly when the teenager approached.

"*Gut margn,*" the boy responded. His body was like a coiled spring. His shoulders, torso, then one knee jerked.

Their eyes met in a shared recognition. "I'm from Eretz Israel, from a kibbutz," Uzi said in Yiddish, speaking low. "Do you know what a kibbutz is?"

The boy shrugged, busying himself lining up a row of white asparagus stalks.

"It's a large group living together, many families creating one family where everyone is equal. We have orange groves and fields of vegetables, and we raise herds of sheep and cows. But we are building something bigger." Uzi paused, certain that the boy understood. "A nation. Together we are stronger than any of us alone. We are building a country for the Jews where we hold ourselves proud, never having to hide, and we're willing to fight for it."

The boy's eyes brightened with interest. "Do you fight with guns?"

"Only if we must. My name is Uzi Yarden. What's yours?"

"Arthur Durand."

"When do you finish working today? We can talk then."

"Seven o'clock. I live here. I sleep in the attic."

Just then, a woman approached. She was in her forties and wore an elegant hat and what Uzi could tell was a city dress—so different from the simple printed cotton shifts that the village women wore under their aprons. She didn't carry a basket; she was neither delivering produce nor shopping. Her differences put Uzi on alert.

"*Gut margn,*" she said. "Who exactly are you?"

"Uzi Yarden. And you?"

"I am Ruth Morgenstern. I am from the Jewish Organization for the Protection of Children."

"Nice to meet you. I hear that OSE has been doing an incredible job."

"I'd like to inform you that if you want to recruit Arthur for your Zionist project, you must go through us."

So, word about him had spread even further. Uzi was annoyed by the woman's tone but conceded that if OSE had placed Arthur here,

Ruth Morgenstern's request was reasonable. She must have a dossier on his family and his health history. Uzi tore half a page from his notebook and handed it to her with a pencil. "Ruth—"

"Mrs. Morgenstern," she corrected.

"Mrs. Morgenstern, please write down how we may contact you. After I speak with Arthur, of course."

The boy stopped pretending to arrange vegetables. His eyes were fixed on Uzi, but his arm jerked, then a knee shook, as if his body were inhabited by mice. At least someone was checking on him in this godforsaken enclave, Uzi thought. This nervous boy wasn't completely abandoned.

"What I mean is that we have a department that handles children heading to Palestine," Ruth said. "No need to duplicate efforts."

"You're right that there's no need to duplicate efforts—if indeed that's what we're doing." Uzi leveled his gaze at her. "The question is, when will a kid such as Arthur actually travel there?" Both of them knew the British were blocking entry of Holocaust survivors.

"Our Tel Aviv office receives the entry certificates to Palestine and distributes them among *legitimate* organizations," she replied.

The place she called Palestine, as the British did, was the country the *yishuv* and Diaspora Jews hoping to live there referred to as Eretz Israel. Her use of the British name told Uzi that she wasn't buying into the Zionist nation-building dream of Jewish sovereignty in the Holy Land.

"First, we've waited two thousand years to return to our homeland. We owe it to these children to settle them with no further delays." Piqued by her insinuation, he added, "Second, for the record, Youth Aliyah is a legitimate organization headed by the distinguished Henrietta Szold. The Haganah's involvement in this project has the support of most Israelis. It's the bureaucracy—of both the British rulers and organizations like yours—that the Youth Aliyah is circumventing."

"Arthur!" someone called from inside the store.

"We won't put our children in danger." The woman laid a gentle hand on Arthur's shoulder and said to him, "If what you want is to go to Palestine, we'll transfer you to our institution in Toulouse. You'll even study Hebrew there."

Arthur's eyes darted between Ruth Morgenstern and Uzi. Uzi hated the fact that the boy was a witness to the confrontation, especially one this futile. Hilda would not engage in a conflict with OSE over one child who was already being supervised. Yet instead of living in Israel and learning Hebrew, Arthur would wait in France for months on end to restart his interrupted life. What unending anxiety must fill the soul of a boy like this, standing between two adults representing two opposing worldviews.

"Arthur!" The grocer leaned against the doorway.

"He's yours," Uzi said to Ruth Morgenstern. He tipped his head in respect to the grocer and pulled Arthur to the side. He reached into his backpack and took out the mezuzah he'd found. "You're in good hands, young man. To show my faith that you will have a home in the Holy Land, here is something that one day you'll place on the threshold of your home." He touched Arthur's arm. "Shalom."

He mounted his bike and pedaled away, nagged by another thought: he'd had an opportunity to lead Ruth Morgenstern to the drunkard's house and show her Daniel's tattoo. This boy had been born to Jewish parents, clearly, not to the people in whose house he now lived. With the adoptive or foster mother dead, let OSE launch the bureaucratic investigation so this beautiful, sunny boy would be adopted by a family who deserved him.

Why hadn't he? Because, Uzi answered himself, he didn't want the boy removed before he presented him with that wood-carved train and sang him the *rake'vet* song. Because lingering for months before being adopted by a family in England or the United States wasn't what he wanted for Daniel.

Chapter Thirty-Five

UZI YARDEN

Loire Valley, France
September 1946

UZI FINISHED BATHING Daniel in Madame Therrien's tub and dressed him in the last of his clean clothes. He crouched, and Daniel jumped on his back for a ride to his house. Laughing, Daniel kicked at Uzi's sides with his bare feet, calling out, *"Au galop! Au galop!"* Uzi broke into a short run.

The drunkard was in the kitchen, noisily rooting through the cabinets. When Uzi entered and slid Daniel off his back, the man looked surprised. Either he didn't recognize Uzi or he hadn't noticed that the boy was missing.

"I'll tuck you into bed," Uzi told Daniel. Ignoring the man, he walked upstairs. In the trunk he found a clean sheet and replaced the soiled one. He collected all of Daniel's dirty clothes and placed them in an equally filthy pillowcase. Daniel climbed into bed. Uzi regretted that today hadn't been a market day. In his travels through the countryside—a fruitless chase after children whose tracks had evaporated—he had found no toy maker.

Suddenly, Daniel jumped up from under the cover and hugged Uzi's neck. Uzi held him, feeling the warmth of the thin body, smelling the fresh scent of Madame Therrien's industrial soap powder. The prospect of never seeing the boy again saddened him, as did his grave concern about this child's well-being.

At the sound of heavy footsteps coming up, Uzi laid the boy back down and jiggled the coins in his pocket.

From his cot, Daniel cried, *"Je veux Maman!"*

"Maman est morte." The man's tone was gruff. Daniel began to bawl.

Uzi's heart contracted. *"Bon enfant,"* he said to the man and handed him some coins. The man mumbled something and walked out. Uzi was certain that he was heading to the tavern around the corner.

The cry that tore out of Daniel took over the whole of his little being, the loss greater than his body could contain. *"Maman, Maman!"*

Uzi dropped onto the bare wood-plank floor and took him in his arms. Holding him tight, he rocked him and sang a Hebrew lullaby, then another, until the crying turned into hiccups. Exhausted, Daniel finally fell asleep.

Uzi lowered him into his cot, then kissed the crown of his head, the light brown hair now clean and dry. "Shalom," he whispered, his heart filled with regret.

He returned to Madame Therrien's and handed her Daniel's soiled clothes along with a ten-franc note. He took out his ration card with another bill. "Daniel. *Manger.*" She smiled her understanding. Why hadn't this kind, childless widow taken the boy in? Uzi turned up his palms in a gesture of inquiring. "Daniel. *Maman?*"

"Amour. Nazi." Madame Therrien grabbed her own neck and pulled up as if hanging.

She had to repeat the mime before Uzi comprehended. Daniel's adoptive mother had had an affair with a German and was hanged for it. By whom? Did the stigma of her liaison taint the little boy too? Or was Daniel shunned because of his Jewish star?

Uzi was in his room, studying his growing stack of French flash cards in the wan light of a bare bulb, when Madame Therrien knocked on his door. She signaled for him to come downstairs.

There, in the parlor, stood Arthur. He shifted his weight from one foot to the other, then an arm jerked. "You didn't come as you said you would." The boy's tone was belligerent, probably to cover his disappointment.

"So sorry. I thought it was settled with the lady from OSE," Uzi replied. "Hasn't she been taking care of you? Is she the one who found you your job?"

Arthur shrugged as if the answers were irrelevant.

"How old are you?"

"I'll be fifteen in December."

Fourteen, then, the age of Uzi's youngest brother. "Why aren't you in school?"

"I didn't like it."

"What exactly didn't you like?"

Arthur didn't reply. His body didn't stop twitching.

"You're here to talk to me," Uzi said in a soft tone. "Please tell me what happened there."

"I don't have a head for books," Arthur mumbled. "I like doing things with my hands. They were always after me to sit on my ass and study—math, reading, history, geography, prayers."

"Okay. I get it. Would you care for some tea?"

Arthur nodded.

After Madame Therrien brought two chamomile teas, Uzi said to Arthur, "If you'd like, I can tell you more about Eretz Israel, but please understand that I can't take you with me. OSE will make the arrangements for your emigration."

"In Eretz Israel, will I learn to fight with a gun?"

"Why do you want a gun?"

"To kill Nazis."

What rage roiled in his rib cage to create these nervous tics? Uzi rested his arm on Arthur's, guessing that the boy craved human touch. "Fortunately, there are no Nazis in Eretz Israel. We have other enemies. However, our aim is not to fight them but to find ways to live peacefully with them."

For the next forty-five minutes, they drank tea and ate bread and cheese, and Uzi spoke about the country's challenges and miracles. Arthur's body calmed as he listened. He could concentrate,

Uzi thought. Life in a kibbutz, an industrious life of physical work, would suit him. How unfair it was for Arthur to waste months waiting for an indifferent world to act. How unfair that after six million Jews had been killed, the world held the survivors in its clutches so those who had barely made it out alive still had to seek its approval to rehabilitate themselves.

After Arthur departed, Madame Therrien showed Uzi a small item he'd left on the table: the mezuzah.

As Uzi scooped it up, he understood. The boy didn't need more promises or dreams.

Chapter Thirty-Six

CLAUDETTE

Château de Valençay, France
Summer 1945

REACHING THE CHÂTEAU in the midst of a storm, Claudette was shocked to discover that the expansive area outside the front gate was filled with wooden huts. The former grassy plaza, once ringed by the stately orangery, immaculate horse barns, and elegant sentry lodging, looked like a Barcelona slum. As Father Hugo drove his horse-drawn covered cart through the wrought-iron gates, Claudette saw through the sheets of rain that even inside the château's grounds, the formerly beautiful gardens were crisscrossed with laundry lines.

In his office, Monsieur Vincent told Claudette, "I protected everything I could. I had sworn loyalty to the late duke and to his ancestors' legacy, and I would have given my life to protect the estate and its assets." He wheezed when he gulped air. "I'm proud that all the treasures we hid are intact! They are being transferred to the conservancy of the state, which will preserve their history."

"I'm talking about my baby whom you promised to—"

He cut her off. "The Boche confiscated the herds and the horses. Without laborers, I couldn't cultivate the vineyards, orchards, and fields, so I let the women and children harvest whatever grew wild. Yet they still went hungry. We were eating rutabaga—animal feed!" He coughed.

"But my baby!" Claudette yelled, a monumental transgression. She would not be intimidated; she was a mother wild with grief. A lioness searching for her cub. "How could you? You knew that I was with the duchess! You knew that I would come back for him."

"You have no idea what was going on here! The villagers fled to the château grounds so I could negotiate for their safety in supposedly German territory. Who could care for an infant?"

"Who took him? Where is he?" she cried.

Monsieur Vincent's tone was pleading: "It was complete chaos. Léonie had been killed. Father Sauveterre was dying. Our remaining men had been sent into slavery in Germany. Hunger—do you know what that is like? That's what we had here. You were living in comfort in Spain. Here, the Boche soldiers settled in our homes, stealing everything—a piece of rope, a single parsnip. We'd hardly reconciled ourselves to their presence when a murderous regiment advanced toward us, scorching the earth and massacring everyone in every village along the way. What was anyone supposed to do with your *bastard* baby?" He spat out the word. "Luckily, some childless couple took him."

"Who?"

"I don't know. We were just grateful someone did, given what you'd done to him."

"What did I do to him?"

"A tattoo of a Jewish star? Were you mad?"

"It was supposed to be tiny." She swallowed. "Who got him? Where did Benjamin go?"

"Sorry. I wasn't in the church that day. I was here, dealing with more than enough for one person." Monsieur Vincent straightened in his chair. "I managed to convince the general of the Waffen-SS to keep his soldiers from entering the château grounds because it belonged to a German duke. I saved the treasures and I saved the townspeople sheltering here." He pulled out a handkerchief and coughed into it.

"Who in the village facilitated the adoptions?" Claudette asked.

"The midwife." Monsieur Vincent stopped and gazed at Claudette as if a thought had just occurred to him. "Was it she who tattooed his foot?"

Claudette nodded. A muscle in her back spasmed.

"Now I get it. I knew you weren't that stupid. It's proof that Madame Duchamp was losing her mind even before she stopped making sense altogether. The last time she assisted a woman in labor, she walked out in the middle of the delivery, forgetting why she was there. Luckily, a neighbor saw her wandering in the street, heard the birthing mother's screams, and rushed inside. She saved the young woman's life."

"Where is Madame Duchamp now?"

"Maybe in an asylum, although I can't imagine who operates one. Even if she's alive, no one will get anything out of her."

Claudette's entire being collapsed. She gasped for air. Benjamin was lost to her. How could she accept that he was gone forever?

Outside, heavy clouds went on emptying their gray, low-hanging bellies.

"Claudette, at least he's alive, something I can't say to many mothers. I'm sure that whoever adopted your son is giving him a good home. It was in the middle of the war, so they must have been rich people of influence who could provide him with everything or they wouldn't have taken him."

Her loud sobs almost drowned out his words.

"I'm so sorry." Monsieur Vincent went out and returned with a glass of tea. "Is there anything I can do for you?"

She managed to speak through her tears. "My baby's father is supposed to come looking for me. Has anyone asked?"

He shook his head.

"He'll come. His name is Raphaël Baume. His father is Isaac Baume. He may come too."

"How did you get yourself involved with them?"

"Whatever you think of Jews, these men are very decent people." She tried to control her trembling voice. "When they come, please let them know where I am."

"And where is that?"

She had no home. No one to turn to. "I'll let you know." She wiped her face with her sleeve. "My suitcase was stolen. There might still be trunks of old clothes in the upstairs chambers. May I look so I can fashion myself something?"

He exhaled. "You helped store centuries' worth of uniforms and evening gowns of the duke's ancestors, so you know they must be preserved. But you may check for items that can't be salvaged from dampness or moth."

She would visit her chamber, where Raphaël had made love to her and where she had felt the certitude of being a mother to Benjamin even as he was being nursed elsewhere by Léonie.

Lightning slashed the sky, followed by a roar of thunder. Claudette had imagined the worst-case scenario of Benjamin not recognizing her, hiding behind Léonie's skirts, believing that his nursemaid was his mother. Never had she envisioned this nightmare.

Monsieur Vincent lifted the letter she had delivered. "The duchess asked that I provide you with lodging. The château is no longer hers to make requests, but out of loyalty to the family, I can permit you to room with some of the staff on the grounds." He added, "Or you'll find Fabienne Couture accommodating. She lost both her sons."

Was Claudette supposed to thank him? She wouldn't. Not when Benjamin was gone.

Chapter Thirty-Seven

SHARON

Cherbourg, France
December 1968

HANUKKAH WILL BEGIN in a couple of weeks, and the eighth night of candle-lighting will be the day before Christmas Eve. A few days earlier, when the tide is high in these Normandy waters, Saar Seven will launch. It will be the first time Sharon sees a boat glide out of the hangar on massive tracks and hit the freezing ocean water with a tumultuous splash.

She is organizing the event that will take place in the afternoon and will be attended by local dignitaries. She's procured paper napkins printed with the Israeli navy's insignia from a supplier in Caen and placed an order with Café Parisien to serve food and alcohol in the hangar following the ceremony.

The four wives of the officers in the Israeli mission are planning the Hanukkah party. Dr. Hubert Vaiseman, the dentist who heads the town's Jewish community, has secured the use of the church as a quasi-synagogue for families like Rachelle's, Jews who put down roots here when they couldn't afford to sail to America.

The Christmas lights that already glitter in the streets and shops add to the exhilaration of the upcoming festivities, and the excitement is palpable among the seamen at evening café gatherings. The tradition of Hanukkah that commemorates the rededication of the Temple in Jerusalem after the Romans had desecrated it is deeply anchored in Israel's secular society. Like the Rosh Hashanah celebration on Sharon's arrival did, the upcoming Festival of Lights infuses her with a sense of shared culture. The wives' planning committee gives recipes to local bakeries for batches of latkes—fried grated-potato pancakes—and *sufganiyot*, jam-filled doughnuts sprinkled with confectioners' sugar. A chocolatier is at work creating Bible-themed foil-wrapped chocolate coins for the children. Cases of champagne and a matching number of bottles of orange juice, which most of the Israeli servicemen prefer, are ordered.

Even the recalcitrant Pazit has volunteered to instruct the fifteen local Jewish children on how to cut and glue colorful paper into the symbols of the holiday—menorahs, oil jars, candles, and dreidels.

Even after Saar Seven's launch, Sharon hears no mention of the obvious fact that the boat's freedom to leave and sail to Israel will be the second test of de Gaulle's resolve to enforce the embargo. The challenge weighs heavily like the winter clouds auguring rain while the bustle of Hannukah preparations continues on the ground below.

When Sharon has lunch at Rachelle's grandmother's apartment, the old woman takes her hand and, voice trembling with emotion, says, "We were proud of Israel before, but meeting these young men—these strong Jewish servicemen in our community—our hearts are overflowing with pride. If only we had had Israel then—"

Then means "the Holocaust." Sharon imagines the hopelessness and desperation this woman must have endured twenty-five years earlier. How amazing it is that the Israeli navy's mission has revived this congregation and that Sharon, herself a daughter of a hunted Frenchwoman, is part of this team.

"Now will you find my granddaughter a nice Israeli husband?" the old woman adds.

Rachelle laughs, but Sharon has someone in mind. Later, she tells Rachelle about her new roommate Ehud, a reserve officer who's just arrived for a month.

"Unmarried?" Rachelle asks.

Sharon giggles. "Single. An adorable hydroponic desert farmer with degrees in philosophy and theater."

"Checks off everything on my wish list!"

That night Sharon brings her flute to the church and joins Naomi at the piano. A seaman has a guitar, and Kadmon, with his baritone voice, is the lead singer of the string of Hanukkah songs. Pazit is given a tambourine and a triangle to complete this odd musical ensemble.

This is the first time Sharon has played her instrument since *it* happened. How mistaken her initial reluctance to work for the navy was. It has offered her such a sense of camaraderie and personal accomplishment, she thinks as the familiar Jewish melodies fill the church.

The next afternoon, she joins the line of a dozen seamen at the post office and waits to place an international call to Savta. It takes over an hour before the operator summons her to the booth.

"I miss you so much!" she tells Savta, her heart billowing at hearing the voice that has soothed her for her entire life. She is unsure whether the accompanying crackling emanates from the cables stretching under the sea for six thousand kilometers or from Savta's excitement.

"Yes, I received the suitcase with my flute and the winter clothes," Sharon yells into the mouthpiece. "Thank you so much for the new sweater! It's gorgeous. And the business suit is perfect for this weather. My new winter coat picks up the color in the plaid." She loves the mundane conversation. "Most important, Savta, tell me: How are you feeling?"

"No point in complaining about age." Savta reports that she plays cards a few afternoons a week, and afterward there's always someone to go to a café or a movie with. The entire family comes for Friday-night dinner, which keeps her busy shopping and cooking starting on Wednesday. She is free of labor on Saturdays, when she visits one of her children's homes for the cholent lunch.

Sharon thinks of Savta's six-bedroom apartment, mostly empty now, once home to a bustling family, often with rambunctious children, including herself. Savta is alone. "Please don't save on the cleaning woman's services," Sharon says.

"She comes every week, and your cousins take turns daily refilling my kerosene heater." Sharon hears Savta's smile as she adds, "So, how is Diaspora?"

Sharon giggles. "Diaspora does me good, as you said it would."

"I was hoping it would be Paris, not some godforsaken town with no cultural life."

"I get there sometimes. I send you postcards from every museum I visit! You'll also be glad to know that I gained a couple of kilos."

Neither mentions that there is no news of the *Dakar,* that the wait for the funeral is stretching beyond what anyone thought possible almost eleven months earlier.

When Sharon returns to the office, she's surprised to find Danny there, drumming his fingers on his desk while staring at the black telephone. He's been out at sea every day, testing Saar Seven since its launch. "I've ordered a call to the kibbutz secretary," he says. "My parents are waiting there, but the international operator is not calling back." As an officer, Danny is entitled to place personal international calls despite their exorbitant cost. He glances at his watch. "I must return to my crew. Please call the operator to cancel so we won't be charged."

Sharon does. An hour later the phone rings, and the international operator informs Sharon that the requested party is on the line.

"It's been canceled," Sharon says, but already she hears excited voices. "I'm sorry," she tells whoever is on the other end of the line. "Danny waited for an hour, but then had to leave."

"This is his father." The man has a nicotine-cured voice, and Sharon recognizes the confident, no-nonsense cadence of a kibbutznik's speech, typical of men and women rooted in the country's soil and soul. "We understand the call of duty."

"I'm sure he'll try again tomorrow," she says. "Happy Hanukkah."

"To you too."

"Wait!" The three minutes are already charged. "Since I have you on the phone, my name is Sharon, and I work with the team.

Danny wanted to lend me his advanced math textbook. Would you know where it is?"

"Sure. Right here on the shelf. I'll drop it off at your liaison office in Haifa."

"Thanks!" She hesitates. There's no better time. "Mr. Yarden, may I ask you a personal question?"

"Uzi. Only my wife calls me Mr. Yarden, when she's cross with me. What is it?"

"Since we're in France, I'd like to help Danny trace his roots. Would you be able to give me any information? Where did you find him?"

Uzi coughs. "It was in a region with lots of castles."

"The Dordogne? The Loire Valley? Provence?"

"Couldn't tell you if you hung me upside down by my toes. I had a nice landlady by the name of Madame T-something."

"Was it a city, town, an isolated farm?"

"A village, but even then I couldn't pronounce its name. Sorry, it was a very intense time." He pauses. "I have a letter in French that never served any purpose. Danny can have it."

"Great. Thank you very much." What possible explanation can she give Danny when he receives this old letter and learns of her request? Last time she badgered him, he came close to losing his cool. And she'd agreed to leave his life alone.

"How is his French now?" Uzi asks.

"Perfect. Most four-year-olds would have forgotten it."

"My brother kept it up with him until he got killed in the Sinai campaign."

Why would a kibbutz member of an Israel-born family be fluent in a language other than Hebrew and possibly Yiddish? "You had a brother who spoke French?" she asks.

"The one time I served as a Youth Aliyah agent, before they found more qualified candidates, I also brought back with me a teenage boy, Arthur. My parents adopted him. Every family in the area kibbutzim adopted at least one child. Danny was a gift to me and my wife. Arthur to my parents."

"So sorry to hear that he was killed." A teenager gets rescued from the Holocaust only to lose his life in one of Israel's wars—like her own mother. "Was Arthur from the same village as Danny?"

"Yes, but he was under the care of some other Jewish organization, not the Youth Aliyah."

"What was his full name?"

"Arthur Durand. It was changed to Arnon Yarden."

"Thanks, Uzi." She makes a quick calculation. In 1956, when the Sinai campaign took place, Danny was fourteen. "I'll give Danny your regards. I'm sure that he'll reschedule the call. Happy Hanukkah to your family."

From the other end of the line comes a chorus of voices, as if rehearsed: "Happy Hanukkah!" It tells Sharon that a whole group of relatives is gathered around the phone for this eagerly anticipated conversation with their boy.

She glances at the wall clock. She's used two more expensive minutes beyond the first three. "Shalom," she says.

"Shalom upon all of Israel," Uzi says and adds, "Good luck to you guys up there, whatever it is that you're doing."

After Sharon hangs up, her hand remains on the receiver. She and her grandparents created a tight unit within their large extended family. Although she had a horde of aunts and uncles and seventeen cousins, none of them ever gathered by the phone to hear her voice.

Perhaps this rich circle of love is the reason Danny doesn't wish to shake its foundation. She has no business poking her nose into his personal affairs.

Chapter Thirty-Eight

CLAUDETTE

Loire Valley, France
Fall 1945–Spring 1946

S HE LIVED WITH Madame Couture. They hoped to get sewing work, but few could afford even the cost of repairing old clothes. Claudette was grateful when, in the fall, she found a job with a pleasant young cheese seller. Fernand had returned from the war early after losing an arm and an eye.

Today was market day in Buzançais, and Claudette accompanied him in his cart. He was dexterous with his left arm and his right-arm hook prosthesis. He needed her help slicing cheese and wrapping it for customers. His wife was still running a fever after the birth of their third child, and there was no doctor around to help.

He set up a chair for Claudette in his stall. Its selection of cheese was meager; few milk-producing sheep and cows had escaped the Boche's looting. While he explained to Claudette his system of presenting, cutting, and weighing cheese, Claudette scanned the street and its customers. She cast her gaze low, searching for a three-year-old boy.

Would she recognize Benjamin? She'd seen him in her mind's eye every minute since she'd left. At six weeks old, he was already focusing his gaze on her when she spoke to him, as if he were trying to imprint her face on his memory. He broke into a delightful giggle when she imitated his babbling. Benjamin had a joyful disposition. His eyes and mouth and smile were Raphaël's. And that cute cleft chin? She had no idea if it vanished when a baby lost his facial fat.

Hours later, her nostrils stinging from the tangy cheese, Claudette had not seen a single one of the many passing children who could possibly be her son.

And then a woman stopped at the cheese counter. Her little boy tried to pull away from her grip. "Stay here. Don't get lost," she warned him. Carrying her basket in her other hand, she could only nod her chin toward the cheeses that she would like Claudette to slice. "One hundred and fifty grams of this, and two hundred grams of that."

But Claudette was examining the boy. Were his brown-speckled green eyes similar to Raphaël's?

"Does he have a tattoo at the bottom of his foot?" Claudette asked the woman.

"Excuse me?"

"Does your boy have a blue mark at the bottom of his foot?" she repeated.

"No, he doesn't! I—"

Fernand broke in. "Madame, we'll cut the cheese for you. Anything else?"

After the woman left, he turned to Claudette. "What is this nonsense?"

She lowered her eyes. "Sorry." She shouldn't alienate him. Tomorrow he would be traveling to market day in Vendoeuvres and the day after to Mézières. On Saturday, the big market was in Loches. These trips were her only way to scout for Benjamin. Sooner or later, whoever had adopted him would be out shopping in the same market as she was. It might take months or years. She would never stop hoping and searching.

The next day, one of their customers was accompanied by a boy who could have been Benjamin, but this time Claudette waited until the boy and his grandmother had departed. She stepped away from the cheese stall, followed the woman, and caught up to her as she was buying cauliflower. The boy was free to move, but he circled around her, never running away to get lost in the crowd. Claudette liked that. An obedient child, a careful one.

When the grandmother finished paying, Claudette said, "Excuse me, madame. Does your boy have a tattoo on the bottom of his foot?"

"I don't understand your question."

"Never mind. Please forgive the intrusion. He's a very cute boy."

At the end of the week, Fernand insisted that Claudette explain why she was hounding people. Bursting into tears, she confessed the truth, certain that he would let her go. She would lose her chance to travel with him—and the little income she was earning.

To her surprise, he said that she could continue to work for him as long as she didn't bother customers at his stall. "Mothers will have sympathy for you. So many babies died of malnutrition and lack of medical care," he said. "My wife and I lost a little girl."

"I'm sorry." Perhaps adoption hadn't been the worst of all possible outcomes, not if Benjamin was in good health and being fed.

"What kind of tattoo is it?" Fernand asked. "A bird, a cross, a word?"

Claudette was aware that she was gaining a reputation as a crippled mother gone soft in the head. "When I find Benjamin, you'll see."

❧

WINTER WAS BEHIND them. Raphaël had not appeared. Father Hugo kept in touch with other churches and reported that no Jews had returned to the area. The many French transit camps in which Jews had been held before being transported to Auschwitz had long been emptied. After all these tragic confirmations of the Jews' fate, Claudette's trust in Raphaël's resilience dissolved. If he were alive, he would have returned by now. Her heart hollowed at the double loss. She had to accept that Raphaël was gone forever, but not Benjamin. Her son was alive somewhere not far from here. Hope was the only light in the dark pit into which she had sunk.

In Madame Couture's kitchen, Claudette picked up a yellow chick from the box in which she was raising a dozen of them. Holding the fluffy yellow baby creature in her palm gave her a minute of comfort. She brought her lips to its head. Benjamin would have loved to stroke the fuzz. When her chicks matured and produced eggs, she would never kill any of them for food.

At the sound of Fernand's cart's wheels, she put down the chick and walked out. Today was a bright spring day in the market of Châteauroux, a large town that attracted many shoppers.

Fernand was busy restocking his table with wheels of cheese when a great commotion rose up in the street. An excited mob approached, cheering, taunting. Claudette heard the cruelty in their collective tone before she understood the dirty words they flung against a woman: *"Putain."* "Boche lover." "Whore." "Traitor."

The disorganized procession neared Fernand's stall, and a shriek pierced the air. The scream was a woman's, but it sounded inhuman in its tortured pain.

Claudette's skin contracted in horror. She stepped from behind the counter to catch a glimpse. She'd heard about retaliation against women who had fraternized with German soldiers; she had been disgusted by the thought of these women's treachery. But this?

The woman the mob dragged forward was completely naked. Her screams continued as her limbs were pulled in different directions. Then her arms were pinned back. Three men yelled into her face, pinching her breasts, grabbing her crotch. A fourth one yanked the mane of her hair and wrenched her neck so far back that Claudette feared it might break. Only the many hands holding the woman kept the body from crumpling to the ground. A man directed a hard kick with his work boot into the woman's groin. Her body jerked. She screeched in pain.

No one came to her aid. Some onlookers were wide-eyed with

horror, their hands on their mouths. Others nodded sadly; still others raised their fists in approval.

Fernand joined Claudette. "So many collaborators are being purged," he whispered. "My cousin saw a public hanging here, one of a woman like this one. Why not leave justice to God?"

The woman struggled against her captors. The blades of a pair of large scissors, the kind Madame Couture used to cut fabric, glimmered in the sunlight. Chunks of hair were chopped off so close to the woman's scalp that they left streaks of blood.

No one helped the woman as she continued to scream, her voice now hoarse.

Only when her head was bald did the men let her drop to the ground. She convulsed. More people approached and kicked her. She stopped jerking.

The mob finally dispersed.

In the silence, Claudette took a blanket out of Fernand's cart and, using her new cane for support, limped toward the crumpled body on the ground. Whether she was alive or dead, Claudette would give her some dignity. That was the Christian—and Jewish—thing to do.

She was about to return to Fernand's stall when she heard a familiar voice, clear as a bell. "Claudette, is that you?"

She swiveled to see a cart heaped with woven baskets. Standing next to it was Solange.

Chapter Thirty-Nine

SHARON

Cherbourg, France
December 1968

A*RTHUR DURAND.* S*HARON*'s heart sings with excitement as she rides her bike to Rachelle's office at *La Presse de la Manche*. The cold, wet ocean wind slaps her knit hat and raises the flaps of her coat. Her gloved hands grip the bike handles tighter and she bends low. Her lips and nose freeze as she rides along the open canal and over the bridge.

At the front of the newspaper building, she stashes her bike and pulls out a handkerchief to wipe her cold, damp face. Her exhilaration mounts.

She enters the office and takes off her gloves; Rachelle rubs her bloodless fingers between her palms. "Herbal tea?" She plugs in the percolator.

Sharon peels off her coat and one of her two sweaters to let warm air reach her skin. "Didn't you tell me that Jewish organizations kept track of children? I need your help in finding out where an orphaned Jewish boy by the name of Arthur Durand lived. It might be somewhere in the Loire Valley, Provence, or the Dordogne."

"OSE had institutions in the southern part of the free zone. The Loire Valley was a major escape route, but it was too close to the demarcation line for most Jews to stay." Rachelle places a strainer with tea leaves over a mug and pours hot water over them. The herby aroma of chamomile wafts up as she hands the tea to Sharon.

Sharon wraps her fingers around the warm mug. "Who do I write to?"

"Write to?" Rachelle steps to a filing cabinet and opens a drawer.

She roots through folders and pulls out a large envelope. "Remember my missing grandfather? When I searched ships' manifests from the 1940s for his name, I also ordered any lists available from Jewish organizations to find other relatives." She settles in front of a side table supporting a large machine with a tall, opaque screen. Her back is to Sharon as she pulls smaller envelopes from the big one and leafs through them. She selects a filmstrip.

"Do you have it all here?" Sharon asks in amazement.

"Who knows? The microfiche are a mess. Many notes were written by hand during wartime. Some were coded for safety reasons and then decoded, but with errors. It will take days to go over them all." She scribbles on a piece of paper. "Arthur Durand, Arthur Durand," she mumbles, then turns to Sharon. "Before I start, tell me, why am I doing this?"

Sharon hesitates. There's no good explanation for why she's investigating someone's background. Worse, if she confesses her fixation with Danny's tattoo to Rachelle, she might suspect Sharon of having amorous intentions toward him and tell Dominique.

Sharon hates not being candid. "It's confidential," she says, trusting Rachelle's reverence for military secrets.

WHEN SHARON RETURNS to the newspaper office at the end of the workday, she is filled with anticipation.

Rachelle apologizes. "I could give it only an hour before I was called on assignment." She points to an open ledger on her desk. "I'm on a money-trail project. A local politician—"

"How about if I continue? I have all evening."

"Be my guest. I'm meeting Ehud at ten."

"Glad to hear that my matchmaking worked out," Sharon says. "My *savta* would say that I've secured myself a place in the next world."

Rachelle laughs. "That's exactly what my grandmother said about you." A blush floods her face. "He's really wonderful. We've connected so well."

"In what language?"

"My broken English and the language of love, of course."

"Let me know when you're ready to start your Hebrew lessons." Sharon turns to the pile of small envelopes. "Is there any geographical logic here?"

"I can tell you what's not here. In the summer of 1940, Paris and its surroundings were cleared of Jews; they fled or were deported." She makes a sweeping gesture. "All of Normandy was in the occupied zone. No Jews, no institutions—and no lists. Only in November 1942 did the Nazis advance south and take control of the free zone."

"That leaves most of France."

Rachelle leafs through the envelopes. "There are lists here of children who were smuggled to Switzerland—"

"Let's exclude those."

Rachelle returns to her desk while Sharon settles in front of the screen. She picks up a filmstrip, places it on a glass tray, and adjusts the focus dial. Dozens of names pop up, each representing a tragic story of a Jewish child and a family devastated by persecution and death.

She decides to scan the typed lists first, which proves to be a challenging task; many are faint from an overused typewriter ribbon or muddled by misshapen or missing letters in the typewriter's carousel.

Hours later, the cleaning woman's wet mop chases her out. Sharon has found nothing.

For two more evenings, she returns after work for the painstaking search. *Arthur Durand, please be here somewhere.* On Sharon's third session, she tackles the handwritten notes, scribbled in cursive on torn notebook pages and even on what looks like the insides of cigarette packets. Straining her eyes to read a list written in pencil, Sharon imagines a wartime shortage of ink or, perhaps, a notetaker using a pencil, ready to erase everything in the face of danger.

Two hours later, she comes across the name. *Durand, Arthur.* Her heart skips a beat. She reads the few words in the next column: *Born:*

1932. Parents: Hershel and Perla Durand, presumed dead. Siblings: three, missing. Disability: none. Transferred 1944 to Chât—

The loopy cursive handwriting is impossible to read. Sharon calls, "Rachelle, would you please come here?"

Rachelle ambles over and leans on Sharon's shoulder. "Could it be Châtillon-sur-Indre?"

"Have you heard of it? Where is it?"

"The Indre is both a region and a river." Rachelle leaves to search the map library and returns ten minutes later. "There's a small village in the Loire Valley by that name. Population thirty-six hundred. The nearest city—eighty kilometers northwest—is Tours."

Sharon's excitement at the discovery is tempered by the question of what she can possibly do with this information.

Chapter Forty

SHARON

Cherbourg, France
December 1968

SHARON IS TRANSLATING technical engineering instructions from French to Hebrew when two seamen return from their yearly visit home and deliver a locked canvas mail pouch from headquarters. She sorts through the mail at her desk. Among the manila folders of new recruits is a letter addressed to Admiral Yaniv marked HIGHLY CONFIDENTIAL and URGENT and sealed with a red wax stamp. A large envelope is addressed to Commander Daniel Yarden. It's from Uzi Yarden.

Fingering Danny's envelope, she guesses that it's the math book and perhaps also the French letter. She could slash open the envelope, as she does all invoices and correspondence, then claim that it was done in error. She could remove the letter, and if Uzi Yarden hasn't mentioned it in his cover note, Danny will never know.

That's devious. So unlike her. *Enough snooping, yenta,* she tells herself. She must take responsibility and face the inevitable storm when Danny learns of her talk with his father. She sighs and places the unopened envelope on Danny's desk. Holding the urgent letter to Yaniv, she goes searching for him in the shipyard.

So much could be urgent and highly confidential. Now that Egypt is known to have missiles, Israel must be developing its response. The first six Saars already in Israel will not be fitted with arms until the final six arrive, and, Sharon guesses, for political reasons, additional time will pass before their combat designation is revealed.

Any sea-battle training Danny and his crew begin later this month with Saar Seven must include whatever new weapon Israel is developing—except that it's not here. She imagines that it is some futuristic armament that will change the outcome of any sea battle. It has to. The Saars project is a race against time.

The sentry at the entrance to the hangar lets her in. The sight of the immense, cavernous structure makes Sharon catch her breath anew. Full-size ships in various stages of construction line one side of the space, each looking like Gulliver tied down and explored by an army of Lilliputians. The hundreds of workers on ladders and scaffolding, probing, screwing, hammering, wear overalls color-coded by trade: electricians, welders, mechanics. A separate crew keeps the floor scrubbed. There is none of the sticky oil that gums up the floors in her uncle's factory.

"I know where the office is," she tells a sentry who insists on accompanying her. He stays with her, though, as she makes her way through a side corridor.

Yaniv is planted in front of a wall covered with blueprints. At her approach, he turns and raises his eyebrows in question, his sour expression letting her know that she's interrupting him. "What is it?"

She extends her hand. "I didn't want to leave this on your desk."

He takes it from her, tests the firmness of the envelope's glued edges, and checks the strength of the red wax seal. Then he says, "I hear that you're doing an excellent job at everything we throw at you. We'll need you in the coming months."

Soon, purchasing, customs, filing, weather reports, and translations will have to run without her. "I'm here only until the *Dakar* is found."

Just as she says it, it dawns on her: She should have connected the dots. "Admiral, weren't you the one in charge of refurbishing it in Southampton?"

"I was." He holds her gaze. His gruff demeanor melts. "There's not an hour that I don't churn in my head what could have gone wrong. One day we'll have an answer. One day *soon*, I hope. We can't risk our other submarines until we know."

She can find no more words. Churning it all in her head gets her nowhere. "Would you let me know if there's any news?"

"Through the official channels, of course. Families are notified first."

She swallows. She hates the reminder that she was only Alon's fiancée. Seven years together, a planned wedding—and she has no standing.

Walking away, Sharon mulls over the fate of Israel's two other submarines. If the navy has frozen their use until it figures out what went wrong with the *Dakar,* the long coast of Israel is not being protected. The two remaining destroyers are aging, and France won't sell Israel any spare parts. Her enemies know that. They'll pounce soon.

Back in the office, she once again fingers the envelope on Danny's desk, tempted to open it and remove the letter, because if Danny finds it, all hell will break loose. She can't imagine him screaming, but she must expect it. What can she say in her defense? That whether he agrees with her or not, the mystery of his tattoo *is* her onion? She can't justify her nosiness by her curiosity about her mother.

Danny is right, of course. What is a little private matter of a tattoo in the face of existential danger?

She sets down the packet, bracing herself for the inevitable confrontation.

Midafternoon, Danny stops by her work area and drops the math book on her desk. "Ready for your lessons?"

She winces and looks down, waiting for him to say more. The book's corners are frayed, and geometric pen doodles fill all the white spaces on the cover. She flips it open, goes past the title page and table of contents. Unfamiliar letters and complex equations stare at her. Calculations are scribbled in the margins.

"Sorry about the book's poor condition. I bought it used."

"It looks very difficult."

"You're smart. We'll take baby steps. How about an hour after work today? Get a grid notebook from supply. I'll be back at seventeen hundred hours."

Maybe Uzi couldn't find the letter, or maybe he included it but made no mention that he was sending it at the request of someone named Sharon. Relieved, she pushes the math book aside and continues filling out multipage customs forms for navigation equipment from Italy.

Before five, with a crisp new grid notebook on her desk, she sharpens a couple of pencils and places a rubber eraser next to them. She fans through the pages of the dreaded textbook, doubting her ability to conquer the equations.

She halts at the sight of a piece of paper tucked inside the back cover. She unfolds it and feels her heart stop. It is a letter on a lined notebook page, browned in places, and written in French.

Chapter Forty-One

CLAUDETTE

Loire Valley, France
Spring 1946

As their last acts, the Nazis had burned villages during their retreat. Ruins were visible everywhere in La Guerche-sur-l'Aubois, where Claudette was back, living with Solange, her two little girls, and Dorothée, her ailing mother. Mémère's home on the main road was a pile of cinders. Luckily, some houses like Dorothée Poincaré's on side streets had been spared.

Claudette was a hundred and forty kilometers from Valençay. She'd exhausted the markets in that vicinity, but with Solange, she could explore villages far outside the cheese seller's territory. She didn't feel as alone now as she had when living with Madame Couture, both of them immersed in their own grief, their respective sorrows separating them like two islands wedged in a river as life flowed past.

Now that spring was here, Claudette planted a vegetable garden. She had missed the feel of the clumps of earth between her fingers and the sight of the first brazen leaf that poked up its head in search of sun—and she loved gardening with Solange's adorable little girls, ages four and five, at her side. Their little arms around her neck when they thanked her for the dresses she sewed for their dolls gave her minute reprieves from her anguish. And having their little bodies in her lap while she read them the stories of Babar brought her closer to her little Benjamin. She hoped his adoptive parents were equally loving, bestowing on him the same tenderness and care.

Their home was the refuge of three disabled women. The cooking stove posed dangers to Solange—she might scorch precious food, scald the hands that wove baskets for their livelihood, or set a sleeve on fire. Dorothée suffered dizzy spells that kept her lying on the living-room sofa. She wove small jute baskets with her eyes closed while instructing Claudette how to cook—Claudette, the cripple whom Mémère had kept away from the stove for fear of an accident.

On weekends and some Wednesdays, the little girls were sent into a neighbor's care while Claudette and Solange traveled to the markets. Claudette was Solange's eyes on the road, and Solange acted as Claudette's voice. She didn't hesitate to ask any passing strangers— not just those who were accompanied by little boys—whether they had heard about a boy with a blue tattoo at the bottom of his foot.

In the evenings, after the girls and Dorothée were in bed, the two of them sat by the fire. While Solange wove rattan, Claudette read aloud from the many new romance books published after the war. The virginal princesses had been replaced with confident, capable heroines with soft hearts for their lovers. *Relentless Search*, *Unforgettable Woman*, and *A Hero's Return* told sensuous stories of courage and valor. The two of them giggled like the teenagers they once were, the only difference being that now, each had known a great love.

Solange's husband had developed abdominal pain and died five weeks later. The midwife in the village where he had been serving as a social worker touched his enlarged belly and told Solange that no doctor could save him.

Claudette confessed her love for a Jew. She talked about Raphaël and his father. "I have you and your husband to thank for directing them to Château de Valençay," Claudette said, then added, "Even if you didn't like Jews."

"My husband taught me to be a better person," Solange replied. "'God's Chosen People,' he said."

"Yes, Raphaël was an admirable man. So smart too." Claudette was grateful for the memories of his bright eyes and lean body, of his kisses and caresses.

His boy was somewhere. She had to find him for both their sakes. In her inquiries about a three-and-a-half-year-old boy with a blue tattoo, she never revealed its design, and she asked Father Hugo not to describe it in his probes of his colleagues. Only someone with reliable information would know about the Jewish star.

No one had heard of such a boy.

And then it happened. The day was bright, with the first buds of cherry blossoms. The long morning in the market had been profitable; Solange sold many baskets, and Claudette had been kept busy mending clothes at a side table. It was almost two o'clock when they finished packing up the cart and entered a nearby tavern for a meal.

While waiting for their pea soup to arrive, Solange rose to address the room in a way that Claudette would never have dared. Solange's past public inquiries had been met with either indifferent glances she had been unable to see or crude jokes to which she responded with her sharp tongue, drawing laughter.

Claudette was jolted to hear a drunken man say, "Tattooed with that star of the Jews?"

"Yes!" Claudette jumped up from her seat. "Where have you seen him?"

"I heard, not saw." The man waved his hand. His speech was slurred. "Gone the way of all the Jews."

"Spell it out," Solange called to him. "What are you saying?"

"The Boche got him and his Jew-loving family."

"But how, exactly?" Solange pressed.

The man mimed raising a rifle and shooting. "Boom, boom."

Shot? The Nazis shot a baby? Claudette's heart broke into a million pieces all over again. She crumpled into herself, trying to control the scream that threatened to tear out of her.

Still standing, Solange squeezed Claudette's shoulder and went on. "Where was it?"

Claudette saw the man waving his arm in the direction of the outside world. Then he gulped the rest of his beer and dropped his head on the table.

"What's his answer?" Solange asked the man on her other side.

"Nothing. He's a known drunkard and a liar," he replied.

But Claudette knew that this wasn't a lie. The drunkard had identified the star tattoo—and not just any star, but the six-pointed Star of David. He'd implied that Benjamin's adoptive family was not Jewish but had sheltered a Jew.

Benjamin, the innocent soul, was dead. He had been killed because she had marked him for the Boche. Her little cherub didn't even have the comfort of sitting at Jesus's feet.

Claudette's wail filled the tavern. She fell sobbing into Solange's arms.

Chapter Forty-Two

UZI YARDEN

Loire Valley, France
Late September 1946

UZI FELT MORE at ease when he arrived at his new base in Argenton-sur-Creuse even though this was a bustling town, unlike the tiny enclave of Châtillon-sur-Indre. He walked on a stone bridge over a wide river bisecting the town and stopped to lean on the railing, felted with green moss. Charming two- and three-story houses constructed of various colorful materials lined both sides of the river, and majestic weeping willow trees drooped into the water. To the east, a bridge over massive, arched rock foundations had been gutted in its center. Twisted metal rods of a railway testified to Nazi air bombing.

No need to search for a room here. Father Patrick, a Catholic priest, was to host him in the church with its carved medieval façade.

"I thought Catholics baptize our children and won't give them back," Uzi had said to Hilda when she had handed him this address.

"Some of them do that, and the drama of legal cases draws media attention, especially since the Catholics battling for custody get the blessing of the archbishop. Is there a more blatant form of anti-Semitism?" she replied. "Luckily, many more Catholics were our allies during the occupation. They saved Jews with faked baptism papers."

Stepping outside the church compound the first morning, Uzi heard the shrill buzz of a knife sharpener. The man and his heavy stone wheel were stationed on the street corner, where a line of customers had formed. He pumped the pedal to sharpen scissors, axes, and scythes.

Uzi guessed that this craftsman traversed the area. He waited until the early rush of customers had subsided, then approached with his folding pocketknife. When the man finished filing it, Uzi showed him the flash card that said *Enfant juif?*

The man raised his protective glasses, revealing lids almost devoid of lashes, and examined Uzi. Nodding, he pointed to where they stood, then he pointed to the clock tower and signaled with his fingers the number eighteen. That was six o'clock here. Uzi gave the man a thumbs-up, excited about the prospect of finding another Jewish child who had eluded Hilda's and OSE's sights.

The sky was bright blue, but the temperature had dropped. Uzi entered a used-clothing store and, for the first time in his life, bought a piece of clothing for himself. The long wool jacket was worn at the elbows and cuffs but had no bad odor.

He still had a whole day of work.

The mother superior of a nearby convent allowed him entrance into the enclosed courtyard, then led him through a long, high-ceilinged, moldy corridor. At the desk in her office, she consulted Hilda's letter about the ten-year-old Eloise. Her face was a stern mask.

"She's in a good Christian home," she finally said in English.

"I'd like to check it myself."

She rose and left the room. Uzi waited for almost an hour, wondering whether she was secreting the girl somewhere. Finally, she returned. "I've prayed for guidance," she said. The grimness didn't leave her face as she wrote down an address on a piece of paper.

Back in town, Uzi looked through the barred fence of a school at girls in blue-and-white uniforms and braided hair running around during recess. As in the kibbutz, they jumped rope and played hopscotch. A half a dozen clustered together, their heads close, probably exchanging secrets. He didn't know which was Eloise—formerly Leah. According to Hilda, the girl's Jewish parents had been deported in 1942. That first winter, her brother, a decade older, had kept her with him in a forest camp of Résistance fighters. When an action against the Boche failed and some of his comrades were captured, he was certain that under torture they'd reveal the location of the camp. He brought Leah to the convent and left to join another cell, never to be heard from again.

Uzi waited until an hour after the end of the school day to visit the home where the mother superior had placed her. It was a stone house with a garden wall whose climbing bougainvillea was now devoid of flowers. Through the iron gate, he glimpsed a garden with beds of late-blooming vegetables and herbs.

The gate was unlocked, but Uzi pulled on the bell's string. A woman came out of the house.

"*Bonjour,*" Uzi said. "*Je suis de Palestine.*" He presented Hilda's letter.

The woman read it, flinched, and pointed to the bench. "*Attendez,*" she said, then walked to the field behind the house. Uzi heard her calling someone.

Several minutes passed. The white lace curtains on the window shifted, and a girl looked out at him. He recognized her from the schoolyard. She let the curtain drop.

Finally, a broad-shouldered man in work clothes entered the yard from the field. Bits of grass and leaves were stuck to his boots. Uzi rose and extended his hand. The man took it in a hearty shake, then began to speak.

"*Je ne parle pas français,*" Uzi said.

With a solicitous gesture, the man directed him into the house. The table had been set with a vase of fresh flowers on a lacy tablecloth, coffee mugs, plates, and even a cake. Uzi took in the pleasant room—upholstered couches and a rug in front of the fireplace. Above the mantel hung a framed picture of Jesus with a golden halo.

The couple sat on one side of the table, Eloise between them, her face drained of color. The man kissed her head and took her hand. The woman wrapped her arm around her. Then she let go of the girl to pour Uzi coffee and cut a slice of cake for him. Its ingredients, Uzi thought, must have cost them a few ration coupons.

They spoke, husband and wife taking turns, using short sentences as if that might help Uzi understand. What he understood clearly was what was in front of him: a picture of love and the promise to protect Eloise. He sensed that they had been expecting a stranger to show up one day and claim her.

An image flashed through his head of the neglected Daniel. If he were in a loving home like this, Uzi would never consider removing him. And then he heard Hilda's voice telling him, *It's us or them. If you don't take her, another organization will, because in today's atmosphere, national identity overrides family.*

What's the right moral judgment? Uzi looked at Eloise's eyes. They widened in fear the more her parents talked. He couldn't be the one whose presence filled a child with terror. He wouldn't manipulate the word *parent* to crush the security she had found after her previous world shattered.

He pressed his palms together in supplication and looked at the girl, trying to convey that he wouldn't cause her harm. He pushed himself away from the table. Eloise would never become Leah again, would never reclaim her Jewish identity for the collective good of her people. Already ignorant of the traditions of her dead parents, she was one more child lost to their tribe.

When he departed, he wished he could say in French "God be with you."

At six o'clock, Uzi joined the knife sharpener. He rolled his heavy equipment to a nearby shop to store it for the night, then began his trek out of town, Uzi following. They crossed a wide field and entered the woods.

As they walked deeper, trepidation crawled into Uzi's heart. His experience in the tavern was still fresh in his mind. What if the man was part of a gang conspiring to kill this Jewish man somewhere his body could never be found? Uzi picked up a straight, short branch. Walking on, he broke off leaves and offshoots, stripping the stick bare. He was ready for a *kapap* fight if needed.

At the line where the trees ended, the earth opened onto a limestone quarry gouged into a hill. The sun cast orange-pink hues on the chiseled, whitish walls that dropped into a low basin. Excavated years ago for the construction of houses and mansions, the quarry had long ended its usefulness. Now pigeons flew in and out of fissures where seeds had sprouted into shrubs and trees.

Uzi followed the knife sharpener on the downward slope toward a shack tucked against the side of a wall. Three men were idling outside, smoking. The knife sharpener stopped, and Uzi, perplexed, did too.

"Enfant juif?" Uzi whispered, and the man nodded.

When a man emerged from the shack buttoning his pants, Uzi tasted blood in his mouth; he had bitten the inside of his cheek. His mind caught up with the rest of him when the next man deposited coins into the palm of a stocky man with a thick neck standing to the side of the shack, then entered.

LIVING IN THE house adjacent to the church for the week gave Uzi time at the end of each day to spend with his new charges, which included a boy and a girl brought in by local people. He loved getting to know the children rather than depositing each one and rushing back the long distance to Madame Therrien's to prepare for the next day's hunt. He taught them Hebrew songs and the hora dance and played tunes on his harmonica for them. In Father Patrick's office, he showed them on the world globe the pinprick dot that was Eretz Israel.

He asked the Yiddish-speakers among them to translate for the others when he described how, in the lowland reaching the Mediterranean, settlers had created cultivatable land by drying up the swamps of foul standing water that had been a breeding ground for malaria-carrying mosquitoes. "It was backbreaking work, digging drainage channels. But you know what? They planted eucalyptus trees to drink up excess water, and little by little, since the start of the century, Jews have been reclaiming the land with their sweat." His grandparents and parents had salvaged the land of their people. He was working on the next chapter—bringing in the people to live there.

When no words existed to communicate with those children who didn't know Yiddish, Uzi's hugs did. Zehava would have been as surprised as he was to see him this engaged. He'd never been particularly interested in children, but these were *his* children. In his head, he replayed the moment each had been found. Each one felt like a birth. The young features were carved into his memory, though he was aware that he saw only the outside. He couldn't begin to fathom the agony each had to be suffering. The rock lodged in each little chest would never lift, even if it grew lighter with time and the new ideology that would fire up their young spirits.

And then there was Daniel, whose absence here was a void. Uzi missed the radiant smile and the feel of his underfed body. The boy had suffered the wrath of the entire village because of his adoptive mother's transgression or his Jewish tattoo—or both.

On Uzi's fifth morning, as he was crossing the garden, Rivka, the sixteen-year-old he had rescued in the quarry, signaled for him to approach. He sat down at the far end of her bench and registered that some color had returned to her pallid cheeks. Four evenings earlier, he had paid her captor two thousand francs, entered the shack, and wrapped the scrawny, naked body in his jacket. He carried Rivka in his arms the entire long trek back to the church, all the while assuring her in Yiddish that he wouldn't hurt her, that there were good people who were committed to helping her. When they arrived at the church, the priest summoned a doctor, who said that she could benefit from a new drug called penicillin, still unavailable to the public in France. Uzi placed a phone call to Hilda, and late that night, Robert Weintraub showed up in his jeep. He brought penicillin and a box of food. "I also threw in here iodine, aspirin, sulfa powder, and bandages," he said.

"Thanks," Uzi said, laughing. "We're not in a combat zone. Our kids only scrape their knees."

Robert had pointed to the box. "There's chocolate for that."

"Are you eating?" Uzi asked Rivka now, treading carefully with his questions. He was acutely aware of the harm men had caused her. In time, he hoped, she would learn that there were also decent men in the world.

"What if he comes looking for me?" she asked.

Uzi understood that she hadn't seen the financial transaction that had taken place outside her prison shack. "He won't. You're safe. And in a couple days, we'll start the long journey to Eretz Israel."

"I just want to get very far away from here," she whispered.

"Can you tell me about your family?"

She looked up at the sky as if plucking memories from the slow-moving clouds. When she spoke, her voice was so low that he had to lean forward to hear her.

"We were six. My oldest brother and sister were born in a town outside Krakow. My second sister, Bettina, and I were born in Paris a year apart. My parents had a candy shop, and we lived above it. All the girls in my class were my friends because they loved coming over after school." The little sad smile that graced Rivka's face faded quickly. "We escaped Paris when the Nazis came. Lived on the road. Once we rented a house for a while. Then we had to leave, and we slept in our covered cart. That's when we got caught and were sent to the Drancy labor camp." She stopped and closed her eyes.

"Go on," he said softly.

"I don't know how long we stayed there. Maybe weeks or months. We heard that we were going to be deported to Germany or Poland—no one told us anything. There was no food. Everything smelled so bad, even my parents." Tears streamed down her face. Uzi handed her his handkerchief. "I was so stupid that when a guard offered to take me to be a companion to his sick mother, I begged my parents to let me go. I was conceited about having been chosen over Bettina, who was always the smart one. All I wanted was to get away from their stink."

"You were eleven years old?"

She sniffled and nodded. "The guard's mother's house was near the camp. I heard the trains and knew—I just knew that my family had been taken away. I felt remorse. I missed them so much and regretted leaving. I wanted to be deported on a train, too, so I could find them in their new camp." Rivka sobbed. "I was bored without Bettina. There was not even a piece of paper and a pencil to draw."

"Do you like to draw?"

"I was good at it once."

Uzi made a mental note to ask Robert Weintraub for a sketch pad and colored pencils.

She went on. "I took care of the guard's mother for about two years, until she died. I didn't know then how lucky I was that the old woman had been kind to me, and her son brought us food from the camp's kitchen."

She blotted her eyes with Uzi's handkerchief.

"The guard always warned me not to be seen by the police. He said that they shot Jews. For my protection, after his mother died, he found me a new job with another family." Rivka's shoulders shook. "They had five older boys."

Cold traversed Uzi's spine. He imagined the vicious Vichy police outside and the beasts of men inside, and this child, then thirteen, repeatedly raped with no relief. He wished he could gather her in his arms. "You'll love Eretz Israel," he said, "and you'll make a new life." Was healing possible for a girl whose childhood had been eviscerated so cruelly?

Chapter Forty-Three

SHARON

Cherbourg, France
December 1968

THE FIRST THIRTY minutes Sharon spends on calculus with Danny are torture. As much as she tries to concentrate, her mind is on another track. He explains something, but in her head she's asking him, *Do you know that your name used to be Benjamin-Pierre Pelletier? Did your father ever tell you that a man named Florian Robillard relinquished his parental rights to you? Robillard must have been your adoptive father, but Pelletier is not a Jewish name—did your Jewish mother marry a Christian? What Christian would have tattooed you with the Star of David?*

"You are not paying attention," Danny says, his one eyebrow raised in amusement. "I'm talking basic stuff, the level you must have already studied."

"I scored ninety-five, but it was two and a half years ago." She presses on her temples, hating the idea that he thinks she's stupid. For months, she's been trying to excel in his eyes, feasting on every word of praise, and now she's blowing it. *There is the name of a witness on the letter, Evelyne Therrien. Perhaps she was Uzi's landlady? He said her name started with a T.* "I'm sorry. I'm tired," Sharon mumbles, annoyed with herself.

Danny's green eyes examine her from behind his glasses.

She cringes at his kind patience; she wishes that he'd just call it quits. "Thanks for trying so hard. Maybe tomorrow?" she says.

He scratches the back of his head. It was just shaved by one of the recruits, who also reached deep into the chin cleft. "I'm unavailable until next week. Elazar can start a refresher course. Maybe take a look at Pazit's textbook?"

She fakes enthusiasm. "A great idea." She will say whatever it takes to end this math-tutoring session. What she was unable to decipher were the two official red stamps that were tilted when they hit the paper and have faded since. One has the figure 46 in its center, which could be the year 1946. Or is it part of a district number? On the second stamp, less than half the postmark circle shows four letters: *ndre*. It could be the Indre region Rachelle had mentioned or Châtillon-sur-Indre, the village.

Frustrated at herself for wasting Danny's goodwill and probably losing some of his respect, Sharon rides her bike home, letting the cold sea breeze clear her head. There's nothing more she can do to learn about what happened all those years ago unless she travels to that village where Arthur Durand once lived.

Back in her apartment, she examines her map of France. She locates Tours. The Loire Valley is far. She would have to take a series of trains, more than a day's journey, and then spend a few days in the area to investigate. She would start by trying to locate Florian Robillard, presumably Danny's adoptive father.

Or perhaps not.

In any military scheme, there is an exit strategy or a point at which a decision must be made to abort: a pilot jumps off his burning plane; a captain orders the evacuation of a sinking ship. It's time to abort her quest. She will reveal her findings to Danny and leave it to him to decide his course of action.

Most likely, he will do nothing. It's his call.

Chapter Forty-Four

SHARON

Cherbourg, France
December 1968

IN TWO DAYS, the first candle will usher in Hanukkah. The sky darkens by midafternoon, nearing the shortest day of the year. Sharon is about to leave the office for her music rehearsal when a messenger delivers a telegram. "For Mademoiselle Bloomenthal." He touches his cap and hurries away.

It can't be about the *Dakar*. Yaniv would have received a phone call before it was made public. With trembling fingers, Sharon rips open the edge of the bright yellow envelope.

```
My mother is ill. Come home. Aunt Dvora.
```

Sharon's body wakes up to absorb the blow before her brain processes the words. The room spins, and she leans on the desk. She rereads the one line, her lips trembling. *Savta*. When they spoke on the phone a few days ago, Savta sounded well and in good spirits. Did she have a heart attack? Has she been diagnosed with the unmentionable?

Savta, Savta. Not another loss!

The dispassionate Aunt Dvora wouldn't have summoned her unless the situation was dire. Couldn't she have splurged on two more words to spell it out? *No tears now*, Sharon tells herself. *There's no time*. Her mind shifts into high gear, charting her next steps. Leave for Israel, of course. She must book a commercial airline flight; her paid-for charter-company return ticket is valid only with advance notice and when there are enough passengers to fill a plane. Buying a commercial ticket will cost all the thousands of francs she's saved. She glances at her watch. Forty-five minutes before the bank closes, but her savings booklet is in her apartment. Her passport is locked here in the office, along with Yaniv's, Kadmon's, and Danny's guns, and only they have the key. They've been working in the hangar all day. She must call different airline offices in Paris. Now? No. Go home first for the savings booklet, then to the bank. Return here, find Danny and notify him of her resignation, and ask him to open the safe. Then rush back home to pack. She'll take everything, of course. No soldier leaves stuff behind. By that time, though, the last train out of Cherbourg will have left. She must wait until the morning train, which arrives in Paris in the early afternoon, but she'll still need over two hours to reach Orly and clear customs. Actually, three hours, since she will have to shop among the airline counters for the next available flight with or without a layover in Athens or Istanbul. She'll probably be too late to catch any flights that evening and she'll have to spend the night at the airport, sleeping on a bench to save the hotel cost. That means that she won't be leaving France for two more days.

What will have happened to Savta by then? *Savta, wait for me.*

Adrenaline rushes through her. There's no time to send a telegram to Aunt Dvora that she's coming. Sharon dons her coat and hops on her bike. There's no time to notify everybody that she'll be missing the holiday celebration she's been so looking forward to.

How mad they'll be at her, leaving them all in the lurch. Including her musical ensemble. Preoccupied with one loss, she viewed herself as only a visitor here. Yet now, when she can't say a proper goodbye, she understands how Rachelle, Danny, Rina, Elazar, and Naomi have filled her new world. She belongs with them. She hates to leave the circle of their friendship.

What choice does she have?

Sharon's skin is cold and sticky under her sweater by the time she returns to the office. It is after five o'clock. Neither Kadmon nor

Danny are in, so she rushes to the hangar in search of either one of them. The sentry looks at her curiously; she's aware of her wild hair, frizzy from the bike ride, and her nose red from the cold. Her satchel is slung across her coat, heavy with all her cash; the French paper currency is twice the size of Israel's. Not waiting for the second sentry to accompany her, Sharon bursts into the center aisle between the ships. She runs the length of a soccer field, her eyes scanning the working crews.

"Mademoiselle Bloomenthal?" Félix Amiot pulls away from a worktable where he was examining machine parts with men in orange overalls. He wipes his hands on a rag.

She stops. She hates to be rude and brush him off. He must see what the sentry has just seen.

"Anything the matter?" he asks.

"Sorry," she mumbles. "A crisis at home. I must leave for Israel. Have you seen Kadmon or Danny?"

His hand rises toward the corridor. "How are you getting to Orly?"

She has no time for chitchat. "Sorry, I'm in a rush." She starts for the opening between two ships.

"Let me fly you there in my plane," he says.

She swivels on her heel and stares at him.

"This way you can catch an early flight," he adds.

"I—I—" she stammers. "I can't impose on you—"

"No imposition. I am heading to Paris for a morning meeting. I can land in Orly instead of the private airport I use. It's all the same to me." He looks at his watch. "We can depart anytime this evening."

"Oh God." She can barely get out the words: "Thank you so much!"

AMIOT'S UNIFORMED CHAUFFEUR enters her apartment at eight thirty just as she buckles the second of her two suitcases. Before packing her flute in its case, Sharon held it with a sinking feeling, thinking of the people she is letting down.

In deference to Amiot and his private plane, she's dressed in her wool suit rather than her comfortable corduroy pants and sweater. Those are rolled in her backpack; she'll change into them at the airport before she sleeps on a bench tonight. She's managed to shower, press-iron her hair after it dried, and apply a touch of blush on her cheeks so she doesn't look as frazzled as she feels. *Savta,* she thinks, *hang on. I'm coming. I'll make you all better.*

Only when she is in the chauffeur-driven car does she exhale, releasing the air that's been trapped in her lungs. She scribbled a note for her roommates, and on her way down the stairs, she knocked on Naomi's door to tell her the news. Rachelle will be disappointed too. They were about to start their Hebrew lessons. Failing to reach the Frenchwoman at her office, Sharon left a note with Danny to pass along through Dominique.

"Are you angry that I'm leaving the mission in the lurch?" Sharon asked him when he retrieved her passport.

"Lousy timing, kiddo. Take the calculus book with you in case you're delayed." He hugged her. Breathing the starch of his collared shirt, Sharon wished that the feel of his arms around her would linger. Then a pang in her heart reminded her that she had sleuthed behind his back. If only she hadn't been pressed for time, she would have confessed and ended this saga.

In her head, she repeats her mantra: *Savta, hang on. I'm coming. I'll make you all better.*

Chapter Forty-Five

UZI YARDEN

Loire Valley, France
October 1946

A COUPLE OF DAYS after his talk with Rivka, Uzi was on the bus back to Châteauroux with seven children. If anyone had asked him at the start of his mission how many kids he expected to rescue, he would have said dozens. Now he glanced at the handful of children staring out the window, their silent, shocked numbness a response to yet another seismic shift in their lives. He reminded himself of a Talmud saying: *Whoever saves a single soul is considered to have saved an entire world.*

The bus crossed a bridge over the Creuse River. Underneath, a low dam allowed water to gush over its rim in a copious, raucous cascade. Uzi glanced at Rivka, the oldest in the group. Now properly outfitted for the weather in a wool dress and a thick cardigan, her hair combed and braided, she showed no outward signs of the depredation of an abandoned child thrown into the path of a pimp. She'd told Uzi that her father's sister had left for Palestine, and she knew her married name, so Uzi had promised to help search for her. As he would for Sarah's brother.

For the past year in Palestine, each day at noon, Uzi turned on the radio in the packing shed and blasted it so he could hear it while working among the trees. Kol Israel radio announced for a full hour the names of Holocaust survivors from Germany, Bulgaria, Poland, Hungary, Austria, Italy, Yugoslavia, and Ukraine who were now living in Israel and searching for surviving relatives or neighbors from their European hometowns. Behind each name, there were tragedies beyond the grasp of the human mind. In every village that was no more, like the razed Jewish quarter of Marseille, there had been dynamic Jewish life.

Across the aisle from Uzi, Manuel sat with his new friend, a pale girl with translucent skin and straw-colored hair whom Uzi had found in a monastery. He hoped that the little girl, Guylaine, renamed Gilla, was emotionally strong enough for the arduous trip ahead and that Martha, who sat behind these two eight-year-olds, would keep them calm when the time came.

Now that Uzi was attached to these children and the ones waiting for him with Pastor Gaspard, worry gnawed at him. How could he lead them through the dangerous journey? Up to this point, his focus had been on rescuing them from a life of rootlessness and lost identity. The next phase of his mission was about to launch. He would accompany his children and those found by other agents on the train to Marseille. There, the children would wait at the displaced-persons camp while he joined the team preparing the boat, *Hatikvah*—"the hope."

Uzi shifted his gaze to the window and stared at the magnificent red, yellow, and orange of the tree crests. The adults knew, although it was beyond the grasp of most of the children, how risky the clandestine operation would be. That was why it was unsuitable for young children; they might slow the group's fast pace or cry out and break the silence, exposing them all. Had he done the right thing, removing young Gilla from the safety of the nuns who had sheltered her? The alternative, though—leaving her behind in the convent—was unthinkable.

As was leaving Daniel.

IT WAS UZI's last day in the Châteauroux area and the Loire Valley before he departed with the children to Marseille. He had planned to use his free day to finally explore the baroque splendor of mansions, their façades carved from soft chalk stone into elaborate columns, arches, intricate garlands, and crowns. Instead, he rooted through the trunk of used children's clothes in Pastor Gaspard's church and selected a pair of shoes, two unmatched socks, and a small coat. Uzi would not discuss Daniel's case with Hilda, knowing her response. He wouldn't even ask for Pastor Gaspard's help in composing the letter he needed.

It had been over a week since Uzi left Châtillon-sur-Indre. Guilt at having walked out on Daniel gnawed at him. How could he have left that adorable boy in those deplorable conditions? He now knew without a doubt what had to be done. He wished he could alert Zehava; he would have sent her a telegram if there were a functioning post office nearby.

He copied a string of words from his dictionary. *You. Write. Last name. Father. Permission. Take. Boy. Birth date. Birth parents. Registration. Signature. Money. Witness. Date.*

In the busy town of Châteauroux he had found a wood-carver selling bowls, boxes, and stools. On his shelf sat a train with three cars behind the engine. At Daniel's age, Uzi had loved his and had been scolded for refusing to share it. "No one owns personal property in the kibbutz," he was told. Eventually, as he grew up, Uzi grasped the wisdom of communal life, but the earlier thrill remained in his memory. He wanted to give Daniel the same.

He had left his bike as a gift for Father Patrick's staff in Argenton, so he hitchhiked to Châtillon-sur-Indre. When the farmer let him off, the place where Uzi had spent a week felt as welcoming as home. The air was crisp, and Uzi would have liked, for once, to relax at a café with a cup of coffee or climb up the ancient, abandoned tower in the center of town and get a view of the surrounding land.

Madame Therrien opened the door and appeared surprised to see him.

Hoping that she had been keeping Daniel, Uzi scanned the parlor. Seeing no signs of the boy, he stepped into the kitchen and pointed to the house behind hers.

She shook her head sadly. "No Daniel." She made a hand gesture like a bird taking flight.

Gone? *"Où?"* he asked. Where to?

She raised both hands in a show of ignorance. *"Orphelinat?"*

The word was close enough to the English word *orphanage*. Uzi's heart sank. Where had Daniel been taken to? What was the process for retrieving him from an institution? How could he officially adopt him? Zehava would surely fall in love with him. She and Uzi had agreed on three or four children, their contribution to Jewish revival in their homeland. They would just start earlier than planned, with a child who was already four years old.

But where was he? Uzi had no idea what kind of documents Daniel's adoptive father had signed or whether permission had been required to remove a neglected child from his home. Whatever the scenario, Uzi needed a signed letter from this man authorizing him to take over.

Uzi pointed to his list of words, led Madame Therrien to the dining table, and put a pen and a clean sheet of paper in front of her. He was unsure of her level of literacy, and indeed, she erased, corrected, erased again, then finally copied it all onto another clean sheet.

Moments later, Uzi waved three thousand-franc notes in front of Daniel's adoptive father. The man filled out some blanks and signed the paper. The lines for Daniel's birth parents' names were left empty.

Satisfied with the signature, Uzi folded the letter. *"Plus documents?"* Uzi asked, using the English word with the French pronunciation.

"No." The man reached for the money.

UZI HADN'T IMAGINED that he would ever be heading back to the town hall, but it was the only official place he could think of to notarize his new document. Rounding the corner, he saw the crown of blond curls as the young clerk bent to water the front bushes. She sent him a big smile, put down the watering can, then stretched like a cat. The fabric of her cotton dress pressed against her breasts, and she looked straight at him as if gauging her effect on him.

Discomfort rushed through him at the sexual overture.

Just then, fast footsteps behind him made him turn. Arthur.

"You're back!" the boy exclaimed.

Uzi ruffled his hair. "How have you been?"

"I'm coming with you." Arthur tugged on the large canvas bag hanging across his chest.

"We've talked about it," Uzi replied. "Ruth Morgenstern is in charge."

"I want to come with *you*." Arthur's tone was stubborn, challenging.

How he hated to refuse this lonely child. Uzi suppressed his irritation at being sidetracked. He had to get on with the task of locating Daniel. "I'm really sorry, but OSE won't let me take you along."

Arthur cracked his knuckles, and a twitch traversed his face.

Uzi put his hand on the boy's shoulder. "Right now, though, would you do me a favor?"

"Only if I can come with you to Palestine."

Uzi shook his head. "It's out of my hands." He saw the secretary step inside the door and wait for him in the shadow. "I don't have time right now," he mumbled, then walked in. *"Bonjour,"* he called to the secretary.

She said something in French, smiling widely.

There was a movement to his side. Arthur must have reconsidered the favor.

"Please ask her to have a document stamped," Uzi said in Yiddish.

Arthur asked her, listened to what she said, and reported, "She says that the mayor is not here."

"When will he be back?"

"Next week, she says."

"Can she sign instead?"

"She says you know what to do if you want her to sign."

"Sure I do." Uzi smiled at the woman, then stepped around her to her desk.

She called out something behind him. He quickly scanned the wheel of hanging stamps to the right of the typewriter, similar to the one in the kibbutz secretariat. He slipped the signed paper out of his pocket with his left hand, grabbed the largest stamp, hit the ink pad, and stamped his paper.

Behind him, the woman yelled.

"Please tell her that I am really sorry. I can't wait for next week," Uzi told Arthur over his shoulder. He lifted the second-largest stamp and brought it down hard. Hopefully one of them was the correct one.

She lunged, trying to grab the paper. He raised it above his head and started to retreat to the door; he wouldn't attempt a martial-arts move that would have left a male opponent flat on the floor. *"Pardon,"* Uzi told her. *"Pardon."*

From behind her, Arthur grabbed her dress. She stopped, pivoted, and swatted at him.

"Let her go. Now!" Uzi ordered. "We do not attack women." He folded the letter, tucked it in one pocket, and peeled a bill off the wad of cash in his other pocket. He placed his hand on his heart to indicate his gratitude. "Arthur, please tell her that I am really sorry."

Her face set in anger, the woman yanked the bill from his out-stretched hand and, puffing with indignation, walked back to her desk.

At the door, Uzi stopped. "I'm not done here. Arthur, would you please ask her where there's an orphanage around here? A state orphanage."

"I'm not going to any orphanage!"

At her desk, the woman was reapplying her lipstick. The money seemed to have placated her.

"Please. It's not for you. I'm looking for a little boy."

"Daniel?" Arthur said.

"Yes. Do you know where he is?"

"And what if I do?"

"Please take me there."

"Not unless I go to Palestine with you. If you don't take me, I'll run there myself."

Uzi looked at the eager, determined face, the scrunched-up features hardened by so many blows. He wasn't here to start a tug-of-war between Jewish organizations, yet how could he allow this child to be a victim of bureaucracy?

He wrapped his arms around the boy's thin shoulders and brought Arthur close to his chest. A moment later he felt the wetness of tears soaking his shirt and knew that this was the first hug this boy had received in years.

Chapter Forty-Six

SHARON

Tel Aviv, Israel
January 1969

O N ALLENBY STREET, shoppers carry heavy food baskets from the nearby produce market, and pedestrians stroll leisurely before sunset. The sun sets early this time of year, but today, at least, the weather has been unseasonably mild, and Sharon took Savta to her favorite fabric store. They concluded the successful trip with fabric for a new suit for Sharon, a Simplicity paper pattern, beautiful buttons, and soft material for the lining. Now they are celebrating in a café with milkshakes and airy chocolate cakes under mounds of whipped cream.

Sharon tucks several liroth under her saucer and picks up their packages. "Enough excitement for you for one day," she tells Savta and pulls her to her feet. She helps her button up her coat. "We'll start the sewing tomorrow."

Savta scans the crowd. "It reminds me of my evenings in Paris. Did I tell you about my time there?"

"Plenty, except that you keep the juicy details to yourself."

"I was young once, you know." A smile bunches up Savta's slack cheeks. "Paris was at her best. The avant-garde era. Like *La Bohème* without the starvation."

Just last week they attended that opera. "I'm dying to hear what you did." Sharon raises her arm to hail a taxi. She wishes she had known the young Esther as a friend, a woman who was her own person, not just a wife and mother.

She forgets about it when the two of them slide into a taxi, where the radio is blaring, and the driver greets them with enthusiasm. "Another one is home!"

"Another what?" asks Savta.

"A Saar. Saar Seven is here!"

What? Excitement and pride course through Sharon, and Savta whispers in her ear, "Is that related to what you did in Cherbourg?"

Sharon blinks her eyes in an affirmative response, a wide grin on her face.

They hurry up the stairs to the apartment, and Sharon vaults to the TV. She wastes precious minutes readjusting the rabbit-ear antennas before the grainy screen finally comes into focus.

There is only one Hebrew station, a government one, and in the evening, after its daylong school programming, the channel broadcasts a documentary, an experts' roundtable, or an artistic performance. Right now, the black-and-white picture that Sharon is staring at is of Danny standing in front of a battery of journalists. Behind him, she recognizes the side of a Saar. On the deck above are seamen whose faces she can't make out. *Danny.*

"That's your commander!" Savta exclaims when she catches up with her.

"Yes, Danny Yarden." Even his name sounds sensuous to Sharon's ears. It's been only a month since she left, and here he is, in her living room. She recalls his friendly goodbye hug. She wishes she hadn't held back the desire to tighten her arms around him in a message he would have understood.

Even before hearing the details of Saar Seven's arrival, Sharon knows that, in the same maneuver that was used to snatch Saar Six from under the nose of the French, Danny captained Saar Seven to Israel. But this time, no one is praised for it; Danny is questioned by a journalist from a leading newspaper about this second act of defiance. "Why strain Israel's relationship with France any further, especially before the French election that might bring to power a more accommodating partner?"

"We've acted legally. Our contract with the French government is not under dispute."

The film clip loops and restarts with the boat's arrival in the Kishon port a couple of hours earlier. Then it's back to Danny responding to a barrage of reporters' questions. He is unfazed and completely at ease despite the microphones shoved into his face.

"That's a mensch," Savta says, meaning a man of honor and integrity.

Sharon is glued to yet another rerun when the phone rings.

"You must have heard," Danny says with no preliminaries.

"I'm watching you talking to reporters." She laughs, loving his voice, basking in their camaraderie. "Some real jerks."

"We wouldn't be Jews if we didn't disagree with one another in a dozen different ways," he replies. "Listen, sweetheart. I'm heading to Jerusalem to brief the prime minister. In the morning I'll be taking the train to Tel Aviv to catch a bus to Ayelet HaShachar to see my parents. Let's meet at nine hundred hours at the same café where you surprised me by taking the job." She hears the smile in his voice.

He just called her *sweetheart*, not *kiddo*.

She telephones a cousin to stay with Savta tomorrow for a couple of hours. The pool of available relatives is still large when Savta is mobile. It won't be this easy, Sharon knows, when the cancer progresses and caring for Savta means hands-on nursing. Savta has refused any aggressive, debilitating treatment. The prognosis is clear.

In the morning, excitement runs in Sharon's veins while she feathers her eyelashes with mascara and zips up the new wool skirt she sewed under Savta's guidance. The fact that Danny is squeezing this meeting into his very tight schedule—the bus ride to his kibbutz in the Galilee will take hours—makes her feel appreciated, a chosen friend. Deeper, there's their bond of orphanhood, even if it matters only to her. There is so much she plans to tell him.

First, she'll confess about Uzi Yarden's letter. Surely when Danny visits, his father will mention her request. Sharon will also report to Danny what she discovered: Pelletier, Châtillon-sur-Indre, Robillard. It will be up to him to pursue it further. The geographical distance from France has given her perspective, and what she sees is embarrassing. Her nosing around was beyond chutzpah; it was obnoxiously prying. It was her need, not Danny's, that made her home in on his past like a searchlight beam. *The worst yenta*, Savta would have said.

The temperatures have dropped, and the clouds seem to be wrapped in dripping cheesecloth. Sharon heads out, and minutes later, in the steam-filled café, she secures a spot by the large window. She wipes the fog off the glass pane with a napkin, and through the cleared arch, she sees Danny approach. His shoulders are hunched forward against the wind, and the hood of his jacket doesn't fully cover the face she's so often peered into over mugs of coffee and steins of beer.

He enters, takes off his wet glasses, wipes them while scanning the room, then puts them back on and crosses the space between them in a few long strides.

"You're looking great!" He holds her at arm's length and scrutinizes her face with a softer gaze than she would have expected. Then he gives her *la bise*. His cheek exudes chill and dampness, like a puppy's nose, and it feels intimate.

She laughs. "It's been only a month since I left."

"It feels longer." He peels off his jacket while asking the waiter, who just brought coffee to their table, "Is the cinnamon cake already baked? I have only half an hour."

"Thirty minutes?" Sharon asks when the waiter walks away. She has so many questions—how the Hanukkah party she missed went, who her replacement is, whether Rina had a boy or a girl. She wants to know if there's any news about Rachelle and Ehud and whether Dominique finally landed a "male" assignment.

First, though, she must reveal to Danny his name!

"Actually, forty-five minutes till my bus departs." Before Sharon has a chance to bring up her questions, he asks, "How are you doing with your math?"

"Hardly cracking the book. My *savta*—"

He places his hand on hers, and she feels the warmth of the rough skin. "It's been a year since the *Dakar*'s disappearance," he says.

She withdraws her hand. "Eleven and a half months."

"*Almost* a year," he corrects himself. The waiter brings his cake, and when he's gone, Danny says, "You have the rest of the winter to study. Take the math exam in late June and apply to the Technion to start in September."

She lets out a nervous laugh. "You have my life mapped out for me?"

"If it were up to me, you'd be back in Cherbourg."

"How are things going there?" She can't inquire here about his meeting with the prime minister, but his response gives her a glimpse into it.

"We're dealing with a major French reaction." He looks at his watch. "That's why I have time only to say hello to my parents today and watch the Galilee sunrise tomorrow before heading down to the airport to catch a flight back."

She swallows. *Chutzpah*, she reminds herself. "Will you find time—whenever you're not overburdened—to check on your family roots in France?"

His head snaps back. "Sharon, not that again."

"But why not? I'd kill to have information about my mother, and I've found—"

He cuts her off. "I'm Holocausted out. All the stories turn out the same: deportations, camps, incinerators. I'm committed to making sure it doesn't happen again." In a more tempered tone, he adds, "That is my life's mission."

"But—"

"We're under threat of imminent attack by Arab seacraft equipped with Soviet missiles. If they get close enough, they'll wipe out Tel Aviv and Haifa. I'm concentrating on how to respond." He leans over the table, motions to her to do the same, and whispers, "We are on the verge of a crucial, game-changing solution."

She likes his coffee-laced warm breath on her cheek. "What kind?" she whispers back.

"Even more exciting than the Saars." He straightens, gulps the last of his coffee, and wraps his untouched cake in paper napkins. "Got to run."

"There's so much I want to tell you—" she begins, but he interrupts.

"Write me a letter, okay? I'd love to stay in touch."

She can walk him the few blocks to the bus. Perhaps she'll blurt out the names even if he doesn't want to hear. But before she puts on her coat, he throws her two more air kisses and rushes out the door. Through the glass, she sees him break into a trot. She grabs her satchel and steps out in a daze. He made an effort to see her but left an echo of unease, of an unfulfilled promise.

What if she hadn't withdrawn her hand? Was he trying to tell her something, to create an intimate moment, thinking that almost a year had passed and she was ready for him? Sharon banishes the ridiculous fantasy. Yet his hand did cover hers. Would he have given her a hug before leaving or kissed her if she had not erected the wall of her mourning?

The drizzle has stopped, and the clouds are dispersed by the sun's rays like startled pigeons. Sharon walks home to Savta. How long will it be before she loses the last person who loves her?

She mulls over Danny's confidential security hint. She learned in her intelligence unit a year ago that tests in the desert for some mysterious defense system had failed; code-named Gabriel, it ended up exploding. The scientists weren't optimistic then. They needed years, not months, and a vast budget despite an uncertain return.

Israel's enemies know its weakness. The next war can't be far off. Its threat casts a dark shadow on Sharon's mood, even if this January day promises to be bright after all.

She crosses the small park where nannies are arriving with prams and strollers. She recalls the many hours when Savta watched her play in the sandbox or stood with arms outstretched when Sharon swung from the jungle gym, ready to catch her if she fell. Soon there will be no one to watch out for her, no one to catch her as Savta did after Alon's death. Sharon wants to cry.

Chapter Forty-Seven

UZI YARDEN

Loire Valley, France
October 1946

A CHAIN-LINK FENCE ENCLOSED the front yard of a red-brick, one-story schoolhouse. About a hundred children of all ages played and fought. Uzi stood outside the closed gate, Arthur at his side.

"Do you see him?" Uzi asked.

"No."

There was no bell to ring for entrance. No supervising adult was in sight.

"Let's find someone in authority," Uzi said, and released the latch on the gate.

Arthur didn't move.

"Are you coming?"

"No way."

Uzi wondered whether Arthur had run away from this orphanage and if that was why he knew its location, halfway to Châteauroux. "Wait here, then."

Inside the building, he followed the odor of sour cabbage and frying potatoes to the cafeteria. Past empty rows of wooden tables and benches, he found the kitchen, where a stooped man, white hair sticking out from under his beret, stood on a stool stirring a huge cauldron.

"Bonjour," Uzi called out three times. He stepped into the man's line of sight.

The man raised rheumy eyes and harrumphed, then pointed with his wooden spoon to a side door.

A short back corridor led to a couple of closed doors. When no one answered Uzi's knock on the first, he pressed the handle and found himself in a tomb of documents. Papers and folders were piled on the desk a meter high, and more were heaped on the floor. A bookshelf overflowed with so many documents and binders that they spilled out and formed a hill of papers. The lone chair was buried under more files. Papers dropped through its open side arms.

Confounded, Uzi started scanning the top of the mess for the name Daniel. If the boy had been brought here this past week, his dossier might still be visible. The state might even have the names of his biological parents.

He found no document that started with the name Daniel.

He halted his frantic rooting through the files. The important question was where the boy himself was. Had he been sent to another institution? Uzi had only two hours before he had to make his way back to Châteauroux and get the children ready for the trip the next morning.

He turned and strode down the longer corridor lined with classrooms. He heard the scraping of furniture, and through a small window set in a door, he saw a middle-aged woman writing on a blackboard.

"Parent," Uzi said. He searched his backpack for his signed letter.

The woman harrumphed something and continued to write.

From outside came shouts of boys. Mayhem seemed to have broken out. Uzi rushed outside to see, hoping that the commotion would attract someone in charge.

As he had suspected, a group of teenage boys were scuffling. Five of them kicked two who struggled on the ground. Excited girls formed a circle, watching. Uzi noticed Arthur still standing outside the gate, ready to bolt.

Uzi was about to break into the fighting mess of bodies when a burly man in his thirties wearing a brown jacket and tie showed up. He pushed through the circle, yanked the attackers away, and pulled the boys up from the ground. They were obviously in pain; one was doubled over. To Uzi's surprise, the man grabbed each by the ear and dragged them inside, as if they were the aggressors.

Uzi had begun to follow them when Arthur, still by the gate, called him. "What is it?" Uzi asked, irritated. He had to talk to the teacher before the man disappeared somewhere in the building.

"The little children's area is in the back," Arthur said.

Uzi's suspicion that Arthur knew the place was confirmed. "Why don't you go check while I talk to that teacher?"

In one of the classrooms, he saw the two boys who had been beaten sitting on chairs, weeping. Uzi was horrified to see their arms had been tied behind them. He untied the boys and stroked each one's head. Just then, he saw Arthur in the window, gesturing for him to come out.

Uzi had barely stepped out the door when a little boy ran toward him. "Daniel!"

The boy threw himself at him, hugging his legs. He raised his head, and the glee in the smile on his dirty, tear-streaked face broke Uzi's heart. *This boy will never again cry with no one to comfort him.* He lifted him and pressed him to his chest. "How are you, young man?" Uzi asked in Hebrew.

Daniel clasped Uzi's neck and planted a wet kiss on his cheek. Uzi wrapped his free arm around Arthur's shoulders and pulled him close on his other side. "Thank you, Arthur. You did a great mitzvah."

Uzi imagined how this must look, this small family unit he'd just created. This was the moment that would forever mark the turning point in his life. He envisioned his own parents adopting Arthur. *You'll be my brother,* Uzi wanted to tell the teen.

He led the boys to the drinking trough, where he washed Daniel's face and hands and patted them dry with the lining of his own jacket. *My son,* he thought. *My son, Daniel.*

He looked at the brick building. He still needed permission to remove Daniel from here, and he had to get his file. Then he thought of the office buried in papers and the teacher's educational methods. He had seen enough. There was no time to spare.

"Let's go," he said to Arthur and took Daniel's hand. Never would he let go of that little trusting hand.

Chapter Forty-Eight

UZI YARDEN

Loire Valley, France
October 1946

I N THE CHÂTEAUROUX station, Uzi, an agent named Abraham, and sixteen children waited for the train to Marseille. Abraham was an Algerian Jew in his late fifties who had been recruited because he spoke French. His face was drawn with fatigue, and he barked contradicting orders at the children, poking them with a thick finger.

"We have a long wait—an hour or two if we're lucky, half a day if we're not," Uzi said to him. "Do you want the children sitting on the ground or standing in a straight line for as long as it takes?"

"I'm too old for this." Abraham wiped his brow with a large stained handkerchief.

Uzi gathered a group of the oldest children, Arthur, Rivka, and two others. "The train ride is your first exercise in leadership training. Ready?" His eyes locked with each of the four. "Leadership means persuasion without using physical force. It means *teaching* the young ones to take responsibility for themselves. Show them what to do when they can't manage; don't do everything for them."

"How, exactly?" Arthur asked.

"We have twelve kids besides the four of you. You four will be my right hands. Each of you is in charge of three younger ones; be like a big brother or sister to them." He gestured across the train platform, filled with passengers and packages. "You'll watch them and play quiet games. Do not let them run around. Absolutely no hide-and-seek. If one kid gets lost, we will all miss our train. When the train arrives, hold hands and rush in with your group. Make sure no one is missing. The train will be crowded. Find a spot where all of you can sit together, even if it's on the floor. Comfort the younger ones if they are scared, play with them, take them to the lavatory."

"Wipe their asses?" Arthur asked.

Uzi laughed. "They may be scared of the hole over the speeding tracks." He scanned the faces turned to him, bewilderment written on their brows. "It's your first assignment, but you are not on your own. I'm here as *your* big brother. My job is to help you manage." He smiled. "Let's start. Each of you select three kids you already know."

Uzi sensed someone watching him. He turned his head to see a tall, emaciated young woman peeking from behind a steel column. She stepped out. Her back was straight, proud, despite the flour-sack dress she wore under a frayed wool shawl. Her dark hair was uncombed but gathered up at the back. What struck Uzi were the intensity and curiosity in her brown eyes.

He turned fully toward her. "Shalom," he said, perplexed.

Her eyes didn't leave his face.

"What's your name?" he asked in Yiddish.

"J-J-Judith Katz." It sounded as if she were uttering it for the first time in years. "Yehudit," she added to confirm her Jewishness.

"I'm Uzi. Uzi Yarden."

"May I come with you?" She gestured in the direction of the children. "I can help with them."

Uzi reached into a bag of food tied to his backpack and took out one of the wax-paper-wrapped sandwiches. "First, eat."

"*Toda raba,*" she said, thanking him in Hebrew, and accepted the sandwich. She took a small bite. Then another. He was impressed by how she controlled her hunger, not devouring the sandwich. Judging by her thinness, she had had little nourishment in recent months. "I've been eating lots of apples and berries," she volunteered as if reading his thoughts. "Once I stole a salami, but I couldn't eat it because it wasn't kosher."

He liked her forthrightness. He handed her his water canteen and she drank a little, took another bite of the sandwich, then wiped her mouth with the back of her hand. "Where are you from? How come you're at this train station?" he asked.

"I'm from Lyon. I've been riding trains."

"What do you mean?"

She threw a furtive glance around her, then whispered, "I was hoping to find relatives. Or anyone I know. They could be anywhere, right? So I've been taking whatever train comes along."

"How old are you?"

"Seventeen." She gestured again to the children, now in four clusters. "Please. I heard you talk to them. God sent me a sign to stop searching in France. It was my parents' dream to go to Eretz Israel. Please let me come with you."

"Yes, of course." He wouldn't ask her now about where she had spent the war years or how she had survived or about her lost family. Not yet. It was heart-wrenchingly clear that she was alone in the world.

She gave him a bright smile. Her teeth were straight; a dimple formed in one cheek, and her dark eyes shone with gratitude. She was beautiful.

She disappeared and returned minutes later with a bundle and a folded blanket. Uzi recalled Miriam talking about children living in train stations. Judith must have been sleeping in one of the broken train cars he'd glimpsed behind the station building. He imagined her rising with hope at the sound of every approaching train, then retreating in despair when no one she knew disembarked. How long did she scout a station before she gave up and caught the next train? She probably couldn't ride far before the conductor ordered the ticketless passenger off the train.

So much courage was packed in this thin teenager's heart! Gratitude flooded Uzi at the chance to save another child. If Judith weren't the size of a grown woman, he would have hugged her to let her know that she was no longer alone. "You'll have a home in Eretz

Israel," he said, "and a family of Jews waiting for you." He stepped over to the station office to purchase another ticket.

When Uzi returned, Abraham was sleeping, his suitcase resting on the ground between his legs. Two girls were fighting over a doll. Judith was there, her back to him, mediating. A nine-year-old boy, Reuven, was lying by the edge of the platform, reaching down. Uzi saw the boy scoot forward until half his body hung down over the tracks.

In a few quick steps, Uzi closed the gap between the two of them. With a stick, the boy was trying to fish up a rag. Uzi's first instinct was to pull him up and scold him for putting himself in danger, then he recalled the children with spoons. It would take time for these kids, who had absolutely no possessions, to stop seeing value in everything, even a worthless piece of cloth. Uzi stretched out next to Reuven and fished out the rag. Then he got up, helped the boy dust himself off, and, his hand on Reuven's shoulder, guided him back to his cluster and the quasi-leader who should have been supervising him.

Keeping an eye on sixteen children through two train changes and in crowded cars and stations would be a challenge. Watching Judith talking to a boy, Uzi had a feeling that she would be an asset—she could take over the role of the ineffectual Abraham.

Chapter Forty-Nine

UZI YARDEN

Marseille, France
October 1946

U ZI WAS ASTONISHED to discover how well organized the displaced-persons camp in Marseille was despite the overcrowding. Hilda had told him that dozens of such camps had been set up since Nazi concentration camps had been liberated. The sheer volume of Jewish refugees streaming out of Poland, Italy, Austria, France, and Germany strained the best plans and intentions. The Americans built tent cities and provided food and supplies, but the Jews set up schools, health clinics, and a system of governance. Uzi was struck by the way family-like groups formed, offering both adults and children, even if temporarily, a semblance of normalcy.

His days were spent helping with the last preparations of the *Hatikvah* in a fishing port several kilometers east of Marseille, away from spying eyes. The ship had been refurbished by members of the Jewish Brigade—former battalions of Jews from Palestine who had fought within the British army against the Nazis. They had fitted the cargo hold with rows of shelves with mattresses for the hundreds of refugees who would be making the weeklong Mediterranean crossing.

Examining these narrow sleeping berths, Uzi recalled his voyage three weeks earlier. He had been seasick, and by the end, his body was empty of fluids, drained of its last energy. That freight ship had carried just a few passengers, and when the sea was calm, he could breathe fresh air on the deck. Sailing on the *Hatikvah* would be a nightmarish journey for the hundreds of malnourished, traumatized, and often sick people crammed together. All Uzi could do now was haul in canisters of fresh water, sacks of flour, and cans of cooking oil. Crates of late-season cauliflower, carrots, onions, apples, and potatoes were brought on board. Uzi encountered ruta-baga for the first time, the feed for farm animals that French people ate during the war. Giant wheels of yellow cheese would provide the only protein during the journey. There would be no salami or sau-sage. Those could easily last the length of a journey, but they weren't kosher and their presence would have contaminated the galley, uten-sils, and food for the many passengers who kept kosher. There was no source for the thousands of eggs needed for such a crowd. Milk for the children would be delivered at the last minute, since it could stay fresh for only a couple of days.

The preparations did not ease Uzi's apprehension. Getting hun-dreds of people out of France would be the easy part. The hard part—the clandestine entry into Eretz Israel—was still ahead. In the camp, boys and girls Arthur's age were being trained as Haga-nah dispatchers and deputy organizers, helping with nighttime drills. Arthur was flourishing in his temporary quasi-family circle and even enjoyed the few hours a day he sat in class. In front of Uzi's eyes, the anxious boy had matured into a youth with a sense of pur-pose. His nervous tics had mostly disappeared.

"I've sent a telegram telling my parents to expect you," Uzi told him when the two of them took a walk at dusk, Uzi's arm around Arthur's shoulders. "They will love you and I know you'll like them."

"Only if they don't make me swallow that disgusting fish oil."

Uzi laughed. In camp each day, the children had to gulp a table-spoon of fish oil before the midday meal. It was a foul-tasting but nutrient-filled supplement meant to help make up for their years of deprivation. "I hated it too. Sorry. You need it as long as you are growing."

The greater surprise for Uzi was Judith. She seemed to be ev-erywhere in camp, taking on assignments, delivering messages, or-ganizing. Uzi couldn't count the number of languages he'd heard her speak as she cajoled warring tent neighbors into peaceful co-existence, interpreted a camp coordinator's request for an American officer. When he took Daniel to the nurses' station to treat a cut, Judith was there, interpreting for the patient. Uzi had seen her sitting on the ground surrounded by children as she played the flute. On Friday night in the community hall, she accompanied the crowd's sing-along on the piano. Her undernourished body was filling out, her hair was shiny and braided, and her new used clothes were clean and mended. She wore pants like the *yishuv* women who helped around the camp but unlike most European women, who wore skirts and dresses.

She seemed like everyone's rock, but who supported her?

"May we take a walk after you're done?" Uzi asked her while she played the piano one night.

She nodded with a smile while her fingers ran over the keys.

He returned after tucking Daniel into bed and found her surrounded by young men, all eager to engage her in conversation and offer her treats.

She extricated herself from their circle, and the two of them emerged into the cool night. They walked along the dirt path near the camp's fence and chatted about the place and the large cast of characters that inhabited it.

"How do you feel about the upcoming departure?" Uzi finally asked, and added, "It's natural to be apprehensive."

"I'm not afraid. It's a dream come true." Her gaze shifted to the night sky, where constellations of stars twinkled. "But what if any member of my family is still alive? I may never reunite with them."

"If you need to stay in France longer, just say so."

She shook her head. "I've been training with my kids for the night disembarkation. I'm eager to make it happen for us all."

"You are a natural-born leader. Israel needs you. I see you moving up fast in our ranks."

"If you mean Haganah, that's exactly what I want to do."

He returned to the tent he shared with ten other Haganah organizers. Daniel was sleeping in Uzi's cot, clutching the engine of his new train. Uzi waited until midnight, then woke him up and carried him outside.

Unlike when they played in the daytime, in the quiet of the night, Uzi trained Daniel to keep silent. *"Sheket,"* he said, silence, placing his finger on the boy's lips.

The first time, thinking that this was another game, Daniel giggled, but he caught on fast. At the word *sheket,* he stopped his chattering. Silent, his eyes wide to penetrate the darkness, he hugged Uzi's neck and the two of them made a round of the camp. The night sounds were different from the bustling of the day. Nightfowl returned. Insects trilled and buzzed. Groans of carnal pleasure seeped from the canvas tents of the lucky couples who had managed to secure a measure of privacy. Others sneaked behind the prefabricated administrative offices. Young people took passionately to life-affirming sexual activity. Mature adults who had lost their first families let loose the primal instinct to replace unbearable losses.

In the dark, Daniel learned to hold back his curiosity about the sudden cry of a night bird or a sexual climax and to greet passing guards with only a wave of his hand. When Uzi was satisfied with the exercise, he carried Daniel back to bed and the two of them fell asleep.

Two days before the ship was to sail, it was Daniel's turn to receive his travel documents. Instead of dropping him off at the nursery school, where he would get a breakfast of milk and oatmeal porridge, Uzi handed Daniel a buttered bread roll and took him to the camp's registration office.

"Arthur Durand has an official French ID, issued when his parents emigrated from Poland. I have a Palestinian passport," Uzi told the secretary. He pointed at Daniel. "I need a travel passage for him. I'm adopting him."

"Lucky boy. He's really cute." She gave Uzi a form and instructed him to have Daniel's photo taken at the next tent.

Two dozen people were queued up at the makeshift passport office. When Uzi's turn arrived, he stepped up to the desk of a bespectacled, cheerful man. Uzi withdrew the signed French letter along with the form he'd just filled out and pointed to the blank spaces. "I don't have his date of birth or the names of his Jewish birth parents."

The man consulted the letter. "The boy's name is Benjamin-Pierre?"

Uzi was taken aback. He'd never tried to decipher the cursive letters beyond confirming that the drunkard had signed it. "He goes by the name Daniel."

"Doesn't matter. Anyway, you're giving him a new last name." The clerk peered over the desk at Daniel, then asked him something in French.

Daniel raised four fingers.

He asked another question in French and laughed at the boy's answer. "He says that his birthday is Wednesday. In that case, let's make today's date, minus four years, his official birthday." As he scribbled on the form Uzi had partially filled out, he mumbled, "Daniel Yarden, born October sixth, 1942." Again he peered down at Daniel and said something in French.

Daniel grinned and turned to Uzi. "Abba," he said. "Abba."

The sudden uttering of the Hebrew word for "Dad" sent warmth through Uzi. "Does he know what it means?" he asked the clerk.

"I asked him if he was accepting you as his father, and this was his answer."

"Abba, Abba." Daniel laughed, repeating the word he must have learned in nursery school. Uzi lifted him in his arms and threw him up in the air.

"All set." The clerk entered the information in his ledger. "His photo should be developed tonight. Come back tomorrow for his travel pass."

"Is this travel pass a French passport?"

The man chuckled. With a wide sweep of his hand, he indicated the camp outside. "How many of these refugees do you think have the original documents needed for legal passports? And do you see here the consuls of Hungary or Poland to issue them? We make do with great artists." He crooked his finger at the people standing behind Uzi. "Next."

A couple in their late forties approached, holding hands. As Uzi walked away, he heard the woman say to the clerk, "We got married last night, and I need to change my last name."

"Mazel tov," Uzi called, and a chorus of others in the queue joined in. Within seconds, a small circle of people were dancing the hora, sweeping in the newlyweds and the clerks. "Mazel tov," Daniel echoed, repeating the new words while his little feet followed Uzi's in the dance.

Uzi stopped to root in his backpack. He pulled out a small shiny object and handed it to the woman. "This mezuzah was on the threshold of a house right here in Marseille. The neighborhood is no more. May your marriage symbolize the continuity of our people in Eretz Israel."

Chapter Fifty

SHARON

Tel Aviv, Israel
September 1969

SEPTEMBER IS STILL hot, and the dreaded loss has happened. It's been two weeks since Savta's passing and a week since the end of the shivah—the seven days of mourning for a loved one. Sharon's aunts empty cabinets and shelves, breaking up the only home she ever had. The six siblings will sell this large apartment and give Sharon one-seventh of the proceeds, her late father's share. It won't be enough for her to purchase even a tiny apartment of her own. She'll have to move in with Uncle Pinchas and his wife.

From the dining room, Sharon hears the heated voices of her aunts challenging Dvora's claim to the oil painting of red anemones. Sharon packed away two of Savta's framed needlepoints before they became the family's property. Nothing is hers in the only home she's ever lived in.

She steps out to the veranda and closes the door, grateful for a passing motorbike's accelerating *vroom*. This second-floor oasis filled with clusters of cacti and blooming plants was Savta's perch. Her agile hands never stopped crocheting or knitting as she watched the street, ready to chat with passing neighbors.

The swallows are chirping on the ancient sycamore tree. Savta complained about the figs dropping from the tree onto her terrace. They rotted fast, staining the Moroccan tiles and drawing flies, thus requiring twice-daily sweeping. But Savta had basked in the shade of the saucer-size leaves. Now Sharon sits in Savta's caned rocking chair, her feet on the ottoman, inhaling the figs' familiar sweet, dusty smell.

Unlike Alon's life, which was cut short, Savta's had been long and rich, filled with joys and sorrows. Instead of fighting the cancer, she accepted her inevitable demise. "It's all right to say goodbye," she told Sharon toward the end. "That's the natural cycle of life." Her heart breaking, Sharon understood. Yet after months of grueling days of caring, the freedom from the responsibility is not a relief but a burden. Sharon has no more excuses; she must make a decision about her next steps and her long-term path. It's called growing up.

On the street below, a bus pulls out of the station just as a soldier with a rifle strapped across his chest runs to catch it. The driver stops the bus, something he would never do for a civilian. He waits for the soldier and lets him in.

Sharon can't allow such nonevents to constitute her days. She needs to set a goal for herself. She's a capable woman. Her rising to the challenges in Cherbourg proved it. But what can she do? The *Dakar* has not been found. Three other submarines sank this past year under mysterious circumstances—one French, one Soviet, and one American. A widow of one of the *Dakar* sailors has already remarried. This past week, friends have invited Sharon to picnics, discos, and concerts. As if trying to swim up to the surface of a lake of sadness, Sharon joined them a few times in order to remind herself what normal life felt like. Last night, around a campfire on the beach, her friends talked about their university studies and promising new jobs.

She picks up today's newspaper. She circled some help-wanted ads earlier but hasn't made any calls. Should she try to get a one-year drafting certificate? Take an advanced math course? Why not study both at the same time?

How scared she had been a year ago to travel abroad, yet within twenty-four hours, she was hopping from one European capital to another. She did it because Danny trusted her abilities. She should trust them too. When she's ready, that is.

Uncle Pinchas steps onto the terrace and places his hand on her shoulder. She doesn't turn, but she raises her palm and rests it on his hand. "You'll be okay, sweetheart," he says. "Our home is your home. Forever."

"Thank you."

"I'll send two guys from my factory to haul your stuff from here."

"I need them to move Savta's dinner set to the Golans' basement," she says. Savta willed her the entire twenty-person china set with Grandpa's initials, but Aunt Dvora already commandeered the tea- and coffee-pots. "If it's not stored, the cups and saucers will disappear too," Sharon adds.

The two of them listen to the birds chirping and warbling, then he says, "I remember the night I drove my parents to pick you up. A temporary cease-fire had been negotiated, but no one trusted it. Snipers acted on their own. The road from Tel Aviv to Haifa was only two unmarked lanes then, and with my car's headlights painted over, I might easily have veered into a ditch. On the way back, my parents sat with you in the back seat and cried. I asked to adopt you—Mina and I already had our three boys and we wanted a girl—but my parents wouldn't hear of it."

Aunt Mina is a talkative, birdlike woman, well intentioned but overbearing. Sharon is grateful to have had Savta as a mother. "Thank God Aunt Dvora didn't claim me," Sharon says, and they both laugh. In their family circle, Dvora, who studied law and became a judge, is the one who sows discord, as the raised voices in the living room testify.

Uncle Pinchas points to the newspaper with the circled help-wanted ads. "It would be a great help to me if you filled in for my secretary when she takes her six-month maternity leave."

"Sorry. I'd like to help you, but I can't commit for that long." Sharon lets her hand drop. She hates the idea of doing payroll and bookkeeping in the low-ceilinged office over Uncle Pinchas's machine factory. The screeching of the iron grinders in the tight space gives her a headache. Similar noises from machines in Félix Amiot's hangar, a much larger, busier place—and immaculately clean—inspired awe.

Cherbourg. During her four months there, she was filled with a sense of purpose. She took part in a project of national importance. For all she knows, work on the boats has ceased and the hangar stands empty. Pompidou was elected president in June, and despite his promises during the campaign, he clamped down on the embargo in a televised anti-Semitic rant. He banned selling any military materials "to the Middle East," a cynical act affecting only Israel because Syria, Jordan, Lebanon, and Egypt were being equipped by Russia. Since then, no new Saar has arrived in Israel.

She wrote to Danny. His response was warm, albeit brief; he told her about taking a fun trip to Vaudéville. Of course he couldn't reveal any details about his work, but couldn't he have written more than a few lines in response to her two-page letter?

Then she received a letter from Rachelle, who gushed about her wedding plans; she and Ehud would be married in his moshav in the Negev as soon as her parents finalized their early retirement and immigrated to Israel. She added that Danny and Dominique had broken up when she'd pressed him for a marriage commitment but said she wasn't about to make Israel her home.

As much as Sharon liked Dominique, she felt a twinge of triumph at the news. Danny has begun to fill her romantic fantasies, and she often has to remind herself that she is not in his league. He's probably already found another sophisticated girlfriend like Dominique.

In his next brief letter, he made no mention of his personal life or whom he had taken to the concert he'd attended at the Paris Opera, but after describing it, he added, *I wish you could hear the amazing voices and see the exquisite set.*

He didn't write *I wish you were there with me*, she thought. He signed it *With friendship*, but there was nothing personal in their uneven correspondence. Danny liked her as his former efficient employee; she shouldn't presume there was more to it than that. She should stop deluding herself. She did not write back.

When the apartment finally empties of visitors, Sharon walks through the bare rooms where she no longer belongs. She'll take the bus to visit the Golans. She wants to suggest a ceremony by the beach to help them reenter the world, even if they're merely going through the motions. The images of Alon suffocating will forever play in all their heads. For Sharon, the pain of his loss hasn't subsided as much as expanded to all parts of her body, its load redistributed to make it bearable.

Indeed, in feigning normalcy, since her return from Cherbourg, she has spent an occasional night with Tomer, either in his room or hers. This past Shabbat afternoon, they sat at a café by the seashore over lemonade and cake and watched the luminous sunset. It should have felt romantic. As they held hands over the table, Sharon wondered why she even bothered.

In her room, a box of books sits on the floor. She spots the math textbook on top and plucks it out. If she puts her mind to it, could she reach the stellar grade needed to go to the Technion?

Holding the tattered textbook, she recalls asking Uzi Yarden for it.

And then it hits her. A loose end that was too far-fetched to follow. Yet—

She places a call to Ayelet HaShachar and asks the secretary to leave a message for Uzi Yarden to call her.

A few hours later, he does. She recognizes his smoke-cured voice. "Uzi Yarden here. Someone left a message for me?"

"Thanks, it's Sharon Bloomenthal. We spoke last year when I worked with Danny in France. Thank you for sending the math book and the letter."

"Did it help?"

"I left before I had a chance to follow up on the letter. Something else came up, though. I think you might have some information for me."

"What is it?"

"Danny told me that you were a Youth Aliyah agent in 1946. I know that there were dozens of clandestine voyages with hundreds of passengers each," she says, her tone apologetic. "But just in case—" She pauses, feeling silly. "Would you happen to recall whether you met a young woman—a seventeen-year-old, really—by the name of Judith Katz?"

"Of course! I remember her well."

Sharon gasps. "You do? She was my mother!"

"You were the baby she left? So sorry. Such a tragedy. Your father too." Sharon hears the catch in his voice. "We lost so many comrades in the battles around here."

She slides along the wall to the floor and twists the phone cord around her finger. Incredulity spreads through her. The first and only person she's ever found who knew her mother turns out to be Danny's adoptive father. "What do you remember about her? What kind of person was she?"

"Sweet. Resilient. Bright. Musical. Beautiful. Courageous. Hugely talented. Great with people. Spoke many languages."

Sharon smiles into the phone. Music and languages, just as she had guessed. "My *savta* said she was good with children."

"Amazingly so. So loving. So mature for her age. She kept the children engaged and organized in the DP camp and then on the ship. The kids had experienced horrific traumas. She mothered them all. Danny, too, adored her."

The cold tile beneath Sharon chills the heat that floods her. All her yenta nosing had one purpose: to lead to this very moment. For twenty-one years, she's been trying to find the elusive trail to her mother—she even took the job in France to discover details about her Youth Aliyah experience—and suddenly it's here. Now. At the end of the phone line.

"I should travel tomorrow to visit you in Ayelet HaShachar to hear more," Sharon says, "but I can't wait. Tell me everything now."

"Of course. Since her kibbutz was nearby, we kept in touch after she settled there. We all worked very hard but did Friday-night hora dances together." He pauses. "Amiram adored her. They were very happy about the pregnancy and were so looking forward to your birth. She was very strong and worked till the end."

"Did you meet her in the DP camp?"

"Oh, no." Uzi tells her how Judith approached him at the train station. "For two years she rode trains, hoping to bump into members of her family. There was hardly any other way for European survivors to find one another."

"Oh God." Sharon can't help the moan that escapes her. The misery of loss she has known was so much greater for Judith. "Where in France did she grow up?"

"I sincerely don't recall," he says. "To her, bumping into my group as it was heading to Eretz Israel was God's sign for her to pursue her parents' dream."

"Was she religious?"

"A believer. She kept kosher." He pauses. "The Holocaust caused many adults to turn atheist. For children, during the worst times, God was the only one from whom they could draw protection and guidance."

"I can't imagine how scared the children were," Sharon says. "Do you know where she passed the war years?"

"The family's housekeeper kept her in her village and told everyone she was her niece so she could attend school."

"She wasn't in a concentration camp?" Sharon asks, relieved that her mother had been spared that Nazi torture at least.

"No. Judith even studied Latin with some priest. It must have helped her with languages. At the village, she learned to care for farm animals. She loved the idea of living the agricultural life in Israel but was too musical to pass up a scholarship at a conservatory. Before the War of Independence, while pregnant, she traveled to Haifa for weekly lessons."

"What instrument did she play?"

"Sometimes piano, but mostly the flute. It was far easier to carry around."

The flute! The hairs on Sharon's arms stand up. Of all the instruments in the world, they both favored the same one.

Uzi goes on, and Sharon hears the affection in his voice and can tell that he's smiling. "Life had a lot to offer her—in addition to finding a great love and having you."

"All my life I've waited to learn about her past." Sharon sniffles. "My grandparents and I used to drive up to the yearly Galilee ceremony, but I stopped going when I discovered that no one had actually known my mother."

"Thank you for giving me the chance to do a mitzvah," he replies. "I'm so sorry that you were deprived of a lifetime with your mother. Judith was an extraordinary young woman. I sense that you are like her."

Am I? Am I as special as Judith? After they hang up, Sharon remains seated on the cool tiles and sobs. Never had she imagined that the circuitous quest would lead her to the man who'd helped Judith Katz set out on the journey to Israel—and to Amiram's arms.

Judith. "Ima," Sharon says. She never called Savta by this Hebrew word for "Mommy," even though that's what Savta was, nor did she utter the word to Judith's photos. For the first time, there is something real about her mother to hang on to. "Ima," Sharon whispers again. "I now know who I am. Your daughter."

The conversation with Uzi marks the end of her quest. There can be no more. It's time to pick up her life. How right Danny was to choose not to let the past cripple him in the pursuit of his future. She should too.

When the phone rings again, she decides not to answer it. She needs to digest Uzi's stories. The phone stops ringing then starts again twice more. Finally Sharon picks it up. She groans when the operator announces, "Hold on for an overseas call." Only rich

Americans can afford the cost of such a condolence call. Some distant relative Sharon has never heard of will try his halting yeshiva Hebrew on her.

"I'm sorry for your loss," says a man in Israeli Hebrew.

"Danny!" The sound of his voice shoots right through her.

"I've just heard. So sorry. It must have been a tough few months, but it's still tougher when the end arrives."

She wouldn't give voice to the relief of death for both the pain-racked patient and the overworked caregiver. "Are you still in the *Umbrellas* enterprise? I've seen nothing in the media."

"Oh, yes. It's a hectic business here. Have you applied to the Technion?"

She's embarrassed to admit how shiftless she feels. "Made no progress in my math."

"In that case, I seriously need you here. Would you consider returning?"

"I can't afford the cost of a flight."

"Our expense, of course. Just say yes."

"Yes."

"Tonight?"

Part III

BELONGING:
Some men are born out of their due place. Accident has cast them amid certain surroundings, but they have always a nostalgia for a home they know not.

—W. SOMERSET MAUGHAM, THE MOON AND SIXPENCE

Chapter Fifty-One

SHARON

Loire Valley, France
October 1969

I N ORLY, AN airport that she knows well, Sharon reattaches her suitcase to the wheels with their rubber cords and hops on the train to Paris. She is supposed to make her way with no delay to Gare Saint-Lazare for the northbound train to Cherbourg. Danny is expecting her by this evening. She is looking forward to life among the members of the small Israeli community—even to the changing cast of characters of the reservists. And to seeing him.

Yet when she enters the city, instead of heading to Gare Saint-Lazare, she rides the Métro to Gare d'Austerlitz, where trains leave for points southwest, including the Loire Valley.

What is she doing? she asks herself. Last month, Danny urged her to return immediately, but she had to wait for Aunt Dvora to stop bickering over possessions, for Savta's apartment to be sold, and for the lawyers to divide the proceeds. Uncle Pinchas invested Sharon's share in a fund that would provide her with some income. She no longer has a home. She broke up with Tomer, and last night stayed at the Golans'.

She spent a sleepless night in the bedroom where she and Alon had passed so many hours laughing, making love, and listening to Elvis Presley and a new group called the Beatles. The four framed botany posters she had bought for him at a used-book store still hung on the wall. How excited Alon had been about this present! Lying on the mattress that still held the imprint of his body, Sharon cried as she recalled their early tentative forays into the hidden landscapes of each other's bodies. Kissing for hours had left their lips sore. They had no idea how to proceed until they got hold of an instruction book and studied it as if it were a school assignment, albeit an exhilarating one. In the following months and years, growing together deepened their love. Would she ever find that security in another man's arms?

Alon would remain forever young, his life experiences never fully formed, while she, since his death, has continued to grow in unexpected directions. Danny had seen her potential and challenged her. His condolence phone call had left her curious as to what he had in store for her, but she wanted to prove to him that his continuing trust in her was well placed.

Yet now she is in the wrong train station in Paris. It's been ten months since she left Cherbourg—what's another day or two? She's taking a cue from Judith, the strong-willed teenager who rode trains all over France, fueled by her own determination. Sharon now knows that the woman whose facial features so resemble hers also bequeathed her daughter her courage and resourcefulness.

This new sense of identity overrides Sharon's resolve to abandon the mystery of Danny's tattoo. The chutzpah required to piece that puzzle together takes Judith's kind of doggedness.

Sharon deposits her suitcase in a keyed locker, keeping only her satchel, stuffed with the basic necessities for one or two nights. Her passport and money are zipped into her coat's inside pocket. She purchases a ticket to Châtillon-sur-Indre via Tours.

Next, she places a collect call to the Cherbourg office.

A man's voice accepts the charges and tells her that Commander Yarden is out. "It's Sharon. Please tell him that I'm delayed in Paris on a personal matter."

"You'd better call again. Try him tonight at his apartment." He gives her an unfamiliar phone number. Is Danny back with Dominique, and have they set up house together? Sharon suppresses the pang of jealousy.

"To whom am I speaking?" she asks.

"Yaniv."

He's still in Cherbourg? Heat rushes to her face. "Sorry. I'll try to finish in twenty-four hours."

"That's three weeks too long."

"I told Danny that I was tied up with my grandmother's estate."

"I'll give him your message. Shalom." Yaniv hangs up.

What is going on at the mission that requires her presence so urgently? Sharon looks at the giant clock. Her train to Tours leaves in ten minutes. Yaniv's unpleasant attitude is not new, but he made it clear that she should abandon her senseless pursuit and rush to catch the last train to Cherbourg. A military urgency trumps any personal whim.

But then again, she's a civilian and an insignificant cog in the team's machine, whatever crisis they're facing up there. Chutzpah. This is her only chance to follow the leads she abandoned last December. It's probably a futile chase. If she gets nowhere, it will force her to drop her obsession, her worst yenta streak.

But if she learns something, it will be a life-affirming gift for Danny, as her conversation with Uzi was for her.

It's near dusk when she gets off the train at the Châtillon-sur-Indre station. She stands in the weather shelter, stunned that there is nothing around. There is not even a ticket-office shack. A sign directs arrivals to a distant line of houses Sharon can barely detect in the mist.

She begins to walk. At a nearby farm, a dog barks. In response, chickens set up a confused clattering before they settle down again. The air is cold. She is slipping on her gloves when a van with pictures of cakes, baguettes, and croissants on its side pulls up next to her.

A woman in her thirties rolls down her window. "Need a ride?"

"I'm looking for a hotel in Châtillon-sur-Indre."

"There's only a rooming house. Hop in. Three francs for the lift."

On the short drive, the woman explains that whenever she delivers baked goods, she swings by the station for stray passengers.

"Do you know Florian Robillard?" Sharon asks.

"No one by that name here."

Sharon will check the church records first thing in the morning.

The village is clustered around the ruins of a tall, narrow, windowless tower missing its top that looks like a giant headless scarecrow. Green moss sprouts on its crumbling façade.

The baker drops Sharon off at a corner of a triangular plaza next to a charming cottage built of half-hewn lumber. A lit sign reads CHAMBRES.

"Come in the morning for a chocolate croissant," the baker calls after her. "You won't find a better one in all of Paris."

Sharon rings the bell twice before a woman her age opens the door. She wears her honey-colored hair in an old-fashioned style of braids wrapped around her head.

"Yes, there is a room available." The young woman's body blocks the way. She examines Sharon from head to toe before she steps aside to let her in. "I'm Anne-Marie Niquet. May I ask what is the purpose of your visit here?"

Irritated, Sharon says, "Why do you need to know?"

"We rarely get late arrivals, not in the offseason." Anne-Marie eyes Sharon. "And certainly not foreigners. May I see your passport?"

A passport is required by law at every hotel, so Sharon hands it to her. "What's the price of a room? Are you the owner?"

"My mother, Madame Niquet, is the owner. My father is a policeman. They are upstairs," the girl adds as if informing this stranger that she's not alone here.

After Anne-Marie copies down the details of Sharon's passport, she leads her to the second floor. Of the two available rooms, Sharon selects the one nearer the bathroom at the end of the corridor. "Will it be possible to get something to eat? I didn't see any restaurant open."

Seemingly no longer suspicious, Anne-Marie says that she'll serve her downstairs.

The browned cheese topping the rich onion soup is broiled to a tasty crust. When Sharon finishes, she asks to use the phone to make a call within France.

Anne-Marie gives the number to the operator. Minutes later, Danny is on the line.

"I'm glad you caught me," he says. "What's this business of staying in Paris? Never mind, it works out well, because tomorrow you need to meet six clowns at Orly."

"What?" Sharon's mind reels. She is hundreds of miles away from the airport. "Six? It's always been three or four."

"Still the same drill. One guy is a doctor, and he already informed someone that he plans to take a shopping vacation in Paris."

Why would a doctor be pulled from his duties in Israel, where the health system, as Sharon knows well from Savta's illness, is stretched beyond capacity? Doctors usually serve their yearly reserve duty in local IDF installations. What is going on in Cherbourg that requires flying in a doctor for a month or two? And why, after all the precautions, are they bringing in a large, potentially visible group?

"Hello? Are you there?" Danny asks.

"What time does the flight land?"

"Fifteen hundred hours. Air France, flight three-fifty-nine from Rome."

"All right." Sharon sighs. So much for her trip here. This is a sign that she should abort this investigation. She is tired. She woke at dawn to catch the flight from Tel Aviv, and now it looks like tomorrow will be another long day. Anne-Marie turned on the radiator in her room, and all Sharon wants now is a shower and a warm, comfortable bed.

There's a minute pause before Danny says, "Can't wait to see you."

Sharon loves the warmth in his voice and must remind herself that it does not mean what she would like it to. He's merely glad to have his trusty assistant back.

After she hangs up, she asks Anne-Marie, "When is the first train to Tours?"

"Five after seven."

It is a long walk to the station; Sharon will have to leave at six fifteen. The worst part is that, although she's here, she won't even be able to visit the church, where she hoped to start her inquiry.

"What was that language you spoke on the phone?" Anne-Marie asks.

"Hebrew. The language of the Bible. You saw my Israeli passport."

"We love your people. My mother especially; she taught me to pray for them. We did it a lot when you had that war a couple of years ago."

"Thanks. The Six-Day War in June 1967. A David versus Goliath story."

"You were wonderful. Very inspiring."

Inspiring in what way? What do they know about war in such a sleepy little enclave in the middle of nowhere?

Chapter Fifty-Two

Loire Valley, France
October 1969

BAKING SMELLS AWAKEN Sharon minutes before her alarm clock goes off. It's still pitch-dark outside when she comes downstairs, carrying her satchel and coat.

Madame Niquet introduces herself and serves her a fresh brioche. Sharon shaves butter from a small bowl and watches it melt in the brioche's steaming center. When she's done, she wants another but must rush to the station. The train might not even stop if there are no waiting passengers. She hopes she'll have only a short wait in Tours for a train to Paris and then enough time to get back to Orly.

Madame Niquet fills Sharon's coffee cup. Instead of stepping away, she pulls over a chair and sits down. Her gray hair is gathered in a chignon, and she's missing a front tooth. Her fingers are veined and gnarled. "I was very happy to hear from my daughter that you are from the Holy Land," she says.

"She told me that you pray for us. Thank you."

"Once I had a guest from Palestine. A very considerate young man."

"It's Israel. That's the name of my country."

"I mean that it was Palestine at the time," Madame Niquet says.

"When was that?"

"After the war. There were terrible food shortages, but this man gave his ration coupons to feed a child."

Sharon gathers up her satchel. "Thank you for your hospitality. It's a very long walk to the train station." She stops to look at the woman. "Wait. Did you live here in 1946?"

Madame Niquet nods. "I was a war widow. My first husband was killed on the Maginot Line."

"Sorry to hear that." Sharon hates the platitudes she's heard all her life yet can never come up with a better expression of sympathy. She takes a deep breath. "It's a weird question, but did you happen to know a little boy with a blue tattoo at the bottom of his foot?"

"Daniel!" Madame Niquet explodes. "Of course. He lived right there." She points toward the back window.

Sharon's heart skips a beat. It can't be this easy. *No! Yes!* She drops back onto her chair and searches her inside coat pocket for the letter that Uzi Yarden sent her. She encased it in a plastic sleeve for protection, and now her fingers shake as she straightens it on the table.

"That's me! I wrote it," Madame Niquet says. She points to the signature of the witness. "Evelyne Therrien, that was my name then. I remarried two years later."

Thank you, Arthur Durand, Arnon Yarden. Sharon's hand clutches her throat with the magnitude of the moment. *Thank you! If it weren't for you, I'd never have known to come to this forgotten little village.* She glances at her watch. No way can she make the train if she stays even a minute longer. The next train passes by in three hours, and who knows when she'll catch a connection to Paris in Tours? The doctor and his "clowns," as Danny called them, will be waiting—or they'll have disappeared on a shopping trip.

Yet how can she not hear the rest of the story?

"It says Benjamin-Pierre, not Daniel." Sharon points to the letter.

"My friend had always hoped to have a son named Daniel. Since the baby was so young, it made no difference to him."

Sharon places her hand on her heart. "Tell me everything."

"How come you have this letter?"

"I'm on assignment to learn more about Daniel's roots."

Evelyne Niquet's voice rises with excitement. "My Daniel? Where is he?"

"He's an officer in the Israeli navy."

"My little Daniel?" Evelyne Niquet's tone is filled with wonder and tears. "He captains ships for Israel?"

Sharon nods. It's too early to reveal that he's in France, albeit very far from here. "Exactly."

Evelyne Niquet counts on her fingers. "He must be twenty-seven."

Her hands trembling, Sharon takes out copies of Danny's photos from the January media write-ups. They are grainy but clear. One is an official portrait. In the other, he stands tall and erect in front of a battery of journalists.

The Frenchwoman looks at them, wipes her eyes, then brings the portrait to her lips and kisses it. "My little Daniel," she whispers.

"Keep it," Sharon says. "Tell me what happened before Mr. Yarden came."

"The war was a terrible time. The Boche were brutal. If not for my vegetable garden, my mother and I would have starved. And then, after the Nazis massacred the people in Tulle and Oradour-sur-Glane, villagers were fleeing in every direction, like scattered chickens, not knowing where to go. They flooded our village even though we weren't any safer here." She gulps air. "Someone brought to the church two toddlers from Valençay."

"Valençay?"

"That's a château north of here, and there's a village adjacent to it."

Valençay, Sharon thinks. Her heart sings at the new lead. "Was Daniel one of them?"

Evelyne Niquet nods. "My neighbor Régine Robillard, who had lost three pregnancies, took him. He was about a year and a half old, maybe a little more, and starting to talk a bit. He was so precious." Evelyne Niquet wipes away a tear. "I would have taken him in, but the priest gave the babies only to families that had both parents, even if the father was a no-good drunkard."

"Was he, her husband, a drunkard?"

Evelyne Niquet shrugs. "Yes, but in the priest's opinion, he was good enough to adopt a kid."

"There's a difference between taking in a child and adopting him."

"These were orphaned babies, and Daniel was so beautiful, and he had this ringing laughter that I can still hear in my head—Régine fell in love with him instantly." Evelyne Niquet pauses. "A day or two later, she discovered the blue tattoo on his foot. It was a shock. She'd never expected to shelter a Jewish child, and now both of them were in danger. She feared that if her husband found out, he might blurt it out in the tavern or even just hand Daniel to the Nazis. It was a terrible strain to keep the boy in shoes."

From upstairs comes the sound of someone walking. Cabinet doors open and close; there's a cough, water running in a sink.

"Who was his biological mother?" Sharon asks.

"I have no idea."

"She must have been Jewish, because Judaism follows the line through the mother," Sharon says.

"Daniel's last name didn't sound foreign, like the Jewish refugees'. I don't recall it now."

"Pelletier?" Sharon's finger is on the letter.

"Yes, that's it." Evelyne Niquet holds Sharon's gaze. Her eyes, under wrinkled lids, are bright blue. "Régine loved this boy with all her heart, and he immediately started calling her Maman." Her voice breaks. She rises, gets a glass of water, and returns to the table. "No one in town ever talked of the atrocities, not then and not now. We're all neighbors. We live with what no one speaks of, yet we cannot hide anything or ever forget what happened, what people did."

"What atrocities?" Sharon whispers.

Evelyne Niquet casts her eyes down. "Terrible things happened here."

"To Daniel? To Madame Robillard?"

Evelyne Niquet glances toward her daughter, who is standing in the doorway to the kitchen, a sprig of mint in her hand. "It's time you hear it," she says to Anne-Marie and takes a deep breath. "Régine thought that the best way to protect her Jewish boy was to befriend a Boche, an officer who was living in my house, in the room upstairs, the one with the tub. That's where the enemy settled, in our midst. He ordered me and my mother around, but he brought produce. My mother cooked for him, and I spit in his plate before serving him." She stops, seemingly lost in her memories.

"Régine?" Sharon prompts her.

"He was *not* a nice man, the Boche. Loud, bad-mannered. I disagreed with her idea that, should anyone find out about Daniel, this crude German would protect him."

The dozens of stories that Sharon has heard about World War II and the Holocaust whirl in her head. Danny asserted that they were all the same, but each was a unique human tale, and this one is turning out to be more bizarre than most. "So what happened?"

"What happened was that the war ended—though it went on longer than people think, because there was still a lot of fighting going on for months. The Boche didn't lay down their arms; the Allies progressed into some areas and not others, leaving voids where the Résistance was at odds with the new French army. Our police chief, a Communist, was always quarreling with his deputies, who were Gaullists. All that time, we were still starving."

"Where was your tenant?"

"The only good thing was that he left, thank God." Evelyne Niquet puts her hand over Sharon's. "Who would ever have imagined that our people would be worse than the Nazis?"

No one could be worse than Nazis, Sharon thinks, then recalls the Vichy police, everyday Frenchmen in uniform who captured Jewish children and sent them to their death. "What did they do?"

"The purging. Have you heard of it?"

Sharon shakes her head. "No."

"Revenge disguised as justice. Enemies settling scores. After the war, Communists and collaborators were given punishments without the benefit of a trial. People accused each other of betrayal for the sin of holding different ideologies. The nationalists went on a rampage." Evelyne Niquet crosses herself. "Some people, they shot in the forest, out of sight. Others they hanged at the tower for the whole world to see."

A thought of Félix Amiot flits through Sharon's mind, and she wonders how he escaped the purge. What regrets he must be living with. He's been tireless in his efforts to make amends, yet Jews like Rachelle refuse to forgive him.

Evelyne Niquet points outside. "The tower in the center of town carries our shame." She tightens her fist around a handkerchief. "They constructed their hanging poles there and noosed whomever they thought was a traitor. Régine included." She cries openly. "I begged them. They had already beaten her and shaved off her hair. She was naked, bruised, and bleeding, and now the rope was around her neck. I fell down on my knees and vouched for her honesty, yelling and crying and telling them that it was a huge mistake, that nothing had passed between her and my tenant. I knew that God would forgive my lie. How could Régine's good intentions to protect the boy be so unjustly punished?" Evelyne Niquet raises her apron to her face and sobs into it. Sharon can barely decipher her broken words. "They pushed me out of the way and just kicked the box from under her."

The blood drains from Sharon's face. War made visible what had lain hidden—the bestiality of human nature reared its ugly head. "How awful. How awful" is all she can utter.

"We all know who did what then. We have never trusted each other again." Evelyne Niquet continues to weep into her apron, and Sharon places her arm around the shaking shoulders. Danny was loved by this woman, and he has no recollection of it.

Minutes pass. The grandfather clock chimes the hour. Sharon can't believe that she is shirking her responsibilities, but she can't leave, not until she hears everything that Evelyne Niquet remembers. In a soft tone, she asks, "What happened to Daniel?"

The Frenchwoman collects herself. "The poor little boy was left alone with the drunkard, who didn't care whether he was alive or dead. By now everyone knew about the tattoo, and the priest would not allow me to take him in, saying that there were enough Christian orphans needing our charitable hearts, that caring for one of them was what Jesus wanted from me."

"So you did?"

"My mother and I took care of a very sick girl for a while, until her soul went to heaven. God forgive me, but I never loved her like I did Daniel, and after she died, I asked again for the priest's permission to take him in. The poor boy was so neglected. He would have starved if it were up to Robillard. But the priest said that Jews were no longer in mortal danger and that this boy was cursed with the cardinal sin of his adulterous mother." She sniffles.

The cardinal sin of his adulterous mother. The words echo in Sharon's head and anger rises at that anonymous, cruel priest. And she had thought that rabbis were harsh. Would this priest have interceded and saved this woman from hanging if he had not believed that she deserved this gruesome death? Didn't he see the sacrifice of a loving mother?

"And that's when Uzi Yarden showed up?"

"Sometime later. When he came, I was certain that God had heard my prayers. A man arrived from Palestine searching for children—he didn't tell me that, but within hours everyone in the village knew what this stranger was here for. And here was a Jewish boy that no one wanted. I was shocked that Monsieur Yarden refused to take him. I couldn't understand why, because he seemed so charmed by Daniel; he sang to him, fed and bathed him, played with him. But then he left without him. My heart broke. Daniel had been rejected even by his own people."

"Obviously, he did take him."

"I didn't know that until now—you're telling me such good news!" Madame Niquet takes Sharon's hand between hers and brings it up for a kiss. "Is he married? Does he have children?"

"He's totally devoted to his military responsibilities." Sharon inhales deeply. "You didn't know that Monsieur Yarden returned?"

"Oh, yes, I did." Evelyne Niquet taps on the letter. "A week later he showed up again. By then the priest had sent Daniel to an orphanage. I helped Monsieur Yarden write this letter, and Florian Robillard signed it in exchange for a lot of money. But where was Daniel? I didn't know what happened afterward. All these years I wondered." Her voice breaks again. "In my prayers I followed my little boy. When I had my own daughter and showered her with love, I hoped that someone was doing the same for him." She smiles through her tears. "I'm so happy to hear that my little Daniel is an Israeli captain!"

"He was well loved. Uzi Yarden adopted him, and then he and his wife had more children."

"Did Daniel fight in that Six-Day War?" Anne-Marie breaks in.

It is too complicated to explain that the war was so short and fought mostly from the air and the ground; Israel's navy wasn't capable of fighting a war against Russian-equipped enemy fleets. "He was an officer on active duty," Sharon says for the women's comfort. One day soon, she thinks, she must bring him here, if only for the sake of the neighbor who cared so deeply for him.

At the sound of boots coming down the stairs, Sharon lifts her gaze and sees a small-framed man in a police uniform approaching. He looks quizzically at his crying wife and reaches out tenderly to touch her cheek. "What happened?" he asks Anne-Marie.

"Maman has just told a very sad story."

Chapter Fifty-Three

Loire Valley and Paris, France
October 1969

S HARON WANTS TO stay and see the village, as if its alleys and splotched stones might reveal more secrets, but Danny's assignment is pressing. "I've missed my train and I must get to Paris as soon as possible," she tells the Niquets. "Are there any buses to Tours?"

"I'll drive you." Officer Lucas Niquet points outside to the black-and-white police Citroën. "That's the least I can do for an important visitor from the Holy Land who's brought my wife such wonderful news that she can't stop crying."

As he drives, the tower comes into view. It juts into the blue sky, unapologetic despite the layers of pigeon droppings, as if showing that the passing centuries haven't dimmed its dominance. How amazing that the young Uzi Yarden was here, Sharon thinks. He surely climbed to the top to get a view of the surrounding valleys. Maybe he had no idea about the tragedy that had taken place at the foot of the tower. Sharon cranes her neck to see the spot, conjuring the horrific sight of hanging contraptions twenty-four years earlier. Danny's adoptive mother would never have fraternized with a Nazi had it not been for her little boy's blue star tattoo.

Why would Danny's parents mark their infant with such a dangerous identifier?

Lucas Niquet drives onto a one-lane road filled with ruts and potholes. They pass a lumberyard and a silo with a water trough. Three boys in school uniforms walk on a dirt path. The road cuts through an open field, and when a car comes from the opposite direction, both vehicles shift to the edges of the broken asphalt. Sharon's knuckles are already white from holding on to her seat when, in a harrowing close encounter, a truck sends their car into the field.

Unfazed, the officer straightens out his vehicle and pulls back onto the road.

Sharon waits to calm down before she asks, "Did you know Daniel?"

"He was gone by the time I returned from the Nazis' forced labor. I recall my wife telling me about him." He shakes his head in amazement. "It's incredible that the story is resurfacing."

Forced labor? For a split second Sharon thinks that he's referring to concentration camps, but then recalls Rachelle telling her about the Vichy government shipping half a million able-bodied Frenchmen to Germany's ammunition factories. It's never right to compare suffering, but the French also had their share of misery.

Sharon looks out the window at corduroy-like rows of vineyards radiating up the undulating hills. A silvery ribbon of a river runs alongside the main thoroughfare. A majestic château looms on the horizon, but then a forest blocks it from view.

"Where is Valençay?" she asks.

"About an hour's drive north."

"Is the château still standing?"

"Oh, yes. It's a tourist attraction. Nothing to do with us. We live our simple lives, keep to ourselves." By way of explanation, he adds, "Many châteaux operate vineyards, grow wheat, or raise cattle, and the adjacent villages' economies are attached to them. In Châtillon-sur-Indre, there's no duke lording over us."

"And Valençay has a duke?"

"Not since the war. The last duchess never returned. She lost the estate, like so many members of the nobility did. I heard that she lived in poverty in Paris, even served as a personal maid to a former friend of hers. Then one day she was selling cosmetics in a department store, and an old admirer showed up—the owner of Hennessy Cognac, no less. She married him, and he gave her back the lifestyle to which she had been accustomed."

"A fairy-tale ending." One day, Sharon thinks. One day she will have to visit that place. How can she not try to find out about the Pelletier family? If Danny's Jewish mother was deported, could the non-Jewish father—someone named Pelletier—still be alive?

WHEN THE CONDUCTOR on the train from Tours announces Paris's Montparnasse station, Sharon realizes that she assumed all trains on this line went to Gare d'Austerlitz. How irresponsible of her not to check every detail. She's now in Paris but nowhere near her stored suitcase.

She glances at her watch. She has an hour to travel to Orly before the new recruits land. Even allowing for fifteen minutes for them to get through passport control, if she tries to retrieve her suitcase, she'll be late to meet them and might lose them altogether. Her only option is to meet them first, then schlep all six of them across Paris to fetch her valise. But then they are likely to miss the last train to Cherbourg.

What a mess. Perspiration erupts on her neck. She has no choice but to abandon her suitcase until her next trip to Paris, whenever that might be. Even if all she has now are the clothes she's wearing, her duty takes priority. She won't compound her mistake.

In her head, she runs through every detail to ensure that she's not overlooking anything else. Ah—she must confirm the flight's arrival time.

A huge sign on the building across from the Montparnasse terminal blinks AIR FRANCE in red and blue. Weaving her way through taxis, cars, and buses, Sharon rushes over. A pleasant clerk, her hair in a beehive, informs her that flight 359 from Rome was canceled. "Our ground personnel secured seats for the passengers on other airlines," she adds.

"Which flights?"

"Names of passengers, please?"

Sharon's old unease grows. Had the men been given alternate

plans in case of eventualities like this, as she had recommended last year? The Mossad would never have been this amateurish about an operation, even a small one like this, a peg in a much larger scheme.

She places a call to the office from a phone booth. "I need the names of all six guys to find out the flights they're on," she tells Danny. "Do they have my name and description? Do they know their final destination?"

"I doubt it."

"Do they know one another?"

"Like before, they are selected from different units."

She fumes. "I might lose one or two."

The only positive outcome of the delay is that she can steal forty minutes, take the Métro, and fetch her valise before leaving for Orly.

At the airport, she stops by the roped-off area opposite the passport control booths. A throng of people—some whole families— wait to welcome arrivals. A dozen flights have landed. Sharon has no idea what the men look like or how she can signal to them that she is their liaison. Six men, after all the careful drills of no more than four.

A child drops his ice cream cone, and the mother wipes his hands but does not bother to pick up the pink-and-brown mess. Sharon watches to see who will step into it and, distracted, almost misses an unusual movement behind one of the booths. She looks up and sees a female agent scanning the three long lines of passengers. The woman pulls out five men in blue windbreakers.

Sharon recognizes the jackets sold for decades by Atta. This Israeli brand manufactures functional garments worn by farmers and townspeople interested in durability, not fashion. Sharon swallows hard. Her men will be interrogated. The first question will expose that they don't know their destination. An inspection of their suitcases will reveal an Israeli navy uniform tucked in each.

Five men are being questioned. Suppressing her alarm, Sharon puts on her sunglasses and pulls a French magazine from her satchel. She pretends to read it while she searches for the sixth man. She spots him, wearing the same jacket, at the farthest booth to the left, his passport already held by an officer. From the Israeli's unconcerned stance, it's clear that he can't see that his colleagues have been detained. He seems to be chatting amiably with the officer.

Sharon watches their banter and catches a snippet of what sounds like Hebrew, although she can't make out the words.

She can't believe her audacity and the risk she's taking, but she glides along the rope to a spot near the booth, leans forward, and says in Hebrew, "Officer, would you please process the others over there?"

He frowns and looks over at the female agent who is holding the five men's passports. His glance shifts back to Sharon.

"Please." She points at her watch as if time is pressing. She smiles while her dread grows.

He rises, puts on his hard cap with its center insignia, and steps out of his booth. When he reaches the female agent, she points to something in the passports. Sharon is unsure if she should feel relieved when he takes charge. Holding the stack of passports, he walks back to his booth, the five men in tow.

Sharon seethes. Nothing illegal here, she reminds herself, but nevertheless, it's a mess. Having revealed her connection to the men, she may be the one interrogated. What will she say?

The officer processes the passports and hands them back to the men. Then, as they file down the center aisle to the exit, he approaches Sharon at the separating rope.

He turns slightly, his back to his colleagues. "So this is your Ping-Pong team?" he asks in Hebrew with a Moroccan accent.

Ping-Pong? Catching his drift, Sharon collects herself. "They are here to *win* the Ping-Pong tournament. I'm grateful for your assistance."

"A national pride." He adds quietly, "Tell your headquarters that next time they issue passports, they should not use consecutive numbers."

THE LUGGAGE CAROUSEL rolls lazily across the hall. The coffee Sharon drank in the morning boils in her stomach. She is furious. At Danny, for sure, because he is her supervisor, but also at those above him who are scheming something big to which she isn't privy. How high does it reach? To Yaniv and the naval top brass in Haifa. Perhaps also to the Tel Aviv IDF headquarters. And what about Moka Limon, the revered retired admiral who claims to be no more than a diplomat in Paris? He's her contact if she is detained. What kind of a spy ring is he running—probably all over Europe—if he can't get these very basic details straight?

Sharon's old anger at the navy's failure to locate the *Dakar*—to take responsibility for its sinking in the first place—flares up. It has no outlet. There's no one to rail against. It is down in the trenches that mistakes are discovered, often too late. People die—suffocate in the belly of a submarine—because of human errors.

Luckily, these recruits have the sense to disperse along the length of the luggage conveyor belt. Sharon lets out all the air in her lungs to start afresh. Right now, she has a job to do; she does not have the luxury of giving in to her emotions. Still, the sheer luck of having the crisis handled by a Jewish-French national who must have lived in Israel keeps her nerves on edge. From now on, she will insist on coordinating a background story. And those Atta jackets? Most Israelis don't own winter coats, but they are a necessity in Northern Europe's winter. Until they receive the heavy jackets with fake-fur collars that the French navy supplies them, she should buy a cartload of used overcoats from Paris's flea market.

Tonight, she'll have a serious talk with Danny—about more than this fiasco.

Chapter Fifty-Four

Cherbourg, France
October 1969

EXITING THE TRAIN with the six men after dark in Cherbourg, Sharon inhales the salty smell of the ocean. It is stronger than that of the Mediterranean.

She is pleasantly surprised to see Naomi waiting on the platform. "I thought you'd be back in Israel!" She hugs her friend, thinking of Naomi's son, the lone soldier, still cut off from his family while his mother provides support to her husband on his national security job. "How is Pazit doing?"

"You can ask her yourself, since you'll be sharing her room."

Sharon winces. "What do you mean?"

"We're overcrowded. Let's get the men into a taxi." Naomi motions to a man in civilian clothes and tells four of the new recruits to follow him. She invites the doctor and another man to her car.

She drops them off at the Atlantic Hotel. "Someone will be by to brief you. Stay in your room. Don't leave." She adds, "That's an order from above."

"What's going on?" Sharon asks when the two of them are finally alone a few blocks away from the building she knows so well.

"A lot, but it's not up to me to brief you."

"Pompidou's clamping down harder on the arms embargo? I thought that everything here had stopped."

"I'm so sorry about your grandmother," Naomi says, in an obvious change of subject. She squeezes Sharon's hand. "But I'm so glad that you're back."

"I'm ready to rehearse with our musical ensemble."

Naomi groans. "I doubt that anyone has the time for it."

In the ten months Sharon has been gone, Pazit seems to have

adjusted to the new culture. Black eyeliner defines her eyes; she's even painted slanted eyelashes underneath them, Twiggy-style. Blowing bubble gum, she points to the second bed in her room, then to a chalk line drawn on the floor. "This is your side." She opens a door in the armoire. "Keep your stuff here."

Irritated, Sharon sits down on her bed. She's never shared a room except occasionally during IDF night duty when no one had an assigned cot and just dropped onto whatever one was available. She adds this complaint to the list of issues to bring up with Danny.

Trying to break the ice, she asks Pazit whether she's made friends.

"Yes," the girl replies, then she turns up the volume on her transistor radio, and the room fills with a Beatles song. Having silenced any further conversation, Pazit dances to the beat. "'Back in the USSR. Back in the USSR.'"

In the hall, Sharon places a call to the office. When no one answers, she settles on the living-room couch with Naomi. Elazar is out. Two Israeli men show up, silent and tired. They shower, grab a plate of sandwiches Naomi has prepared, and take it to the third bedroom. Naomi serves Sharon coffee and cake, and the two of them chat about everyone they know, avoiding the elephant in the room.

At eleven o'clock, Pazit's music is finally turned off by her mother's decree, and Sharon falls asleep. The shrill ring of the phone in the hallway pierces her dreams of Châtillon-sur-Indre. A minute later, Naomi informs her that Danny will pick her up shortly.

The night is cold and moonless. Sharon stands close to the building entrance, wearing her coat, hat, scarf, and gloves, and wonders how long this night will be. Anticipation at seeing Danny for the first time since January swells in her. She wishes she weren't half asleep and that her teeth would stop chattering.

He pulls up in a Renault and lets Elazar out, and after a brief hello to him, Sharon slips into the passenger seat. She leans over and kisses Danny's cheek.

"Great to see you, sweetheart." His hand touches her arm, then rests on her sleeve as if he has forgotten it, and he gazes at Sharon for what seems a long time. In the car's whitish light, his face looks drawn.

She glances at his hand, wondering what to make of the gesture. And that *sweetheart* again. He withdraws his hand and grabs the stick shift.

The boy with the blue star tattoo, she thinks, and rests her palms on the vent to warm them. When she reveals to him what she's found, he won't be able to hold back his excitement. His reluctance will melt when she tells him about Evelyne Niquet's love for him.

"I was going to drive to the office where we can chat, but I'm beat," he says. "Do you mind if we talk in the car?"

"The sooner you enlighten me about what's going on, the better."

"Let me start by showing you something."

"I also have something important to tell you."

"I'll go first." He drives three blocks toward Napoléon's canal, turns left then crosses the bridge. He swings into the wide water basin parallel to the canal's east side. The marine repair shops and windowless warehouses are deserted for the night.

He stops the car but keeps the motor running. "What do you see?"

She strains her eyes in the dark. She can't even detect the streetlamps on the opposite bank. "Nothing. A ship is blocking my view."

"Stand outside and look," he tells her.

"Must I?" She's exhausted, but she buttons her coat and scrambles out. Salt-carrying wind blows from the ocean onto the oil-slicked water, where the mast sides of four Saars loom. Four? They are anchored side by side, looking like huge, proud sentries. Sharon lets out a yelp, then slips back into the car.

"Four Saars? Docked right here? Unprotected?" she whispers. When she left, the French navy kept each completed boat in its highly secure west-end harbor—and there was never more than one at a time there.

"After I captained Saar Seven out without a champagne party, our French naval friends punished our 'ungentlemanly' act by removing their protection. Each subsequent boat that has come out of

CMN was launched into the water—the fourth one only ten days ago—but it can only dock here."

"The Saars' production has continued all along? Is Saar Twelve coming too?"

"Last year's civil unrest is still fresh in the government's memory, so Amiot exploits it to keep his people employed," Danny replies. She knows he's referring to the general strike that started in May 1968 with the students' revolution and quickly spread to include all labor unions in France. Danny lights a cigarette. "With only one *official* crew, we rotate taking out one boat for testing and training, but we return it at nightfall."

"And this has been going on for nine months?"

Danny points his cigarette toward the Atlantic Hotel on one side, then to one of the buildings diagonally across the canal. "We are running our own surveillance for any unwelcome activity."

"That's why you need more men," she states.

"There's more. The saga of the five remaining boats has turned into an international crisis. Amiot is beside himself because he's heavily invested financially. Our government won't pay him the balance until the French government assures us they will allow the boats to be delivered. The Germans designed and partially subsidized the project; the Italians have a stake in the development of the navigation systems. The French—well, it depends on whom you're talking to." Danny cranks open the window and blows out smoke. "The mayor of Cherbourg is incensed that this political conflict has landed right on his belly button. He's petrified of a Palestinian attack in the center of town. He's pressuring Pompidou to get it over with, but at the same time the mayor has been warned to keep it quiet; media exposure increases the risk that one terrorist cell or another will take it upon itself to sabotage the boats."

She recalls that Amiot saw to it that no local paper ever reported on the Israelis' presence in Cherbourg. "How long can anyone hold back the media?"

Danny's cigarette points somewhere east. "Not long now. The French are about to launch their first nuclear submarine with great fanfare right next door to CMN. The media circus will come to town. Who's going to miss the sight of our Saars?"

"When is Saar Twelve being launched?"

"The sun and moon align on December twenty-third, but we won't wait that long. Amiot is rushing the production."

Sharon recalls that in these Normandy waters, high tide can reach fourteen meters, making it possible for a boat to slide on tracks out of its cradle and into the water. The urgency to launch before the highest tide means a crisis of immense proportions. "What if the Saar is not ready? There have been so many technical issues before. The propellers—"

He cuts her off. "Waiting till January is not an option."

On the silent dock, a Peugeot passes by. Two men wave at Danny, stop by a distant lamppost, and step out. Each with his hand on his right hip, they walk around, check with a flashlight behind a cluster of oil barrels, climb on top of two fishing dinghies moored on planks, disappear behind a warehouse, and reappear from its other end, their flashlights searching its roofline. One of the men takes out a walkie-talkie and speaks into it. They climb back into their car and drive slowly the length of the dock to the bridge.

Sharon doesn't realize that she's been holding her breath until the men—and their not-quite-concealed pistols—are out of sight. "Do we have a trained commando unit here, ready to defend our boats on French soil?"

"That's one possibility we must be prepared to address."

Scenes from an action movie flash in her mind—the rat-a-tat-tat of machine guns, bursts of fire, men wearing keffiyehs yelling the war cry "Allahu Akbar." No, it would be quieter—explosives planted under the boats. It means that the Israeli crew here also includes frogmen.

Existential fear floods her brain cells. "What's the other possibility?" she asks.

"We must be ready for the moment that we get the green light and all five boats are released to leave." Danny sucks on his cigarette. "You see the problem?"

"It takes twenty-two men to crew each boat." Until now, the core crew manning each boat, supported by some trained reservists, sailed it home and flew back for the launching and testing of the next boat. "You need a hundred and ten men," she says.

"In our tiny navy, there isn't a large pool of officers and seamen from which to draw. The training to operate these particular boats, the first in the world with this fast yet small design, takes months, not weeks. We started last year at all levels with your guys. This past summer, we graduated the naval academy earlier than scheduled and put the cadets on a fast track to command the Saars—less time than we view as safe and necessary for the many situations that arise at sea."

"Is that why I'm sharing a room with Pazit?"

"Would you rather have your own room in Valognes?"

The desolate village where Amiot gave the Israeli mission the use of a second apartment building is too far. Sharon says nothing. The steam of their breath coats the windows.

Danny continues, "The townsfolk loved us when our work supported over one thousand families. Now that manufacturing is about to end, unemployment here is rising. Amiot can't accept and finance new orders until he's reimbursed for the personal investment he made to keep his company afloat. Into this unfriendly mix, can we drop over eighty new Israelis?"

"Can't they be trained on the seven boats already in Israel?"

"We run exercises there too. Less than half the crews are here. The Mediterranean Sea, though, is a sleeping baby compared with conditions in the Atlantic Ocean." Danny rolls down his window and tosses his cigarette into a puddle. "We hide some officers among the Israeli families. The seamen are on the boats."

That explains the two men at Naomi and Elazar's small apartment. So men are living on these boats? Sharon examines the four vessels' silhouettes against the wan glow of a moon struggling to break through clouds. Not even a pinprick of light twinkles in the portholes. It's hard to believe that anyone is inside.

"The first time I reported to Kadmon, I told him that more careful planning was needed, and he asked me to write a proposal. I did, but it hadn't been implemented when I left. Who at headquarters makes the travel arrangements? Given what you're telling me about the situation, you can't let their incompetence continue. Today's recruits were caught at Orly." She proceeds to report how, by sheer luck, the men were saved from questioning that would have brought in the highest levels of law enforcement. Her voice gets heated. "Now that the scope is expanding, you need the Mossad to take over."

"That would require Jerusalem to approve Operation Noa."

Operation Noa. She lets the new name sink in, although it reveals nothing about its nature. "Are you saying that our heads of state and defense are not on board with what's being planned here?"

"Limon made Golda and Dayan *aware* of it." Danny pauses. "They've accepted losing the fifty Mirage aircraft; they don't want to risk further escalating tensions with France over a few boats."

"This is crazy. These preparations are not merely a comma separating the legal from the illegal, as you once described it. Is Moka Limon running his own show? This is not just insubordination—it's insurrection!"

Danny takes a deep breath. "Do you want to leave?"

"I should. Never in the IDF's twenty-year history has there been a known case of mutiny, much less one of this scale." She turns her face away and stares into the darkness.

"Limon views the Saars as crucial for defending Israel's shores—and its Red Sea access," Danny says, referring to the port of Eilat in the south. "We—the boats—are the tip of the spear."

The tip of the spear is the first to penetrate an enemy. "I can't believe that you brought me into this," she mumbles in anger. She agrees with Limon, but she doesn't presume to know more than her Six-Day War heroes Golda Meir and Moshe Dayan. Anyway, an army is structured on obedience. How can she go along with this scheme—this defiance—minor player that she is? She recalls handing the fake passports to the "Norwegians." She overcame her hesitancy when it seemed to be a harmless infraction, strategically necessary. Now the scheme is huge. She understands its importance to the country's defense, yet to be part of it, knowing that it's outside her government's knowledge?

For a few moments, the hum of the running motor and the heater's soft whistle are the only sounds heard in the car. Moka Limon, she thinks. The man who, in his youth, commanded the fleet of refugee boats dodging the British blockade to reach Palestine. Judith Katz had been one of these refugees. If not for the Haganah's daring during those years, hundreds of thousands of Holocaust survivors would not have been able to escape Europe and find a new home in Israel. Judith Katz included. Sharon would not be here, recruited to help in Israel's defense.

The silence stretches between her and Danny. Finally, he yawns, shifts the car into gear, and begins to back out. It jolts Sharon out of her thoughts.

It's settled, then. She's staying.

"Wait," she says. Danny is exhausted, but how can she not tell him? "I said I have something personal to tell you. It's about your ta—"

"Please." He cuts her off. "Me—I need some shut-eye." He rubs the stubble on his cheeks and touches the cleft chin that must feel coarser. A small smile appears on his tired face. "Sweetheart, we'll talk about you or me, as they say, 'after the war.' In the meantime, I'm glad that you're back."

Sweetheart again. Danny really is half asleep, she thinks. "You haven't told me what my assignment is."

"Feed the men."

Chapter Fifty-Five

Cherbourg, France
November—Early December 1969

IF FEEDING LESS than half a crew is this taxing, Sharon can't imagine what it would take to feed one hundred and ten hungry men three meals a day. No shopping in town is possible, not in any meaningful quantity. Over a dozen low-ranking seamen who used to be housed and fed in the French navy barracks are now squeezed into her building's first-floor apartment, which Kadmon filled with cots. They eat on the boats, as do the officers who are housed with the Israeli families or in the Atlantic Hotel, where they get only partial board.

How long can this impossible situation be sustained? The greatest risk is keeping the men's presence inconspicuous. Sharon worries that every day increases the odds of exposure. The shipyard daytime workers might notice unfamiliar faces on the decks; a neighbor might complain at the grocery store that there are too many guests next door; a sailor might carp to his French girlfriend about overcrowding belowdecks. And a Parisian journalist privy to the goings-on in Pompidou's government might come sniffing around and break the story.

Daily, Sharon travels in her rented van near and far in the Cotentin Peninsula, shopping for food. At each supermarket, she fills one cart with a reasonable amount of rice, beans, chocolate, crackers, cereal, margarine, cigarettes, cookies, marmalade, oatmeal, and canned fruit and vegetables, enough for a large family. At each farm, she buys dozens of eggs for her supposed bakery in Bayeux. At each dairy farm, she buys one huge wheel of cheese weighing thirty or forty kilos, a block of butter, and a hip-high canister of fresh milk, even though she needs four. She can't return to the same chicken and dairy farms for a couple of weeks. She drives for hours to the cities of Caen and Rouen to purchase wholesale sacks of flour and sugar and cans of cooking oil under the pretense that she owns a restaurant. She buys loads of baguettes daily—never more than half a dozen from each of the many bakeries she visits daily—and shows up at the weekend markets early to pick up cases of fresh string beans, parsnips, cabbages, and carrots. She moves her van to the other end of the market and buys only two sacks of potatoes and a kilo of roasted coffee beans, then drives to the next town market for another kilo of coffee and crates of apples "for my pies." As if she were foraging for precious objects, she collects slaughtered chickens cleaned of their feathers and innards—tasks that can't be executed in a ship's tiny galley. In this region that is so rich with cattle and sheep and industrious fishing villages, she can't buy meat because of the IDF's kosher regulation, nor can she draw attention to herself by buying trout and sea bass for more than two dozen hungry men at a time.

Her contact is Kadmon. He works in the formerly busy office with just one new man, Rear Admiral Vaknin, who is quiet with a distinguished professorial look down to his plaid jacket with leather elbow patches. From the charts on his walls and his locked office door, Sharon suspects he's a military strategist devising battle games.

Kadmon hands Sharon lists and cash. On her return from her shopping trips, she leaves the full van parked next to the office and gets a ride home from the gate of CMN with one of the workmen. In the morning she retrieves the key to the now-empty van. She imagines the seamen unloading it at the dock under a night sky tinged with a predawn glow. Her crates, sacks, and canisters are silently loaded onto the first boat, then transferred to the next boat in the chain, where each cook examines the produce to plan nutritious meals.

She's been doing this for seven weeks now, seven days a week. She's exhausted. She hasn't been alone with Danny since that first evening, and she's seen him only three times at Friday dinners. *The boy with the blue star tattoo.* Every day, for the whole day, along with a small crew of officers and seamen, he takes out one of the boats—never more, even though he has the personnel hiding in their hulls. She fantasizes about accosting him on the dock one night and blurting out everything she's learned of his past. Against the odds, he'd be grateful. He'd hug her in delight; he'd kiss her—

She brushes her longing away. It's just a young woman's infatuation with her handsome boss. If Danny had the time, he would find himself another girlfriend like Dominique—accomplished, sophisticated. What he needs most now is for Sharon to support his mission and not become a major headache. How could she drop a bombshell into his life when he feels like the future of Israel rests on his shoulders? His emotions are on high alert, focused on his men and his boats, on preparing for the inevitable next war, a war that, the Arabs threaten, would "finish Hitler's job."

Sharon can't imagine how the crews can train for sea battles against four or five Russian-equipped navies without the benefit of arms on deck to practice. But train for battle they must. A small news item buried deep in an Israeli paper informs readers that a fishing dinghy off Israel's southern coast exploded. A report that arrived at the office revealed a crucial detail about it: the dinghy was hit by a missile. Egypt had tested the accuracy of the new Russian-made sea missile against a distant small target. It proved incredibly precise.

If Sharon is this stressed and tired, Danny, *Benjamin-Pierre*, must be more so. The long trips to the countryside give her hours of time to reflect and second-guess herself. Yet, she can't block the names that flash through her head while she drives: *Pelletier. Châtillon-sur-Indre. Valençay. Robillard.*

She inserts a cassette into the tape deck, turns up the volume, and belts out Israeli songs to drown out the names. She sings "Speak to Me with Flowers." She doesn't regret having traveled to the Loire Valley when she did. Valençay would, one day, be key to solving the puzzle—but it would be up to Danny to pursue it to find the answers. She modulates her voice to the quieter, melodious "Maybe None of It Had Happened." But it all happened.

At a farm stand, she buys two crates of leafy greens and accepts the offer of a cup of hot tea sweetened with honey. Back on the road, Sharon lets her eyes feast on the sights: the contrast between textured, ancient forests and smooth, mowed fields; between foaming ocean waves crashing against rocks and the softly rippling hills. If only it weren't winter. It starts to rain, and a gust of wind whips her van so hard that Sharon forgoes a drive to the fishing villages along the coast of Lower Normandy. She turns inland, following her map on which she marked each farm and what it sells.

At nightfall, she returns to her new lodging: Rachelle's living room. Rachelle insisted that Sharon's alternative—living in the isolated, distant Valognes—was no life for a young woman. The evenings in Cherbourg, though, are also quiet, so different from the boisterous nightlife of the year before. The Israeli seamen who once relished platters of oysters and clams in the cafés and danced until midnight in discos are now under a strict curfew. The mood is somber. Since Rina's husband is always at sea, she returned to Haifa with her two babies so her mother could help her. Naomi and Elazar are packing to leave; his drafting job using a pencil and a ruler has ended. Even Yaniv's family is gone, although he stays, often locked with Vaknin in the latter's office.

Whatever Operation Noa is, it may never take place if Golda doesn't give her approval.

Just before Sharon falls asleep, in that state between wakefulness and dreams, something occurs to her: If the brewing scheme is against France's explicit embargo but is carried out without the Israeli government's authorization, the latter can't be held responsible. The only head to roll would be Limon's. But if some mishap brings the ploy to light before Operation Noa is launched, would the team—herself included—be viewed as coconspirators in an insurgency?

She bolts upright, throwing off her covers. If she were still serving in the IDF, she'd be court-martialed along with the others in classified proceedings. Now, as the only civilian on the team, she would be on her own in an open criminal court. As outrageous as it seems, she and Limon would take the public brunt of this insurrection.

There is no one to consult. No Israeli attorney around. The simplest solution would be to extricate herself from this potential mess and leave. But how can she? There's no one here who will get into the van early tomorrow morning for a shopping expedition. Overriding all else, she is committed with every fiber of her body to doing whatever has to be done for Israel's defense.

"It's the best I can do for you, Alon," she whispers.

THIS YEAR, HANUKKAH falls in the first week of December. Unlike last year, only Sharon, Naomi, Pazit, and a handful of Israeli seamen join the tiny local Jewish community to celebrate the first night of candle-lighting. They sing with the Jewish families that gather at the church. This year, the words of "Rock of Ages" hold a deeper meaning for Sharon. The bloody victory of the Six-Day War took place only eighteen months ago. Who knows what's to come? She belts out the second stanza in full voice:

Furiously they assailed us,
But Thine arm availed us
And Thy word broke their sword,
When our own strength failed us.
And Thy word broke their sword,
When our own strength failed us.

She sings it again every evening when she visits the four boats— each night a different one—where the hiding seamen light menorahs brought over by recent arrivals. She delivered decorations made by the children to hang in the crammed crew messes and purchased yeast for the fried *punchkes*. Anything to give the men a sense of home. She watches their bright-eyed faces aglow around the menorah, the icon of Judaism. Secular or Traditionalist, every Israeli reveres this symbol of freedom and national identity.

When Sharon climbs onto and off a boat after dark, she does so with the help of the team's security. They squeeze her visit between the CMN night watcher's and the patrolling police cruiser, then drive her home. There, lounging on the huge beanbags, Sharon helps Rachelle with her Hebrew lessons. She's inspired to tackle her own old high-school math textbook. Soon she'll be ready for Danny's calculus textbook—if an engineer were available to tutor her.

Some nights she takes out her flute and practices before retiring to bed. Deep breaths, pure sounds, and measured phrases are a reprieve from the tensions of the day.

Rachelle doesn't usually ask questions, but tonight, when Sharon puts away her music, she says, "I smell something in the air."

"You smell Pompidou's foul odor of anti-Semitism."

Unlike the past, though, the Jews will no longer be its victims.

Chapter Fifty-Six

Cherbourg and Loire Valley, France
Mid-December 1969

I N MID-DECEMBER, THREE days before Saar Twelve is to slip into the water at high tide, France's first nuclear submarine will be launched to great fanfare. Sharon's trepidation grows at the sight of flags going up in the adjacent shipyard. Dignitaries in black limousines stream into town, and journalists prowl about. At ceremony time, she rushes home to watch the French minister of defense's speech on TV. When asked by a reporter in front of the cameras about the fate of the Israeli boats docked in the center canal, he replies that the problem "is about to be resolved."

How? What's brewing on the French side? Sharon leaves Rachelle's apartment and walks the streets. She scrutinizes the cafés and passersby, trying to memorize the faces of out-of-towners. She doesn't know what she's looking for beyond anything that strikes her as being suspicious. The men who compose the Israeli security team are trained to deal with a physical confrontation, but they don't speak French and might miss cultural nuances that could indicate danger.

Three days later, her teeth chattering against the December wind, she scans the crowd again when Saar Twelve is launched and is relieved that the journalists have left town. Unlike last year's launch, though, French navy officials are glaringly absent despite their personal friendships with Kadmon, Yaniv, and Danny. The official Israeli crew in uniform stands at attention, a solid wall of determination. They salute the flag of Israel waving from the mast here, in the port where Jews escaped annihilation. Sharon is a civilian, but she can't help saluting the flag too. Pride in her homeland swells in her, even more than it did at the only launch she witnessed before, that of Saar Seven. Her country is so far away, yet, at this moment, it is inside her.

And she imagines Alon at the launch of the *Dakar* two years ago in Southampton, just across the English Channel. He stood tall, one of the men in the proud line. He's also with her now.

Amiot delivers an impassioned speech and ends it with the traditional boat christening: smashing a champagne bottle against the Saar's prow.

The big moment arrives. A tugboat pulls the boat forward on its tracks and it slides into the harbor with a deafening splash. Freezing water sprays three stories high to the cheers of hundreds of CMN workers and onlookers. There is no public party afterward as in previous launches, and the officers' celebratory dinner at the Café Parisien is hurried, since Amiot and Yaniv are leaving and the others must get back to work. Not the townspeople, though. Over a thousand CMN tradesmen are now out of work.

TONIGHT'S FRIDAY DINNER is Naomi and Elazar's last one before they depart. If Danny shows up, Sharon will ask him to take a walk with her. She wishes it were a romantic stroll on a spring night, but that is not to be. She'll spill her information whether Danny wishes to hear it or not. It's his story to follow because she'll never get to Valençay.

Arriving back late from her day of shopping, she immediately notices Danny's absence but is pleasantly surprised to spot Amiot among the dozen people at the table. He's been in Paris negotiating, pleading, and pulling strings among politicians and industry leaders in his attempts to break the political gridlock.

"Mademoiselle," he says, and rises to pull a chair out for her.

"Thanks." She blushes at his European manners. Amiot's good nature notwithstanding—he hasn't turned his ire against the Israeli government that is withholding payment—her wariness of his motives remains unchanged. It is further stoked by Rachelle's uncompromising view of Nazi collaborators. "Sure, it was noble of him to save Chanel Perfumes for his Jewish friends and prevent Coco Chanel from stealing their share," Rachelle argued, "but the scent of Chanel Number Five rising to the high heavens didn't stop Nazi bombs from falling from airplanes that Amiot built and killing hundreds of thousands."

Amiot's apparently genuine goodwill toward Israel may be only his economic interest, Sharon thinks, perhaps tempered by remorse. "I'm glad that you've been able to escape *gai* Paris for a visit to cold Cherbourg," she says to him.

"Quite a mess, hey?" he says. It's unclear whether he is referring to the weather or the political predicament. He pours red wine into her glass. "Have you given any thought to architecture school in France?"

She lets out a nervous laugh. "It's an idea." An impractical one.

"Here's another idea for you. Tomorrow I'll be taking my granddaughter Christine to Orléans. She's working on her high-school paper and needs to visit the Cathédrale Sainte-Croix. It's Saturday, so I presume you'll be off?"

Sharon smiles and glances at Kadmon; he's engaged in a deep conversation. Saturdays are lucrative market days, and she hasn't taken a day off yet.

Amiot goes on. "Christine will be thrilled if you join us; she was quite taken with you when you met."

Sharon recalls that last year, the four-year age gap between her and Christine felt like four cultural light-years. "Where is Orléans?" she asks.

"In the Loire Valley." Amiot doesn't seem to hear the *ping* of Sharon's heart. "Just looking down from the plane at all those castles is a fascinating lesson in architecture."

She swallows. She can't imagine a grandfather who flies his grandchild on a private plane for a high-school assignment. A grandfather who is so attentive but who nevertheless fed the Nazi war machine.

"Do you know Château de Valençay?" Sharon asks, disbelieving the fortuitous break.

"Sure. We can drive there for lunch and taste their excellent wine."

~

IF THIS IS the same plane that flew her to Paris a year before, this morning it is subject to more vagaries of air pressure. Or is she more nervous? The opportunity to make inquiries at Valençay is incredible luck. Sharon fights the nausea that rises in her. The roar of the engines, so close, thrums in her temples. Nibbling on crackers, she appreciates that Christine has stopped chattering about her paper about Jeanne d'Arc.

With another churn of her stomach, Sharon gathers her hair into a loose braid and thinks of the reservists, young men who have never been at sea but who have been plunged into the brutal winter conditions. That's why each ship has a reservist doctor on board, himself a sea virgin.

Amiot, who commandeered the pilot seat for takeoff, relinquishes it to his copilot and sits across the aisle from Sharon. "It's a perfectly clear day. Would you like the pilot to take the scenic route or the shortest one?"

"The scenic route, please," Christine says.

"Are you okay with it?" Amiot asks Sharon.

She munches on a cracker. "Yes."

"Great," he says. "He'll start southwest at the mouth of the Loire River at Saint-Nazaire and will fly low along it so the two of you can see it in all its glory."

The view that opens to Sharon from the air is a series of fairy-tale postcards. She forgets her unease when fortresses and châteaux pop up below as if they were mere Monopoly pieces. Massive and ancient, they perch along silver-blue rivers, sit atop soaring cliffs, nestle in thick forests, and lord over grayish-green fields.

"Fortresses were built for defense from the thirteenth century well into the sixteenth," Amiot explains. "From the seventeenth century on, kings and noblemen built houses for themselves or their mistresses. Moats still kept outsiders out, but we see fewer buttressed walls against enemy attacks."

Sharon takes in the mix of conical, triangular, and peaked roofs, of turrets and towers topping stone behemoths. Amiot points out the styles: Here's a medieval, and this is a French Renaissance. Royals with more flamboyant tastes chose baroque. There is so much of everything that Sharon's head spins.

Then, below her, a geometric carpet of boxed hedges form squares, each with a different interior design. Moments later, another formal garden dazzles her with its curlicued hedges enclosing bright vegetation. The pale winter sun glints off lakes, reflecting pools, and tributaries of the Loire.

Valençay, she thinks, filled with anticipation. *I'm coming*.

A black limousine awaits them on the runway, and the uniformed chauffeur drives them to the city of Orléans. The glittering holiday lights zigzagging over the streets are dazzling. Before exiting the car for his meeting, Amiot says to Sharon, "It's an hour-and-a-half drive from here to Valençay. How important is it for you?"

"That's the purpose of my trip today!" she cries, then softens her tone. "Sorry. Maybe I can head there now while the two of you are busy?"

"Aren't you coming to the cathedral with me?" Christine's lips pull down in a pout.

"Very well," Amiot tells them, "both your wishes will be met. First the one, then the other."

Minutes later, the limousine deposits Sharon and Christine in front of a majestic cathedral. Christine's feet barely touch the ground as she skips up the stairs, her braids flying.

"The story of Jeanne d'Arc appears in medieval stained-glass windows depicting her life story. Orléans was her hometown," Christine says as the two of them enter the cavernous church filled with ribbed pillars and arched ceiling vaults. "I'm also interested in the craft of jewel-colored glass—cutting it and fixing it with lead that will last centuries." She clicks a series of photographs with what looks like an expensive camera, then pulls two sketch pads out of a canvas bag. "My grandpa says you can draw."

The two of them fold their coats and sit down on the freezing stone floor, cross-legged, each copying a different piece of glass art that had started as merely sand and fire.

But Sharon hates wasting her time. Every few minutes, she raises her eyes to the church entrance, on the lookout for the chauffeur who will drive them to Valençay.

Chapter Fifty-Seven

Château de Valençay, France
Mid-December 1969

AMAZINGLY, TO SAVE the long drive, Félix Amiot arranged for a helicopter to fly them to Valençay. The ride feels bumpier than the plane, and they're buffeted by winds from hills and valleys, but soon the helicopter lands on a mowed field on the grounds of the château.

"It is rumored that during World War Two, Duchess de Castellane allowed the Allies to drop ammunition and land missions here," Amiot says.

Sharon scans the winter-dormant manicured gardens, the huge castle. "Where's the village?"

"Didn't you say you wanted to visit this château? We have a lunch set up for us in the famous wine cellar."

She cringes, hating to seem ungrateful. What business could she possibly have inside the château? "I must speak to the priest at the village church."

"Very well. After lunch?" Amiot smiles. "Will you share with us what this is about? Certainly not naval business."

Heat floods her face. "It's too complicated and personal."

A young man with bouffant hair and what must be eighteenth-century attire welcomes them and launches into a thirty-minute guided tour. Sharon struggles to seem interested in the tapestries, furniture, sculptures, Chinese cloisonné jars, ancient swords, uniforms, and paintings of ancestors. All she wants is to find out about this Pelletier woman who gave birth to Danny.

Lunch is an elaborate affair. There is no restaurant on the premises; Amiot has arranged for a chef along with fine china and crystal. All because she asked to visit Valençay? With all of Amiot's good intentions, she's here, but at the wrong spot, wasting two hours on dining and wine tasting.

She hates to be rude. "It will get dark at four o'clock," she says.

"It's one thing that the French take seriously. We don't rush through meals." Christine scoffs. "But we must eat little so as not to get fat."

Sharon is relieved when the young man reappears—until he suggests a visit to the greenhouses. She can take it no more. "Do you know anyone who lived or worked here in 1946?"

"The family of the former business manager has been in service here since the Duke of Talleyrand was Napoléon's ambassador. I can take you to his cottage."

"Go ahead," Amiot tells her. "We'll have our coffee."

Sharon glances at her watch. She's stretching Amiot's and Christine's patience. "Let's do it fast," she whispers to the guide, and dons her coat and gloves. She is glad to step outside of the vast château and its cold enormous walls.

At a cottage constructed of half-hewn timber, the guide taps the knocker, and when a dog barks from inside, he opens the door for Sharon to step in.

The room is lit by several lamps and sconces, yet its heavy furniture makes it seem dark. The fireplace glows orange, and an old man with a large belly and sparse tufts of hair sits near it, a plaid blanket covering his knees. The man's hand is resting on the head of a hound to quiet him. The dog seems unsure if the newcomer poses a threat. Its tail wags at the end of a coiled body, prepared to pounce.

"Please meet Vincent Voclain, whose family has been in the service of Valençay since 1814," the guide says.

"It's a pleasure to meet you. I am Sharon Bloomenthal, and I promise not to take too much of your time."

"Sit down, please, young lady." The old man points to an ornately carved chair upholstered in brocade. "What can I do for you?"

She sits at the edge of the chair, ready to leave after a polite exchange of niceties. "You wouldn't happen to know a family named Pelletier? They may have lived in the area around the time of the Second World War."

"I don't know a family, but there was a seamstress in the service of the duchess by that name. Claudette Pelletier. The duchess took her along when she fled to Spain after the invasion."

"Do you know if she was Jewish?"

"I know she wasn't, although she got involved with them."

"What do you mean?"

He shakes his head sadly. "Such a shame she brought upon herself, getting herself in the family way. She acted as if she were blessed. I would have forced the man to marry any house staff so tricked, but Claudette refused to reveal the identity of the father of her baby."

"Was the baby a boy or a girl?"

"A boy."

Sharon grabs the arms of her chair. "Was his father Jewish?"

Vincent Voclain rubs his rheumy eyes. "Only when Claudette returned from Spain and asked me to notify her if he came looking for her—only then did she admit that he was Jewish."

The little wine Sharon has drunk must be making her swoon. Could this be the beginning of the thread? An unwed Catholic mother and a Jewish father? Every possibility Sharon imagined is unraveling with this implausible version. "Did she give his name?"

The old man sighs. "I can't recall. Such mayhem at the time."

"Was her baby in Spain too?"

Vincent Voclain's face turns red. He waves his finger at Sharon. "Don't you start with me about that baby too!"

The dog at his feet rises and growls.

Sharon's heart races. She leans forward and reaches out toward the dog. "I'm here on a friendly quest," she says quietly to Monsieur Voclain. "I don't mean to upset you. I'm just curious about this story."

"There's no story. During the war, children disappeared. Many died. This one was lucky that he didn't." Monsieur Voclain raises his voice. "I did all I could for the many members of the staff who had problems. Don't you barge in here blaming me, young lady! He was saved after Léonie's death."

"Who was Léonie?"

Vincent Voclain's agitation grows, and he yells, but his words are jumbled and shot out at machine-gun speed, and Sharon can't decipher any of them.

The guide touches her arm. "Mademoiselle, it's better if we leave."

A woman comes into the room and hands the old man a vial. She holds his forehead as he gulps down its contents, then flattens the flying hair. "Look what you've started," she says to Sharon.

"Sorry." She is not. She's not responsible for his temper. Questions swirl in her head. The old man's memory might mix up events; the seamstress and her connection to the boy that was saved after Léonie's death is not fully established. At the door, Sharon stops and looks at the old man, who has calmed down. "Thank you, monsieur, for your time."

His eyes closed, he nods.

She takes a deep breath. "Did Claudette Pelletier ever find her baby?"

"She should have." His voice is tired. "How many babies have a Jewish star tattooed on the bottom of one foot?"

SHARON WALKS AROUND the château. She would skip like a little girl if it were not for the guide in costume. *Claudette Pelletier*, her heart sings.

Early dusk casts the fields beyond in a purple haze. On the open ground in front of the château, the helicopter is waiting, its engine thrumming. Félix Amiot and Christine come out of the guest quarters.

"I'm bored." Christine yawns. "Can we leave now?"

Sharon is so close, she can taste her success. She's annoyed at the spoiled teenager who's gotten what she wanted from the trip. *Muster chutzpah,* she tells herself. A motor is revving in her head. Somewhere around here, there must be someone who knows more about Claudette Pelletier.

"I truly apologize for holding you up, but it's important," Sharon says. "You've been so generous. But I haven't been to the church, which was my destination in the first place."

"I knew you were a spy," Christine says.

Sharon smiles to placate her. "Only a private detective."

"We promised," Amiot tells his granddaughter. "How about if we take an after-lunch walk?" He gestures to the helicopter pilot to kill the engine and asks the guide to drive them.

The car exits the château grounds through a stone gate, and the village's main street stretches out before them. Sharon wishes she could make small talk, be polite to her host, who has been so accommodating. Instead, she stares at the double row of houses and stores. The name Claudette Pelletier hums in her head. She peers at a middle-aged woman at an intersection, then at two women chatting in front of a house. Could one of them be Danny's mother?

Claudette was not Jewish. The magnitude of this discovery takes Sharon's breath away. That means that Danny, according to Jewish law, is not Jewish. If that is entered in his military or government records, the rabbis will not allow him to marry a Jewish woman without first converting to Judaism, a rigorous, lengthy process. The secular kibbutznik would never give in to such Orthodox tyranny. The irony is that he broke up with Dominique because she didn't share his vision for the Jews' life in their own country.

More important, what will this crucial piece of information do to his sense of himself? A man who, for as long as he has lived, has sported a tattoo of the Star of David but who is not, in fact, Jewish.

Learning about her mother anchored Sharon's identity. It will do the opposite for Danny. He would be better off never knowing. She should stop her investigation.

"You are both so tired. Sorry to test your patience," she tells Amiot. "Let's head back and not waste more time."

His eyebrows raise quizzically and Christine groans just as the car stops in front of the church. Not wishing to seem even more flighty, Sharon climbs out. What has she done?

At this late hour, the door is locked. Her heart racing, Sharon knocks, then waits, hoping no one will open it. Time to abort.

"Knock again," Christine calls to her.

A man wearing a priest's collar opens the wicket door. He has smiling eyes; their corners crinkle down into grooved crescents. "Mademoiselle? I'm Father Hugo."

"I am Sharon Bloomenthal. May I bother you for a few minutes?"

Inside, he motions to a tall wooden box that she figures is a confession booth. "No, no," she says. "I just want to ask you whether you knew a parishioner by the name of Claudette Pelletier. A seamstress to the duchess."

"Certainly. She came back after the war looking for her son." With a grimace, the priest sits down on the nearest pew. "Sorry, my knees are acting up."

A second person who knew Claudette Pelletier! Sharon's excitement percolates in her chest, mixed with dread.

"The poor woman was seriously crippled, couldn't walk much. For a while we all tried to help her find her boy. We knew he had been adopted but not where or by whom. Then she moved away." The priest raises his eyes to Sharon. "Obviously, you know something."

Sharon can't keep herself from smiling. "He is an Israeli naval officer."

"Jewish after all," the priest mumbles. "She wanted her Benjamin to belong to the Chosen People. That tattoo . . ." He lets his words trail off.

Seriously crippled? "Is Claudette Pelletier still alive?"

"Last I heard, which must be at least two years ago, she was still living with her blind friend, that woman who sells woven baskets in markets. I don't know where their home is." The priest presses his forehead as if racking his brain. "Solange. That's the blind girl's name. A big talker. She was young when she lost her husband, so Claudette helped her raise her children."

"You say the boy's name was Benjamin?" Sharon asks.

"Benjamin-Pierre Pelletier."

This final confirmation of the name in Evelyne Niquet's letter causes something inside Sharon to quiver. She presses her palms together. "Would you happen to know the name of his father? I've been told that some churches keep records. Maybe you know his date of birth?"

"I'll have someone look through old files in the basement and I will call you."

How amazing would it be if Danny's father survived? Her quest has taken on a life of its own.

***

"THIS HAS BEEN one of my best days ever," Sharon says to Félix Amiot on the flight back. As the plane flies over the clouds, the stars seem near enough for Sharon to touch them. The droning of the engines that bothered her in the morning is soothing now. Her nausea has evaporated, and she can't stop smiling.

Curiosity sparkling in his gray eyes, Amiot asks, "What was it all about?"

Christine giggles. "You're so full of secrets."

Sharon laughs. "Thanks to your patience, I learned that the mother of someone I care about may be alive."

"Is he a new boyfriend?" Christine asks, and Amiot's eyebrows shoot up.

"Just someone special."

Amiot reaches inside a leather-upholstered compartment, withdraws a bottle of cognac, and pours it into three crystal glasses. He hands one to Sharon and one to Christine. "*L'chaim*. I like being an accomplice to a conspiracy."

Christine chirps, "Pépère, speaking of a conspiracy, I read in the paper that the defense minister hinted that the Israeli boats might be sold to another country. Will you finally get your money?"

"The politicians must know something we don't." He swishes the liquid in his glass and tosses a glance at Sharon as if she might be privy to some confidential information.

Except that she's not. Kadmon shares with her only what she needs to know at her civilian level. She sips from her glass, and the velvety liquid burns pleasantly as it slides down her throat. "Monsieur Amiot," she says, "I have no words to thank you. Once again, you've shown me such generosity."

The sides of his mouth rise in a smile of acknowledgment, but a cloud traverses his face. He leans his head back against the headrest and closes his eyes. In the dim yellow light of the plane, his features are slack with age and fatigue. Sharon is surprised by the wave of fondness that washes over her.

"Pépère will do anything for the people who work for him," Christine whispers. "Half the French aviation industry used to be his. He risked it all for them."

Not wishing to discuss World War II and Amiot's regrettable share in it, Sharon says, "I've heard that he invented a hundred patents."

"There were many Jews among his workers. He hired people with no skills solely so he could arrange fake papers for them," Christine continues. "You may have heard how he rescued Chanel for the Wertheimer brothers. But did you know that he gave *millions* of francs to the Résistance and financed the smuggling of Jewish children to Switzerland?"

"I had no idea. You are blessed to have such a grandfather."

Christine grins. "My mother thinks he spoils me. What about your family? Are your parents still married?"

"In heaven, maybe. They were killed in our War of Independence." Sharon adds, "Like my friend, I knew nothing about my mother."

"But now you know that his may not be dead?"

Yes, Claudette Pelletier might be alive, but she is Christian, and Danny was born out of wedlock. Sharon is at a loss as to how to reveal it to him. She had not set out to shatter Danny's identity.

She's furious at herself. She's not the courageous Judith Katz's daughter; she's a busybody who sticks her nose into other people's affairs and wreaks havoc on their lives. She downs the last of her cognac and closes her eyes. She won't tell Danny any of it, she decides, and she locks her pinkies in a promise to herself. Enough.

Chapter Fifty-Eight

Cherbourg, France
Mid-December 1969

I T IS LATE when she enters Rachelle's apartment after the Valençay excursion. Her friend's bedroom door is closed. The lava lamp in the living room casts kaleidoscopic colors and shapes on the walls and ceiling, an apt ending for this extraordinary day.

The light on the Electronic Secretary, the answering machine that *La Presse de la Manche* installed for Rachelle, is blinking. Among the many recorded messages for Rachelle, there is one for Sharon: Kadmon dictating a list of food items she should gather up tomorrow. She checks the pouch with cash that she keeps separate from her own. There's enough for an early Sunday-market run.

There's also a message from Danny. "Hi, kiddo. I'm glad that you took a day off. You deserve more for the fantastic job you do. On behalf of everyone, thank you."

She replays the message, loving his voice, basking in his praise—except that he's reverted to *kiddo*. Gone is the *sweetheart* he'd adopted over the months of her absence. She's only his very efficient employee. She reminds herself of her promise to herself to share none of her findings with Danny.

Or should she stick to that decision? How disrespectful it is to hold such crucial information from a man of integrity! Sharon opens the Monopoly game and grabs one of the dice. Even number, she'll tell him. Odd, she'll take the information to her grave.

The die falls on four.

Danny answers the operator's call as quickly as if he sleeps with the phone at his side. "Danny here," he says, an officer at the ready.

"It's me. Sorry to call so late. We must talk."

"Something happened?"

"Yes, but it's not about the boats. It's personal."

"Are you all right? Anyone sick?"

"Not that. It's—it's about you. Danny—"

"Sharon. Please," he says, cutting her off. "Can we save it for 'after the war'?"

"About the tattoo—"

"Sharon, sweetheart. Stop right now! I'm trying to catch three hours of sleep before we fire up the engines."

"Oh." The word *sweetheart* disarms her. "I didn't think you had to be up for that too," she says meekly. The engines. Over the past two nights, the extreme cold has posed a risk to the boats' engines, the Israeli navy informed the French. They must be restarted at night to prevent irreversible damage. However, each time an engine is fired up, it sounds like a cannon shot. And each boat has four engines. Five boats means twenty huge blasts and exhaust filling the air with acrid smoke. Last winter, only one boat at a time was kept at the vast French naval port northwest of town, and the detonations occurred at a considerable distance. Now that the Saars are moored in the center of town, the enormous nightly explosions wake up the entire populace. Babies scream in terror, and war-traumatized men vault out of their beds and hunt for cover. Teachers complain about students falling asleep in class, and incensed mothers flood the mayor's office. The mayor is already at his wits' end. Christmas is coming, and there is no solution in sight.

But Sharon knows that the engines are designed to withstand variations in temperature. All this blasting is a ruse meant to make such nighttime detonations routine. Operation Noa must be about to launch, and the unnecessary explosions ensure that no one will pay attention when the boats are actually about to slip away.

"Can we please find five minutes to talk?" she asks.

"Wait until after you know what." He adds, "You're doing a superb job. We—I—couldn't have managed without us."

"Thanks, but—" *Valençay. Claudette Pelletier.*

"Good night, Sharon." Suddenly, the soft way he utters her name sounds sweet, as though he's said it in his head many times.

She will accept his refusal. She will not call Evelyne in Châtillon-sur-Indre. She will take her discovery to the grave.

SHARON SET HER alarm for five o'clock to hit the Sunday shopping early. Outside, a storm is raging. There will be no outdoor stalls, but farmers will appreciate her trekking up to their barns. Sharon listens to the howling wind, stealing a few extra moments of warmth under the covers in her flannel pajamas and wool socks. In the past, when a storm advanced straight inland, it flattened villages. She imagines that along the shore, the legendary squall tosses fishing craft like a French chef sautéing vegetables. To avoid the worst of the weather, Sharon mentally charts a route inland, along farms nestled on the south side of hills, a modicum of protection from the wind's fury.

She pulls the covers over her head and breathes in the heat of her own body. It's the kind of day when she and Alon would have stayed in bed. It surprises her that when her body shudders with a moan, Danny takes Alon's place under the covers. He uttered her name in his beautiful voice: *Sweetheart.*

Was there more in that term of endearment than mere friendship? If pressed to make an intelligence assessment of the facts, she would conclude that it was only her imagination. Or maybe not? Danny is probably already out to sea with his crew after barely a few hours of sleep.

The thought of the seamen's bravery inspires Sharon to push herself out of bed to heed her own call of duty.

Seven hours later, she returns home, soaking wet, shivering, and exhausted. Her boots are covered with mud, and her fingers are numb with cold. Rachelle is out for her three-hour Sunday lunch at her parents' home. The apartment is dark because the metal shutters are closed against the storm. They rattle with every gust of wind.

Sharon turns on the lights, hangs up her coat, removes her water-logged clothes, and warms her hands over the radiator. She plugs in the electric kettle.

Next to the phone, the Electronic Secretary is blinking. Sharon ignores the messages meant for Rachelle but stops at one for her from Father Hugo.

"There was water in the basement. We didn't see that until we pulled up some boxes. It will be a while before we sort out which documents can be salvaged. So sorry for not being more helpful. *Joyeux Noël.*"

How Sharon wishes she had Danny's father's name to search through the Holocaust archives. If a branch of Danny's Jewish family is still alive, it might offset the distressing fact that Claudette Pelletier is not Jewish.

Thankfully, Danny knows none of this. Decisions are better made in daylight. Danny's Jewish identity is imbued with his Zionist vision. He has dedicated his life to the security of Israel, the very survival of the Jews to whom he belongs. Who is she to sabotage his zeal?

If Danny were younger—just entering the naval academy—could he have lost his security clearance?

She presses the play button again and almost misses the robotic time stamp announcing a message from six o'clock in the morning, after she left.

"Hi, Sharon." Danny's voice fills the room. "Sorry I couldn't talk last night. I'm heading out for a rough day. I know what you want to discuss, and I apologize that I can't allow us to express our feelings yet." As he pauses, wonder mixed with heat spreads through Sharon. He goes on, "Let's just get through this tough time together, each doing our part. Okay?"

"Danny," she whispers, letting herself waken to feelings she's tried to suppress for so long. Pictures of him flit through her head—the twinkle in his green eyes when he likes her witty comments;

his water-dripping body emerging from the sea; his warm voice when he commands, so self-assured that it conveys authority without harshness. That voice has now revealed what she never dared believe. A year and a half ago, she was awkward and inexperienced, scared of venturing out of the familiar. He saw who she was beneath the crust of her youth.

"Yes," she whispers, her hand over her heart. "Oh, yes." A window opens wide into a sunny day on the beach. This time it is she who runs into his arms, and they fall into the water with a splash, their bodies intertwined.

The fantasy is halted by the thought of what she's churned up—and the consequences to him. She must force herself to unknow what is already lodged in her brain.

Rain pelts the metal shutters; it sounds as if clubs were hitting them. Anxiety about Danny and his men at sea gnaws at Sharon. The Saar was designed for the mild Mediterranean, not this ferocious Atlantic Ocean storm. She has seen the sky-high waves hitting the giant boulders enclosing the harbor. What hubris makes men challenge the English Channel time and again?

No more indulging in her emotions. She's exhausted. It's only two o'clock in the afternoon. Sharon sips her tea, stretches out on the couch, and pulls the duvet over her head.

The phone rings. Cobwebs of sleep make her want to refuse the call from Châtillon-sur-Indre, but she hears Evelyne say, *"Joyeux Noël."*

"To you and your family too."

"Have you found out anything more about Daniel's family?"

"Well . . ." Sharon drags out the word. She's supposed to unknow what she can't get out of her mind. And Evelyne Niquet is not yet aware that Danny is actually in France; explaining why he is unavailable would be a breach of security. "His birth mother may be alive," Sharon blurts out.

"That would be incredible. The best Christmas gift!" Evelyne says. "Can you imagine how she would feel if she found him?"

Groggy and still plagued by the dilemma, Sharon describes her visit to Valençay.

"Someone in the markets must know where she and that blind friend live," Evelyne says.

Sharon winces. Right now, all she wants to do is sleep. Her guard is down. Hadn't she decided to stop this investigation? "Let's talk after Noël."

They hang up, and Sharon drops into deep slumber.

She swims up from the bottom of an ocean to a soft touch on her shoulder and Rachelle's voice telling her that the Norwegians are in town.

Her ersatz Norwegians from a year ago? How would Rachelle know about them? Their visit was never with the Israeli mission. Their official business was with the French government and Félix Amiot. Sharon sits up, unsure if she heard the words or dreamed them. "What are you saying?" She rubs her eyes.

"We got the scoop at the newspaper."

"Weren't you at your parents'?"

"I was called in." Rachelle takes a deep breath. "The five boats have been sold to a Norwegian company called Starboat. Contracts are being signed right now."

Starboat. Sharon swallows. "Who's signing?"

"The French acquisition minister has approved the buyers, an oil-exploration outfit. He's been pressuring Moka Limon for weeks to relinquish Israel's rights to the boats, but Limon wouldn't relent— until now. He finally agreed." Rachelle's face falls. "I'm so sorry. I know how much they meant for Israel. Also for my own future there, where I will raise my family."

"It's happening now?" Sharon can hardly breathe at the realization that the complex ruse is playing out. People believe it. The fictional sale, which started when she outfitted the "Norwegians" in Paris, is reaching a climax.

"They're in Hotel Sofitel," Rachelle says, "signing the contract before Amiot leaves for Christmas in the South of France."

"I need a moment." Sharon goes into the lavatory, where she can think. The next step of Operation Noa is about to launch.

Thirty minutes later, she's in Kadmon's office. "I know you can't tell me anything, but I'm part of the team, not merely an outside civilian."

"Let's just say that the Israeli government has made a magnanimous gesture toward the French to relieve them of the embarrassment they've created for themselves." Kadmon's handlebar mustache twitches, and his tone turns sarcastic. "What's most interesting is that, rather than sailing the boats away themselves, the Norwegian buyers insist that trained Israeli crews deliver them in a month or so."

"Our guys can't remain trapped in the boats for another month," she says.

Kadmon lays his hand on a pile of documents. "First thing, since it's only a matter of clearing customs, let's make sure that every single paper is in order." He pushes a typed list toward her. "Second, we must plan for three thousand meals."

"Three thousand?" She raises both palms in a gesture of astonishment while her brain calculates what he means: They must feed one hundred and ten men three meals a day for nine days. Not a month from now, but in a couple of days. The schedule of nine days at sea barely allows for delays caused by refueling, an incapacitated boat, or having to ride out a storm in a safe harbor.

"Meat too," he says. "The men are screaming about their imposed kosher."

"You'll need more than one cow." She runs through all the butchers she knows. Even a hundred steaks will make only one nonkosher feast.

"Salami would be great," Kadmon goes on. "Christmas is in four days. I've rented two more vans and have French-speaking reservists to drive them. You'll instruct the guys on where to shop. Since it's holiday time, an overflowing cart in a supermarket won't be that unusual."

Sharon digests all she knows. More than one hundred men are here at the ready. The majority must have arrived while she was driving around the countryside. "How come I didn't pick up new recruits?"

"Each group was led by one of the guys you guided here." He smiles. "And we made sure they had cover stories—and no identical jackets."

Outside the window, night has fallen. The rain has stopped. Since it's Sunday, there are no cars in the parking lot. The night watchman starts his first round.

"Has Golda given her approval for a breakout?" Sharon asks.

Kadmon looks at her for a long minute, his face a mask, and says nothing.

She takes a deep breath. During her time in Intelligence, she witnessed schemes planned down to the last detail, some at great cost, despite the possibility that they might be aborted. None was of the scale of Operation Noa. Now, all these months of preparations, thousands of hours of work, a vast outlay of money, and all the men arriving and hiding here might go to waste. She can't imagine the staggering price tag of what might come to naught.

IT'S A RELIEF that the two reservists—a graphic designer and a plastics factory foreman—are both urbane and French-speaking. They divide the shopping areas for the next two days, and Sharon returns to Rachelle's apartment. In the holiday spirit, to demonstrate normalcy, twenty Israeli seamen will receive passes and will congregate in a café. Sharon would have liked to join the hilarity, but she'd rather not bump into "Jorgen" and his partner while they are in town. A mere flick of the eyes might tip off an alert outsider that they know each other.

She's marinating chicken breasts for dinner and Rachelle is simmering the lemon-butter sauce when the phone rings. Sharon wipes her hands on her apron and picks up.

The operator announces, "Officer Lucas Niquet for Mademoiselle Bloomenthal."

"One of my colleagues knows the women," he says after she accepts the call.

"What?"

"My wife told me about your conversation. They live in La Guerche-sur-l'Aubois, and he'll visit them in the morning."

"My God." Sharon drops into a chair. Her mouth is dry. Claudette Pelletier is alive. Danny's non-Jewish mother is real. "Would you be able to pass her Daniel's photos?"

If only she could witness the moment that Claudette Pelletier holds Danny's photos. Sharon has never felt the emotion of doing a mitzvah, a good deed, as deeply as she does now. She would have done it a hundred times, even against Danny's objections, just to bring happiness to the heart of a mother who searched for years for her lost baby.

What Claudette Pelletier will not know is that her Israeli naval officer son is right now in France but is as unaware of her and as unreachable as if he were across the sea.

Chapter Fifty-Nine

Cherbourg, France
Late December 1969

CHRISTMAS LIGHTS SPARKLE in windows, and a giant pine tree is placed in the plaza. Behind their steamy glass, the cafés serve *vin chaud,* warm red wine spiked with cognac, cinnamon, and orange. At home, Rachelle welcomes Sharon with *chocolat chaud à l'ancienne,* a mug of rich, dark, and thick hot chocolate.

The holiday cheer does little to quell Sharon's sense of foreboding. Images of the *Dakar*'s fate almost two years before return in full force. Ten days after its launch, Saar Twelve is out for testing every day. So many things can go wrong, and with the designated remaining shipyard crew in a festive mood, Sharon doubts that every problem is remedied. If spare parts are needed from Germany or Italy, they'll take weeks to arrive.

After dropping off her full van for the last time before everything closes for the holiday, Sharon lingers in the plaza to listen to a children's choir singing Christmas carols. The sweet voices bring her a moment of reprieve from worrying about Operation Noa, except that the nagging question of Claudette Pelletier remains. It's been two days since Officer Niquet's colleague checked the women's home and found it empty. They were still making the rounds among the Noël markets, he surmised. Christmas Eve is tomorrow, and Officer Niquet is certain that they will return by then.

Sharon steps into a perfumery to buy Rachelle her favorite scent, Je Reviens. The shop owner raises her eyebrows. "What's with you Israelis? You've emptied my shelves. If only you'd told me you were leaving, I would have ordered a larger supply."

Leaving? The word hit Sharon. The seamen living in the open have been instructed not to close their bank accounts. Those who have formed friendships with locals were told to accept invitations for future dates. Most important, they have been warned not to engage in shopping sprees. Apparently, they succumbed to the temptation of buying perfume for the women in their lives and, Sharon guesses, cartons of cigarettes for themselves—while also filling orders for their hidden colleagues. The town has been put on alert.

With deliberate nonchalance, Sharon says to the perfume seller, "The Norwegians won't be taking possession of the boats for at least another month. Please order for me two bottles of Je Reviens. No rush." She, at least, will be around to retrieve her order.

As she approaches Rachelle's apartment building, she sees her friend hurrying toward her.

"Thank God you're here!" Rachelle is breathless as she pulls Sharon into the vestibule. "I've just heard very disturbing news. The editor ordered us not to publish it, but your team should be aware of it."

"What is it?"

"The RG commander has sent a confidential memo to his superiors in Paris reporting unusual activity on the boats. He suspects that the sale to Norway is fictitious and that instead of sailing next month, the boats will be leaving as early as next week—going to Israel, not Norway."

A shiver travels down Sharon's spine. Operation Noa has been exposed. The elaborate ploy has failed. And the ramifications? Beyond her imagination.

Her voice trembling, she asks, "What's RG?"

"The intelligence arm of the police."

"Did you see the memo?"

"A carbon copy of it. The original was mailed at noon."

"Do you know anyone in the post office?"

"My old schoolmate is the assistant manager. Why?"

"Run over and see whether you can intercept that memo. Call me at the office."

Rachelle jumps into her car, and Sharon takes the steps two at a time, unlocks the apartment door with shaking fingers, and lunges at the phone. Luckily, the operator puts the call through, and when Kadmon picks up, Sharon breathes into the mouthpiece code words that an Israeli educated in Passover culture would understand. "The maiden Noa is naked."

By the time she reaches the office in a taxi, the top brass is there, including Moka Limon, who must have stayed in town.

Rachelle calls a few minutes later. "He'll delay it—" she begins, and Sharon cuts her off. "Say no more over the phone. Thanks."

"If *La Presse de la Manche* got a copy of the memo, other newspapers may have one too," Yaniv says. "We've run out of time."

"Any journalist who sniffs out the Oslo address of Starboat will find that it's only a mailbox," Kadmon adds.

Only a mailbox? Sharon assumed that the subterfuge had a tighter foundation—at least the address was someone's office, with typewriters clicking. A company with a functioning front. Why such a flimsy, amateurish game plan that can easily be exposed?

Smoke hangs below the ceiling as the men puff on their cigarettes, grind out the finished ones, and light others. The air is as thick as the tension in the small room.

"It's twenty-four hours to Christmas Eve." Limon scans the team, locking eyes with each man. "If the memo is delayed until tomorrow, we'll be in luck—if there's no one at the other end to move it up through the channels. However, one astute clerk who has the ear of a cousin high up in government will kill us." He takes a deep breath. "There's no choice. The five boats must escape tomorrow night, when the town is busy having Christmas Eve dinner."

"All five?" Kadmon asks. "The fresh paint in Saar Twelve smells so strong that our hidden guys must sleep in the other boats."

"And there's a leak in the gun deck," Danny adds. "Plus, we're still waiting for some navigation equipment from Italy."

Vaknin, the military strategist who hasn't yet spoken, now says,

"We'd be better off taking only four boats rather than risking all five getting stuck because of this one."

"Four or five boats, the radio system to communicate among them is not yet installed," Kadmon says.

There is silence as the men contemplate this hurdle.

"Would walkie-talkies do?" Sharon says, then feels silly at her unsophisticated suggestion.

Kadmon, though, perks up. "Check first thing in the morning if there are five still available in the toy stores," he tells her. "And get two hundred batteries for each. My son runs out of them in an hour and a half of play."

Where can she find a thousand batteries?

And all this, Sharon thinks, will happen only if Limon gets Golda's and Dayan's clearance. The heavy smoke in the small office makes it hard for her to breathe. She rises and steps out for fresh air. Just before she closes the door behind her, she hears Limon speak.

"Operation Noa is on," he announces. "The Gabriels are ready back home. The Saars will break out tomorrow before midnight. All five."

Sharon walks away in a daze. The Gabriels. These are surely the new missiles that were tested and are now powerful weapons. Limon has just blurted out top secret information believing she was out of earshot. She recalls Danny hinting in Tel Aviv that something "more exciting than the Saars" was in the works. Now she knows for sure. Israel's new missiles must be a match for the Russians'. Nothing less will do. Their launchers will be mounted on all twelve Saars, readying them for battle.

The signs are all there. A war is coming. That's why Limon wouldn't—couldn't—give up even one boat.

⁓

CHRISTMAS EVE IS tonight. It's three o'clock in the afternoon when Sharon crosses the canal on foot on her way home. In spite of the bitter cold, she breaks into a sweat in anticipation of what's coming tonight. Without the French navy's accurate weather service, the team relies on public reports from Radio France and the BBC across the English Channel. Both predict a gale-force-nine storm.

Sharon's day has been hectic; she traveled to toy shops everywhere to find walkie-talkies, doubles of each of five sets in case one breaks. The two reservists helped procure some of the batteries and did the final food shopping. The huge quantities will be loaded onto the boats only when the town settles down for its Christmas Eve meal. Sharon is designated to deliver a bottle of cognac on behalf of the Israeli team to the lone sentry at the port's watchtower, who will be missing the holiday at home. With all the men on alert confined to the boats, those who double as the security teams won't be on the lookout for the occasional police cruiser making its rounds.

Most daunting, how can five boats moored in the center of town slip out unnoticed? The blasts of the engines alone should alert even a drunken sentry.

The wind has died down despite the forecast. Sharon is wrapping her scarf to cover the bottom of her face against the cold when she catches sight of three Israeli seamen hauling bicycles into the water.

"What in the world are you doing?" she calls.

"Getting rid of the bikes," one replies. "By order."

"Whose order?"

"Danny Yarden's."

"Dump the bikes here? Are you nuts? Stop it right now." She scans the boats. "Where is he?"

"At the Hotel Sofitel."

She bursts into the hotel's bar and to her surprise finds Danny perched on a barstool, chatting with Moka Limon and two Frenchmen.

"Here you are," Limon says to her in French. He's rarely spoken to her; she is way below his rank. "Would you join us for hot spicy wine?"

"Thanks." Sharon turns and addresses Danny in Hebrew. "Your guys are dumping bicycles in the canal in full sight. Supposedly by your order."

"Idiots." He bristles. "They're supposed to be discreet. We can't just abandon dozens of bikes on the dock." He motions to a junior officer and orders him to handle the crisis. "And remind the men that anyone who says goodbye to his local girlfriend will be subject to court-martial."

He doesn't leave his spot, though, and the interrupted conversation with the Frenchmen resumes. Sharon is piqued but sips her mulled wine and listens as the men chat about a new lottery method in the United States to select draftees to Vietnam; a Rolling Stones concert in California at which a woman was trampled to death; and Charles Manson announcing that he'll defend himself in the Tate-LaBianca murder trial in a few months.

How can Danny suddenly have time for idle chitchat when he's been avoiding her for weeks? Clinking glasses with the Frenchmen, he and Limon toast the sale of the boats to the Norwegian company. Sharon gets that they are making a public show of being unhurried. But how can they be so insouciant? Not only the boats but also the fate of one hundred and ten men hang in the balance.

After the two Frenchmen depart, Limon tells Sharon, "Nine o'clock tonight, we're having a celebratory dinner. No spouses. Just our team." He excuses himself and joins a group of French officers at a table across the room. Danny remains seated, his eyes on Sharon, examining her features.

"What?" She wonders if her mascara is smudged or if this is related to his phone message.

"You're very pretty," he says.

She blushes, suddenly overwhelmed by the words uttered face-to-face, not through a recording machine. "Did you have too much to drink?" she asks lightly and instantly regrets breaking the tone he set.

He slides off his stool and motions with his chin toward a corner table with a sofa. There, he speaks in a low voice, covering one side of his mouth as if someone who can read lips is watching.

"Here is your next assignment: After we break out tonight—hopefully without being apprehended—you'll clean up the mess. The notarized authorizations for you to close our bank accounts are in the office safe." He takes his key ring and removes a key. "Talk to Dr. Vaiseman, the dentist, about selling the cars. You'll also help him get the families left behind packed and ready to leave."

"Isn't Kadmon staying?" she asks.

"There's the possibility that he might be detained."

Arrested? Sharon sits back, filled again with the significance of what's about to take place. "What about stamping the crews' passports?"

"Why am I not surprised that you've nailed the one weakness in the plan?" Danny shakes his head. "Leaving without the exit stamp is the only illegal hiccup. The men won't be able to return to France for a very long time, if ever."

The consequences for Danny hit Sharon. He'll never come back to France. He'll never meet his birth mother.

This is it. All her prior decisions fly out the door. "Claudette Pelletier," she blurts out.

"What?"

"Claudette. Pelletier. That's your birth mother's name."

Danny stares at her.

"And she. Is. Alive."

The green in his eyes behind the glasses darkens. "How is it possible?" he whispers. "Wasn't she murdered by the Nazis?"

"She lives in the Loire Valley."

"She survived?"

Sharon winces. "There's more."

"What?"

"She and your father weren't married."

He swallows. "She gave me up for adoption?"

"She lost you in the mayhem of the war. She searched for you for years."

He takes off his glasses. "God Almighty," he murmurs. "How? How did you find out?"

"I did some sleuthing. Sorry I did it behind your back. No, I'm not sorry I broke my promise." Her voice cracks. "I would have been happy if anyone did this for me."

Danny drops his face into his hands. For a long moment all she hears is heavy breathing, as if he's trying to control a sob. Then, while the fingers of his left hand cover his face, his right hand slides along the table and finds hers. He wraps his hand around Sharon's. "She's *alive?*" he whispers. "She *lost* me?"

She feels the warm skin, callused from hours on the helms of ships, the long fingers strong and delicate enough to manipulate complex instruments.

She still hasn't dropped the second bombshell. She begins with a small detail. "Your name at birth was Benjamin-Pierre Pelletier."

"Benjamin?" He lets out a soft chuckle and repeats the name with a French accent, as if tasting it. "Benjamin-Pierre Pelletier."

In her peripheral vision, Sharon catches Limon approaching. She dabs her eyes with a napkin while Limon's glance darts from her to Danny, whose face is still covered. Sharon figures that he suspects that this is a lovers' quarrel. "It's not what you think," she tells Limon.

Danny raises his head, wipes his glasses, and takes a sip of water.

"There's no time for private sentiments," Limon says. "Did you brief her?" When Danny nods, Limon says to Sharon, "When you're done here, in a week or so, call my Paris office and they'll arrange for your flight back home."

"I'll be persona non grata in France," Danny murmurs to her. "I won't be able to come back."

"Unfortunately, so will I. This is bigger than any of us," Limon says, his tone stern.

Sharon looks up at him. What price will this war hero pay, former chief of the navy, now a diplomat revered by the French whose wife moves in Parisian high society? He can't guess that Danny's personal stake is of an entirely different nature.

Limon squints at his watch and tells Danny, "A briefing in my room in six minutes."

Sharon stands up. Outside, the calm weather still holds. The bar clock shows it's almost four. The clock in her heart beats toward a major crisis. Had she launched her search months earlier, she might at least have set a phone appointment for Claudette Pelletier and her son. He would have learned the rest of the story much earlier and could have grappled with what Sharon is still holding back. Instead, massive ripple effects might cause him a painful identity crisis.

All of which is her fault.

Danny rises too and touches her shoulder. "I'll catch up with you later." His pinkie lingers on her neck, and its warmth traverses her spine.

"The women are not back home," Officer Niquet reports when Sharon reaches him close to dinnertime. "They're probably visiting some relatives for the holiday."

Sharon is numb with confusion. "Thank you, and *joyeux Noël* to you and your family."

"Next year you'll join us," he says.

"Wouldn't that be great?" Of course she won't be here. As Sharon lowers the phone's handset into its cradle slowly, her stomach rumbles. Danny leaves tonight, never to be allowed back in France. Where is that woman?

Would Claudette Pelletier travel to Israel to meet him? Her physical limitations make it doubtful.

From the apartment next door come cheerful sounds of a family at their Christmas Eve table, which Rachelle has joined. A little girl sings in a clear, bell-like voice. Sharon looks out at the building across the street; in three lit windows, she sees more families gathered. Pine trees glitter with red bows and gold tinsel. She plugs in the lava lamp, picks up her flute, and plays Rimsky-Korsakov's "Chanson Indoue" to the melancholic dance of kaleidoscopic colors.

It's now 8:35. She grabs her coat to go to the dinner at the hotel. The weather has changed drastically again—and for the worse. When she tries to leave the building, the wind is as brutal as the radio forecast predicted. No taxi will be available, she knows. She trudges back upstairs, knocks on the neighbor's door, and apologizes as she asks Rachelle to drive her the short distance.

"This will turn into a gale-force-nine storm," Rachelle says while she struggles to keep the car from being blown into the open canal by gusts of winds. "Why not postpone the dinner? No one in her right mind would venture outside. Will someone bring you back?"

"Moka Limon's chauffeur." After he drives her up the ramp in his Peugeot to deliver the cognac to the sentry.

"Good, because I won't go out again."

The wind is so violent that when Rachelle stops in front of the hotel, Sharon can't push open the car door. A concierge tethered to the hotel door by a rope pulls her out, grabs both her arms, and drags her into the lobby.

As Sharon swipes water off her coat, her heart sinks with foreboding. Seas like this are treacherous. For the Israeli navy, though, the damage would be incalculable if . . .

She refuses to finish the thought.

Chapter Sixty

Cherbourg, France
Late December 1969

DANNY WAITS FOR her in the small vestibule outside the private dining room. In a low voice, he says, "I have so many questions. I don't know where to begin."

Sharon throws her coat, hat, and scarf over a nearby couch and pulls out a brush to tame her hair. "Let me give you a quick summary." She starts with Arthur Durand. "The letter Uzi sent wasn't clear on the name of the village. Without Rachelle's lists, I wouldn't have known where to look."

"Who was Claudette Pelletier?"

Was. Sharon's heart goes out to him. He hasn't come to grips with the fact that his birth mother is alive. "In her youth she was a seamstress to the duchess of Valençay." Sharon pauses. "She's disabled."

"A recent injury? Damage from a concentration camp?"

Sharon doesn't have the courage to reveal that part yet. "My impression is that she was always disabled."

"How did she *lose* me?"

"I don't know. I'll travel to meet her after I tie up loose ends here."

"How did a Jewish girl get the name Pelletier if she wasn't married to a Frenchman?"

Sharon swallows hard. This is the moment she's dreaded.

"She isn't Jewish." She finally utters the words she promised herself she never would. "Only your father was."

Danny stares at her, and she can almost hear the wheels in his head spin with a realization of what every secular Israeli knows. "I'm not going through a conversion with those Orthodox rabbis," he says in suppressed fury. "Never!"

"No one needs to know. It stays between us." Sharon's tone is soft. "And it doesn't change who you are."

"Of course it does." Danny turns and pounds the wall with his palm. "I've been fighting for the survival of my people—what I thought were my people."

She rests her hand on his arm. "They are your people. They belong to you, and you to them. You grew up in a kibbutz. What else can you be? And your father was Jewish. He probably perished in the Holocaust."

Danny swivels back to face her, his nostrils flare in a way she's never seen before. "That should make me feel better? Does my father's murder give me the credentials I need as a career Israeli naval officer?"

"All of it combined is what makes you an Israeli. It's the spirit of our country that makes me an Israeli. Our ethnicity is our religion."

"I am not even entitled to Israeli citizenship!"

"Nonsense." Her timing could not have been worse. What has she done? "Danny, you had a French adoptive mother who protected you as a Jew—"

"So my Jewishness is defined by Hitler and Pétain?" Danny drops onto the arm of the nearby sofa.

"Imagine an alternative scenario," she says. "Imagine that Uzi Yarden hadn't found you. You would have grown up Christian, hiding your tattoo and knowing in your heart that you belonged with the Jewish people."

He lowers his chin to his chest. She rests her palm on his shoulder, and he raises his hand to hold on to hers. She lets the moment linger, feeling atoms rushing between their fingers. He is adjusting, resetting some internal wheels.

Yaniv passes by on his way to the dining room. "Is everything all right?"

Danny rises to his feet. Just then, a blast of wind smacks the huge windows on the corridor side.

"How can you sail in such weather?" Sharon calls to Yaniv. Her voice is shrill. "The Saars were never built for these seas!"

Yaniv peers outside. "It may change by midnight."

His calm enrages her. "And if it doesn't? It's suicide!" she yells. "Like the *Dakar*!"

Danny touches her arm to calm her. "The wind may not subside, but it will shift direction to the northwest."

The technicality of a storm's direction is beyond her. "A gale-force-nine storm?"

"We've taken everything into consideration," Yaniv tells her.

"Everything?" She's a civilian, unbound by military protocol, she reminds herself. Suppressing her fury, she tries to deliver her words in a professional manner. "In our intelligence unit, worse-case scenarios remained open as possibilities. Have you also taken into consideration that the French might *bomb* the boats?"

Yaniv's hand pauses on the handle of the door to the dining room. "Sharon, if you can't hack the stress, you shouldn't be here."

She opens her mouth, but before she can reply, he tells Danny, "Please make sure she doesn't ruin our dinner," and disappears inside.

Sharon fumes. "So now he silences me?"

"It's tonight or likely never," Danny says. "He'll be commanding Saar Twelve."

"Sorry," she mumbles. She's not, but she can appreciate the courage of this experienced admiral in commanding the most problematic boat. It doesn't quell her fears.

Danny takes her hands. "I'm the one who should apologize for my outburst."

"It's my fault. Given what's going on around you, I promised my-self I'd keep my mouth shut," she says. "Then, when you said that you might never return to France, I spilled it out at the worst possible moment."

"There's a lot to think about. I'll deal with it another time.

Tonight, I owe you my thanks." He smiles into her eyes. "You're beyond amazing."

Sharon looks up into his face, imprinting his features on her memory in case she never sees him again. Her fingers, intertwined with his, feel as if they are on fire. Fear and anguish flood her. She's grown accustomed to carrying around the ache for Alon. Now, on the verge of healing by the touch of this man, she's on the edge of another abyss.

She can't take another loss if Danny's boat sinks or gets bombed. She will never find peace again, or love. "If I were religious, I would pray," she whispers.

His hand still holds hers. "Sometimes, at sea, I envy the Traditionalists. They have someone to believe in."

"So you forgive me for butting into your onions?"

"You certainly have a way of being exasperating at times." He scoffs. "Just one last question for tonight." She giggles as they both remember her many last questions. "Why? Why did you do this sleuthing?"

She sighs. "I'm a yenta who can't leave puzzles unsolved. It's my worst trait."

"I missed it on your psychometric test," he says, smiling.

An officer pokes his head out of the dining room. "Danny?"

Danny waves him away. "Coming." After the man closes the door, he turns to look at Sharon again, his gaze tender. "I said we'd talk about us when this is over. Just in case, may I leave you something as a down payment?"

"What's that?" she asks, knowing the answer as he bends toward her. His lips gently touch hers.

IN THE DINING room, the other four captains are already seated. To Sharon's surprise, Amiot is there, and he half rises as she enters.

"Monsieur, I thought that you'd left for the French Riviera," she says.

"And miss this important night?"

Sharon takes a seat at an available chair at the end of the table. The man she has been suspecting as an anti-Semite, or a *former* anti-Semite, is in on the conspiracy to deceive his own government.

She sips the consommé, so light and airy and different from the heavy Jewish chicken soup. From his seat, Danny sends her a sad smile. She lowers her gaze so he doesn't see her eyes brimming with tears again. If he is intercepted tonight, he might spend time in a French jail, at least until all five crews are cleared of wrongdoing. That would be preferable to having any of them founder in the storm.

The winds might subside by the time the Saars reach Portugal waters. The risk of France bombing the boats from the air will remain, not only once they're outside Cherbourg's harbor but along the entire length of the Mediterranean on their weeklong sail home. Considering the huge public defiance of the embargo—and given the oversize ego and temperament of the French—Sharon gives this intelligence analysis a high probability. She glances at Yaniv, Vaknin, and Limon. Are they really gambling on a war with France?

Two waiters wheel in trays of food, then disappear, closing the door behind them. Sharon crumples her cloth napkin in her lap, her nails digging into the fabric. Her stomach tightens.

For a while, quiet conversation and subdued laughter is heard around the table. The tension of the coming hours is as thick as the béchamel sauce over her lamb. Sharon pushes her plate away.

Moka Limon stands up and, with ceremonial flare, makes a toast to Félix Amiot, a dear, devoted friend of Israel. He circulates a signed check around the table. "Gentlemen—and one lady—you'll never see such a large check in your life. Five million dollars—the balance on the ten million contracted with CMN." When the check is returned to him, he hands it to Amiot. "From the Norwegians, with our thanks."

Amiot chuckles. Sharon can see that his helping Israel is not about resolving the economic woes of his enterprise. Given the stigma he's carried for twenty-five years—and the public trial that banned him forever from his beloved aviation industry—his loyalty to France will surely be questioned again. Will he be prosecuted for treason? This seventy-year-old genius has chosen the moral path.

From her seat, Sharon sends him a smile. Despite the generational gap, their time together has brought them closer. He's fond of her, she knows. He's a special friend and she wishes to keep him in her life, yet she will probably never see him again.

"My dear friends, I promise to visit you in Israel very soon," he says in English and lifts his glass. When the cheers and good wishes die down, he asks Danny in French, "Young man, will you step outside with me, please?"

A puzzled expression on his face, Danny rises. Amiot crooks his finger toward Sharon. "You too."

They ride the elevator in silence. Danny tosses Sharon a perplexed look. She shrugs. She can't imagine why Amiot would waste Danny's precious moments at such an important juncture.

Danny glances at his watch. "Monsieur Amiot, I'm a bit busy tonight—"

"I imagine that you are," the Frenchman replies.

At the third floor, he exits, Sharon and Danny following as he walks down a corridor. He stops at a door and knocks.

She hears a rustle on the other side; Christmas carols play on the television.

The door is opened by a tall, thin woman with braided hair who smiles, but her eyes are vacant. She steps to the side. Behind her, facing the door, is a woman in a wheelchair whose gray hair is braided the same way. A brown blanket is thrown over her knees.

Sharon's breath catches and she hears Danny gasp. His body freezes. His eyes lock with the woman's for a long moment.

The woman is wearing a plaid wool jacket and listing to one side in her wheelchair. Claudette Pelletier looks fragile and older than what Sharon guesses her age to be, about fifty. Behind her, the blind woman fumbles her way to the television and turns it off. The room falls silent except for their breathing and the wind howling outside.

"Benjamin! Oh, my baby," Claudette cries. "You're the spitting image of my Raphaël!"

Danny takes a step forward and halts. "God in heaven," he mumbles. Sharon can see only the side of his face but she can read the incredulity in the raised eyebrows and slack jaw. "I can't believe it."

The woman breaks into a sob and reaches her arms up.

He drops to his knees in front of the wheelchair. Sharon registers the instant kindness he's showing to the woman whose existence he hadn't known about until this afternoon and whom he'd never sought. Or perhaps he'd buried any natural curiosity.

"My baby Benjamin," the woman cries again. She takes his face in her hands. They search each other's features, then Danny wraps his arms around her.

Her heart beating fast with the significance of the moment, Sharon signals to Amiot to give them privacy. The two of them inch toward the door, but she glances back to see Danny drop down on the carpet. He unlaces his right shoe. Sharon stops moving. She can't tear her eyes away from the unfolding scene.

"Thankfully, I darned my sock." Danny chuckles as he removes it and raises up his foot for Claudette to see.

Claudette passes a gentle finger over his foot. It tickles Danny, and he withdraws a bit, but extends it again to let her touch more.

Solange approaches, reaches out, and feels his foot.

He wiggles his toes. "It tickles," he says, laughing in an easy way as he does when joking around the office. The two women laugh with him.

Solange asks to touch his face, and her fingers trace his features, then run down his back. He rises to his knees to face Claudette. "So tall and handsome," Solange says.

"You darned your sock?" Claudette reaches for it and checks the stitches.

"I do it for my crew too," he says. "It relaxes me during down-time at sea."

She laughs. "That's my son for sure."

Sharon can hardly contain her elation, more for Claudette than Danny. This mother had searched for her lost son, had ached for him for twenty-seven years. Sharon goes to the door and joins Amiot outside. "So extraordinarily kind of you," she says.

He smiles the sad smile that she now recognizes, a smile that cracks through a cloud of stigma and possible regrets. "Due to the weather, I couldn't fly them here," he tells her. "I had a driver pick them up. Unfortunately, Claudette Pelletier's condition forced them to stop frequently. They stayed overnight at a hotel."

"But how did you know?"

"You'd given me the big clue. 'The mother of someone I care about may be alive.'" He chuckles. "My lawyer sent an investigator to speak with both of the men you visited, and he knew how to search for Madame Pelletier."

She doesn't correct him and say that it is *Mademoiselle* Pelletier. "How did you figure out that she was Danny's mother?"

"He's the only one on your team born in France." Amiot raises his eyebrows. "Is it true that he has a blue Star of David tattooed on the bottom of his foot?"

She giggles. "If not for that clue, I doubt we'd be here right now."

Danny comes out. "What an emotional encounter, but my men are waiting," he says to both of them, and dabs his eyes with a handkerchief. Then he turns to Amiot. "How can I thank you for your thoughtfulness?"

"Bring your boat safely home."

Chapter Sixty-One

Cherbourg, France
Late December 1969

IT'S PAST MIDNIGHT. Solange, the talkative blind woman, has fallen asleep on one of the two beds in the room. The storm outside roars. Sharon pulls an upholstered chair next to Claudette's wheelchair, and the two of them stare out the large window into the darkness. Only the outlines of the five Saars are visible in the canal. Their engines haven't yet blasted. Despite her trepidation, Sharon no longer wants to see the operation aborted. All will be lost. Israel won't have its full naval fighting capacity for the next war. Its shores—the Mediterranean Sea, bordered by Egypt on one side and Lebanon and Syria on the other, and the Red Sea, flanked by Jordan, Saudi Arabia, Yemen, Egypt, Sudan, and Eritrea—will be unprotected.

There is no movement on the docks. A couple of streetlamps throw yellow cones of light webbed sideways by sheets of rain. Sharon knows that in a residential building on the other side of the canal, Kadmon is watching through his binoculars. Limon is in his suite somewhere in this hotel, probably twisting the radio dial in search of weather forecasts from France and England.

At Sharon's side, Claudette fidgets and lets out a groan.

"May I help you get into bed?" Sharon asks. "You'll be more comfortable."

"And miss seeing my son navigating a boat for Israel?" She smiles. "Did you see his blue tattoo?"

Sharon lets out a little laugh. She loved seeing Danny open himself so graciously to the unexpected gift of meeting Claudette. She loved witnessing the tenderness mixed with play between them. She also loved how, after she walked him to the elevator, they stole one more moment together. This time they kissed long and hard.

Now the memory of his lean, muscular body as she pressed into him arouses the whole of her.

"Are you his girlfriend?" Claudette asks.

"Almost. Hopefully soon." Sharon places her hand on her heart to still it. "When all this is over."

When the news of the Saars' escape breaks in a few days, she'll call Uzi Yarden and convey the regards of the woman who was once his landlady. And when Sharon is back in Israel, she will check Yad Vashem's archives for records of Isaac Baume and Raphaël Baume—the names Claudette gave her. She's learned that Raphaël had a sister who was deported and probably perished, but a younger brother had been sheltered in a monastery. How amazing would it be if he had survived?

At two in the morning, Sharon slaps her own cheeks to fight off sleep. She helps Claudette to the bathroom, then splashes cold water on her own face and thinks of the men in the boats below, all awake, all waiting. Returning to her seat by the window, Sharon wishes again that she believed in prayer.

While Claudette dozes off in her wheelchair, Sharon contemplates the journey she has made in Danny's convoluted history—and in her own. It all comes down to belonging, belonging to something larger than herself. For some people, it's belonging to a shared faith; for others, a shared ideology. For some, it is a matter of love; for others, a matter of family. But her arc of belonging—and Danny's—comes from their national spirit, one defined not by the Holocaust but by the common destiny of connecting with the past, present, and future of the Jewish people. Belonging to Israel is central to their identity.

Just then she hears the blasts—the blessed blasts of twenty engines firing in a thunderous burst. "Hooray!" she calls out.

In her bed, Solange sits bolt upright with a loud yelp. Claudette claps enthusiastically. She pushes herself out of the wheelchair, grabs the windowsill, and stands. Solange comes over and puts her arm around her waist, propping her up. Sharon leans against the window, the cold glass pressed against her burning forehead.

Mast lights come on. Two by two, the first four boats begin to glide forward, the fifth one close behind. Claudette narrates the scene for her friend. A hundred meters out, darkness swallows the boats. In the storm, Sharon can't even make out the light of the sentry watchtower. She holds her breath, recalling the young man to whom she handed the cognac; he was as bewildered as her fresh recruits. No doubt he had been placed on duty to free the senior staff to go home for their Christmas Eve dinner.

She hopes that the rest of Limon's and Yaniv's gambles prove equally prescient.

All is silent except for the breathing of the three women and the roaring wind outside. In her head, Sharon accompanies the Saars sailing against the ferocious waves through the harbor, past the French navy port, then to the ancient set of breakers, after which they are met with mountain-high waves.

At any point, they might be intercepted by the French navy. Will they be forced back to harbor by cannon fire?

Thirty minutes pass. And then, under the lamppost's cone of illumination, Sharon spots a lone figure in a long coat, its collar turned up. Moka Limon is holding on to the post with one hand and waving goodbye with the other.

"They're out!" Sharon cries.

"My Benjamin," Claudette says, awe in her voice. "How proud Isaac Baume would be to see his grandson a captain of a Jewish boat!"

Postscript

THE LAST FIVE Saars slipped out of Cherbourg undetected in a gale-force-nine storm at two thirty on Christmas morning. Several hours later, a visiting British journalist noticed their absence and notified his editor in London. It took two days before the international newswire buzzed with the scoop. By then, the Saars were being refueled off the shore of Portugal via another Israeli invention: all five boats suckled like puppies simultaneously from a mother ship that had been waiting for them. Since the boats had supposedly been sold to a company in Norway, media outlets sent helicopters to search the North Sea. It wasn't until the Saars passed through the Strait of Gibraltar and into the Mediterranean that their destination become apparent. Against maritime laws, the Saars carried no flags or identifying numbers, but as they passed Gibraltar, the British signaled to Kimche, *Bon voyage!*

The French were furious at the deception, though a quick internal scrutiny of the paperwork confirmed that no French law had been broken. The French defense minister Michel Debré (Catholic grandson of a rabbi) ordered the French air force to bomb the boats, but the chief of staff refused the order. President Georges Pompidou decided not to escalate the incident that had already made a mockery of the French in the international media. The press praised the Israelis for their ingenuity and upheld Israel's right to the contracted purchase.

This novel is a fictional imagining of the preceding fifteen months. I took the liberty of altering the timing of Saar Six's departure and fictionalizing the characters while staying close to the historical background. I have constructed situations based on real-life personalities: Moka Limon, Félix Amiot, and Duchess Silvia de Castellane. For an accurate historical account of the Boats of Cherbourg, I invite readers to check out the articles in the Jewish Virtual Library and excellent books written by Abraham Rabinovich (English) and Justin Lecarpentier (French).

The Saars participated in the 1973 Yom Kippur War, which Israel nearly lost on all fronts but the sea. The ships employed the newly developed Israeli sea-skimming, anti-ship missiles—Gabriels—that changed naval warfare and won Israel's victory over both the Egyptian and Syrian navies.

With the help of advanced sonar technology, the submarine *Dakar* was found between Cyprus and Crete thirty-one years after it disappeared. The cause of its sinking was determined to be a mechanical malfunction, not a hostile attack. The deaths of the sixty-nine men were "swift and violent." When it was found, in late May 1999, Israel finally went into official mourning.

Youth Aliyah, under the early leadership of Henrietta Szold, founder of Hadassah, rescued over twenty thousand Jewish children before, during, and immediately after the Holocaust. These youngsters grew up to leave their marks on Israel's military, political, economic, agricultural, scientific, cultural, and academic maps.

Hadassah continues to operate youth villages in Israel for at-risk children.

Author's Note

IN MAY 2018, I visited the Clandestine Immigration and Naval Museum in Haifa in the company of Admiral Hadar Kimche. The year before, I conducted extensive interviews with this modest then-eighty-nine-year-old commander of the legendary story of the Boats of Cherbourg. Hadar (who asked me to address him by his first name) introduced me then to over a dozen officers who had been involved in the breakout. On the 2018 Haifa visit, he took me to view one of the twelve missile-carrying boats, Saars, that had caused an international crisis in 1969 and four years later brought Israel naval victories in the Yom Kippur War.

I had not anticipated how the mere name of the museum would affect me, a reminder of the tight connection between the clandestine immigration to Palestine before the State of Israel was established in 1948 and the Israeli navy that was created upon the country's birth. Four aging, barely floating vessels that had been refurbished after the Holocaust to transport thousands of Jewish survivors from Europe to the Promised Land were once again pressed into service, this time for the nascent Israeli navy.

Having grown up in Israel as part of its first generation, I had been fed detailed accounts of the clandestine immigration—Jews entering the country illegally because the British, who had been given a mandate in 1922 by the League of Nations (the precursor to the United Nations) to administer the land for the purpose of creating a home for the Jews, had reneged on the directive. Not only had they handed 76 percent of the Jewish-designated land to the Hashemites (creating Jordan), but in the wake of the Holocaust—when over three million displaced Jewish survivors who had escaped the Nazis' incinerators had no place to go—Britain blocked the Jews' entry to the remaining 24 percent of the land they had named Palestine.

Both this gross injustice and the heroism of the thousands who defied the British blockade were infused into my DNA, as were the horrors of the genocide of six million Jews that preceded it.

In 1969, twenty-one years after Israel was born, the astounding breakout of the Boats of Cherbourg dominated international headlines. The boats, all commissioned, designed, and paid for by Israel, had been built in a private shipyard in a Normandy port, but their delivery was blocked due to a new French arms embargo on Israel. Two years later, in 1971, I learned that a small project I worked on while serving in the Israel Defense Forces had played a minuscule part in the vision, daring, and flawless execution of the boats' escape.

Only twenty years later did the Israeli navy declassify the identity of the person who had executed this heroic operation: Admiral Hadar Kimche.

What I instantly noticed on this visit, as I read the museum's full name through the prism and wisdom of the passing five decades, was how all of these events—the Holocaust in Europe, the clandestine immigration to Palestine, and the escape of the Boats of Cherbourg—were interwoven and how close, timewise, they had been. In the spectrum of human history, and even in the shorter arc of the Jews' exile for two thousand years from their homeland, these three events occurred in the span of less than thirty years. Only the blink of an eye.

And then I read the inscription at the museum entrance, and the significance of history came rushing in, like a tidal wave:

> *Your path led through the sea, your way through the mighty waters, though your footprints were not seen.*
> —*Psalm* 77:19

Even on land, history's footprints can disappear just as quickly as if they were marked on water—and more so as the globe entered yet another century.

In the context of the clandestine immigration, there was a human-interest story that had touched me deeply but seemed to not have been fully explored:

While growing up in Tel Aviv, on rare occasions I encountered Holocaust orphans who had been saved by Youth Aliyah. All older than me, they had been absorbed in youth villages or kibbutzim or were brought to Israel by surviving relatives.

Such was my friend David's adopted older brother, a nameless five-year-old who was handed to David's father by a monk. Since no one had come to claim this boy, the monk said, would this Jew take him? Such was Charlotte, who, at age four, was saved by a Red Cross nurse from Vel d'Hiv (where the Jews of Paris had been rounded up and deported to Auschwitz)—only to be removed from that second mother's home at age eight by an organization that placed her in a Jewish orphanage. Such was Miriam, who had been baptized by the time her Jewish father returned. When the twelve-year-old refused to leave her new family, he kidnapped her and took her to Palestine, where her distraught mother, who had lost two other children, waited. Such was Jacob, who for years labored on the farm of his Christian rescuers, abused and starving, receiving no schooling or medical care, until he was bought with cash by a Youth Aliyah agent.

There are as many unique, heartbreaking stories as there are children who survived. I did not want to tell another Holocaust story but to explore what happened afterward. How were these children found? Did an agent from the Jewish community in Palestine—the *yishuv*—knock on the door of every farmhouse and ask whether by any chance there was a Jewish child he could take across the sea to a place where people spoke a language the child wouldn't understand? Yet it happened, and in this novel I set out to explore not stories of trauma and loss, but a Youth Aliyah agent's journey to heal these children's scarred hearts.

The Boy with the Star Tattoo links all these events that have dwelled in my psyche. Each episode in this extraordinary historical saga stands on its own. Woven together, they create a story of the resilience and fortitude of the Jews who reasserted their right to self-determination in their own homeland. Without Israel, we Jews would have been the Kurds and Romani of the world—landless, oppressed, disrespected, and exploited. Israel continues to offer refuge to Jews whenever the need arises, and given that, along with the nation's achievements in science, technology, and medicine, Jews everywhere can walk tall. We belong.

Talia Carner, January 2024

Acknowledgments

M Y VERY FIRST thanks are to my hero Rear Admiral Hadar Kimche, who in 1969 commanded the escape of Israel's boats from Cherbourg, Normandy. Since I first met him in 2017, he has been generous with his time and knowledge. He introduced me to other officers, including Commander Eli Kama, Captain Arieh Ronna, Lieutenant Commander Gadi Ben Zeev, and others who are no longer with us—Major General Micha Ram (1942–2018) and Major General Shlomo Erell (1920–2018)—all of whom shared with me fascinating details about the project.

I am grateful to family members of the Israeli team in Cherbourg: Yossi Wexler-Halfon, son of Brigadier General Yitzhak Wexler-Halfon; Orni Ben-Dor, daughter of Commander Zeev Bar-Zeev Farkash; Captain Sheli Shahal, daughter of Commander Haim Shahal; Tami Ozri, daughter of Rear Admiral Hadar Kimche; and Esther Tabak, wife of Commander Moishe Tabak. Their stories about living in Cherbourg gave me the nuanced flavor of life there.

My thanks also to seamen Moshe Levi and Avraham Avizemer, whose perspectives added color, and Avi Brillant, son of Commander Edmond Wilhelm Brillant, who added his engineering expertise.

An amazing coincidence happened when a friend, the French journalist Serge Farnel, attended a writers' conference. At lunch, he sat across from the aging Yves Bonnet, former deputy for *La Manche* in the National Assembly and a member of France's Committee for National Defense and the Armed Forces. Farnel's initiative opened for me a channel to experts on the French side of the saga: in 1969, when the event described in this book took place, Yves Bonnet was in charge of French security in the region. He introduced me to M. Pierre Balmer, CEO of *Constructions Mécaniques de Normandie* (CMN, the shipyard founded by Félix Amiot, where the boats were built), who invited me to visit the highly secure facility, now manufacturing nuclear submarines. The visit gave me the in-person experience of the vast place, down to its smell of machine oil. Standing in front of a life-size sculpture of the controversial Félix Amiot, I knew that he would be a character in my novel.

The librarians at the Library of Cherbourg and Bibliothèque Départementale de la Manche helped me search microfiche, but it was Justin Lecarpentier who generously shared with me his trove of photographs, original documents, and archived film clips. An author of several books about the Cherbourg affair and Félix Amiot's biographer, he produced and aired, in 2019, the fiftieth-anniversary documentary about the event. Justin continued to patiently answer my questions as they popped up.

And finally, on the French side, I would like to thank the charming René Moirand, former journalist at *La Presse de la Manche*, who covered the Cherbourg event. Even though he had caught a whiff of the upcoming escape, he did not break the news. Moirand invited me and my husband for a weekend at his country home in the French Alps and regaled me with stories that gave me both his inside view as a townsperson and the international aspect of the event.

My two visits to Cherbourg were memorable because of my hosts Michel Niciejewski and Emmanuel de La Fonchais, owners of the magnificent bed-and-breakfast La Manoire de la Fieffe. I can't imagine a better writing retreat than their beautiful manor set in botanical gardens.

The second thread of this novel, that of Youth Aliyah, was launched with a primer about France's Holocaust history by Eliot Nidam-Orvieto at the International Institute for Holocaust Research, Yad Vashem, Israel. I first learned from him about the search to rescue Jewish orphans and the custody battles with the Church that baptized many. My thanks, too, to Ariel Sion, archive director, Bibliothèque du Mémorial de la Shoah, Paris; Boaz Cohen, chair, Holocaust Studies Program, Western Galilee College, Israel; and Katy Hazan and Dominique Rotermund, Œuvre de secours aux enfants Archives and History, Paris, France. All of them helped me understand the post–World War II mood in France and how Jewish children became caught in the competition to replenish the lost populations of Europe. The only former Youth Aliyah agent I could find still alive was Idith Yanai-Charuvi; she gave me an inside understanding of the process of rescuing Jewish orphans in Europe and bringing them to Israel.

The second French location of the novel, the Loire Valley, began with a passing comment by Olivier Vidal, a French architect living in New York, about Château de Valençay and the story of Duchess Silvia de Castellane. On my visit to the château, Fanny Chauffeteau, *assistante de conservation*, gave me a guided tour to its secret chambers and hidden turrets.

With the COVID-19 pandemic grounding me, I selected the specific villages in the Loire Valley where the rest of the plot unfolded with the help via Zoom of tour guide Manuel de Croutte, concierge Summer Jauneaud, and historians Susan Walter and Simon Brand. Finally, in late 2021, my daughter, Eden Yariv Goldberg, drove me to visit these locations. Thank you all for the introduction to this history-filled region.

For additional information, I thank Keren Haliva and Dalit Hasson for their feedback regarding women in IDF Intelligence in the late 1960s; Dr. Charles Polit for medical information regarding disability; and Lisa McLaughlin, for her lesson about the use of fieldstone in house construction.

This book would not have started had it not been for investigative journalist Meira Gaunt, who initiated a call to Hadar Kimche and turned my abstract idea into a doable writing project. And the novel could not have progressed without the support of my writing group, Two Bridges, administered by Walter Cummins.

But it was the patience of readers with red pens, each contributing significant observations and comments, that vaulted this complex novel to the finish line: Sue O'Neill, Lisa Bernard, Astrid Cook,

Andrew Gross, Becky Stowe, Diane Goullard, Linda Davies, and, especially, Emily White, my adviser on each of my novels so far.

My agent Annelise Robey and her colleague Logan Harper from the Jane Rotrosen Agency have cheered me from the sidelines. My wonderful editor at HarperCollins, Tessa Woodward, along with her assistant, Madelyn Blaney, ably coordinated a fantastic team— from Lisa Glover, Tracy Roe, and Joe Jasko, who cleaned up my drafts, to Kerry Rubenstein, who designed the striking cover art, and followed by Amelia Wood and Tess Day in marketing and publicity. Their combined hard work shepherded the manuscript from the chip inside my computer into your hands, the reader. Thank you all! I can't imagine a better dream team to birth my novel.

And, as always, there is Ron, who once again sacrificed our private time to allow me days, weeks, months, and years of writing this story. Fascinated by the research that unfolded with a string of coincidences that opened new doors, he encouraged me to pursue them and accompanied me on three of my five trips to France.

Glossary

caserne—(French) Military barrack.

cholent—(Yiddish) A savory slow-cooked stew for Shabbat with meat, barley, potatoes, and beans. It was developed over the centuries to conform to Jewish laws that prohibit cooking on the Sabbath.

chutzpah—(Yiddish, Hebrew) Daring; audacity with insolence. Having the "gall" or "nerve" to say or act on one's self-confidence.

CMN—Constructions Mécaniques de Normandie, the shipyard founded and run by Félix Amiot in Normandy, France.

DP camp—Displaced-persons camp; these were established throughout Europe shortly after World War II to care for the millions of homeless, nation-less refugees.

Eretz Israel—Meaning "the Land of Israel"; it was the traditional Jewish name favored by the residents of the Jewish territory before the formal establishment of the State of Israel.

fedayeen—(Arabic) Arab guerrillas, especially those operating against Jews in Israel and Palestine; Islamic militants.

gonif—(Yiddish) A thief.

Holocaust—The genocide of European Jews during World War II. Between 1941 and 1945, Nazi Germany and its collaborators systematically murdered six million Jews across German-occupied Europe.

IDF—Israel Defense Forces; it combines all branches of the armed and information forces under one umbrella.

kishkes—(Yiddish) Guts.

kosher, kashrut—(Yiddish, Hebrew) The Jewish observance of strict dietary rules and religious practices of food preparation.

League of Nations—The precursor to the United Nations, established in 1919 by the Treaty of Versailles to promote international cooperation and peace.

Maquis—(French) Guerrilla bands of French Résistance fighters during the Nazi occupation of France in World War II; they operated out of forests.

mezuzah—(Yiddish, Hebrew) A case containing a parchment inscribed with religious texts and attached to the doorpost of a Jewish house as a sign of faith.

mitzvah—(Yiddish, Hebrew) A good deed; a meritorious or charitable act.

mohel—(Yiddish, Hebrew) A person who performs the Jewish rite of circumcision.

moshav—(Hebrew) An agricultural cooperative of independent farms. Unlike a kibbutz, where everything—from buying clothes to child-rearing practices—is decided and owned communally, in a moshav, residents own their own homes and farms and manage their core family lives and economics independently but share heavy agricultural machinery, purchase fertilizers in bulk, and market their produce together.

OSE—Œuvre de secours aux enfants, a Jewish charity in France that rescued children and ran orphanages.

punchke—(Yiddish) A Hanukkah delicacy of fist-size fried balls of dough stuffed with jam and sprinkled with confectioners' sugar.

savta—(Hebrew) Grandmother.

shmi—(Hebrew) "My name."

tsuris—(Yiddish) Troubles, hardships.

Yad Vashem—(Hebrew) Central Holocaust memorial located in Jerusalem.

yenta—(Yiddish) An old busybody, someone who gossips or meddles in other people's affairs.

yishuv—(Hebrew) The autonomous body of Jewish residents in Mandatory Palestine prior to the establishment of the State of Israel. It was run by the de facto government of the Jewish agency.

Youth Aliyah—A Jewish organization that rescued thousands of Jewish children from the Nazis during the Third Reich and arranged for their resettlement in Palestine in kibbutzim and youth villages that became both homes and schools.